THE
CHOSEN
ONES

ALSO BY CAROL WYER

DI ROBYN CARTER SERIES
Little Girl Lost
Secrets of the Dead
The Missing Girls
The Silent Children

Life Swap
Grumpy Old Menopause
How Not to Murder Your Grumpy
Grumpies On Board
Mini Skirts and Laughter Lines
Surfing in Stilettos
Just Add Spice
Love Hurts
Take a Chance on Me

THE CHOSEN ONES

CAROL WYER

bookouture

Published by Bookouture in 2018

An imprint of StoryFire Ltd.

Carmelite House
50 Victoria Embankment
London EC4Y 0DZ

www.bookouture.com

ISBN: 978-1-78681-501-9
eBook ISBN: 978-1-78681-500-2

For Alison Daughtrey-Drew

PROLOGUE

Jordan Kilby didn't hear the car. He was only aware of the rush of cold air as the vehicle drove past so closely, he felt metal against his elbow. His reaction had been swift and violent. Tugging the handlebar to the left, he'd met with gravel and a raised kerb. The bike had ridden it and toppled, taking him with it.

He lay sprawled on the damp grass verge, chest rising and falling quickly, his heart hammering like it would explode. His legs were entangled with the front wheel and his wrist exploded with pain when he attempted to lift it. He didn't dare check his other limbs for fear of what he'd discover. He cursed the motorist who had almost killed him. Then he cursed himself and the cans of beer that had dulled his senses and made him deaf to the vehicle's approach.

He stared into the dark starless night and cursed the clouds that covered the moon and had made him invisible to other road users. Then it struck him, the car had been crawling past, not travelling at high speed. He hadn't heard any engine noise.

Ahead of him, the vehicle had drawn to a halt and the driver's door opened. Jordan turned his head, squinted into the darkness and swallowed hard. A lump formed in his throat and stuck there. He recognised the car. He knew who had driven him off the road. The driver approached him, slowly, casually, as if prolonging the anticipation of what was to come. Inside Jordan's head, a terrified voice screamed at him to get up, make good his escape, but he knew it was futile. His limbs refused to cooperate.

As the person drew closer to him, the clouds above parted for a moment, allowing moonlight to fall on them both and on the object gleaming in the person's gloved hand. More terrifying was the look on his attacker's face. Jordan's mouth opened and closed, no sound escaping. His mind curled into a ball like a terrified animal, leaving him unable to function. He couldn't even plead for his life. He waited as his assailant smiled at him, pressed two fingers to his lips and then held them aloft to Jordan, the gesture of a kiss.

Jordan was never going to walk away from this.

CHAPTER ONE

DAY ONE – MONDAY, 5 JUNE, MORNING

The crows were to blame. Their hoarse caws had penetrated Jane Marsh's dreams and as their cries had grown louder, they'd towed her from her cosy, sleepy state into full consciousness. Opening one eye, she read the digital display on her clock and sighed. It was only 5 a.m. She still had two hours before she had to get up and make the journey to town with her bread, cakes and jams for the farmers' market. She needed those two hours to rest up. She wasn't getting any younger and every minute in bed was savoured. Two more precious hours and she couldn't enjoy them because of the bloody crows.

She kicked off the bedcovers, swung her legs over the side of the aged divan and ambled to the window to see what all the fuss was about. Her husband, Toby, was already downstairs, grabbing an early cup of tea while listening to Radio 4 before he started work on the John Deere. It had been misfiring and he wanted to give it a quick look over before he was forced to call in the engineer. Farming wasn't as lucrative as some of the locals imagined it to be, and Toby was used to being a crop farmer, mechanic and jack of all trades. He wasn't miserly, but he'd rather resolve any mechanical issues himself than pay handsomely for call-out charges.

The commotion was coming from the far field. Crows were circling excitedly around a scarecrow her husband had erected. One or two were landing and pulling at its face. Fat lot of good it was doing. The crows were supposed to be put off by it not landing on it and pecking at it. She slipped on her dressing gown and padded to the top of the stairs.

It was a bright, crisp morning, heralding a beautiful June day. Toby had wanted to collect silage before the rain arrived. She hoped he got the tractor fixed in time. That was another problem with farming: you were hampered by the perversities of the weather – one day it was as warm as the south of Spain, the next, wet and humid. The weather forecast had predicted a few days of hot and sticky weather. At the moment there wasn't a cloud in sight. *Good day for selling jams*, she mused. She entered the farmhouse kitchen with its smell of old pine furniture that had been there ever since they'd moved in. The house had belonged to Toby's parents. Jane wasn't keen on the dark oppressive furniture that made the place seem lost in a bygone age: the outdated kitchen table, stained over the years, and the wooden floor to ceiling dresser that held their best china plates, but retained a deep-rooted smell. They'd never been able to afford new furniture or a complete kitchen revamp, and although she wasn't fond of any of it, she'd got used to it. It somehow belonged to the house. That was the main problem with living in the place – it was outmoded and reminded her that time was ticking by too quickly. Their twelve-year-old Labrador, Brandy, raised her head from her basket and stared in Jane's direction, with milky eyes. Her tail thumped on detecting the arrival of her mistress. Jane caressed the animal, hands running through her oily coat. Yes, they were all getting old.

Toby, mug of tea in one hand, was flicking through a tractor operational manual, lost in terminology she would never understand. He only looked up when she approached the sink, and he threw her a smile.

'You're up early. Thought you didn't have to get off until seven.'

'I don't,' she said. 'It's the crows. They're making a right racket outside. I couldn't sleep. They're pestering that new scarecrow you put up.'

Toby put his manual aside and cocked his head, eyebrows furrowed.

'Scarecrow? I haven't put up any new scarecrow,' he said.

Jane's face clouded in confusion. 'Then what is it they're attacking in the field?'

CHAPTER TWO

DAY ONE – MONDAY, 5 JUNE, MORNING

Silence hung in the offices of R&J Associates, broken only by the odd snuffle coming from Duke, the Staffordshire bull terrier, who'd been confined to his basket for almost half an hour, and was clearly bored.

Ross Cunningham scratched his nose and shrugged. He gazed at his cousin, Robyn, dressed casually in jeans and a loose-fitting baby blue jumper that brightened her sallow complexion. She was wearing the same intense expression she'd worn ever since they'd sat down to discuss his findings. For the last four months, he'd been trying to help her determine the validity of a photograph she'd received that hinted her fiancé Davies had not been killed in an ambush near Marrakesh in March 2015, over two years ago.

It was proving a difficult task, and in spite of Ross's contacts and skills as a private investigator, he'd found little to confirm it had not been a hoax. Robyn, as usual, wasn't giving up until she had all the facts and at the moment they were still missing vital information, in the shape of Peter Cross, Davies' superior, the man who'd know for sure if Davies had been alive that day.

'We can say with almost certainty, the photograph was taken at Birmingham Airport,' said Robyn for the third time.

Ross nodded. Robyn always chewed information over and over until it made sense to her. Her mind never stayed quiet. If something didn't feel right, she'd pick at it, worry it, until it fitted in with her thoughts or conclusions.

'And Davies' name wasn't on the passenger list for the flight that got into Birmingham that day?'

'The airline ran checks on all their flights from Morocco that arrived in the UK before three o'clock, and Davies wasn't on any of them.'

'Which means one of three things: he used an alias, he took a private flight arranged by intelligence, or that photograph is a fake. Pretty much the same three thoughts that have been bouncing about since I received the wretched picture.' She dragged a hand through her long, dark hair.

They'd set up a whiteboard like the ones Robyn favoured at work. The photograph in question took centre position. Robyn scowled at it and threw down the latest email Ross had handed her.

'I don't know why she's suddenly backed off.' The 'she' in question was Peter Cross's ex-secretary, Daphne Hastings, who'd promised to talk to Ross back in March but since then had cancelled their meeting. 'You don't suppose Peter Cross put pressure on her?'

Ross tilted his head and grimaced a response. It was almost a rhetorical question that both had pondered on several occasions. The email had been Ross's latest attempt to get the woman to change her mind. She'd replied saying she was bound by the Official Secrets Act and couldn't talk to anyone about her work, or about those connected to it.

'I'm pretty much done with this,' said Robyn, pushing her chair back from the desk. 'We've wasted hours of free time chasing our tails. I haven't heard anything about or from Davies since January, when I got this photograph. There have been no further incidents or sightings of him, and the surveillance cameras you set up for me after that intruder got into my garden have yielded nothing.'

'Well, at least I've stopped worrying about you possibly being in danger.' Ross gave a weak smile. 'For a while there, I thought somebody was after you.'

Robyn agreed it had been on her mind as well. 'I've decided it has to be a hoax. What I can't work out is why somebody would send this to me. It's a cruel prank to play on anybody. That's what keeps bringing me back to the thought there might be some truth in it.'

Ross agreed with her. 'We've got as far as we can, Robyn. Sorry. I really wanted to find out something positive, if only to give you closure on this. I know how it eats into you. I feel like I've let you down.' His face crumpled. Robyn stared at the man who'd stood by her when life was unbearable, the man she'd always looked up to. Ross was her only close relation and he'd gone out of his way to support her. His craggy features looked mournful, and as she glanced from him to Duke, with his eyes downcast and head hanging over his basket, she choked back a laugh. 'You do realise you resemble that animal a little more every day,' she said, aiming for levity.

Ross grinned. 'You mean, I'm in great physical shape, of course?' He patted his flat stomach. Weeks of long walks with Duke and sticking to his wife Jeanette's strict diet had paid off. *He is looking good*, Robyn thought to herself.

'Of course. Listen, you haven't let me down. I've spent far too long even considering the possibility of Davies being alive, or a more sinister scenario. The fact remains, if he was alive, he'd have contacted me by now. The hidden cameras haven't revealed anyone or any suspicious activity in or around my house, over the four months they've been in situ. I'm going to have to accept this photograph for what it is – a hoax – and move on. However, if I find out who set me up and wasted my time, and more importantly, got me half-believing Davies was alive, I'll throttle that person.'

'You'll have to join the queue. I'm at the front of it,' Ross replied. 'And I think Jeanette wants a few strong words with them too. She's been most upset about this. Says it's completely unfair you've been targeted like this.'

Robyn smiled at the thought of petite Jeanette, with immaculately coiffured hair, dressed in one of her 1940s outfits, being cross on her behalf. She might rise to shaking her fist at somebody, but that was about the extent of the range of her anger. Jeanette was the kindest, sweetest person on the planet.

'Now that, I'd like to see,' said Robyn.

'You'd be surprised. Right, we'll call it a day and I'll get on with some PI work. I have yet another insurance claim to look into. The fun never stops, does it?'

'Want me to walk Duke for you?'

At the mention of his name, the animal raised his head.

'He's part of my ploy. I'll be taking Duke on a nice long stroll past my quarry's house on the off chance we'll catch the man doing something he shouldn't be doing. No one gives a dog walker a second glance. You up for it, Detective Duke?'

'I'll get off too. I need to get some shopping. Schrödinger ate my last tin of tuna this morning. I'd better stock the cupboard again.'

Creases formed around Ross's eyes again. 'My cousin, Catlady.'

'You mean Catwoman, the feline, femme fatale of Gotham City.'

'No, I definitely mean Catlady. You've become one of those women who buys gourmet tins of cat food, or who cooks pieces of organic chicken for their feline friend. Duke gets whatever is left over. No pampering for him.'

'That's because, like his owner, he's a guzzle guts.'

Ross held up his hands. 'Me-ow! You win. Anyway, it's good to see you smile.' He studied her carefully. 'Give me a call if you need anything, or if you want me to pick this back up.'

'Cheers. I think we'll lay it to rest.'

Robyn trotted back down to her car and reflected again on the photograph of Davies. Five months had passed since its arrival.

There'd been plenty of time for whoever was responsible to have made him or herself known. She had to let it go.

As she bounded lightly from the bottom stair and into the building's entrance, her mobile buzzed. She noted the caller ID.

'Hi Mitz. Everything okay?'

Sergeant Mitz Patel's voice was composed. 'Sorry, guv. I know it's your day off but there's been a suspicious death in Colton. Looks like a murder.'

'Stay on the line and give me the details. I'm on my way.'

As Robyn rushed outside to her aged VW Golf, phone clutched to her ear, she was completely unaware of the man observing her from inside a black Audi. He waited until she'd left, then pulled away from the kerb, lips moving as he spoke into a hands-free phone.

CHAPTER THREE

The village of Colton, a thirty-minute drive from Stafford, held a timeless charm, enhanced by its medieval church and an ancient stone bridge that traversed a quaint brook. The bridge today was obliterated from view by the emergency vehicles that littered the lane.

Robyn parked in the first available space and headed towards the commotion. Villagers had gathered near the scene and she had to repeatedly ask them to move so she could make her way to the field, now cordoned off with police tape. She called out, 'If any of you believe you saw any suspicious movements or activity here yesterday, or this morning, please make yourself known to the officers, who will take a statement from you. If not, would you please kindly move away. Thank you for your cooperation.'

A makeshift tent had been erected around the victim, and several officers were combing the area around it. She recognised several of them, eyes fixed to the ground as they hunted for any evidence.

She donned her white protective clothing, flashed her warrant at the officer guarding the tent entrance and entered. Mitz was inside, his face unreadable.

'SOCO?'

'Matt was first officer on the scene.'

Matt Higham was her other sergeant, a competent officer whose take on life always kept the team buoyed up. He was their joker, light-hearted and at ease with most situations. Today, his face was etched with concern, his usually bright eyes downcast. He was recording the scene with his bodycam, ensuring he'd captured every minute detail.

Robyn was struck by the victim's crucified pose. The killer had ensured the man's arms were tightly bound to the wooden pole fixed crudely to a large stake. A thin belt had been tied around his neck to further attach him to the post. At about five foot six, he only just reached Robyn's shoulders. He was slight in build, almost delicately so, his hooded top and jeans hung limply on his slender frame. He had been an ordinary-looking young man whose most attractive attribute was his dark wavy hair that hung just below his ears and lifted his sharp features.

Robyn had an instant flashback to a weekend spent in Paris with Davies. The scene reminded her of a painting she'd seen at the Louvre, of the crucifixion of Jesus. Had this man been deliberately arranged to emulate that well-known tableau, or was it simply to create the impression of a scarecrow? The man's face bore several marks where small pieces of flesh had been ripped from his cheeks. On the ground below him was a sheet, scrunched and positioned at his feet. It was stained bright red with blood.

'Any identification?' she asked.

Mitz held up a black wallet in a transparent plastic bag. 'This was found about 100 metres from the road.' He pointed towards a marker stuck in the ground near the field entrance. 'There's ten pounds in it and a credit card. Name is Jordan Kilby. Waiting for more information.'

'Nothing else? No mobile phone? Car or house keys?'

Mitz shook his head. An involuntary shiver ran through Robyn's body as she looked at the gruesome sight in front of her. It took a few moments for her to be able to study the young man's face and wonder why somebody would torture and murder him this way.

Harry McKenzie, the pathologist, had arrived ahead of Robyn and was checking Jordan over for clues as to time and cause of death. He spoke quietly. 'There are several superficial lacerations to the exposed skin, largely around the facial region, most certainly made after his death.'

Matt spoke up. 'The farmer, Toby Marsh, who discovered him, said crows were attacking him. He stood by the body and kept them away until we arrived. There used to be a scarecrow here but it disintegrated over time and only the post remained.'

Harry nodded. 'There are marks on his hands and face produced by something sharp – could be beaks. Have you recorded everything here?'

Matt spoke. 'All done. Did you want to move the body?'

'In a sec. I'll need to determine cause of death although it's probably due to…'

He lifted Jordan's hooded top carefully. Mitz turned away at the sight of the bright red intestines bulging from the stomach wound.

'You okay?' mouthed Robyn.

Mitz nodded. 'Just caught me unawares. I'll be fine.'

The sight before them was one of the grisliest Robyn had seen. Between the murder and the crows, Jordan Kilby was a complete mess.

'Connor, do you want this?' Harry called.

Connor Richards appeared instantly. 'What have you got?'

'Another feather but you never know. It might yield something.'

Connor lifted the black feather, trapped under the hooded top, and placed it in a plastic evidence bag. Robyn nodded in his direction. Connor, in charge of Forensics for the last six months, had moved from Southern Ireland to take up the position. Robyn was glad he'd done so. He ensured the department ran efficiently and was as much a workaholic as her. She liked his gentle demeanour and ability to remain completely unflustered no matter how daunting the task. He winked at her.

'This reminds me of the Hitchcock film *The Birds*,' he said. 'That scared me rigid. I was only fifteen when I watched it.'

Harry continued studying the incision on Jordan's abdomen. 'The most likely cause of death is exsanguination. It looks like the weapon entered his intestines and was driven upwards towards his heart. I'd say it was a very sharp implement. Can we cut him down now, so I can get him back to the lab?'

Connor agreed.

'Any idea of time of death?' Robyn asked.

'Body temperature and state of rigor indicate he's been dead about twelve hours. Probably murdered sometime late last night, between ten thirty and midnight. Death was most likely from a stab wound, puncturing one of the major blood vessels in the abdomen. I'll give you a detailed report confirming that. As you can see, there was significant bleeding, which indicates a cut to an artery – possibly, given the location of the wound, the abdominal aorta. I'm assuming the blood on the sheet is the victim's.'

'We'll get that checked,' said Robyn.

'There's bruising to his right wrist, nothing on his left. Could have been caused through struggling against his bounds, but there's an absence of chafing I'd associate with repetitive move-ment against twine, and these bounds are very tight, making any movement almost impossible. There's no chafing or bruising around his neck. My first impression is he was dead before he was strung up. The crows seen attacking him might have made the marks and tears on his body. I'll have to examine them in more detail to confirm that.'

Robyn stared at the bloodied sheet, like red waves lapping at his feet, and wondered if the killer was sending some message she had yet to comprehend.

Matt joined them. 'I'm done here. Anna is with Mr and Mrs Marsh, the people who found our victim. They live in the farm-house over there.'

Robyn looked into the distance and saw the roof of a farmhouse half-hidden behind oak trees and hedgerows. She didn't need to go across. PC Anna Shamash would get a full statement in her usual efficient yet compassionate manner. 'Good. Head back to the station and write up the details. Harry, you nearly done?'

'I'll only be a few more minutes then we can cut him down and move him out of here.'

Robyn took a last look at the body. Whoever had done this had planned it. They'd known about the post in the field and had brought twine to tie Jordan up. Had they hoped his body would have remained undiscovered long enough to be mutilated by the crows? She left the forensic team to do their job, removed her protective clothing, exited the tent and marched across the field, head down towards the squad cars. This was the crucial golden hour where they had to collect as much evidence as possible, before trails ran dry and witnesses' memories dulled. A handful of locals were still gathered, hoping for news. No doubt rumours were flying.

Mitz, behind her, let out a soft groan. 'Amy Walters is there,' he said.

'Why am I not surprised?' Robyn had had several run-ins with the eager journalist. Amy, who was also writing a book about serial killers, had taken a three-month sabbatical to do research for it. Robyn had heard on the grapevine she was back in Staffordshire, working as a freelance reporter for the *Stafford Gazette*, and was keen to uncover further material for what she hoped would be a bestseller.

Amy's short, blonde, spikey hair stood out among the crowd clustered behind the cordon. Stylish in a fuchsia leather jacket, skinny jeans and with sunglasses propped on her head, she resembled a tourist at a holiday resort rather than a reporter at a murder scene. Robyn noticed she was talking to a couple next to her, undoubtedly recording everything they said.

She spotted PC David Marker talking to a man, holding an eager dog on a lead. 'Instruct David to canvas the area and ask the crowd if anybody saw any unusual activity. There'll be a briefing at three. Ring me if you need more time here.'

She watched Matt drive away. He'd ensure all the footage from the scene was loaded for them to watch. 'If Connor finds anything of note, let me know. See you back at the station.'

She strode back to her car and was about to duck into it when she heard a voice she recognised. 'DI Carter, have you anything you'd like to say for the *Stafford Gazette*.'

'Amy, you know I can't comment at this stage.'

'But a body of a young male has been found, hasn't it? Can you confirm that?'

'I can't confirm anything until we've identified the victim and notified the next of kin. Please don't ask me any more questions, Amy. I have an investigation to head and I can't waste time here.'

Amy gave her a knowing smile. 'I'll be in touch.'

'Go through the proper channels. I'm not talking to you,' said Robyn, slamming her car door and driving off, past the field and down the lane.

CHAPTER FOUR

Dark clouds the colour of charcoal had replaced the clear blue skies of the morning. The back of Robyn's neck was damp due to the humidity that wrapped itself around her as soon as she left her car and marched into the station. On days like this she hated the large south-facing windows that heated up her office, making it unbearable to work in.

'No air con?' she asked Matt.

'Broken,' came the reply, 'or budget cuts mean we aren't allowed it on yet. It's not officially summertime and this is freak weather.'

'You can say that again. It's boiling in here.' Robyn picked up the internal phone and punched in a number to request an electric fan.

'I don't care if he has taken the last two. My officers can't conduct an investigation in these conditions. Don't bother. I'll fetch it myself.' She threw the receiver down with a huff.

Matt, hunched over his desk, spoke. 'They've run out of fans. I asked when I came in.'

'We're getting one,' said Robyn. 'I'll make sure we do.'

She stomped out of the office, pulling at the jumper clinging to her body and wishing she'd had the foresight to wear something lighter. It'd been crisp and cool when she'd come back from her morning run and dressed to visit Ross. She hadn't anticipated a sweltering day at work.

DI Tom Shearer's office was a floor above hers. The door was shut so she knocked loudly and waited for him to call. When he did, she plastered a smile on her face, the picture of friendliness. Shearer's face usually wore a permanent look of disappointment and today it was extra miserable with furrowed brows and a glistening sheen of sweat visible on his forehead. He'd rolled up his sleeves and was scowling at some paperwork. The other occupants of the room looked as red-faced and uncomfortable as him. PC Gareth Murray, ruddy-faced at the best of times, resembled a rosy red apple. In spite of the two desk fans whirring noisily, Shearer's office was marginally less disagreeable in temperature than her own.

'Yes, DI Carter,' he said with no preamble and a quick glance up from his paperwork.

'I wondered if we could borrow one of your fans. It's like an oven downstairs.'

'And it feels like the chilled aisle in a supermarket in here, does it? I don't think so. It's impossible to work in here even with the perishing things. They make such a racket. Bloody global warming!'

'So that's a "no" then,' said Robyn, maintaining a fixed smile. She'd learnt a while back, letting Shearer rant for a while was usually the best way to handle him. He'd see reason once he'd had his say.

'There aren't any others available. There's been a run on them for obvious reasons. I'd be most grateful if you'd lend me one of yours.'

Shearer glared at her. 'You'd think in this day and age we'd be able to keep a building cool on the three warm days a year we get.'

Robyn nodded in agreement. Gareth kept his eyes lowered. Shearer had only just begun his tirade. It took a further ten minutes of listening to his pontificating before she escaped with one of the fans.

Back in her office, Matt ran a large hand over the top of his bald head, wiping perspiration from it. He sighed in relief as Robyn plugged in the electric fan and a blast of cool air shot towards him.

'Is it me, or has it got really warm in here?' he asked. 'I'm not going through some sort of male menopause, am I?'

Robyn threw him a grin. Matt could always be counted on to ease any tension.

David Marker had returned and was collecting information from the police database. Robyn settled behind her desk and read through it: 23-year-old Jordan Kilby lived in Newborough, a village set between Burton-on-Trent and Rugeley, with his girlfriend, Rebecca Tomlinson, a 24-year-old admin assistant at Pharmacals Healthcare, a medical facility specialising in distributing wound dressing and drugs to the NHS. Jordan Kilby had no previous convictions, a good track record of employment and had worked as a delivery driver for Speedy Logistics since 2012. On the surface, there was nothing dubious about the man at all, but as Robyn knew, it was surprising what secrets people hid.

'Matt, who's informing the girlfriend?'

'Michelle Watson. She's the new liaison officer. She was in here a minute ago while you were locating a fan. She's headed to Pharmacals Healthcare, that's where the girlfriend, Rebecca, works.'

Robyn read through the rest of the notes quickly. Rebecca Tomlinson had a son, six-year-old Dylan. A quick look at the child's birth certificate revealed no named father and Robyn wondered if it was Jordan. It was always painful to deliver such dreadful news, especially when children were involved. Robyn glanced at her watch. It was only just coming up for one o'clock. There was time for her to accompany Michelle and return for the briefing. The sooner she got some information on Jordan Kilby, the sooner she could track down his killer.

'I'll go with her. It might help me get a feel for Jordan Kilby. Learn a little about him. While I'm out, keep gathering as much as you can.'

─❧─

Pharmacals Healthcare was a futuristic development of six enormous dome-shaped warehouses located in a private business park covering several hectares of land. It was accessed via electric gates manned by a guard in a green uniform bearing the Pharmacals Healthcare logo of a serpent entwined around the letters P and H. He requested both their ID cards and buzzed the reception before allowing them entry.

They drew up outside the office block in front of the first of the warehouses – a glass-fronted building, exposing the starkly furnished offices and admin staff bent over flat-screen computers. Robyn glanced up. It was like a giant square goldfish bowl. All the desks were placed in front of windows with views of either the entrance or over the warehouses and loading bays, so the occupants could watch the comings and goings.

They showed IDs again at reception and asked to speak to Rebecca in private. The receptionist escorted them into a bland room with magnolia walls, an oval-shaped table, six padded seats and a television screen. She scurried off to fetch Rebecca, leaving Robyn staring out of the only window that afforded a view of the back of a warehouse. They waited in heavy silence for the door to open again, and to break the terrible news.

Michelle sat beside Rebecca Tomlinson, ready to offer further support to the young woman who'd let out a howl of distress on learning the dreadful news about Jordan and wept for a full five minutes before being able to speak. Rebecca's full lips trembled as she battled to regain control. She kept her head high, her eyes fixed on Robyn. 'This can't be true. It's not him. Maybe somebody stole his wallet.'

Her accent was pure Brummie, with no trace of her Bajan roots. She tugged at the sleeves of her silk, fire-engine-red blouse, pulling them over coloured bangles in orange and red, far too cheerful for such a sombre occasion.

Robyn shook her head sadly. Rebecca's eyes misted again. 'No,' she whispered. 'Please, no. No. It can't be him.'

She plucked once more at her sleeves, eyes wide, searching Robyn's face for confirmation.

'I'm so sorry,' said Robyn.

'How?' Rebecca could hardly speak the question. 'A traffic accident?'

'No, he—'

Before Robyn could finish, Rebecca shook her head and spoke again, her voice a low moan of anguish. 'Oh no. Oh no. I understand. You're a detective. You're here because my Jordan was killed. Detectives only visit when somebody's died in suspicious circumstances.' She stared at Robyn in horror. 'Did someone murder him?'

'I'm afraid there's a strong possibility he was attacked and killed.' Robyn wasn't going to divulge any of the facts. The heartbroken woman was struggling enough to comprehend what she was being told. There was no need to make it harder for her.

'I knew it.' Her breath turned into a series of involuntary inhalations that quickened as she fought to control her emotions.

'Rebecca, I need to learn as much as I can about Jordan. I know this is impossibly difficult for you. I can come back another time if that's easier.'

Rebecca squared her shoulders and gradually the huh-huh-huh sounds quietened. 'Go ahead. I'm okay.'

Robyn marvelled at this woman's strength.

'How long had you been with Jordan?'

'I met him late last November.'

'So about six months?'

Rebecca confirmed with a brief nod. 'I know we'd not been together long but I knew Jordan was the one – my soulmate. Before I met him, I was a hard-working single mum with a little kid whose father had done a runner as soon as he found out I was pregnant. I had no time for relationships or anyone other than my boy. Then I met Jordan – last November. He delivered a package to Longer Life Health where I worked in Birmingham, and asked me to sign for it. He told me I had the loveliest eyes he'd ever seen, and then apologised for such a cheesy chat-up line. He asked me out there and then. I refused. I told him I had a little boy and no time for a relationship. When I left the office later that day, he was standing outside with a bunch of flowers for me, and a football for Dylan. We spent our first date in Eastside City Park in Birmingham, him and me, playing football with Dylan, and we all laughed and laughed. It was a perfect day.' She blinked away the memory that had lifted the corners of her mouth. 'We moved in with him two weeks later and the last six months have been amazing. He's the best thing that's ever happened to us.'

'Did he confide in you? Did he have any concerns or worries?'

'Yes. There are no secrets between us. He had no major worries. We struggle a bit with money at times, but what couple doesn't? We're a very fortunate, happy couple.' Rebecca was still referring to Jordan in the present tense. Robyn didn't contradict her.

'And he hadn't been acting at all suspiciously?'

Rebecca shook her head.

'No mention of any odd phone calls, misdialled numbers, weird emails or letters?'

'Nothing.'

Rebecca appeared lost in thought for a moment. Fresh tears sprung to her eyes. 'He stayed out last night. He went out with some of his footballing friends. He does that now and again. They head off to a pub, have a lads night, and he'll sometimes crash at one of their houses rather than drive home, especially if he's had too much to drink. He's sensible like that. I'd rather he stayed over. I only worry about him otherwise.' She looked at Michelle who gave her a small smile of encouragement.

'Going out on a Sunday night? I'm not sure I'd be up for that with work the next day,' Michelle said.

The corners of Rebecca's mouth pulled upwards slightly but the smile didn't reach her eyes. 'They're football crazy. They all play for the same local football side. There was some football match showing last night on television, and the landlord at the pub has Sky.'

'When did you last see Jordan?' Robyn asked.

'Yesterday afternoon. We all watched a film together – *Kung Fu Panda* – before he went out.' Her face suddenly took on a faraway look. 'He left just after five. He took his bike because it was a nice evening. I had dinner with Dylan and went to bed at about ten and read. Jordan sent a text at eleven thirty saying he'd had too much to drink, so he was going to stay over at Owen's.'

'Owen?'

'Owen Falcon. He lives in Colton.'

Robyn wrote down the man's name, her pulse quickening as she did so. Colton was where they'd found Jordan's body.

'And that was the last you heard from Jordan?'

Rebecca nodded. 'I sent him a text this morning, before I took Dylan to school, but he didn't reply. I didn't think much of it at the time. He doesn't always get a chance to check his phone when he's got tight drop-off schedules. I figured I'd catch up with him later today… but I won't now, will I? He's not coming home. Oh Lord.' Rebecca drew in a noisy, shuddering breath. Hot tears breached her lengthy eyelashes and splashed onto the table, forming two miniature puddles. Michelle put an arm around her shoulders.

'It's okay. We're going to take you home now. Have you got somebody we can contact, to stay with you?'

Rebecca sniffled noisily. 'Dylan. What will I tell Dylan? He'll be in bits. He loves him so much. How am I going to tell my little boy?'

'PC Michelle Watson is going to stay with you at home for a while. We'll help you through this.' Robyn's heart sank at the sight of the woman, fighting to regain control. Whoever had committed this horrible crime had wrecked more than one life. He'd sabotaged an entire family.

CHAPTER FIVE

PC Anna Shamash was showing signs of wilting in spite of the cool air coming from the electric fan that whirred and clicked as it turned left to right. Her thick dark hair was pulled back from her face in a twisted knot, clipped hastily on her head. Several damp tendrils hung limply around her cheeks. She fanned herself with a manila folder.

'We've taken statements from all the bystanders at Top Field in Colton where we found Jordan, and completed door-to-door enquiries. It's going to take forever to go through all the information. I'll make a start before the briefing.'

'Mitz with you?' asked Robyn.

'Should be back in a few minutes. He sent me on ahead.'

Anna settled into her seat and began typing. Robyn rang Speedy Logistics, the company Jordan worked for, and spoke to his manager, Graham Valence, who was shocked to hear of his death.

'Jordan sent me a text round about eleven thirty last night to say he had an upset stomach and wouldn't be coming in. Some of the lads pull a sickie on a Monday after a heavy weekend, but not Jordan. He never did and it wasn't like him to drop us in it last minute. He was never off sick. He didn't take a day off in the five years he worked for us. Good lad. Kept his head down, did his job and didn't piss about like some of them. I contacted another driver to cover for him. Poor Jordan. I didn't realise it was as serious as that. What was it that killed him?'

'I can't comment other than to say we're investigating the nature of his death.'

'It's a bloody shame. I don't know what else to say. I'll tell the others. We'll want to send someone to attend the funeral.'

'Can you tell me a little about him – who his friends were, what sort of man he was.'

'He was a grafter. He came in, did his job and went off again. He got on with us but none of us are best mates here – not with these schedules. The life of a logistics driver is a lonely one – you load your van, you collect your schedule, you make your drops and if you're unlucky and have a really busy day, you come back and do it all again. There's no social club or canteen. Some of the guys, especially the smokers, hang about in the yard when they finish, but not Jordan. He didn't stay here after his deliveries like some do.'

'He didn't seem unduly worried of late?'

'He was pretty het up last Friday when he returned from his round. I saw him pull up and park the van. Slammed the door and stomped off, head down. I could tell he was annoyed.'

'Did you speak to him?'

'No, he brought his delivery sheets to the main desk, dumped them on the counter and collected his bike he kept there without a word to anyone.'

'Was that normal behaviour?'

'It was a little unusual for him. He wasn't one to lose his rag, although he wasn't chatty at the best of times. He had off days like all of us. It's a stressful job and it'd been a long week. No doubt he'd got cut up on the road or stressed out by traffic or something.'

Robyn rang off, gathered her thoughts and prepared for the briefing. The first drops of heavy rain like fat tears began to patter against the windows, the noise gradually intensifying to compete

with the whirring of the fan. She shut her eyes, pictured Jordan
Kilby and shuddered. What sort of maniac would go to the trouble
of staging such a grim murder scene?

Everyone had returned to headquarters and Robyn began the
meeting as she always did, with her whiteboard at the front of the
office, and pen in hand. She'd attached a photograph of the victim
to the board. He looked ghoulish with his head hanging and his
face ravaged. Beside it, she'd placed a picture of Jordan smiling,
taken from an old Facebook profile.

'Our victim's a delivery driver with no prior convictions. He
lived in Newborough with his girlfriend, Rebecca Tomlinson,
and her son, Dylan. On Sunday evening, he went to a pub with
friends, and sent a text message to Rebecca at eleven thirty to say
he intended on spending the night at Owen Falcon's house. He
sent another message, a few minutes later, to Graham Valence, his
logistics manager, claiming he had an upset stomach and would
be unable to come in to work the next day. He is usually reliable,
so Graham took him at his word, and another delivery driver was
called in to replace him. Although Jordan Kilby's wallet was found,
we've not yet discovered his mobile phone. The forensic team are
completing a thorough search of the entire site, and might come
across it. In the meantime, I'd like Anna to contact his phone
provider and try to triangulate his location when he sent those two
messages. His friend, Owen, lives in Colton, and I want to talk to
him as soon as possible.'

Mitz nodded gravely. 'I'll get hold of him straight after this
meeting.'

They watched the footage from the crime scene and made notes.
As soon as it ended Robyn spoke again. 'It seems particularly sadistic to not only stab him in a premeditated act, but to then string
him up and encourage scavengers to feed on him. The sheet at his

feet looks like it's been deliberately placed there. The more I think about it, the more I believe our murderer is sending a message to us, or to somebody else. Let's bear that in mind as we work through this investigation. Matt, anything to add?'

'Not much, guv. As you can see, the body was tied to an old broom handle attached to a stake. There'd been an old weathered scarecrow hanging from it but it disintegrated and was removed a month ago. Toby Marsh, the farmer, was using the field for silage this year, so didn't bother replacing the scarecrow. He'd intended to lift the post this week before he made the first cut, but had forgotten. He's got problems with one of his cutting machines, so he's not up to speed with his other jobs.

'The perp attached Kilby's wrists to the broom handle, using strong twine, available from most do-it-all stores, or online. Harry McKenzie suggested our victim was tied to the support after he'd been killed. Kilby's neck was fastened to the stake using what we believe to be his own belt, to keep him upright.' Matt replaced his notes and waited for comments.

Robyn spoke. 'When I was there, Harry McKenzie found a black feather from a bird – notably a crow – that might have attacked Mr Kilby. I'm not holding out a lot of hope, but if the killer deliberately placed the feather on his body, we might obtain some DNA from it. It appears from Harry's initial findings, Mr Kilby was stabbed to death in situ. That would mean he chose to, or was forced to, traverse the field at night, then was stabbed while standing beside the stake. I wonder if he arranged a late-night meeting with somebody there. If he did, there might be evidence of that on his mobile. I can't hang about on this, so Anna, please make sure you get all the relevant information from his phone provider and check his call history. Mitz?'

Mitz took a deep breath. 'We conducted a door-to-door and took statements from anyone who thought they'd spotted unusual activity over the last couple of days. There are a few leads that need chasing, notably a black car seen late yesterday evening, travelling very slowly through the village, and pausing by the churchyard.'

'Definitely. David, you okay to do that?'

David raised his thumb in response. Robyn folded her arms and let Mitz continue.

'Mr and Mrs Marsh, the couple who found Jordan Kilby's body, have given full statements. Neither recognised Jordan, but I found out something that might be worth following up. Jordan's father is Nathaniel Jones-Kilby of NJK Properties.'

Robyn's eyebrows lifted high on her forehead. 'That *is* interesting.'

Nathaniel Jones-Kilby owned NJK Properties, a construction and house-building company responsible for purchasing ex-green belt areas and erecting large housing estates on them. He was also a close friend and ally of local MP Stewart Broughton. It had been reported in the papers he'd recently received hate mail due to his continued support for the planned High Speed 2 railway line, which was due to cut through much of the Staffordshire countryside. There had been several heated debates about the planned line through the county, and each time, the ever-present Nathaniel Jones-Kilby had sided vociferously with his friend Stewart Broughton on the subject.

'That HS2 line is, as we've read in the newspapers, a contentious affair and has sparked a lot of fury among local communities. Mr Jones-Kilby is not a popular man. Colton is one of the villages affected by the proposed route, isn't it?' asked Robyn.

Mitz nodded. 'I checked the latest proposals on the government website and it seems the route will not only go through Colton, but will cut through the Marsh's land – through Top Field.'

'That was where Jordan's body was found. Have you spoken to Toby and Jane Marsh about that?'

'Not yet.'

'For what it's worth, I genuinely believe they didn't recognise Jordan Kilby,' said Anna. 'They were both horrified about what had happened. Yet, in light of this, I think we ought to follow this up. They have a motive and they may have been involved.'

Robyn definitely wanted to delve deeper into their backgrounds before she discounted the possibility that either Toby or Jane Marsh was involved. 'If somebody murdered Jordan to get at his father, we'll have plenty of potential suspects. The man is thoroughly disliked. Mitz, drag up as much information on Nathaniel Jones-Kilby as possible before I speak to him. He might be the reason Jordan was murdered. I'll talk to Mr and Mrs Marsh about their land. Have we got anything else?'

David spoke up. 'I've been checking through the statements we took in Colton. Apart from the car mentioned earlier, one witness was walking his dog at about 10.30 p.m. and spotted a van parked outside the village hall. Unfortunately, he didn't get a number plate for it. It was "dark-coloured".'

'What van did Jordan drive?' asked Robyn.

'Dark blue. All the Speedy Logistic vans are dark blue.'

She added the word 'van' to her whiteboard. 'Could it have been Jordan's van?'

David scratched at his chin and grimaced. 'I doubt it. The vehicles stay in the yard at night. I've seen them locked up behind the gates when I've driven past.'

'Anna, when you're done with the telephone company, check all the automatic number plate recognition points and speed cameras in the vicinity for that time. See if any vans, dark or otherwise, went through them.'

David spoke again. 'I checked up on Rebecca Tomlinson, Jordan's girlfriend. There's nothing suspicious to report. Good attendance at school, good grades in her examinations. She was a receptionist for five years at Longer Life Health in Birmingham, which offers alternative treatments to its clients – reiki, shiatsu, Indian head massage, all forms of therapy and homeopathic treatments. The owner said she was an exemplary employee. She

resigned from there the third week of December, and left immediately, and took up the position of admin assistant at Pharmacals
Healthcare 8 January this year. Parents are both deceased. She's a
single mother. No convictions.'

The internal phone interrupted them and Matt answered it.
Robyn wound the meeting up, replacing her pen beside the whiteboard. 'That's about it for now. Let's get cracking on this. There's
a fair bit to get through, but I have faith in you all. Thank you.'

Matt replaced the receiver and called out. 'Guv, there's somebody in reception. Wants to talk to you urgently.'

'Who is it?'

'Desk sergeant didn't say. Just that he's put him in interview
room three.'

Robyn headed downstairs. She had so much to do and she hadn't
got time to waste. She hoped this wouldn't take long. She took a
breath, pushed back the door to the interview room and stopped
in her tracks. She recognised the gentleman sat in a chair, his eyes
dark with anger. He scowled at her.

'I'm Nathaniel Jones-Kilby,' he said without rising from the
seat, 'and I want some answers.'

CHAPTER SIX

DAY ONE – MONDAY, 5 JUNE, AFTERNOON

'Let me say how terribly sorry I am—'

Nathaniel Jones-Kilby lifted a hand and interrupted Robyn. 'We're all very sorry, no one more than me. What I want to know is what are you doing about it?'

'Everything we can, Mr Jones-Kilby. My officers are working flat out on it now.'

'And are you prepared to tell me what happened to my son? So far, all I know is he was murdered. If you won't give me the exact details, I shall have to talk to your superior, DCI Flint. I'm sure he'll tell me what I need to know.'

'Sir, that really isn't necessary.'

Nathaniel stared hard at her. 'Then tell me now. Every single detail.'

'We don't know the cause of death yet, Mr Jones-Kilby. As soon as we do, I'll be sure to contact you. We only know it's likely he was killed and his body left in the field.'

The man in front of her was bristling with anger, anger Robyn felt, that came from fear and from not being in control. This was a man who was used to getting his own way. He ran a very successful and profitable company. He rubbed shoulders with entrepreneurs and other highly motivated men. Here, he had no control. He could not order anyone about or demand they operated the way he wanted them to, and above everything else, he'd just learnt his only son was dead. Robyn would only show him respect, even though she found him uncommonly abrasive.

'Let me assure you, sir, we shall do everything possible to find out not only what happened but who was responsible and bring that person to justice.' Her words were sincere. Robyn felt the same way about every injustice or heinous crime. It was her mission to establish the facts, uncover the truth and do right by those left behind.

Nathaniel glared intently at her. 'Make sure you do, DI Carter, or I shall do everything possible to bring you down.'

With that, he stood up and marched towards the door without looking back, leaving Robyn reeling from his verbal attack. There'd been no need for such harshness. Was his anger disguising guilt?

Mitz stuck his head around the door and waved a piece of paper. 'I've arranged to meet Owen at his house. Want to come with me?'

'Definitely.' She accompanied Mitz to the squad car, her mind now on questions she wished to ask Owen, Nathaniel's rudeness forgotten.

The heavy downpour had cleared the air. Nevertheless, she turned on the car's air conditioning. She refused to get hot and bothered again. The afternoon traffic was beginning to build up and they were stuck in a line of stop-start cars at every traffic light, leading out of Stafford town centre. It was the same most days at this time. At this rate, it would take almost an hour to reach Colton and Robyn didn't want to waste a minute. She gave an exasperated sigh.

'I've had enough of this. Put the siren on.'

Mitz obliged and they pulled out from the queue of traffic, overtaking the line of vehicles. Robyn ignored the surprised looks. She was used to those. Instead she found herself staring at the grey pavements and the occasional tree reflected in the large puddles that spilled into the road to be washed away in noisy waves as they drove through at speed. She wondered how long Jordan Kilby would have remained hanging in the field if it hadn't been for Jane Marsh spotting the crows. He might have been there days, in full sight of everyone yet undiscovered. The thought left her cold.

The town with its roads cluttered with houses gave way to more open countryside and bungalows perched above sloped gardens as they raced into Milford, sped past green verges, wide pavements and old-fashioned phone boxes. Huge horse chestnut trees in leaf dotted along the roadside added to the village's appeal. They shot by the large common, deserted thanks to the rain, and Shugborough Hall, a historic estate Robyn had never visited in all her years of living in Stafford, even though it was only seven miles from her house. The estate had been taken over by the National Trust the year before, and according to David Marker, who was heavily into history, had some 'amazing follies'. With the siren blaring they soon left it – and the entrance to Cannock Chase that lay just beyond – behind them, receding dots in the rear-view mirror. Robyn often cycled through Milford and over the Chase, especially when she had an Ironman contest to prepare for. She had one of those looming, in less than two weeks. She'd upped her regime the last four weeks and had been training hard, not only in her local gym, but also outside, pounding the streets and roads from Stafford to Cannock.

Cars pulled over at the sound of their approaching siren, blurred faces watching them as they sped by. Fields of bright yellow rapeseed raced by her window, and thoughts turned again to Jordan Kilby. She wanted a list of names of all who'd made contact with him the night before. She'd speak to each of them. She wondered how close they all were. Friends didn't always know every detail about each other. Neither did lovers. A vision of Davies flashed before her eyes and she blinked it away. Had Kilby kept things from Rebecca? She suspected he might have, even though Rebecca had been sure they had been open.

They followed the twists and turns of the winding lanes that finally emptied them onto a straight that ran alongside the railway line. A silver train whistled by and for a while ran parallel to them. A large sign, 'No to HS2,' and another, 'HS2 will kill me,' were pinned to ancient oak trees. This was where the new HS2 line would be laid, cutting through these fields and across this land, causing homes to be flattened. Nathaniel Jones-Kilby had been a staunch supporter of the new line. Had it cost him his son's life?

Three swift turns and they drove towards Colton for the second time that day, this time stopping beside one of the houses before the field in which they'd found Jordan Kilby, a few hours earlier. Mitz drew into a driveway and breathed out. 'Not too hairy a ride for you?' he asked with a small grin.

Robyn responded with a grin of her own. 'Nah! I've been with far scarier drivers – David Marker for one.'

Mitz chuckled. David was renowned for his ultra-safe handling of vehicles, which in the past had earned him the nickname 'Slug'.

Owen's detached house was a 1960s brown-brick bungalow, in poor condition with a front porch, wooden slatted blinds at all the windows, and a large, black satellite dish attached to the front wall. His front garden had been replaced by tarmac and a Honda motorbike stood on it, propped up on its stand.

Robyn pressed the bell but when no chimes were heard, rapped loudly at the door. A man appeared and nodded as he scratched at a scraggy beard on a tired, washed-out face. His hooded eyes gave him an appearance of a bird of prey, an image born out further by his rounded shoulders that threw his head forward. Robyn held up her warrant card.

'DI Carter,' she said. The man grunted. 'And this is Sergeant Patel. I believe you spoke to him on the phone.'

'The man rubbed once more at his beard. His voice was lighter than she expected and polite. 'Come in.'

They crossed the threshold into a sitting room. It was surprisingly modern inside the house and very stark, as if its owner only popped in and out, now and again. A large, brown, velvet settee with red cushions and a matching chair appeared to be the only furniture in the room. An enormous television screen dominated one wall. On it two knights fought, the sound of steel clashing against steel amplified by the surround sound speakers, giving the room the feel of a cinema. Owen muted the film and picked up an open can of beer from beside the chair, held it to his lips, sipped and then spoke.

'Can't get my head around it,' he said. 'He was here last night. What happened?'

'I'm sorry, it's an ongoing investigation so I can't release details for now.'

'There's a rumour going around he was found in a field.'

Robyn refused to be drawn in by the questions. Owen chugged the beer. 'Was he attacked or did he top himself?'

'What makes you think he'd commit suicide?'

'I don't really. He had no reason to. He wasn't depressed or taking any medication as far as I know. He wasn't pissed out of his skull or high. He didn't take any drugs. He wasn't that sort of bloke. So, I don't really know what made me say it. Trying to make sense of why Jordan was found dead in a field near my house, I suppose. What do you want from me?' he asked, with a sigh.

'To find out what happened last night.'

Owen wiped foam from his top lip and shrugged. 'Nothing much. We met up with some of the crowd at the Fox and Weasel down the road, to watch the friendly between Ireland and Uruguay. Wrapped it up at about eight fifteen. Jordan came back with me. We had a couple of cans, played *FIFA 17* on the Xbox, then he crashed out on the settee and I went to bed. I thought he was going to stay overnight. I didn't hear him leave. I was well out of it. He had a drop to make first thing, so I guessed he'd gone home to get changed. I got up before eight and he'd already left by then.'

'How would he have got back home?'

'Bicycle. He always cycles in the warmer weather – cycled,' he said, correcting himself. 'He didn't want it to be nicked, so he left it in my garage. Like I said, the pub's only down the road. We walked to it together.'

'And you didn't hear him leave?'

'Nah, I was dead to the world.' He stopped at his own words, took another drink. His can trembled slightly in his hand.

'Did anything happen last night?'

'Like what?' Owen asked.

'Somebody take offence at anything that was said. Maybe somebody took a dislike to Jordan. That sort of thing.' Robyn watched his face as she spoke. Owen's head jerked from one side to the other, an involuntary movement. Was it a sign of nervousness?

'Can't think of anything. We weren't out to cause trouble, if that's what you're suggesting. It was just some mates having a drink. It was quiet in the Fox and Weasel. Only a few others in.'

Robyn made a note. 'And can you give me the names of the others who were there with you?'

'Callum Bishop, Jasper Fletcher and Dean Wells. We know each other from football. We've played for the local team, Blithfield Wanderers, for the last four years. Landlord's our team manager so we usually hang out at the Fox and Weasel.'

'The landlord's the team manager?'

'Yeah. Joe Harris. He doesn't play, but he used to. He manages us now. He sorts out our kit for matches on a Sunday, washes it, all that sort of stuff. And his pub sponsors the team.' Owen rubbed a hand over his face. 'Look, I don't want to be rude, but I've been at work all day, and I'm a bit knackered. Can we wind this up? I don't see what else I can tell you.'

Robyn gave a tight smile. 'I appreciate that, Mr Falcon. We won't keep you much longer. I'd like addresses of where your friends live, any contact details, that sort of thing. Obviously, we're doing our best to find out what happened to Mr Kilby in the hours before his death.'

Owen's shoulders slumped. 'Sure. I didn't mean to be rude. Poor Jordan. He was a good bloke.'

'You see him often?'

'Now and again. More often when it's football season.'

'So, he wasn't an especially close friend.'

Owen laughed loudly, too loudly. 'No, he was okay. We hung out a bit, that's all. He was into some weird shit I didn't get – he liked Marvel characters – not my cup of tea at all.'

'But he stayed over last night?'

'Only cos it was too far for him to ride home after drinking a skinful. He didn't want to fall off his bike. He came back to play me on the Xbox and then decided he was still too pissed to go home. Asked if he could crash here so I said okay.'

'What about the others you met? Did they drive home?'

'Jas was having a night off the booze so he drove. They all live in Rugeley. Jordan doesn't live near any of them.'

'So, he played on the Xbox and then asked to stay over? He didn't think he should go home to his girlfriend?'

Owen let out a snort. 'Rebecca? Nah. I imagine he was glad to get away from her nagging for the night.'

'Nagging?'

'Bossed him about. He was probably glad for some time out.'

'You not keen on Rebecca?'

Owen winced and spoke again. 'It's not that I'm not keen on her. She's a bit too full on for my liking. It was all "hun" this and "hun" that, and touchy-feely stuff all the time when she was with Jordan. Made me feel uncomfortable.'

'You not got a partner, Mr Falcon?' asked Robyn.

He shook his head. 'I prefer my own company. I can't bear all that pressure to please. I had a long-term girlfriend, but we split up. Had a few dates since then but nothing serious.'

'Did Jordan tell you about anything that might have been troubling him?'

'He was a pretty laid-back bloke. I don't think much bothered Jordan.'

'And he was just a friend?'

Owen's eyes flashed for a moment. 'If you are inferring we were involved in a physical relationship, Detective, the answer is no, we weren't.'

'I'll take details of your other friends and let you get on with your evening. Thank you for your help,' said Robyn.

'That's it?'

'For the moment. We might need to ask you more questions later.'

'So, you going to tell me what happened to him or do I have to listen to the crap that's flying around – Jordan hanged himself, he was shot in the head, he was nailed to a post. There's all sorts of rumours.'

'We can't reveal any details for the moment. Please try not to listen to the rumours. You will be told in due course and for now, I'd be grateful if you'd keep our conversation confidential. Don't talk to any journalists or anyone, please.'

Owen studied his can once more. 'Poor bastard,' he said.

As she sat in the car with Mitz, she spotted Owen peering out from between the slats of the blinds. He hadn't seemed terribly upset at his friend's death, and the involuntary shaking suggested he was nervous about something.

'I know what you're going to say,' said Mitz, putting the squad car into gear and reversing out of the driveway. 'Check him out. He was a bit shifty.'

'I love it when the power of telepathy works,' she replied.

'He was definitely hiding something,' Mitz said. 'It was the way he kept jerking his head, and looking away when you asked him questions. It wasn't simply because he was uncomfortable.'

'Maybe that's all it is and he's emotionally challenged so he can't express his feelings. He admitted he doesn't like "touchy-feely" stuff. Or maybe he didn't really like Jordan that much. Just because they played for the same football side doesn't mean they had to like each other.'

'True, but you wouldn't go out for a drink with somebody you didn't much care for, or have them back to your place to play on your Xbox,' said Mitz. 'He's got to be keeping something back from us.'

'I think so too. He said Jordan intended to ride his bike home. I wonder where it is. I'll give Connor a ring and ask him to keep an eye out for it. It might still be at the crime scene somewhere.' She lifted her mobile and then spoke again. 'We might get something more out of Jordan's other friends. Fancy trying any of them now?'

'I have nothing else planned for tonight.'

'You sure? I don't want to overwork you.'

'I'm coming voluntarily,' said Mitz. 'I'll not settle tonight if we don't start building up a picture of what happened. You know what it's like.'

Robyn knew only too well. Once she became involved in a case, nothing else took priority – not even thoughts of her dead fiancé.

CHAPTER SEVEN

The kitchen was a mess of unwashed pans and plates. Callum Bishop sat at the kitchen table, spooning Spaghetti Hoops into a reluctant toddler's mouth. On a far chair, another small boy stared intently at an iPad, ignoring Robyn and Mitz.

'Missus is out so it's my turn to look after the kids. This one won't eat his food and if I don't make him, I'll be in the doghouse, won't I?' he said in a silly voice to the child. 'Come on, George, help me out here, or Daddy will have to eat it all up and tell Mummy that George ate the pasta.' He pretended to eat, making the toddler gurgle and hold out his hands for the spoon. Callum swooped the food into the child's mouth before he could change his mind.

'And that's the last of it. That's lousy about Jordan,' he said, turning his attention from the toddler and wiping his hand on a tea towel. 'Owen rang me before you called. He said Jordan was attacked in Colton.'

'That's right. On the route leading to Rugeley.'

Callum shook his head. 'What a thing to happen.'

'Can you run through last night for us? We're trying to get an idea of his movements,' asked Robyn.

'Met up at the Fox and Weasel just outside Colton, at about five forty-five before kick-off. It was the Ireland versus Uruguay friendly match, on Sky. Stayed for a quick drink afterwards. Joe, our football team manager, wanted to run some new football shirt logos past us. Jasper was on soft drinks, so he drove Dean and me home at eight thirty. Owen and Jordan left before us. That's it.'

'Did Jordan appear to be acting normally?'

Callum shrugged. 'As normal as he ever is.'

'What do you mean by that?'

Callum rubbed a hand over the toddler's soft hair and considered his words before speaking. 'He was a bit of an oddball. He was into comic book stuff – films, memorabilia, and superhero action figures – and cycling. The only common ground we shared was football. He was friendlier with Owen than with any of the rest of us. I've known Jas and Dean for years. Went to the same school as them, lived around Rugeley all our lives. But Jordan was different – he had a privileged upbringing, went to public school and lived in a massive, posh house before he moved out. He tried to fit in with us but he didn't quite manage it. Jordan only began hanging out with us after matches because of Owen. He always looked like he wasn't on the same wavelength, if you get my meaning. Unless he talked about sport, he didn't know what to say.

'Last night, he and Owen stood at the bar while the rest of us sat near the television, glued to the match. I didn't really speak to either of them, only afterwards when Joe pulled out the new shirts. Jordan didn't much care for them and scoffed at them – all pompous-like. He could get like that from time to time. Must have inherited it from his old man. He soon backed down though. Joe told him if he didn't like it he could piss off and play for another team. That shut him up. I thought he was going to cry when Joe said that. He apologised and then left with Owen soon after.'

'I was under the impression Jordan hung out with you all regularly.'

Callum shook his head. 'Only when Owen invited him along. Jordan was a hanger-on. He tried to be one of the lads, especially in front of Owen, and during football matches, but off the pitch he was out of his depth with us.'

'You didn't see either of them after they left the pub?'

''Fraid not.'

'And you came straight home?'

'I was the first to be dropped off. Ask my wife. She'll tell you I was back before nine.'

Robyn was curious about the strange relationship Jordan had with his teammates. None of them appeared to like him much. Owen had denied he was a good friend and now Callum was hinting he didn't especially like the man. She wondered if it was because he'd come from a wealthy family.

'Did Jordan get any stick for being related to Mr Jones-Kilby?' she asked.

'We might have had a few digs at him about it when we first found out who he was, but the truth was, Jordan hated his old man. One day we were ribbing him and he'd had too much to drink. It all spilled out – how he hated his father and blamed him for his mum's death.'

'What happened to his mother?'

'She and Nathaniel split up because he'd been having an affair. She moved out and bought a house somewhere in the Lake District to get away from him. Travelling to it one day, she had a car accident that killed her. Jordan decided it was his father's fault she was on the road that day. Said if his dad hadn't messed up, his parents would never have split up and his mum would never have moved away.

'He was embarrassed to be associated with Nathaniel. NJK Properties have ruined lots of villages in this area by sticking up new housing, and there's a fair amount of resentment round these parts because of Nathaniel's support for the HS2 railway line. There are folk whose houses will be demolished to make way for it, and who will have to move out of the area. Some have lived here for generations and will lose family homes. Jordan was as annoyed as the rest of us. There was a piece in the press about his old man getting hate mail over it. We joshed Jordan. Asked if he'd sent the letters. You should've seen his face. He got proper worked up and red-faced. Said Nathaniel deserved more than fucking rude letters. Never seen him look so angry. There's no point taking the mickey out of somebody who hates their own father that much.'

'He didn't talk about his family, then – his girlfriend, her son?'

'As I said, he wasn't into man-talk or chatting much. It was always about football or cycling. Right cycle bore, he was. Would drone on about the Tour de France and La Vuelta if given half a chance. Personally, I can't be arsed with it. I prefer matches on the pitch. Can't see the attraction of watching cycling.'

The toddler began to get restless and Callum lifted him from his highchair.

'Jordan didn't mention Rebecca or Dylan at all?' Robyn found it odd a man wouldn't want to chat about more than football with friends.

Callum pulled a face at the youngster, who giggled. 'Owen told me before Christmas that Jordan had a girlfriend. That surprised me. I had Jordan down as gay. I even thought at one stage he fancied Owen, the way he hung onto his every word. She used to come to the football matches with that lad of hers – cheered and shouted every time Jordan got the ball. It was a bit embarrassing, if I'm honest. My missus doesn't make that sort of noise. Rebecca joined us at the pub afterwards a couple of times and seemed pleasant enough, but she'd drag Jordan away after one drink, arm in arm – all lovey-dovey stuff. Look, I really have to get these guys to bed now. It's past their bedtime.'

'Of course and thank you, Mr Bishop.'

'Any time,' said Callum with a shrug. 'Jordan was definitely weird, but I'm sorry this has happened to him. Doesn't bear thinking about.'

-⚜-

Back at the car, Mitz punched an address into the satnav and spoke.
'Jasper Fletcher only lives five minutes away.'

'We'll try him.'

The short drive took them out of Rugeley town on the ring road
that ran parallel with the main railway line. A Virgin Express bullet-
shaped train, its livery of red and silver shining in the last rays of
the setting sun, shadowed them for a brief moment before speeding
ahead, taking only seconds to disappear into the distance. Robyn's
thoughts turned again to the HS2 line. Was it possible somebody
had murdered Jordan because of something his father had done? She
chewed over what she already knew while Mitz turned back towards
the town, following commands that took them down several roads,
into a housing estate and out onto a road lined with 1930s houses
with bay windows, two mirror-image houses in one building. They
drew up four houses down, behind a dark blue Ford Fiesta.

'That's his car – it's registered to him – and that's where he lives.
Number 76,' said Mitz, pointing at the house on the right-hand
side.

A skinny woman in her mid to late forties, wearing a careworn
expression, opened the door. Her eyes widened at the sight of
Robyn and Mitz.

'Good evening. I'm sorry to disturb you but we'd like to talk to
Jasper Fletcher, please.'

'Jas? He's my son. He's not in trouble, is he?'

'No. We'd like to talk to him about one of his friends.'

Her eyes bulged, then, realising she was expected to act on
the information; she invited them in, motioning towards a room
ahead of them.

'Go in. I'll fetch Jas.'

She scurried up the stairs, leaving Robyn and Mitz in the hall.
As they walked towards the door she'd indicated, Robyn heard

animal noises in the room on the right, and glanced towards them. An elderly lady, dressed completely in black, hair thin and patchy, was glued to a nature programme, oblivious to the visitors. Mitz followed Robyn into the dining room that looked out onto the back garden, a small plot, completely laid to grass and surrounded by wood-panelled fencing. It lacked colour and care, although somebody had recently dragged a lawnmower across it.

The room smelt old. A lace tablecloth, yellowed with age, covered a dining table. The stiff-backed chairs looked utilitarian rather than comfortable and Robyn found it difficult to imagine anybody enjoying a meal around this table in this room. A dark dresser took up almost one wall and was filled with pieces of patterned crockery and china knick-knacks – the type often purchased at car boot sales.

'Somebody enjoys cross-stitching,' said Mitz, pointing out the framed pieces that adorned another wall. 'Wow, some of these must have taken ages to complete.'

Robyn studied the picture of three flowers resembling tulips with a bee flying above them, next to the quote, 'Be still and know that I am God.' Other patterns, all verses from the bible, were extremely intricate. She marvelled at the one that began 'Blessed are the poor in spirit…' As she read, a shuffling by the door indicated the arrival of Jasper and his mother.

'My mother made them,' said the woman. 'Spends hours at it. Got the patience of a saint. I can't – I'm all fingers and thumbs.'

Jasper, dressed in jogging bottoms and a sweatshirt, gave them a curt nod.

'You want me to stay or go?' asked the woman.

Jasper shrugged. She hovered by the door, her face etched with concern, while Robyn spoke to the young man.

'Hi. I'm Detective Inspector Carter. This is Sergeant Patel. I'm sorry but we have bad news concerning one of your friends – Jordan Kilby.'

Jasper studied her with pale blue eyes. 'Yeah. I already know. Owen rang me.'

'What about Jordan?' Jasper's mother asked.

'Died,' said Jasper. 'Owen says he was murdered.'

The woman let out a small gasp and crossed herself.

Jasper turned towards her. 'Why don't you go and watch telly with Nan? This won't take long.'

'I'll do that. Let me know if you need anything.' She nodded furiously as if to drive home her point before moving off.

'Obviously we'd like to extend our condolences,' said Robyn.

Jasper shrugged. 'We weren't that close.'

'But you saw him regularly and played football with him?'

Jasper slid onto one of the dining chairs and wiped his palms on the tops of his jeans. 'I knew him. I got on okay with him but he wasn't like one of my real mates or anything. I didn't see him outside of the pub.'

Mitz spoke. 'We were hoping you could tell us a little about him.'

'Can't help you,' Jasper said with a shrug. 'You ought to ask Owen about him. He was more of a mate than the rest of us. If you want my honest opinion, Jordan was a bit of a wanker – always cycling everywhere, and clomping into the pub in his cycle shorts and shoes. His girlfriend Rebecca was up herself too. Didn't really hit it off with her. Her kid was okay though – Dylan. Supported Birmingham City. Chatted to him a couple of times.'

'You didn't really like Jordan?'

'I didn't like or dislike him. I had no particular feeling either way. He was a good football player and he didn't piss me off. That's about it.'

'You were with him at the pub last night?'

Jasper nodded. 'Yeah. He wasn't in a talkative mood.'

'What time did he leave?'

'Just before us. He went off with Owen. He didn't want his fancy bike to get nicked so he'd left it at Owen's place. I took the others home in my car. I'd been drinking soft drinks because I'd already binged that weekend and needed a break from the alcohol.'

'Who were "the others"?'

'Dean Wells and Callum Bishop. Dropped Callum off at his house first, then Dean at his flat, and came home. Mum and Nan were just back from church. Nan wanted to watch a drama on television, so I came upstairs and watched a film on Netflix – *The Wall*, a thriller about two soldiers in Iraq. Really good it was.'

'Can anybody vouch for you?'

'Am I a suspect?'

'It's procedure.'

Jasper stared ahead at the wall covered in cross-stitch pictures. 'My mum came in to say she was off to bed and asked me to put out the wheelie bins in the morning. The film lasted about an hour and a half. Turned in soon after. Nan saw me. I went downstairs to pick up my phone charger before I went to bed. She was still watching television.'

'Thank you. Can you think of anything that might help us?'

He screwed up his face. 'Nah. I'm not the bloke to ask. I didn't know much about him at all.'

'If you think of anything, please let us know.'

Jasper shrugged nonchalantly and took the card he was offered. 'Was Owen right? He said Jordan was hanged.'

'We're not releasing details at the moment. You'll be notified in due course. As you appreciate, it's an ongoing investigation.'

'Yeah. You want to check I was here with my mum and nan?'

'If you wouldn't mind.'

He pushed back his chair and loped in front of them to the sitting room. Both women were watching the television. His mother rose as soon as they appeared.

'The police want to know if I was here last night,' said Jasper.

'Of course you were. You were upstairs. I heard you in your room. The walls in these places are very thin,' she said to Robyn.

The elderly lady looked across at the interruption.

'I saw him too,' she said, her voice surprisingly assured and strong. 'Jasper was here. He came downstairs when I was watching the news on BBC One. He's a good boy. I hope you don't think he's been involved in any wrongdoing.'

'We're merely following procedure,' said Robyn with a small smile.

The woman threw her a steely look. 'That's all right then.' She turned her head back to the television, dismissing them in that one gesture.

Robyn thanked them and departed with the sense that Jordan was a lonely individual who, in spite of his network of friends, had nobody he could really count on. Jasper didn't like him much. So far, they'd all suggested he was an oddity. She mulled over Callum's account again. Could Jordan's temper have got the better of him off the pitch and caused a fight? It was something to consider.

They rang the third friend, Dean Wells, but reached the messaging service and had no reply when they banged on the door to his flat. It was now too late in the day to pursue any further enquiries. Robyn had a duty to look after her officers and so she called it a night, sending Mitz off-duty.

As she drove back to her own home, she remembered she needed to buy some food for Schrödinger. She'd get some chicken at the supermarket en route and grill it for them both. She chuckled as she thought about Ross's words. She *was* turning into a Catlady.

CHAPTER EIGHT

Rain had replaced the sunshine of the day before, and as Robyn raced across the car park and into the building, with her coat held over her head to protect her hair from the heavy drops, she almost collided with Tom Shearer by the entrance. He gave a rare smile and held the door open for her.

'Guess we don't need the fans today,' he said.

She shook the coat, sprinkling water over the floor, and returned the smile. She'd tried not to encourage any overfamiliarity with Shearer ever since she'd learned he was the secret admirer who'd sent her a large bunch of anemones on Valentine's Day. Fortunately, he hadn't followed up on that gesture, invited her out or given her any hint he was interested in her in any way other than in a professional capacity. For that, she was grateful. Her restless mind had been struggling with the possibility that Davies was alive. She couldn't have coped with any more emotion, or a relationship with another man. As Shearer strode to his office, head high, shoulders straight, his dark hair flecked attractively with silver streaks, she wondered for a brief second if she ought to encourage him. It'd been over two years since Davies' death. She'd been alone too long.

Anna was in the corridor talking to one of the technicians. Robyn mused that Anna would be as much at home in the technology department as on the crime investigation team. She had worked in computer technology before joining the force and was the best person to ask for anything to do with laptops, phones or the Internet. Anna's face was as intense as usual as she nodded, deep in conversation with the officer. She spotted Robyn at the last moment and pulled away.

'I've got a location for Jordan Kilby's phone Sunday night,' she said. 'The messages sent that night came from Colton. There's a transmitter nearby. I've also received his phone records for the last month. Before I go through them, I wanted to show you something. He didn't have any active social media accounts, but I came across a couple of articles that might be of interest.'

She accompanied Robyn into the office where Mitz was coaxing the coffee machine into life. He greeted them with some news.

'I ran Owen's name through the police database. He was in a young offender's institute from 2003 to 2005 for attacking and injuring two fifteen-year-olds – gang-related incident. He was one of three convicted at the time. Also charged with GBH in 2010 – a brawl in a pub – but the case was dropped by his accuser.'

Robyn's eyebrows shot upwards as she considered the possibility of Owen Falcon attacking his friend. It would have to have been over something serious for Owen to murder him in such an elaborate way, and leave his body strung up in a field close to his home. The picture didn't feel right. Owen wouldn't have murdered him and left himself with such a weak alibi. If the pair had argued, the attack would have been quick and aggressive. She pulled out her Post-it notes and wrote two questions:

Did Owen plan to murder Jordan that night?
Did they argue and fight?

She shut her eyes and considered what she'd written. Both were possible. Owen knew the field – Top Field – and would have known there was an empty stake in the ground. He could have planned it. It wasn't far from his home, which was on a quiet lane. He might have killed Jordan and then disposed of his bike and mobile. Neither had been found yet. In spite of the logic, her instinct said Owen was not responsible.

She opened her eyes and turned her attention to the printout Anna had given her. It was a newspaper article from 2010 entitled, 'Why Do Rich Boys Turn Bad?' – a piece about offspring from wealthy families who'd rebelled. Robyn flicked through the piece and slowed down when she reached the fifth paragraph.

Jordan Kilby, the sixteen-year-old son of successful businessman Nathaniel Jones-Kilby, turned no heads when he arrived at our agreed meeting point in Lichfield. Dressed in a pair of jeans and unremarkable jacket, with a boyish face framed with dark wavy locks, he resembled a member of a boy band. Softly spoken and almost painfully shy, this kid might have just been thrown out of an expensive school, but he doesn't have attitude. In fact, he was reluctant to talk to this journalist about the real reasons behind his expulsion from the £30,000 per year fee-paying school, and denied the rumours it was because of dealing drugs. 'Nothing like that at all. Some days, you have enough of it: the bossing about, the academic expectations, the other, equally screwed-up kids,' said Jordan in a quiet, soft voice that didn't smack of the usual teenage cockiness I expected. 'I didn't want to be controlled any more. I was only at the school because my dad is stinking rich. I'd rather have gone to a more local school. Not every kid at public school fits in.' The school has remained tight-lipped about the reasons for his expulsion and Mr and Mrs Jones-Kilby were both unavailable for comment. As Jordan left, this journalist felt he was less a rebel and more a misunderstood young man. Maybe money doesn't solve every problem.

Anna waited for Robyn to look up from the article before speaking. 'Did you notice the name of the journalist?'

Robyn read the title and name. 'Amy Walters. This must have been one of the very first pieces she wrote.'

'It's not very detailed, but Amy might remember more about Jordan. You know what she's like. She'll have asked a load of questions and only used some of the material.'

'True. Looks like I might be talking to her after all,' said Robyn with a sigh. 'So, the text messages sent from Jordan's phone were sent from Colton. He must have been alive at eleven thirty.'

'Unless the killer sent them,' said Anna.

Robyn let out another sigh. 'Indeed. And given we haven't found Jordan's mobile, that's a possibility.'

Mitz dropped a cup of coffee onto her desk with a smile. 'You'll need that. Joe Harris, the landlord of the Fox and Weasel, is here.'

'Cheers. Let's chat to him,' came Robyn's reply as she took a quick swig of the coffee and steeled herself for another long day of interviews and questioning.

Joe Harris sported a dark grey, neatly trimmed beard and a shaven head. Black eyebrows, like giant caterpillars, crawled across his forehead. The immediate impression was of a villain from a Bond movie, an impression supported by the dark look he threw Robyn when she introduced herself.

'I'd like to extend my condolences,' she said. 'I understand Jordan was one of your regulars and played for your local football team.'

Joe gave a brief nod.

'What can you tell us about Jordan? You must have known him quite well.'

'He was a little eccentric but mad keen on football and cycling. Kept his head down. Got on okay with everyone. Quiet lad.'

'I hear he and Owen got along well.'

'You heard right. Wherever Owen went, Jordan would tag along. Owen took him under his wing. Jordan didn't find it easy to mix. Owen made it easier for him.'

'Good friends?'

'Definitely.'

'You'd say Jordan was a shy type?'

Joe nodded. 'Shy, timid and even a bit scared of his own shadow.'

'How did you meet him? The Fox and Weasel isn't his local pub. It's out of his usual patch.'

'About a year ago. Owen brought him along to one of the training matches and we let him have a kick about with us. I asked him to join the team straight away. He was a cracking player. He turned out to be one of our best. I reckon he could've tried out professionally, he was that good. He sometimes got carried away on the pitch, but nothing over the top. Football matches can be like that. Heat of the moment clashes, the odd foul, a few words spoken out of turn. Nothing terrible. Lads letting off steam, that's all.'

'Callum Bishop told us you revealed the new football shirts to some of the team on Sunday evening.'

'That's right. I'd had brand new logos printed. Thought I'd show them to the lads in the pub before I took them along for the rest of the squad to see. Just to make sure they liked them.'

'And did they?'

He nodded. 'Pretty much. Jordan wasn't too keen but he was in a mard that night.'

'A mard?'

'Bit sulky like. He could get like that sometimes – sullen. Especially after a pint or two. He'd go all moody. Would only give one-word answers. He was best ignored when he was like that. Thought maybe Rebecca had been giving him a hard time.' He laughed. 'He was a bit hen-pecked. We'd rib him about that sometimes. Poor lad. He was quite sensitive really.'

'Can you elaborate?'

'He was a soft touch when it came to her. If she said to be home at a certain time, he'd go racing back, even if a match was only halfway through, or he was enjoying himself. She'd only been living with him for five minutes and was already wearing the trousers. Owen thought Jordan was behaving like a right pussy – sorry, no offence.'

'You met her?'

Joe laughed. 'Yes. She had Jordan by the balls.'

'Did the others bring their wives or girlfriends to the pub?'

Joe shook his head. 'The lads in the football team usually come to the Fox and Weasel to get away from their partners. It's a refuge for them.'

'Surely their spouses go along to support the local football matches.'

'Yeah, now and again, they do. Jordan's girlfriend came to a few matches. Regular cheerleader she was.'

'I'm sure the support was welcome,' said Robyn.

Joe opened his mouth to speak but changed his mind with a slight shake of his head.

'Have you been sponsoring the team for a long time?'

'About five years. I used to play for the Blithfield Wanderers when I was younger. In those days the local shop sponsored the team, but the owners sold up in 2012, and it seemed a shame to let the team fold. I took over as team sponsor and manager. I go along to training matches and the Sunday games. Keep my hand in, as it were.'

'I expect you know the players well.'

He nodded. 'Known a lot of them since they were kids. I used to play with their fathers. Owen, Callum, Jasper and Dean, they've been in the team the longest. The others were new to the team this season, or joined us back end of last year. We get quite a lot of changeover – lads who can't commit on a Sunday or during the week because of families, work, that sort of thing. Those four lads – been faithful to the side – never miss a match.'

'Can you think of anybody who'd bear a grudge against Jordan?'

Joe shook his head. 'Nah, he wasn't the sort to rile anybody. He was quite unlike his father, Nathaniel. Now, I can think of plenty of people who'd like to murder *that* man. Bloody nuisance he is. At least Jordan wasn't a chip off that particular block.'

Robyn left Mitz with Joe Harris so she could drop in on Matt, who was in another room interviewing Dean Wells. Dean looked like a rugby prop – with thick thighs, a round face, shaven head and a bull neck. His responses were similar to the others.

'Jordan didn't join in the banter much, only if there was a match on television then he'd shout and jeer at the referee along with the rest of us.'

'Did you ever see him outside of the pub?'

'Yeah, I sometimes saw him cycling around the roads on his way to work or wherever. I saw him and his girlfriend, Rebecca, playing football with Dylan once at the park in Lichfield. Well, he was playing. She was standing about and cheering when the kid scored a goal. I was there with my nephew. We went across to them to say hello but Rebecca was a bit off with us. I suggested the kids might like to hang out together and play for a bit, but she said they had to go. Jordan looked apologetic but left with her. I asked him about it next time I saw him. He said they really did have to get off. I didn't believe him though. I think she didn't want her little lad to mix with my nephew. Probably thought we weren't good enough for him or something like that.'

'Can you think of anybody who'd want to harm him?'

Dean pulled a face. 'You mean kill him? There's a difference, isn't there? I can think of a couple of people who'd want to punch his lights out, but nobody who'd actually murder him.'

'Who'd want to hurt Jordan?'

'Nah, I wasn't being that serious. He pissed off a few of the opposition now and again – he was a really good player and was our best scorer. Nobody likes to lose, do they?'

Following the interviews that had yielded so little information, Robyn rang Toby and Jane Marsh, the couple who'd found Jordan's body, primarily to confirm their statements, but also to see how they were. Jane Marsh sounded hesitant when she picked up before Robyn explained who she was.

'I almost didn't answer the phone,' said Jane. 'We've had people knocking on the door asking us questions, and the press keep phoning. Toby wanted me to take the phone off the hook. He's outside in the field. Did you want to talk to him?'

'I wondered how you both were. It must have been such a shock to you.'

'It was but I've been a farmer's wife for forty years and I've seen a lot of death – we've lost many an animal over the years – although I've never seen a man hanging from a pole before.'

'We're keeping the details from the public and I very much appreciate your silence on this matter.'

'Oh, it's no problem. I don't want to talk about it anyway. I'd rather try and put it out of my mind. Although I doubt I shall ever forget his face. He was so young.'

'You're aware of his identity, aren't you?'

'We didn't recognise him, but I heard a rumour it was Mr Jones-Kilby's son.'

'You've never met him?'

'No. We've met Mr Jones-Kilby, but not his son. We didn't even know he was married or had children.'

'Are you friends with Mr Jones-Kilby?'

Jane's voice became suddenly suspicious. 'We're not friends. He doesn't have many friends here.'

'Is that because of his part in the proposed HS2 line?'

'That would be one of the reasons. He's ruined quite a few pretty villages around here with his developments, and people in these parts have long memories. But we've personally no grievances against the man.'

'I understand the planned route for the HS2 is over your land.'

'I'd rather not discuss that with you, certainly not without my husband here. It's really none of your business.'

'Then please answer me one last question. Are you angry about losing your land to the HS2 project?'

'No. We're not upset. Not at all. Toby isn't getting any younger and he doesn't want to spend every day of the rest of his life in the fields. In short, it's a blessing in disguise.'

After she'd ended the call, Robyn drew a small question mark beside their names on the whiteboard. They didn't have a concrete alibi, and although she was tempted to eliminate them from the investigation, she couldn't yet, not until she was completely sure of their innocence.

'You got any further details on Owen?' she asked Mitz.

'He's been keeping his nose clean since that GBH incident in 2010,' said Mitz, opening the document he'd received about the incident on his computer.

'What happened exactly?'

'It was over Joy Fairweather, Owen's girlfriend at the time. The whole thing took place at the Bowling Green pub in Lichfield. The plaintiff, Jonathan Bagshaw, made lewd remarks and flirted with Joy. When she rebuffed him, he became offensive. Owen rose to her defence but both men were drunk and a fight ensued. Owen admitted to causing grievous bodily harm, but witnesses claimed he'd been heavily provoked and had only acted in self-defence. In the end, Jonathan Bagshaw dropped the charges.'

Robyn made a non-committal noise. 'I'm not sure. Owen appears to have a history of anger-related incidents. He might have lost his temper and attacked Jordan. We'll talk to him again, if only to exclude him from our enquiries. He said he was asleep and didn't hear Jordan leave the house. That troubles me. We can't prove his whereabouts at the time Jordan was attacked. Do we have any news on Jordan's mobile yet?'

David answered. 'Nothing yet. Connor said they're still hunting for it, along with his bicycle.'

'I wonder if his attacker took the bike, or if it was stolen afterwards. We'll have to see if it turns up. Where's Matt?'

'He and Anna went to Speedy Logistics to talk to Jordan's colleagues.'

'Okay, cheers.'

If Robyn had uncovered further useful information about Jordan, she might not have contacted Amy. Jordan's colleagues had merely confirmed what everyone else had told them: Jordan was little short of a recluse who only ventured out to go cycling, play football or go to work. Jordan Kilby had made little impact on anybody.

Robyn found it strange that a person could have worked somewhere for five years and divulged so little about his personal life. Stranger still, how could he have been part of a local crowd, met up regularly, played football with them, had drinks with them, and yet the so-called friends professed to know little about him? There was something else that niggled her – Rebecca had described Jordan as friendly, and only a confident man would have waited outside with flowers and a football to ask a woman he didn't know out on a date. The accounts didn't tally. It was as if he was two different people – Jordan the recluse and Jordan the romantic.

CHAPTER NINE

DAY TWO – TUESDAY, 6 JUNE, AFTERNOON

It was frustration that drove her to pick up the phone and arrange to meet Amy Walters at the café on the corner of the high street in Stafford. It was one of the few well-known chain coffee houses in town, but had a back room where they would be able to talk more surreptitiously.

The rain had let up but the pavements were still damp. Pedestrians skirted round puddles left by the downpours as they exited shops, cafés and restaurants where they'd been sheltering, and joined the crowds milling about the main square set up with stalls, selling everything from ostrich burgers to homemade candles. Robyn circumnavigated the wide double-buggy pushchair in front of her and avoided the man with samples of glistening caramel fudge laid out on a tray. She liked the centre of Stafford, with its mixture of old and new architecture, the black-and-white Tudor buildings, the high arches of the Oddfellows Hall and the Ancient High House, one of Stafford's main attractions and England's tallest timbered building. Although it was free to enter, Robyn was no historian and hadn't set foot inside. She preferred parks, countryside and open spaces: places where she could breathe deeply, and feel the sun on her skin. Towns, even attractive ones, were stifling.

She glanced up at the bay windows of the Swan Hotel, once a coaching inn, now a smart brasserie and tearoom. Several tables were occupied. At the table closest to the window sat a woman, hands fluttering as she spoke. Opposite her was a young girl, about Amélie's age, dressed in the uniform of the local school, her face animated as the woman spoke. A plate of fat brown scones, and another with pots of bright red strawberry jam and thick cream, sat between them next to a china teapot decorated with poppies. Robyn thought about Amélie, Davies' daughter who lived with her mother, Brigitte, but who often visited Robyn. Amélie would insist on somewhere trendier. She smiled at the imagined scenario and made a mental note to tease the girl by suggesting it.

Amy was playing it cool. The only sign she was keen to talk to Robyn was the slight shuffle as she drew herself to her full height when Robyn entered the café. The guy behind the counter was preparing a latte in a tall glass, lavishing it with the attention an artist might give a painting. Robyn surmised it was for Amy since she was the only person near the counter.

'Make that two, please,' she said.

Amy's eyes glittered mischievously. 'Glad you rang. Saved me pestering the station for information.'

'Spoken like a true journalist. Nice to see you're as dedicated to your vocation as ever and not letting the novel writing take over. How's that going?'

Amy pulled a face, collected the tray of drinks and headed to the back room, leaving Robyn to fish for the money to pay, before joining her.

The back room looked out onto the main road and was empty of customers. A rack of well-thumbed newspapers and tables still piled with dishes and cups indicated it had been busier earlier.

'I need more subject matter,' said Amy. 'Can't write a book about serial killers without a few case studies and juicy parts. You haven't got one for me, have you?'

Robyn shook her head, leaned forward and dropped her voice. 'I might have something interesting for you but I need your thoughts first.'

Amy gave a small smile, raised her glass of coffee and blew gently to cool it. Robyn knew she was playing for time, trying to work out her best strategy and calculate what bargaining tool she possessed. Amy was fearless and work-driven, but for all her faults, unrelenting pushiness being one of them, Robyn felt a grudging respect for the woman.

'I'm listening,' said Amy.

'You're not recording this conversation, are you?'

Amy grinned, reached into her bag, withdrew her phone and placed it in front of her on the table.

'Tsk. You don't trust me, do you, DI Carter?'

In truth, Robyn didn't trust Amy one inch. The woman would definitely sell her soul for a good story. She chose to ignore the comment.

'Back in 2010 you interviewed some rich children who'd gone off the rails. Do you remember the article?'

Amy sipped her coffee. Pink lipstick stained the side of her glass. She nodded slowly. 'It was the very first piece I had accepted by the *Lichfield Gazette*. I've moved on since those days. I rarely write for that paper now. Of course I remember it. I sweated over it for weeks, chasing up wayward offspring, trying to get interviews with them and their uber-wealthy families. I even went round to their homes.' She raised her neatly manicured eyebrows. 'One of the families set their dog on me. I had to leg it all the way down the mile-long drive back to my car. Never ran so fast in all my life.'

Robyn resisted the urge to smile. 'I'd like to know what you really thought about one of them – Jordan Kilby. In the article, you said he was shy and misunderstood rather than a rebel.'

Amy blinked suddenly but swiftly gained control. Robyn sensed a sudden uneasiness and wondered why the name had touched a nerve.

Amy spoke. 'I remember him well. He wasn't like the other brats I spoke to. He really was just a quiet kid. I couldn't get much out of him about why he'd been kicked out of school. School wouldn't say. His parents wouldn't talk. He wasn't prosecuted for any reason. It seemed pointless interviewing him. I suspected his father or mother put him up to it... to clear his name. I couldn't work it out. I didn't think he was especially interesting and wanted to cut his interview from the article, but Nathaniel Jones-Kilby was well known and my editor wanted it left in.'

'You must have extracted more from him than you mentioned in the article. I know you, Amy. You record conversations and only use the sections you think will resonate with your readers. You would have found out more about him. I bet you kept notes from the interview too. You never delete anything you might have a use for in the future. You're too professional for that.'

Amy gazed at her with clear green eyes and smirked. 'Maybe I did. What's in it for me?'

Robyn gave a brief smile. 'In a moment. I promise. His father, Nathaniel Jones-Kilby. Ever interviewed him?'

Amy snorted. She thought for a moment before speaking again. 'Prick of a man. He's self-opinionated and arrogant. He's either threatening to sue the paper for writing about his land-grabbing tactics, or sucking up to the editor, trying to get us to garner support. You heard about the hate mail debacle?'

Robyn had mused over that incident and wondered why he hadn't involved the police. Instead he'd gone directly to the news-paper to complain about receiving hate mail. In Robyn's opinion, it would have made more sense for him to report it to the appropriate authorities. She said as much to Amy, who gave a nod in agreement.

'Exactly. He should have reported it to the police, shouldn't he? But no, he contacted my editor, who sent out a senior reporter to interview him. He got a double-page spread about how unjust it was for him to be receiving hate mail. The whole article was little more than propaganda to get support for the HS2 line, and he played the victim card very well. He even came over as some modern-day white knight, crusading to create new homes for underprivileged people, and championing the new railway line which would increase employment in the area.' Her slim foot waggled in an irritated fashion. 'The article didn't bring up suspected dodgy dealings or potentially corrupt councillors who've allowed him to build in areas that ought to have remained green belt. I'd have used it to dish some dirt on the man, but no, he came out of it very well. Funnily enough, no more letters were sent to him after the article went out. They dried up. I know because I tried to follow it up. Jones-Kilby said the article frightened off whoever was sending them. I don't believe that's the case. I think it was all a publicity stunt.'

'You think he sent the letters to himself?'

Amy nodded. 'Or he asked one of his staff to fabricate them.'

'Why didn't you make a stand or mention it to your editor?'

'I had more important stories to work on.' Her tone suggested otherwise.

Robyn suspected Amy hadn't let it drop and was still digging away. Amy drank her coffee before speaking again.

'He enjoys power.' She paused. Robyn sensed she was trying to decide if she should continue. She did. 'Ever get the impression someone is being bullied? I did when I met Jordan. He seemed so… frail. I half expected him to burst into tears. I think his father, or his mother even, made him come to the interview to quash the rumours. One of them was waiting for him outside the café that day. I watched him slip into a silver Mercedes, and I swear the boy was in tears as he climbed inside it.'

'And what rumours were they?'

'Jordan had been involved in taking drugs, and been expelled. I figured Daddy paid the school to drop any charges, and it was brushed away. Jordan had the chance to deny any wrongdoing during my interview, and was forced to meet me. All supposition, I know, but I have a nose for that sort of thing.'

Robyn agreed. Amy was very sharp and could read people very well.

'Did you have any more contact with him after that interview?'

Amy shrugged. 'Not really. I knew about his mother. Felt very sorry for Jordan. He took it badly. Heard Jones-Kilby bought him the house after her death. It's no secret they fell out majorly. Jordan moved to Newborough and got on with his life. He drives for a local delivery company and keeps out of the limelight. Unlike his father.'

'You're not keen on Nathaniel Jones-Kilby, are you?'

'He's a creep. He's got the local council in his back pocket, very pally with the local MP, and is only keen on the HS2 line because there's something in it for him. I don't know what but I'm sure of it.' Amy sniffed. 'And, being a crack journalist, I've worked out why you wanted to ask me about this family. One of them is dead. One of them was in that field on Sunday. Which one?'

'Jordan,' said Robyn.

Amy's face clouded for a moment. 'Do you think it's to do with his father?'

'Honestly? I don't know. I haven't got any other avenue to pursue at this stage. I'm investigating the possibility it is connected to his dad.'

Amy screwed her eyes up, struggled with a thought then spoke. 'Like you, I'm not keen to share information, especially with the police. As you know, I have my own methods and you have yours. I'm going to be upfront with you now. I don't like him. He's a man with an agenda. Between you and me, I've been digging into his dealings for some time, before the hate mail letters, before HS2. I've collected a fair bit of information on him and his contacts. I'm planning on exposing him and his company and maybe even a few others he deals with. If you need any of it, it's yours. I'll hand over what I've got if it'll help find Jordan's murderer.'

This was most unlike the Amy Walters Robyn knew. There had to be a catch. Amy shifted in her chair, hands resting loosely in her lap, conveying a picture of calm. Only her eyes gave her away, narrowed and anxiously awaiting a response.

'Why would you be so generous?'

'Like I said, I'm not one of his fans, and if his dealings have caused Jordan's death, he should be held responsible.'

'There's something else, Amy. What is it?' Robyn waited while Amy wrestled with her conscience. Eventually she spoke.

'Okay. You'll find out anyway. Jordan phoned me on Sunday afternoon. He said he had something he had to tell me.'

'That's it?'

Amy nodded. 'He said he couldn't talk on the phone. He wanted to meet me. He was going to call me again this week. He needed some proof first to bring to the meeting. He promised to call me yesterday. When I didn't hear from him, I thought he'd maybe gone off the idea, or not got enough evidence. I was going to ring him today. I'd have done so, if you hadn't arranged this meeting.'

'And you've no idea what he was going to tell you?'

'I hoped it was about his father. What else could it be?'

'It's best if you keep out of it, Amy. It might be dangerous.'

'I figured you'd say that. I hear you.'

'I mean it. Stay away from Jones-Kilby and any of his associates. Aside from concerns about your safety, I don't want the investigation compromised.'

Amy gave a broad smile. 'DI Carter, I didn't know you cared so much about me.'

Robyn's eyes were serious. 'Amy, do *not* get involved.'

Amy gave a mock salute. 'What about if I interview his friends? He was chummy with Owen Falcon.'

'No. Sorry, not yet. We can't be certain he isn't involved in some way. I don't want you stepping on any toes. However, I will make sure you get first-hand information and a scoop on it.'

Amy pondered the proposition. Robyn knew it wasn't what she hoped for. She was an investigative journalist who thrived on situations that were challenging. Robyn understood asking her to step away, especially when she'd had a phone call from Jordan, was asking a lot, but she was also sensible enough to know she ought not interfere in or jeopardise a police murder investigation. Amy came to the same conclusion and heaved a sigh. 'You win.'

'And you'll give me what you have on Jones-Kilby?'

Amy nodded, picked up her glass and drained it. 'I want in as soon as you have something. I mean it. No holding back on me.'

Robyn agreed. As much as she didn't want to be beholden to Amy, she needed her information if she was going to go investigate Jones-Kilby and still have a job afterwards.

CHAPTER TEN

As Robyn drove to Newborough to speak again with Rebecca Tomlinson, she reflected on what they'd ascertained so far. Connor and his team were still searching the field where Jordan had been discovered. It was a vast area and she wasn't holding out much hope of them finding a murder weapon or Jordan's bike and mobile phone. The rain had impeded the search, making the grass soggy and more difficult to check.

'Not having much luck,' Connor had said in his usual bright tone when she rang him. 'If it holds off with the rain, we might make headway. Don't give up on us just yet.' She'd never met anybody as permanently optimistic as Connor.

Jordan's phone records had shown he'd only rung a handful of regular numbers during the last month: his girlfriend, an Indian restaurant, work, Amy, and Owen. It didn't seem right that a young man was so friendless. Had he been, as Amy suggested, bullied in his youth? And had that had an effect on his adult life?

They had yet to track down the vehicles – the van and the dark car – spotted in Colton the night Jordan was murdered, and were waiting for Harry to finish examining Jordan's body. Robyn was pretty certain the stab wound had killed him, but she knew from experience to wait for confirmation.

Newborough was renowned in the area for its annual well-dressing festival, where villagers decorated clay-filled boards with petals to create scenes or pictures and adorned the wells in the small village. Robyn and Davies had brought Amélie along to it just after they'd started seeing each other. It had been a soaking wet May bank holiday, but Robyn remembered it with fondness and a tinge of sadness as she drove past the church where she had stood hand in hand with Davies as they'd joined the crowds to admire the colourful tableaux.

Jordan's house was on the outskirts of the village, in remote grounds, and was one of five converted buildings that had once belonged to Grange Hall. The hall was now a private residence set apart from the other houses, reached by a vast, sweeping drive, overhung by ancient horse-chestnut trees.

The Forge was a blue-and-red brick, single-storey building with arched windows. The doorway was similarly arched and flanked by two large, painted cartwheels. There was a sizeable gravelled parking area in front of the house. A dark blue Ford Fiesta stood next to a red Nissan Micra. Robyn drew up next to a Toyota Yaris belonging to the liaison officer, Michelle Watson, and crunched up the gravel pathway.

Michelle opened the door. She shook her head. Rebecca was obviously still in a bad way. Robyn paused before entering the elongated open-plan kitchen with its heavy beams and slate-tiled floor. Rebecca was sat beside a breakfast bar, head in hands, untouched cup of tea in front of her. She lifted wet eyes and spoke as Robyn's boots clattered on the floor.

'Sorry. I can't seem to get a grip. I woke up and thought it was an ordinary day and then remembered.'

'You'll need time, Rebecca,' said Robyn kindly. Around her the place was a happy jumble of kids' toys, DVDs and boxes of cereal, promising surprises inside each packet. A plastic toy giraffe stood on the window ledge above the sink. A child's red sweater was on the back of one of the chairs and a pair of school shoes were abandoned by the back door. Pictures, obviously drawn by a child, were attached to the front of a large American fridge–freezer. The top one caught Robyn's eye. It was of three people standing outside a house: a small, smiley-faced child between a round figure with black hair in a triangular-shaped orange skirt and a tall, stick-like man holding a football. A bright yellow sun had been painted in one corner, as large as the two cartwheels drawn beside the front door of the house. It exuded happiness.

'Do you have any family you can talk to?' Robyn asked.

Rebecca shook her head. 'I lost both my parents when I was sixteen. Our house caught fire. Fire brigade said there'd been an electrical fault in the kitchen – some wire from the toaster – that started the blaze. Dylan's all my family now. Him and Aunt Rose, but she's away at the moment.'

Robyn was deeply saddened. Having lost her own parents when she was nineteen, she knew how difficult it was to accept such a loss and to adjust.

Rebecca gave a brave smile. 'I'll be okay. I always manage and I have Dylan. He's my world. I kept him off school today. I wanted to keep him close. Maybe that sounds strange. Maybe I should have let him go to school. I just couldn't bear to.'

At the mention of her son, Robyn felt another pang. 'How is he? Have you told him?'

The woman nodded. 'He doesn't understand. He thinks Jordan will be back later to play football with him. They play most days when Jordan comes home.'

Michelle pushed a cup of tea towards Robyn, who thanked her. Michelle was young, but with her wide-set eyes and a matronly attitude, she gave off an air of compassion. She sat next to Rebecca and spoke, her voice soft and lilting. 'He's okay for the moment. He's in his room doing a word search puzzle.'

'He loves puzzles. Keeps him occupied for hours,' said Rebecca to Robyn.

'Does your aunt live locally?' Robyn asked.

'Birmingham, but she's in Barbados at the moment. Aunt Rose went back to visit some distant relatives.'

'I hear it's a beautiful place,' said Michelle. 'I'd love to go there – sea, sand, sunshine. Sounds like paradise.'

'I've never actually visited the island. I intended to go, with Jordan and Dylan,' she said, unhappily. 'We'd talked about getting married and holding the wedding, or even just our honeymoon, there. It would have been magical.' Her shoulders drooped as she spoke. 'Jordan came into my life and he made it better. Finally, I found somebody who understood me, loved me, and loved my boy. And now, he's gone. How come life is so unfair?'

Robyn had no answers. She ached for the young woman who'd found happiness at last, only to have it snatched from her. She knew what it was like to battle life alone, to unexpectedly find love, and then be sideswiped by fate again. Rebecca would face another uphill battle and Robyn felt her pain.

A small voice drew Rebecca's attention and a smile tugged at the corners of her mouth at the sight of the little boy clutching a book. Robyn could almost feel the surge of love as it washed over the woman's features, transforming them.

'Hey, my little man,' she said, holding out her arms. The child, no more than six, ran into them, his bare feet pattering on the floor. He was an engaging child, the white smile at odds with the sad, hazel-coloured eyes sunken into his small, round face. He lifted the book.

'I did it,' he said.

His mother examined the page he'd completed and let out an exaggerated puff of pride. 'Did Michelle help you?'

The boy shook his dark hair, so like his mother's, his face now solemn. 'No. I did it by myself.'

'Then you are the cleverest little dude I know.'

He smiled, pulled away and asked, 'How long will Jordan be away?'

Rebecca's face crumpled for a second. She fought to regain control and, placing her hands on the little boy's shoulders, explained once more that Jordan wouldn't be back. Dylan nodded but the blank look on his face indicated he still had not fully understood.

'Why don't I play with you?' said Michelle. 'I'm a great goalie. Want to try and score against me?'

The pair left the room and Robyn caught sight of Michelle waving her arms wildly as Dylan kicked the ball into the back of the small goal erected in the narrow garden. He raised his fists in triumph. Rebecca was watching too. 'I don't know what will happen to us,' she said, quietly. 'We'll have nowhere to live. I thought Jordan owned this house and hoped we could stay for a while, at least until we could find our feet, but his father rang me this morning. He's the real owner and he wants to put it on the market immediately.'

'Nathaniel Jones-Kilby phoned you today?'

'He called the landline first thing this morning. Said he was sorry, but I'd have to make alternative living arrangements. No preamble. No, "How are you?" No mention of Jordan. He just came out with it. No wonder Jordan didn't have any time for the man.' She studied her nails, still painted in bright colours. 'I'll have to find somewhere to rent nearby. We've settled here, begun to make friends. Dylan loves his school. I can't really think about it yet. Jordan's only been gone a day. I still can't believe it – it's all happening too quickly for me.'

Robyn was outraged on her behalf. The man's insensitivity was incomprehensible. 'Have you ever met Mr Jones-Kilby?'

Rebecca shook her head. 'Jordan and him, they didn't get along at all. Jordan rarely mentioned him. I'd not spoken to his father before today. Look, I'm sorry. I shouldn't be burdening you with my problems. Did you want to search the house or ask any questions?'

Robyn nodded. 'I wondered if I might take a look around. Did Jordan have a computer I could take with me to be checked out?'

Rebecca opened her arms wide. 'Help yourself. He had a laptop. Usually kept it in the sitting room.'

Robyn left her watching Dylan running after Michelle, who was now in control of the ball, and headed into the adjacent room. Like Owen, Jordan had a large television flanked by two well-lit display cabinets, each filled with sculptured statues of superheroes whom Robyn recognised – Spider-Man, Captain America, The Hulk – and many she didn't. Two chocolate-brown leather chairs were angled in front of it and behind those, a long settee on which was propped a jigsaw puzzle lid bearing a picture of a Star Wars Stormtrooper. The half-completed puzzle was on the floor, the 300 pieces facing picture-side up, waiting to be slotted into position. A white ceramic heart inscribed with 'Rebecca and Jordan' dangled from a wall light. Robyn's eyes rested on an open-fronted, pine bookcase, crammed top to bottom with superhero DVDs – *The Dark Knight*, *Deadpool*, *The Avengers* – and many more, along with numerous PlayStation games. Her eyes lighted upon one lying on its side, *FIFA 2017*; the same game Jordan had been playing with Owen the night of his murder.

The laptop, attached to a charging unit, had been left on the carpet next to the settee. She unplugged it and lifted it from the floor before walking through the rest of the house. There was more evidence of Jordan's passion with framed prints of Marvel Comics characters and more action figures on display on tables. Also, everywhere she looked there were reminders of the happy family unit Rebecca, Jordan and Dylan had become: in their bedroom, a card bearing the words 'I love you' framed and hung on the wall; on the dresser, a photo of Jordan and Dylan in the garden – Dylan holding the football, face flushed from exertion, happy, full of energy.

She crossed the room and looked outside. Dylan had given up chasing Michelle and was crouched on his haunches on the edge of the patio, staring into space. His demeanour had changed and he seemed a small, forlorn figure, hunched as he was. Michelle had joined him and was chatting to him, one hand on his shoulder. Robyn hoped he'd bounce back soon. It was heartbreaking to compare the contented boy in the photograph and the pitiful lad outside.

She walked through the house, trying to get a feel of Jordan's life. Without Rebecca and Dylan and the trappings they'd brought with them, the place would be little more than a museum to Marvel Comics. Jordan Kilby was the loner everyone said he was.

When Robyn returned to the kitchen, Rebecca was still observing her son from the kitchen window, her eyes moist with fresh tears.

'Are you staying here for a while?' Robyn asked.

Rebecca nodded. 'Until Jordan's father insists I leave, or as soon as I find somewhere to rent. Whichever comes first.'

'I'll let you have this back as soon as possible.' Robyn motioned to the laptop in her hand.

'Please. There are some photos I'd like to copy from it. I might take Dylan out in a minute. Rather than mope about here. It's not doing either of us any good.'

Robyn felt that was a good move. She spotted a bunch of keys hanging on a rack above the draining board. 'Are those your keys?'

Rebecca looked at them as if seeing them for the first time. 'They're Jordan's house keys. He forgot to take them with him on Sunday. He was in such a hurry to get off. I left the back door unlocked for him, but he didn't come home.' Her voice trailed away.

Michelle clattered through the back door with Dylan. Rebecca was in good hands. Robyn left them. She'd get Anna to check through the laptop and tell Connor not to waste any time hunting for keys at the crime scene. As she fumbled for her mobile, it rang. She looked at the display, pulled a face and answered.

'Amy, I can't tell you anything more—' she began but Amy interrupted her.

'You have to come immediately. I'm at Owen Falcon's house. He's dead.'

CHAPTER ELEVEN

MONDAY, 5 JUNE, EVENING

*Owen Falcon curses loudly and tosses the spanner onto the garage floor.
He's tightened the nut as much as he dares, and still a globule of oil
is dripping from the joint, working its way down to join the puddle
beneath it. Bloody bike. It's been nothing but trouble from the day he
bought it. The guy who sold it to him swore it was reliable. Said it
was a great little runner. Joe claimed the bloke was a shifty bastard.
Owen wished he'd told him that before he'd bought the damn bike.
He needs it for work in the morning. He can't phone in and say he's
without transport. That'll sound like he's making it up. He's handy
with all things mechanical and usually can keep the wretched thing
running, but this time, he's stumped. He'll have to ring for a taxi if he
can't fix it. The thought makes him more bad-tempered and he scowls
at the joint. Is it a bust seal?*

*Owen had turned on the radio for company but now Daft Punk's
rapid beat music is getting on his nerves. He stares at the stain on the
garage floor. Normally, he carries out repairs to the bike outside on the
driveway, but every time he tries to work outside, the nosey bloke from
down the road comes past, walking his dog, and stops to talk about
everything and nothing. If he goes past tonight, the man will want to
gossip about Jordan, and Owen can't face that. He doesn't want to talk
about Jordan. Not to anyone.*

He wishes he'd been honest with the detective who'd come around earlier, but he couldn't tell the truth, especially when the truth implicated others. He struggles again with his conscience before turning his attention back to his Honda. The oil is still dribbling. The music seems to be louder and he stands up to turn off the radio, wiping his hands on a rag. As he does so, a shadow falls across the walls. He turns in surprise.

'What are you doing here?' he asks.

He doesn't have a chance to say another word. There's a swift movement from his left and something heavy smashes into the side of his head, knocking him sideways into his bike. It topples over with a clatter, the smell of oil and petrol combining with something else he doesn't recognise filling his nostrils. He crumples onto the floor, stars bursting in his brain, unable to comprehend what's happening. His eyelids flutter once and then Owen Falcon is swallowed by an eternal darkness.

CHAPTER TWELVE

Robyn was glad to see her team had secured the scene, the bright yellow cordon swaying in the breeze. David and Matt, positioned by the front gate, were keeping a few curious neighbours at bay. Mitz and Anna, both suited up in protective clothing, stood directly outside Owen's house. Amy was in her car, waiting for Robyn. As soon as she spotted her, she leapt out and accosted her.

'I didn't touch anything. Called you as soon as I found him.'

Robyn stomped up the path, hardly acknowledging the woman.

'I know you told me to keep out of it but I was only following up as any good journalist would. Mr Falcon was one of Jordan's friends. It was only natural I'd—' Her words dried up on her lips. Robyn marched towards the path and the officers waiting to accompany her to the back door.

'Stay outside. I don't want the scene contaminated.' Robyn's growl was directed at Amy, who tried to maintain eye contact but conceded defeat and turned away.

Robyn donned her own protective suit and led her officers through the open back door and into a laundry room.

'The back door was unlocked. Victim's in the garage. We checked for any vitals but haven't moved him,' said Mitz. He'd smeared a thin layer of vapour rub under his nose. It shimmered like a shiny transparent moustache as he moved this way and that, recording the scene with his body cam.

Music was coming from the open door to a garage, a song about being happy.

Robyn halted in the open doorway. The room, larger than the one she used to do her laundry, was home to a washing machine on top of which stood a basket of dirty washing. It was a smaller version of the adjacent kitchen with painted units and a Belfast sink, next to which stood a cheap bottle of washing detergent. Several pairs of shoes and trainers were littered haphazardly on the floor by the back door. One trainer lay on its back, a black tie-up shoe in the corner of the room.

'They like this when you arrived?' Robyn asked, pointing at the shoes.

Anna nodded. Although the most junior member of the team, Anna had already come across dead bodies and was coping well with this latest discovery.

Robyn took a breath and entered the garage. It was relatively uncluttered – more workshop than garage, with shelves on the wall immediately to her left housing boxes of screws, motorbike spares, oil cans, paint tubes and the like. Next to the shelves stood a heavy-duty workbench, with a T-bar support made from blue steel, on which was a Roberts radio and an open toolbox. Following an unspoken command from Robyn, Anna switched off the loud music. Silence was more appropriate for the scene in front of them. Robyn recognised the sickly odour immediately – the smell of death. Harry, the pathologist, had explained on one occasion that the various putrid smells that emanated from a corpse were due to the mixture of molecules caused by the breakdown of amino acids in the body. Analysis of these molecules helped a pathologist ascertain time of death, but in this case, Robyn already had an idea of when that had happened. She'd spoken to Owen Falcon only the evening before. At most, he'd been dead for twenty-one hours.

Her eyes moved from the open toolbox on the bench to the spanner on the floor, a discarded oily rag, and then to the Honda, a mechanical beast, now twisted on the ground, bleeding oil. Owen was sprawled beside it. A black aureole of fluid encircled his head. His face was crusted with blood, his eyes open in terror, his lips distorted in agony. The reason was immediately apparent – the handle of a large screwdriver protruded from his ear.

Anna swallowed hard and chewed at the gum in her mouth, but her eyes remained focused on the victim. Robyn moved aside to allow Mitz to get clear footage of the man, and looked about the garage. The remainder of the garage floor appeared to be clean. A dustpan and brush stood against the wall near the shelves. A small charging unit and a pair of plastic ramps had been tidily stored at the far end of the garage. A hammer with a wooden handle lay beside the body, its surface stained red-brown. Robyn wondered if it had been used to drive the screwdriver into Owen's head. She glanced at the toolbox on the bench. It was positioned near the open door. The music had been on loudly. She looked again at the bike. It most likely toppled over when Owen fell into it. There might have been a skirmish. He might have struggled and clawed his attacker, in which case, they might get lucky with traces of DNA. She stared again at the body, his grease-covered hands, his nails grimy, his head in a pool of oil and blood, and mentally filed away the image before speaking.

'Everyone been notified?'

'Yes, guv.'

'Anna, make a note of where everything is in this room. I want all the tools examined by Forensics when they arrive, especially the hammer and screwdriver. Also have the radio checked for prints.'

She came away to allow her officers more space and tried to imagine the scene. Could somebody have visited, followed Owen through to the garage, and then turned on him? That would suggest he knew his assailant. Unless he'd telephoned somebody – a mechanic maybe – to help him repair his bike, she reasoned. No, that made little sense and would be too random an act of violence. She cast about the utility room again. Apart from Owen's shoes, presumably kicked out of alignment by the intruder, there was nothing to indicate there'd been a struggle. From what little she'd seen of Owen and his home, he was a tidy man. He would have left his shoes lined up by the back door, not left willy-nilly. There was nothing else she could see that pointed to a struggle. Owen hadn't been dragged through to the garage. He'd been murdered in there.

When she had been here the evening before, the television had been on, and Owen had been drinking a can of beer. She looked in the sitting room. Nothing seemed out of place. The television and Xbox were still there. This wasn't a robbery gone wrong. Somebody had come in through the unlocked back door, or been invited in. That person had either sneaked into the garage and attacked Owen unawares, or had gone in there with him and then killed him. Underlying all of these thoughts was the fact that Owen had known Jordan and both had been killed in Colton within hours of each other. There was no way it could be a coincidence – they just needed the evidence to back it up. Jordan had been stabbed, strung up and left for crows to peck at. Owen had had a screwdriver driven through his ear into his skull. The killer was violent and merciless. She was relieved when a familiar voice shouted, 'Anyone home?' and Connor appeared. Harry trailed in his wake, medical bag in hand. He gave her a nod in greeting.

'Through there,' she said, pointing towards the laundry room. Harry disappeared with another nod.

'Where do you want me to begin?' Connor asked.

'The laundry room. I'm hoping his assailant came through that door and lingered in here before going into the garage. He might have left behind some evidence.'

'We'll get onto it immediately. Had to leave a couple of the team down the road. They're still hunting for a murder weapon in the field. The recent rainfall has made it more difficult, but we had a breakthrough just before I got the call to come here – we found a bicycle abandoned in a ditch behind the field. Sure it belongs to Mr Kilby. Can't see why else a perfectly good bike would be there.'

'Make?'

Connor checked his notepad. 'Sirrus Comp Carbon Disc. It's a lightweight, all-terrain model. Retails at over £1,000.'

Whoever had attacked Jordan hadn't been interested in stealing the expensive bike, unless they'd planned on returning to collect it later.

Connor continued, 'The rain has turned the field into a soggy bog, and messed up any chance of uncovering prints. I'm not confident of turning up any weapon either, not without a huge detail of officers on the lookout. The field is massive. Talk about a needle in a haystack.'

In spite of the tired grin he threw her, Robyn could feel his frustration. 'You might have more luck here. There's a hammer with what looks like bloodstains on it and a whole box of potential weapons in there.'

She arranged for Connor to present all findings at the station the following day, and then headed outside to deal with Amy. She knew the reporter would still be waiting, hoping for news. She was, standing next to her white BMW, and moved towards Robyn once she had removed her protective clothing. The street had begun to fill up with cars and police vans. Matt and David were still in position. She could see Amy jiggling from foot to foot, desperate to make contact with her. She left it as long as possible before she approached the woman.

'I'll ask PC Marker to take a full statement from you,' said Robyn.

Amy's cheeks were flushed pink, not from embarrassment, but excitement. 'Do you think the same person who murdered Jordan has killed Owen Falcon?' she asked.

Robyn refused to be pushed. She gave Amy a steely look. 'Far too early to make any assumptions.'

Amy wasn't going to give up. 'I know I've cheesed you off, but you'd have done the same in my place. I have to stay top of my game and the newspaper would think it peculiar if I hadn't interviewed a few of Jordan's friends. I was the first reporter in Colton when it got out there'd been a body found in Top Field. I had to follow up on that. Owen didn't answer the door when I rang the bell so I went around the back of the house to see if I could raise him. I heard music so I banged on the back door but when he still didn't answer, I tried the door handle. The door was unlocked, so I stuck my head in and called out to him. He didn't respond, so I popped my head through to the garage and, well, you know what I saw. I called you immediately, and then the station.' Amy's eyes were glowing as she spoke. 'I want in. I want to know first-hand what you uncover. I saw Owen Falcon. I saw what his killer did to him, and I'm at liberty to report it as a witness, but I won't if you keep me in the loop.'

Robyn spoke quietly. 'Go back to your office. Write a piece about Jordan, saying we are investigating his death as suspicious. Keep it to the bare minimum. You can't release Owen Falcon's name or any details until you are permitted to do so. Anything you print or say will impede my investigation, and I won't stand for that. Send me the information on Nathaniel Jones-Kilby and keep out of the way until I call you. Clear?'

'You want to know what I think?' said Amy, almost bubbling over with enthusiasm. 'I think the same person who killed Jordan killed his friend in there. And I want in from the start. I'll give you the files we discussed and I'll help in any way possible, but I want to be told the second you have evidence to link these murders. No palming me off like you usually do. Not this time. I saw what that madman did in there. I'll only keep quiet for so long.'

Robyn shrugged her consent and left Amy to give her statement. As loathe as she was to involve the journalist, it would be better to have Amy on board rather than fighting against her every step of the way.

CHAPTER THIRTEEN

DAY TWO – TUESDAY, 6 JUNE, EVENING

Robyn played out every possible scenario again in her head on her return trip to the station and kept returning to the obvious conclusion – she was dealing with the same murderer.

Amy had departed shortly after making her statement, while Robyn had remained at the scene until her officers had the recordings and notes needed to begin the investigation. Once again, David made door-to-door enquiries, and she and Anna had to pacify hysterical locals who thought a madman was on the loose. They'd have to make a statement to calm the public. DCI Flint would decide how to deal with that. It would be impossible to request no coverage. The people of Colton needed to be sure they were safe.

Robyn struggled with her instinct that was certain the two murders were connected, and tried to maintain focus on the facts that suggested otherwise. If Jordan had been murdered on account of his father's business dealings, where did Owen fit in? The only reason Robyn could think of was that he'd known something about Jordan's murder.

She circumnavigated Stafford and avoided her usual route past Cannock Chase, favouring the ring road that took her in via Stafford University. It was here Harry conducted his autopsies, in the recently built pathology department. The university had finally been granted the funds it required and had created a state-of-the-art operating theatre with an observation window through which students could watch Harry and his team working. Forensics and pathology were fast becoming popular courses among students these days, Harry had told her with an air of pride. If students wanted to learn, then they couldn't have a better teacher than him, she mused. She stopped off at the car park outside the pathology block and pressed the button on the outside door to be allowed entry. Security was stringent here – she looked into the surveillance camera and held up her ID card before hearing a click as the door released. Inside it was as clinically clean as a hospital. The young man at the front desk almost stood to attention. He was new to the department, all white teeth and shining eyes.

'How can I help you, Detective?' he asked.

'I'm here to see Laura Whiston.'

He rang through and nodded at Robyn to say she could enter the laboratory. She climbed the wide metal staircase; huge glass windows on one side afforded a view of the vast campus. Another keypad and buzzer and she was in the inner sanctum, a laboratory consisting of machines that whirred and clicked and spurted out information on computer screens, and three desks lined up in front of a glass-fronted room, called the theatre, where they performed the autopsies. There were no bodies on the gurney in the centre of the room. Owen Falcon would be their first of the day.

Laura Whiston was a ball of energy. Tiny-framed at only five foot two inches and with baby soft skin and clear emerald eyes, she looked like a first-year student, not an up-and-coming assistant with several articles in print and a formidable reputation as one of pathology's rising stars. Harry had discovered her due to a chance conversation with an old colleague and had convinced her to join his department. At twenty-four years old, and with a first-class degree from Edinburgh University, Laura was going places.

She was sat on a stool in front of a microscope, examining a miniscule piece of thread, toggling the adjustor to get clearer vision, but stood up the second Robyn entered. With her hand extended, she beamed at Robyn, who'd heard about all about this fireball of enthusiasm, but hadn't yet seen her in action.

'DI Carter, what a privilege to finally meet you,' said Laura.

'Likewise. Harry hasn't stopped singing your praises since you arrived.'

Laura flushed. 'I'm very fortunate to be working with him. He's got a formidable reputation himself up at Edinburgh Uni. I'm delighted he's my mentor here.'

It was Robyn's turn to smile. She had a soft spot for the quiet Scotsman who had helped her on many an investigation. 'He told me to come and see you. You've completed the autopsy on Jordan Kilby?'

Laura nodded furiously. 'All done. I've got the report on my desk. Want the shortened version from me?'

'That would help to speed things up.'

Laura crossed her arms and began explaining what they'd uncovered. 'The contusions to his upper arm appear to have been caused by a blow from a blunt object or from a fall. There was significant swelling around his right wrist as well as soft tissue damage. The stab wound that killed him entered the left third intercostal space approximately half an inch from the left sternal border. Due to the angle of insertion, major blood vessels, notably the aorta, were damaged, and the victim bled heavily. Death was due to exsanguination. There are no defensive wounds on either hand, suggesting he was unconscious at the time of stabbing, or unable to defend himself, most likely because at that time, he was tied up.

'We collected fibres from the wound that matched the clothing he was wearing at the time. We noted several minuscule puncture marks on his scalp we believe resulted from repeated pecking from birds, born out by oil residue found in feathers, evident on his scalp and in superficial wounds on his hands and face.

'In brief, Jordan bled to death fairly quickly, no more than three minutes in our opinion. As for the weapon, based on measurements we took, and the shape and edging to the initial incision, we think you're searching for a large kitchen knife, probably ten inches in length.'

Uncrossing her arms, she said, 'I hope that helps you.'

Robyn whistled softly. The killer had taken a knife in preparation, and laid in wait for his victim. Either he knew Jordan was at Owen's house that night, and waited for him to leave, or he'd chosen the wrong person. Was Owen the intended victim all along and the killer had returned the next day for him? Robyn was struck by another thought. Had Jordan been lured from Owen's house by a phone call or a message? If only Robyn had Jordan's mobile phone, then she'd know for certain. This was one puzzle she was having difficulty putting together. Laura, meanwhile, had collected the report and offered it to her.

'Time of death?' Robyn asked.

'Between eleven and midnight. Can't be more specific than that, I'm afraid.'

'Thanks for this,' said Robyn, taking the file. With that, she left the laboratory, and as she bounced down the stairs, boots clattering on the treads, she spotted Harry driving into the car park. She waited for him to enter the building. He showed his pass, eyes lighting on her. He beckoned her to one side, voice low so the boy at the desk couldn't hear him.

'Most unpleasant act of violence. Screwdriver was drilled through Owen Falcon's ear canal with force, most likely with a heavy tool. My money's on the lump hammer on the floor. He was struck initially with sufficient force to render him immobile. There's little to suggest he fought back. The assailant could have killed him with a blow to the head so I can't understand why they followed up with the screwdriver.' Harry looked unusually upset. He pushed his glasses up the bridge of his nose and stared Robyn in the eyes. You've got your hands full with this one, Robyn. I genuinely hope you catch him soon.'

He patted her shoulder in a fatherly gesture and padded towards the staircase.

Robyn considered his words. If this was the same killer, then she was dealing with a very disturbed individual indeed. She clutched the report more tightly and hastened to her own vehicle. There was no time to waste.

CHAPTER FOURTEEN

Even though she'd been working since eight, Robyn was still alert and eager to press on. However, there was one small problem and he was at home on Leafy Lane – her cat, Schrödinger.

She'd fallen for the feline's charms during an investigation earlier in the year, when his owner had been murdered. He'd only been a kitten at the time, and feeling a mixture of sympathy for the animal and loneliness, Robyn had taken him home with her. Amélie adored the cat and came around most weekends to play with it. It had been a good decision. The girl might not be a blood relative but she was everything to childless Robyn, and a reminder of the man she'd loved.

She checked the app on her mobile. Ross had set up the nanny cam for her, so on the days she was too busy to return home at a civilised hour, she could check on her pet.

She was somewhat of a technophobe, but Ross had convinced her this was simple to use, and it was. She'd found herself checking up on Schrödinger more often of late, not because she was anxious about him – he seemed perfectly content to loaf about the house and pass the hours staring out of the window onto the street – but to share his crazy, wild and happy moments with him. Last time she'd used the app, she'd been treated to the sight of him chasing an empty cotton reel around the floor, tumbling and leaping on it with such enthusiasm it had made her laugh. The nanny cam, favoured by Ross and his clients, gave her a wide-angled view of her sitting room and the chair Schrödinger had commandeered as his own while she was at work.

She activated the app and her sitting room came into view on the small screen – the settee with its cushions still puffed up was empty, and his red ball containing a small bell was where she'd last seen it. The toy, a gift from Amélie, had delighted the cat. Schrödinger wasn't in sight. He might have stayed upstairs. He'd been reluctant to get up when she'd flung back the duvet and gone for her run, even though he'd been at the door awaiting her return. It was unlikely he'd have ventured outside. He didn't seem to like the big outdoors although he'd spend hours people-watching from the back of the settee. She tried the other camera set up in the kitchen and watched as the black cat languished under the table, licking his paws meticulously clean. He was fine for now. She was about to switch off the app when she noticed him suddenly fix his gaze ahead, then stand up, stretch and arch his back, tail flicking as he always did when he greeted her. It was most odd behaviour. Nobody was in the room. She hesitated before switching it off. She had an investigation to oversee, and watching her crazy cat practise his moves wasn't going to solve it.

The office was empty. She'd sent her officers home and requested an early start from them. Matt had been preparing for the briefing in the morning. The whiteboard in the office had been divided into two sections: the first half contained the photographs of Jordan; the second half, a head and shoulders shot of Owen beside another taken in the garage of his head twisted in the dark, bloodied circle of oil with a red screwdriver handle emerging from his ear. Robyn headed across, picked up the marker pen and wrote 'carbon-framed bike' to aid her memory when it came to discussing the matter with her team.

Travelling from the university, she'd reflected on Jordan's bike. It was a model favoured by serious cyclists. From the information she'd gathered, Jordan had been a keen cyclist and during the warmer months preferred to cycle rather than drive. What puzzled her was the lack of a cycling helmet. She'd rung Connor and asked his team to search again in the ditch in the field and at Owen's house in case it had been left there, but it hadn't been found.

She read through the autopsy report on Jordan and again examined the photographs of his body as it hung limply against the stake in the field. She settled in front of her computer and checked her emails. True to her word, Amy had sent her research on Nathaniel Jones-Kilby. It consisted of photographs of town-planning councillors taken from a website, meeting times and places, and a list of sites that he'd purchased over the last ten years, with dates, times and a map showing the locations. There were plans and propositions and a whole bunch of documents that Robyn didn't understand regarding planning restrictions and permissions. Amy had made life easier by summarising her findings in an email.

From: Amy Walters Amy@StaffordGazette.co.uk
Date: 06 June 2017 20.18
Subject: NJK Properties

DI Carter,

I'm entrusting my notes to you and would like to remind you that they are for your eyes only, and not for disclosure. You will most likely come to the same conclusions as me that NJK Properties has been bribing a member, or members, of the planning committee to grant permission for large developments to be constructed in rural areas, previously designated as green belt, or agricultural land. Emails exchanged between Jones-Kilby and senior planning officer Brian Turner which suggest clandestine meetings took place to discuss how best to convince the council to change land purchased by Jones-Kilby from agricultural to commercial are included in the documents I've sent across. Please don't ask how I got the emails. I can't reveal my source, but somebody who questioned the council's decision sent them to me in good faith.

In 2001 NJK Properties purchased a large amount of agricultural land, totalling 200 hectares. All land purchases were on the edges of rural villages with small populations and few amenities. The land designated agricultural was bought at knocked-down prices from struggling farmers affected by the foot and mouth outbreak at the time.

NJK Properties persistently requested planning permission for the sites and was repeatedly refused it until the arrival of a new planning officer – Brian Turner. In 2007, permission for a development of eighty new homes was granted to a site on the outskirts of Bournton. Over the coming years, permissions were granted for all the remaining sites, in spite of protests from villagers and a general feeling that more housing was not required. Locals claimed schools and local amenities would be under pressure and handed in petitions against the building of the estates, but they were not listened to. I've enclosed several articles relating to the protests as covered by the newspapers at the time, none written by me.

I tried to speak to Mr Turner and fellow members of the council, but was refused an interview. Shortly after my attempts to contact them, my editor requested I drop my investigations and made no further attempt to contact any member of the planning committee members, or Mr Jones-Kilby.

Let me know when you're ready to hand over your side of this bargain.

Kind regards,
Amy
Amy Walters Reporter

Robyn heaved a sigh as she opened document after document and considered once again the possibility that Jordan's murder was in some way connected to his father's business. A movement made her glance up. Mitz was back in the room.

'I thought you'd gone home,' she said.

He shook his head. 'I wanted to go back over the statements we took from villagers in Colton to see if I'd missed anything.'

'I'm sure you didn't miss a thing. However, since you're here, can I pick your brains?'

'Certainly.'

'I've been chewing over the possibility that Jordan's murder is somehow linked to his father's business, which, according to Amy Walters, consists of shady deals. I'm going to interview Brian Turner, one of the council members who has had dealings with Nathaniel, tomorrow and see if there's any truth to Amy's claims. Assuming it is true and Jordan was killed because of Nathaniel, where does Owen Falcon fit in? Why is he dead? I can only come up with the idea he might have known about the corruption within Nathaniel Jones-Kilby's business and was blackmailing him.'

Mitz agreed and then offered another suggestion. 'What if Owen actually witnessed Jordan's murder? What if it's not to do with Nathaniel Jones-Kilby at all, and Owen was killed because he knew or saw whoever murdered Jordan?'

Robyn's head bobbed slowly up and down. 'Or Owen was contracted or ordered to kill Jordan and was then silenced by a third party.'

'All scenarios are possible.'

'They are and now I'm even more confused by it all but at least you've given me food for thought. Thanks. Now, go home. This can wait. Go on.'

She watched him as he collected his belongings and left, a hand up in a farewell gesture. It was after nine. She ought to go home too. Schrödinger would be wondering where she was. The thought of him cheered her. It was nice to know somebody was waiting back home.

CHAPTER FIFTEEN

Robyn plodded through long grass that slapped at her ankles and made each terrifying step take forever. The field was full of scarecrows, all with familiar faces – her cousin Ross, his wife Jeanette, Mitz, Anna, David and Matt and then, at the end of the first row, Jordan's girlfriend Rebecca, her mouth stitched up, eyes wide in fear. Robyn couldn't halt. Her legs kept moving, one step after another, as she walked past each of them until she reached the smallest scarecrow, who hung limply against a stake – Dylan. Suddenly the scarecrows began moaning in unison, their cries increasing in volume, louder and louder, until Robyn sat bolt upright in bed, her forehead damp with sweat.

Schrödinger, curled beside her, was unaware of his mistress's distress and slumbered on, his chest rising and falling gently, paws tucked neatly under his body. She rested a hand on his soft fur, grateful for his company, and waited until her racing heart had calmed to the rhythm of his breathing before removing her fingers.

The digital display revealed it was 5 a.m. She shrugged off the duvet, padded to the en-suite bathroom and stood under the shower, letting the hot water beat onto her head and dispel the horror of the dream. She stood until it ran cold, then towel-dried her body and wrapped a smaller towel around her hair, twisting it into a turban and tucking the end underneath to anchor it in place.

Schrödinger didn't budge when she shrugged on her dressing gown and descended the stairs. She didn't switch on the lights, guided instead by the street light outside her house that provided adequate illumination through the glass panel in the front door. There were no noises outside. Robyn enjoyed this time of the day. She'd often take to the streets on her bike, or pound the pavements before the world began to stir. Today, she couldn't bring herself to train for the Ironman event. She'd been spooked by the nightmare and needed to direct her fevered mind to the investigation.

It was on account of the nightmare that Robyn rang Rebecca before heading to the office. She wanted to ensure both mother and son were okay. Robyn replayed the conversation in her mind as she drove to the police station:

'Just seeing how you both are?'

'We're managing. Just about. I still can't get my head around what's happened. It's unreal. Dylan wants to go to school today. Says he misses his friends. He looks so miserable and I don't know what to do for the best. Everything's happening too fast. Three days ago we were happy. Then somebody snatched that happiness away. It's so unfair. I can't believe it.'

'It's only been three days, Rebecca. You need time to adjust.'

'Three horrendously long days, and thanks to Jordan's father kicking us out, I'll have to visit the estate agents for somewhere else to live. I'd like to find somewhere to rent in this area. I don't want to uproot Dylan. It's difficult enough for him without pulling him away from his new friends. I already disrupted his life bringing him here from Birmingham.'

'That makes sense. What about you? How are you?' Robyn had felt a certain admiration for Rebecca's practical outlook, although she detected the sorrow in Rebecca's voice when she'd next spoken.

'How do you think? Some moments I want to scream my head off, rage, hit out, and other times, I want to hide away from everyone and hope everything magically goes back to normal, and that it's all just been a shitty nightmare. But it isn't is it? It's real and I have to put on a brave face for Dylan when inside, I'm a mess. I want to know who did this and watch them go through the same horrendous pain as us. Find the bastard, please.'

'We're doing everything we can, Rebecca.'

'I know you are.' Her words were soft and heavy with sorrow. 'Human resources at work have told me I can take the week off, but I'm probably better at work rather than here, in a house full of memories. Moping isn't going to bring Jordan back, and since I can't even get involved in laying him to rest, I may as well return to my job. His father is taking care of all the funeral arrangements, so I feel redundant. Useless. Like I'm living in a vacuum. DI Carter, this is the hardest thing I've had to do. If I were married to him, or even engaged to him, people would be flocking around, supporting me, saying how sorry they are. I'd be able to remove the memories of him, little by little – his clothes, his belongings, that sort of thing – all in my own time until I could bear to say the final goodbye, and then I'd find closure. As it is, I can't. He's been ripped from me and I'll lose everything to remind me of him as soon as I leave our home. I'll be on my own again. I seem to have always been on my own.'

Robyn understood. She and Rebecca had trodden similar paths – lost parents, lost lovers, kept going.

'It's Robyn,' she had said. 'Forget the DI Carter. Call me Robyn. You'll be okay, Rebecca. You have Dylan.'

She had heard the smile in Rebecca's voice. 'Yes. I have.'

'Are you up to answering a couple of questions? Just say if you're not.'

'Go ahead.'

'Did Jordan take his cycling helmet when he went out?'

There'd been a confused silence. 'He always wore it. Of course, he took it. I can see him, as clear as day, standing by the back door, strapping the helmet on and then hugging Dylan goodbye.'

'Sorry to put you through this again, but did Jordan ever discuss his father's business with you? Maybe mention that his father was involved with the HS2 line?'

'Yes, that came up. Jordan had read about it in the local paper – some article about his father and our local MP – and was annoyed about it. I don't think many people are happy at the thought of the line going through the countryside here. It'll spoil it.'

'The line was due to go through Colton, where Owen lives. Did you ever hear them discuss it? I can imagine Jordan might have been upset or concerned for his friend.'

Robyn hadn't really known why she brought up Owen's name. She'd maybe hoped for a clue that'd point to some common ground that had got them into trouble.

'I never heard him talk about it. If I'm honest, there's a bit of friction between Owen and me. He makes polite conversation, and he isn't rude or anything, but I sometimes get the feeling he resents me being around – or he's uncomfortable with me. There are little signals – for instance, he'll stop speaking mid-sentence if I walk in on him and Jordan having a conversation, like he doesn't want me to be part of it.

'I sound like a jealous cow, don't I? I'm being over-sensitive again. I thought Owen would have rung me or called around to see how we are. He must have heard about what's happened to Jordan by now. He was Jordan's best friend – he was our friend. He came over at least once a week to play on the PlayStation with him. They'd share a couple of beers or we'd all have a takeaway.

Sometimes, I'd watch them play but it bored me rigid, so often I'd play with Dylan, or we'd watch telly in the bedroom. I'm surprised Owen hasn't contacted me. I guess he really doesn't like me.'

Rebecca had to get Dylan ready for school, leaving Robyn surprised by the revelation Owen had visited Jordan's house every week. Owen had claimed he rarely saw Jordan, and Rebecca had just contradicted that statement. Robyn also realised Rebecca was unaware of what had happened to Owen. She had no idea Owen was dead.

Robyn wasn't the first to arrive at the office. David was behind his desk, head down, when she arrived. She didn't disturb him but instead pulled out Jordan's file and looked at what they'd found so far. Connor would be along soon to present his findings and, hopefully, they'd all pool enough information to further the investigation. Robyn wanted to ring Brian Turner at the council offices but it was way too early, so instead she read through the notes she'd made about the crime scenes: Jordan's bloodied body hanging against a stake and Owen's in a pool of blood and grease.

'David, take a look at these crime scene photos. What do you see?'

David studied the picture of Jordan. 'Man hanging on a post like a scarecrow would, with a sheet covered in blood at his feet.'

'Exactly. That sheet seems out of place, doesn't it? If the killer wanted to make Jordan appear to be a scarecrow, he'd have just left him hanging there and not put a sheet down.'

'That's true. Why do you think it's there?'

'Honestly? I don't know. I just have a feeling it's significant.'

The others arrived soon afterwards, Matt, fresh-faced and delighted his baby daughter was at last sleeping through the night, filled up the coffee machine with a fresh packet of grounds.

'Okay, everyone. Let's try and make sense of what we have.' Robyn summarised their findings so far and brought up the subject of the bike and the missing helmet.

'He could have left the helmet in the pub or at Owen's house,' said Matt.

Robyn agreed. 'Sure, although one hasn't been found at Owen's. Forensics would have said something if they'd located it. David, when we finish this, ring Joe Harris, the landlord of the Fox and Weasel, and ask if it's there.'

Mitz spoke up. 'He might have left it at somebody else's house, or the killer took it.'

'Again, that's possible,' said Robyn. 'Either way, it's disappeared.'

'How far is it from Newborough to Colton?' Anna asked.

'About seven and a half miles.'

'Seems strange he'd cycle that way for a drink. It'd be much quicker by car.'

'According to his friends and Rebecca, he was a keen cyclist. He preferred using his bike in better weather. Seven miles isn't that far, would have taken him about forty minutes,' Robyn replied.

'I'd barely last four minutes,' said Matt. 'Give me four wheels any day.'

'Seriously, though,' said Anna, dark eyes turned on Matt, 'I'd have thought he'd have taken his car. The bike isn't a sensible option especially if he intended returning home in the dark after a drink or two.'

Robyn conceded Anna had a point.

Matt considered Anna's words then replied. 'Maybe he always intended spending the night at Owen's house, and planned to ride home in the morning.'

Anna persisted. 'But he texted his girlfriend to let her know he was staying over. If his intention had been to stay at Owen's house, surely he'd have told her before he left home. It's got me wondering if he deliberately used the bike because he knew Owen wouldn't hear him leave. It had no engine. He could go as soon as his friend was asleep and Owen would be none the wiser. That would make sense if he was planning on meeting somebody and didn't want Owen to know about it.'

Robyn was impressed by the thought processes leading to this deduction, even though she couldn't make out its relevance at this stage. She noted it on the board and threw the floor open to each of them.

David was keen to speak. 'My findings might have more significance in light of what Anna's just said. I've been checking up on vehicles spotted in Colton on Sunday afternoon and evening. There were two in particular that we were most interested in – a dark van and a black car. I've yet to trace the owner of the van, but I did come across a witness who claimed they saw a black, or dark grey, Mercedes-Benz driving past the church about nine thirty. They didn't see the whole number plate, but were sure it ended in the letters EXX. I searched the government vehicle registration database and found out that a black, S-Class Mercedes-Benz, with number plate ending in EXX, is registered to NJK Properties.'

Robyn caught her breath. 'Nathaniel Jones-Kilby?'

David nodded. 'Do you think Jordan intended meeting his father in Colton that night?'

Robyn couldn't see why that would be the case, but she certainly had to act on this new information. She'd handle Jones-Kilby herself. She gave a brief nod in response. 'Can we find his vehicle on any cameras?'

'I got in early today and checked through the automatic number plate recognition points around that area, and I've located the car headed towards Abbots Bromley at twelve fifteen.' He held up a photograph showing the car and the number plate. A man resembling Nathaniel Jones-Kilby was at the wheel.

'Great work, David.'

Buoyed by this development, the rest of the team were keen to share what they'd learnt and soon the whiteboard was covered in potential leads. Connor arrived at the office to find the team enthusiastically debating the possibility Owen had been silenced by Jordan's murderer. Robyn waved him across to the board and allowed him to take the floor.

'Got a few things for you,' he said, setting up some transparencies. Unlike Robyn, Connor preferred gadgets and overhead projectors.

'First off, your scarecrow victim.' A picture was projected onto the screen. It showed the bloodied sheet Robyn had been discussing earlier with David.

'This is a cream, cotton, single sheet from a supermarket basics range.' He pointed at the label and enlarged it for all to see. 'It hasn't been washed or used, and indentations where it was folded to fit inside the packaging are still visible. The blood on the sheet is the same type as Jordan Kilby's.'

Connor moved efficiently onto the next picture showing a bicycle, front wheel twisted to an angle, in a ditch.

'Fingerprints lifted from the bike indicate this is indeed the bike he used that evening. There are no other prints on it suggesting the perp was wearing gloves. This is where we located the bike.' A sketch of the field marked 'Top Field' flickered onto the screen. The bike was in a ditch in the adjacent field.

'It has proven impossible to find any footprints, and although grass was flattened in places, we believe that was due to those who arrived after Jordan's death.

'We've found two cigarette butts and a button, possibly from a man's shirt, that might or might not have any significance. They are currently being tested in the laboratory. To date we haven't come across a knife or any weapon that might have been used to kill Jordan Kilby. But earlier this morning we found this.'

He lifted out a plastic bag containing a mobile phone.

'It's a Sony Xperia X Compact mobile phone. It was in the same ditch as the bicycle, only further along and well hidden. It's been wiped clean of prints. I doubt your tech boys will be able to get anything off it because the SIM card has been removed, but it's all yours.'

Robyn let out a soft groan. 'Too much to hope you found the SIM card?'

Connor gave her an apologetic look. He pulled the transparency off the projector with a resigned smile. 'On to Owen Falcon. We can be certain that tools from Mr Falcon's toolbox were used in his murder. Blood found on the lump hammer, wrench and screwdriver all match his own blood group, A-positive. We lifted various fingerprints from the scene and the toolbox. Some are Jordan's. Others might be from visitors, friends or the perp. There are several clear sets of prints in the laundry room, which again match Jordan's. They were notably on the back door and the sink surround. We've lifted fibres from Owen's body that don't match his clothing and are currently checking to see if they match any of his other clothing. He could have picked them up anywhere, from the dirty washing in the basket we found in the laundry room, for instance.

'As you will appreciate, it's still early days, and we've a great deal of work to do. I'm sorry but that's all I have for now.'

Robyn's cheeks lifted in a grateful smile. Investigations weren't easy to conduct. It wasn't as television dramas often portrayed with teams of people in the latest high-tech lab using magical machines that gave instant results. Methods were similar to those that had been employed by forensic scientists for years, and what they needed was time.

'The sheet, Connor. I can't work out why the murderer would take along a sheet and lay it out. It's not like they had to protect the ground from the blood.'

'Might have been used to capture the blood and attract the birds,' he said. 'Carrion are sensitive to compounds given off by rotting corpses but I'm no expert on the subject.'

The nightmare came back to her, and the thought of birds swooping and pecking at Jordan's body caused a shiver to travel through her body. This was one of the most grotesque cases she'd worked on. She brought the meeting to an end and allocated tasks to each of them. She'd decided to tackle Brian Turner and Nathaniel Jones-Kilby personally, and she wasn't going to back down until she had answers.

CHAPTER SIXTEEN

DAY THREE – WEDNESDAY, 7 JUNE, LATE MORNING

Robyn rang the council offices and asked to speak to Brian Turner. The woman was brusque and informed her Mr Turner was busy. Robyn insisted on speaking to him. There was a lengthy pause and then music as she was put on hold. She used the time to choose her opening words. It was eleven minutes before Brian Turner spoke.

'Brian Turner,' he said, curtly.

'Mr Turner, it's DI Carter from the Staffordshire Police Force. I wondered if I could make an appointment to talk to you. We're investigating the death of Jordan Kilby and interviewing everyone connected to him and his father.'

'I don't see how I can be of any help whatsoever.'

'I understand you've had dealings with NJK Properties and that's why I'd like to talk to you.'

There was a lengthy silence as Brian Turner weighed up his options. Eventually he answered her. 'You'll have to talk to my secretary and arrange a time. I'm pretty busy at the moment. Now, if you'll excuse me, I have a meeting to attend.'

The phone went dead immediately, leaving Robyn to redial and ask to be put through to Turner's secretary. After much insistence, she managed to make an appointment for the following afternoon.

The office was quiet with Anna and David working at their computers, gathering the information Robyn had requested. Mitz had been dispatched to the Marshes where he was to quiz them gently about the planned HS2 line, and Matt was interviewing Owen's colleagues at Rugeley Electrical Centre. Robyn swung her chair around and stared out of the window. Across the road from the station, a late-flowering cherry tree was in full pink blossom, its flowers the same colour as Schrödinger's tongue. She picked up her mobile and checked the app. He was curled on the settee, a ball of sooty black fur. She watched him for a minute. It was calming, watching him doze, and allowed her to refocus on the investigation. She'd have to face Nathaniel Jones-Kilby. It couldn't be put off any longer. She rang his office, discovered he was at home for the day, and, without any appointment in place, set off for The Manor House, close to the village of Blithbury, known for its reindeer centre.

The sun had again decided to make an appearance, and Robyn was treated to empty roads flanked by trees bearing fresh, shining green foliage as she drove towards Rugeley and then on to Blithbury. She passed endless fields until she reached the roundabout at Wolseley Garden Centre, a popular weekend destination that not only sold plants but also had a large ball pit for children, and a tearoom. Many people parked here at weekends, not just to peruse the centre but for the wildlife trust centre next door, with its acres of wildlife-friendly gardens, and walks by the River Trent. The summer before, she, Ross and Jeanette had parked up and walked the path alongside the Trent and Mersey Canal, passing gaily coloured houseboats moored there, and watched dragonflies dart over the water. They'd ended up at a picturesque pub with a thatched roof and sat outside in the garden, sipping Pimm's – because Ross decided it was a quintessentially English thing to do – and swatting at wasps. The memory of it made her forget her mission momentarily until she spotted the huge cooling towers of

Rugeley that indicated she was near her destination. The satnav guided her away from the main road and along scenic lanes with which she was not familiar.

Staffordshire was a large county and the labyrinth of lanes and country roads made it almost impossible to know where any place was in relation to another. So it was only through glancing at her GPS that she realised Nathaniel's house was closer to the village of Colton than she'd first imagined, no more than two miles away. He could well have had a legitimate reason for travelling through Colton on Sunday night. She brushed the unsettling thought away. No matter if it irked him – she would ask the question. She had a job to do and it would be unprofessional if she didn't follow up her leads.

Nathaniel had earned a vast amount of money from property, and that wealth was evident in his own outstanding home. The drive traversed stone pillars and wrought-iron gates, and passed through post-and-rail horse paddocks with far-reaching views over farmland, until it reached a turning circle, which revealed the handsome façade of the seventeenth-century manor house.

Robyn speculated at its worth – possibly five or six million. The well-maintained grounds warranted an army of gardeners. She thought of her own patch of garden, no more than twenty feet wide and thirty feet in length, all grassed, with two decent-sized camellia shrubs by her back door that produced pretty pink double-headed flowers each spring, and another shrub that flowered later in the year, bearing huge yellow flowers like small pineapples. She had never learned its name.

Taking a deep breath and steeling herself for confrontation, she crunched over the small stones to the front porch where she rang the bell. As she waited, she tried not to gawp at the enormous brown-brick building with huge towering chimney stacks and sparkling mullioned windows, and instead speculated as to why Jordan had opted for a job as a delivery driver and a small cottage in the country, when he could be following in his father's footsteps and living in opulence like this.

The main door opened and Nathaniel appeared, wearing sunglasses, his mane of dirty-blonde hair swept away from his face. A red-spotted silken handkerchief had been propped up to attention in the breast pocket of his light-grey jacket that he'd teamed with a pale-blue shirt and white slacks. The impression created was of somebody about to attend a party on board a yacht. He lifted and lowered his Ray-Bans to better study Robyn's face; one eyebrow rose quizzically.

'DI Carter. Do you have any news?'

Robyn shook her head. 'Not yet, sir. I was hoping you'd be able to answer some questions for me.'

He removed the sunglasses, held them lightly in his hand and looked at his watch. 'I was about to go out. I have an appointment.'

'I won't take up much of your time.'

'What do you want to know?'

'I'll cut straight to the chase. It's about Sunday night. I understand your car was spotted in Colton village late that night and I was hoping you might enlighten me as to why it was there.'

He twisted the arm of his sunglasses around in his long fingers before speaking. 'Am I under suspicion, DI Carter? Might I remind you, my only son has been killed and you are supposed to be searching for his murderer, not asking me pointless questions.'

'In any investigation, we have to examine everything that is brought to our attention, if only to eliminate people from our enquiries. I'm sure you appreciate that. I have no reason to suspect you, Mr Jones-Kilby, and indeed am deeply sorry for your loss. However, I wouldn't be doing my job properly if I didn't ask you the question.'

She hoped she hadn't been too blunt. Nathaniel appeared to consider her request but did not invite her to step over the threshold or even into the porch.

'Fair enough. At least you're doing something, even if it is time-wasting.' The dour expression on his face did not change. 'I had a late supper at a friend's house. I passed through Colton on my way there.'

'Did you come back through Colton later?'

Nathaniel shook his head. 'No. I returned home a different route.'

'What time would that have been?'

He sighed heavily. 'I don't know. Around twelve thirty.'

Robyn waited for more information but none was forthcoming. She was going to have to ask more questions if she wanted definitive answers. 'For the record, could you give me a name and address of the person?'

His eyes narrowed dangerously. 'I hardly think that'd be necessary, do you? I did not kill my son. I had no idea Jordan was in Colton that night. And I had no reason to do so. Be logical. What possible reason would I have for murdering my own offspring? It beggars belief that you have decided to waste time and no doubt resources to check up on me and come here, to my home, to question me about this. Now, if you'll excuse me, I have an appointment and I don't wish to be late for it. Might I suggest you check out some of his nefarious colleagues or so-called friends before you come knocking at my door?'

'You mean friends like Owen Falcon?'

The lid of his right eye began to nictate. 'Indeed. Good day, DI Carter.'

'Sir, I really need the name and address of the person you were visiting. This is a murder investigation.'

'I shall give that information to your superior and that is all I'm prepared to do.'

He turned his back on her without waiting for further response and shut the door firmly behind him, leaving Robyn wishing she had handled the conversation differently. He was surprisingly brusque. She wondered how cool he'd been with Rebecca when he'd told her to pack up and leave Jordan's house, and shuddered at the thought. The man lacked compassion, and any sympathy she had felt for him over losing his son was fast waning.

It was because of Nathaniel's overbearing attitude that Robyn drove back to the station via Jordan's house. Dylan was not there, but she found Rebecca at home.

'I don't have any news,' Robyn said. 'I came to see how you and Dylan were getting on.'

'That's kind of you. Come in.'

Robyn traipsed after her into the kitchen. Rebecca pulled two mugs from a cupboard and held them aloft. 'You can't leave without a cup of tea, at least.'

Robyn accepted with a smile. 'Have you decided if you're going to stay in the vicinity?'

Rebecca nodded. 'I went to a lettings agency earlier and they have a vacant place near Rangemore which is only a couple of miles from where I work. It's a bit further to drive Dylan to school, but it won't be too bad. I'd rather keep him at the school in Newborough where's he's settled. I said I'd take it immediately.'

Robyn knew the area Rebecca meant. The all-England football training ground at St George's Park was situated close to Rangemore and it was rumoured several famous football players lived in some of the larger rural properties in the area. Dylan would be excited to learn he'd be moving closer to footballers.

'And you might even be able to drop by St George's Park and let him watch the footballers train.'

Rebecca's mouth dropped open a little in surprise. 'Of course! I'd forgotten about the training grounds. I'll definitely have to swing by there now and again.'

Tea ready, she put a mug down in front of Robyn and stood by the sink, stirring her own tea, around and around, with little realisation. 'Can I ask you something, Robyn?' she said, eventually.

'Go ahead.'

'I'm worried Jordan might have been seeing another woman and it got him killed.'

The revelation came as a surprise to Robyn. The look on Rebecca's face suggested she'd given her theory thought and it was eating at her. 'Whatever makes you say that?' she asked.

Rebecca studied the milky tea and slowly removed the spoon, dropping it into the sink. Her speech was laboured, as if she was too scared to voice her thoughts. 'I found something odd.'

'Odd in what way?'

'I was collecting up our stuff – mine and Dylan's – getting ready to move out, and came across a business card for a private investigator in Jordan's beside table drawer. I couldn't work out why he'd have it, and then I got to thinking, what if he had been having an affair with another woman – a married one – and her husband had employed an investigator to check on them both? And what if the husband found out and murdered Jordan? Is that even likely, or am I making insane suggestions?' She picked up a card from the kitchen top and passed it to Robyn.

Robyn glanced at the name on the card. It was her cousin, Ross. 'I doubt this is anything to do with a girlfriend. He'd be unlikely to have a private investigator's number if he was having a relationship with somebody. Jordan might have had this card for years, or it has no significance whatsoever.'

Rebecca gave a cheerless smile. 'I suppose so. Ignore my craziness. I seem to be losing my grip on reality. I wish this was all a bad dream. I so want Jordan to come back home and for this to not be happening. It's all gone so horribly wrong so quickly. One second we're looking at spending our lives together and the next, I have almost nothing to remind me of him. It's too much to bear. I don't even know why I considered the possibility he'd be seeing somebody else. Maybe I'm trying in some ludicrous way to rationalise why he was murdered.'

Robyn endeavoured to coax Rebecca out of her confusion and misery. 'This is nothing. I'm sure he loved you wholeheartedly. I look around at the photos of you all looking so happy, and see the love that is evident in this house, and I'm convinced there was no one else in his life but you and Dylan. I know the investigator. I'll talk to him if you like, just to put your mind at rest.'

Rebecca dropped her head and battled with tears that suddenly formed. 'Thank you. I'm all over the place at the moment, what with packing to move, and everything else. Leaving this, our home, makes it seem so final. Once we walk out of that door for the last time, I'll have lost everything.'

'No, Rebecca, not everything. You'll still have Dylan, and together you'll build another future. It doesn't seem possible at the moment, but you will.' As Robyn spoke, a small voice in her head shouted that she was being hypocritical. Davies had been gone for two years and how much of a future had she carved out for herself? She put an arm around Rebecca, now crying softly, and thought of the callous Nathaniel Jones-Kilby – even though he had just lost his son, he simply wasn't capable of such emotion. She would uncover Jordan's murderer not so much for his benefit but for Rebecca and her little boy – they were the ones who truly deserved her help.

Her thoughts turned back to the card in her hand. Jordan had phoned Amy Walters and wanted to pass her information about something important. He might also have spoken to Ross about it. She'd get hold of her cousin as soon as she could and see if she could make some headway.

CHAPTER SEVENTEEN

DAY THREE – WEDNESDAY, 7 JUNE, AFTERNOON

Robyn had been unable to reach Ross and her attention had been diverted as soon as she reached the office. Mitz had bowled over to her desk with the news that one of Jordan's friends from the football team, Jasper Fetcher, had rung Mitz. He'd had little to say when Robyn had first interviewed him but now he wanted to talk.

The young man, dressed in the traditional bib and braces overalls of a construction worker, had agreed to meet them in Uttoxeter, where he was working on a site. It was market day and the streets had been full of visitors, eager to buy fresh, locally grown produce. The cobbles on Market Square had been covered with stalls and people billowing out onto the road when she and Mitz had crawled past in the squad car.

Jasper had suggested the café hidden up a side street, away from the main thoroughfare, and had chosen a seat at the very back of the room. From where Robyn sat, she had a view of the tall counter and coffee machine that was currently spluttering and hissing.

Robyn and Mitz sat opposite Jasper. The café was busy but it was the only place he'd been prepared to meet them. He rolled a Rizla packet between his fingers for a long time before speaking, all the while his eyes, with their ice-blue irises encircled by dark limbal rings, grazed the room, furtively checking for familiar faces.

'I don't want anyone to know it came from me,' he said. 'If anybody finds out it was me who told you, I'd be next in line for a good kicking.'

Jasper fidgeted uncomfortably.

'I could be wrong about this, but with both Jordan and Owen dead, I thought I should say something. You ought to talk to Darren Sturgeon. He plays football for the Sudbury Dynamos. There was an incident a week ago during a game. We were up against them in a friendly match, and there was some trouble. Darren said something to Owen that set him off. They've both got tempers but this time Owen got really wound up. He and Jordan intentionally fouled Darren, and were both sent off.

'Saturday night, the day before Jordan died, Darren got beaten up outside his local pub. I think Jordan and Owen were behind the attack. I overheard them talking about doing Darren over, so he couldn't play football again. Owen was in a proper mood.'

'And what about Jordan? Why would he attack Darren?'

Jasper snorted. 'Cos Owen asked him to. He was Owen's lap dog. Owen loved it – all the adulation – trailing Jordan about like he was on a lead or something.'

'What did you think of Jordan behaving like this? You told me last time you neither liked nor disliked him.'

'Look, Jordan was a boring tit who hung about with us because he liked playing football and because he was in awe of Owen. He was one of those guys you can't shake off. He'd turn up and sit with us and not say much, just nod, unless he was going on about cycling or football. We used to tease Owen and said he only liked Jordan cos he was rich and was hoping he'd share his fortune. Owen told us to fuck off and Jordan didn't have anything to his own name and we should cut him some slack – so we did at times.'

'Do you think that was the case? Was Owen after some of Jordan's wealth?'

'Owen didn't need anyone's help. He inherited his house from his parents. He wasn't short of a few quid. Not mega-wealthy like, but had enough to get by. He still had to work for a living and he still hung about with his old mates.

'Jordan on the other hand, was one of them posh boys trying to fit in. He wanted people to think he was an ordinary, hard-working bloke who drove a van, when really his old man could have bought him his own delivery business and set him up for life. He was never going to be one of us, was he?'

'So, you think there's a possibility Owen and Jordan attacked Darren Sturgeon following an altercation on the pitch, and Darren took revenge and murdered them?'

Jasper nodded, his eyes darting around the room again. 'It's possible. Darren's a complete basket case. Especially when he gets too much drink down him. But like I said, I don't want anyone to know it came from me. If word gets out I spoke to you, I'll get a bloody good kicking myself. Or worse. Look what's happened already.'

'When did you last speak to Owen, Jasper?'

'Monday when he rang me to tell me Jordan was dead. And today, Joe Harris phoned me to tell me Owen was dead too. Still can't get my fucking head round it all. What the fuck's going on? First Jordan and now Owen. I don't suppose you'll tell me what happened to Owen?'

Robyn shook her head. 'I can't do that.'

Jasper shook his head in dismay. 'I wouldn't be surprised if that bastard Darren didn't round up his nutty mates and set them on Jordan and Owen.' He glanced at his mobile. 'I'm due back at work now. I have to go. You'll keep my name out of it when you talk to him, right? I don't want any trouble from him if I'm wrong about this.'

Robyn agreed to him going, and Jasper scuttled off, eager to be out of the café and away from Robyn and Mitz.

As Robyn and Mitz walked along the main street back towards their car, Mitz made an observation.

'He seemed pretty jittery to me. Do you think he knows more than he was willing to share?'

'That could be the case, or he was worried it'd get out that he'd spoken to us. He might have been more involved in that attack on Darren than he was willing to admit. We'll get hold of Darren Sturgeon and see if he can enlighten us.'

'I'll sort that out.' Mitz pointed the key fob at the car and the indicators flashed red before unlocking the vehicle with a loud blip.

'I think we need to probe into all their backgrounds – the teammates, and maybe some of the opposition. Start with that crowd who hang out at the Fox and Weasel. Can you drop me at Ross's office on the way back? I've got something I want to run past him.'

R&J Associates had been given a makeover. The walls had been freshly painted in sea green and new blinds hung at the window. Ross had splashed out on new furniture too – gone were the old leather armchairs and clunky desk, making way for stylish swivel chairs and a low coffee table.

'Very swish,' said Robyn, admiring the decor. 'Who dragged you into the twenty-first century? Let me guess – Jeanette?'

Ross ran a meaty hand across his head and gave a boyish grin. 'She chose everything. You know me; I'd have left it painted magnolia forever and a day. And there was nothing wrong with those chairs. They were quality. Must say, it looks more cheerful now. Duke, get down! You know where your bed is.'

The Staffie threw him a doleful look, dropped down from the swivel chair and, ignoring his master, sidled up to Robyn. She patted him.

'Ross, I need to ask you about Jordan Kilby. I wondered if he'd contacted you recently.'

One of Ross's heavy eyebrows lifted high. 'Kilby. He was murdered a couple of days ago. I saw it on the evening news.'

'DCI Flint allowed the press to do a brief piece on it, but we're keeping the details of the investigation under wraps. There's been a recent development, and it now looks like we're dealing with a joint homicide. We're under considerable pressure to come up with answers quickly. His father, Nathaniel Jones-Kilby, has friends in high places.'

Ross wrinkled his nose. 'They're the hardest relatives to deal with – so demanding. They think you can turn a case round in an instant. They have no idea that sometimes it can be months or even longer. I blame our culture – they're obsessed with instant gratification, and they watch too many crime dramas where everything's resolved in four, hour-long episodes. I've spent eighteen months looking for a long-lost sister.' His shoulders lifted in resignation. 'I remember Jordan. It was an odd case – one of my first after I qualified as a PI. His mother, Sue Jones-Kilby, died in a car crash but he didn't believe it was an accident. I wasn't going to take the case on at first. I'd seen that sort of reaction before when I worked on the force. You've come across it too. People who can't accept that accidents happen and look to blame others or find reasons as to why something unexplained has occurred.'

'You changed your mind.'

'There was something about the way he spoke and acted that made me curious as to whether there was any truth in what he was saying. He was very calm and he'd thought it through before asking me. He told me he'd got good reason to suspect his father had killed his mother and he wanted to prove it.'

'What made you think he was telling the truth or had grounds for such speculation?'

'You know how it is, Robyn. You've been doing this job for a long time and you've been a PI too. You get hunches about people and cases. Jordan gave me £1,000 in advance to investigate his mother's death. He had a wild idea that his father had first got his mother drunk, and then planted, or had someone plant, a device to cause the car to explode and veer across the road. The look on his face made my guts twist. He looked so unhappy.'

'That was quite an accusation.'

'I thought so too. Jordan wasn't going to be dissuaded. When his father bought him a house of his own, he took it as a sign of a guilty conscience and came to me for help to prove it. I started work but a few days into the job, Jordan rang me and told me he'd changed his mind and he'd rather I didn't pursue the investigation.'

'What did you find out before you were taken off the case?'

Ross stood and crossed the room to one of two filing cabinets where he knelt and pulled out the right-hand bottom drawer. He rooted for a few minutes before emitting a grunt and extracting a file. He returned to his desk and opened the folder, reading the first few paragraphs.

'I always keep notes on all my cases. Never know when you might need them again. This contains everything I found out before Jordan asked me to drop the investigation. He paid me for my time and asked me to forget about the whole affair. Said he was completely wrong and it was emotion that had made him come up with such crazy notions.'

Ross flicked through the first few pages of interviews and notes. 'Nathaniel took his wife to lunch the day she died. According to witnesses at the restaurant, they were discussing financial affairs to do with the divorce settlement and had an argument. She left him and took off in her car. The maître d' confirmed she'd consumed almost all the contents of a bottle of wine. Jones-Kilby had drunk only a little himself. He also said, as soon as she'd left, Jones-Kilby made a phone call, then signalled for the bill and left an extremely generous tip. They might sound seemingly unimportant details but somebody who overheard the conversation stated they clearly heard Nathaniel telling the person at the other end to, "Sort her out once and for all."'

'Why didn't Jordan want to report this all to the police?'

'When I suggested he should take his concerns to the police, he replied his father had many friends and nothing would be investigated.' Ross shut the file and pushed it across the desk to Robyn.

Robyn thumbed through the pages. 'Did you think Nathaniel was responsible for his wife's death?'

Ross lifted his hands, palms up. With a shrug he said, 'For what it's worth, I think there were grounds to suspect his involvement, but it would have taken a forensic team and a lot of investigation to prove it. I was glad when Jordan pulled me off the job. It would have been a shedload of aggravation to prove his father's guilt.'

'Thanks, Ross. I'm okay to keep this?'

'Sure. You think Nathaniel's involved in Jordan's murder?'

'I don't know. It's all… murky at the moment.'

'You'll figure it out,' Ross said with a smile. 'Okay. I have to go. Jeanette's asked me to take her to a doctor's appointment this afternoon. Her car's gone into the garage – needs a new exhaust. It won't be ready until tomorrow evening.'

'I'd best get off too. Say hi to Jeanette for me. Tell her she has impeccable taste.'

'She knows that already. She chose me,' he shouted as Robyn slipped away.

She could still hear his deep chuckling as she bounded from the bottom stair and left the block.

Robyn made the journey from R&J Associates back to the police station on foot. It was a pleasantly warm afternoon and the trip took her through Victoria Park, one of her favourite parts of Stafford. It was awash with colour. Not only were bushes and trees in bloom but the gardeners had created several large displays of multi-coloured blooms in vibrant pinks, reds and oranges that lifted her spirits. She crossed the bridge over the river and paused to let a grey squirrel traverse the bridge, scuttle along the handrail and leap lightly to the ground before scurrying up the nearest tree. She continued along the River Sow using the new towpath, a flotilla of ducks keeping pace as she marched onwards, her mind on Jordan and Owen.

The two were close friends – closer than Owen had suggested. Rebecca had remarked upon it and gone so far as to suggest Owen had been slightly jealous of her arrival on the scene. Jasper and Callum, their footballing friends, had also claimed the duo got along well and would on occasion stand together, set apart from the others. They'd done so in the Fox and Weasel the night Jordan had been murdered. She left the riverbank and, when there was a gap in the traffic, jogged across the busy dual carriageway.

There were various leads to chase up: Darren Sturgeon, the footballer who'd been in a fight with Jordan and Owen, and Joe Harris, landlord of the Fox and Weasel, who might have overheard what the pair was discussing. And there was Nathaniel himself. There remained a possibility he was somehow connected to the deaths, and no matter how harshly he spoke to her, Robyn wasn't giving up on that angle until she was certain he had no involvement whatsoever.

CHAPTER EIGHTEEN

The Fox and Weasel might have been a more attractive pub had somebody attended to the hanging baskets, filled with shrivelled flowers, and removed the pile of cigarette stubs stamped out in a sand-filled flowerpot outside the back door. As it was, the place wore an air of neglect, from the moss growing up through the cracks in the tarmac, to the paint peeling in strips from the yellowed window frames, and the shabby chalkboard advertising the specials for the day, broken and propped against the wall for support. Inside fared slightly better, with dim lighting helping to disguise the stained furniture and scuffed counter. Robyn wondered what it could be that attracted people to drink here, and then judging by the chorus of shouts coming from the public bar, decided it was the large television screen that showed sports all day.

Joe Harris, the landlord, tipped her a nod.

'I was hoping you could tell me more about last Sunday.'

He lifted several empty glasses from a table with one huge hand and moved off behind the bar, where he noisily put them into a dishwasher before speaking.

'Not much else to tell you,' he said.

Robyn glanced about the place, her eyes resting on a group of young men glued to a match. She wandered across to them.

'Who's playing?' she asked a lad in jeans and a black T-shirt with tattoo sleeves that covered not only his arms but the backs of his hands. He spoke without looking away from the screen, a pint of beer in one hand, midway between the table and his mouth.

'Villa.' Then he let out a grunt as the ball was snatched from an attacker and passed to the opposition. The footballer raced towards the goal, slaloming past defenders and aimed for the goal, missing. The crowd at the bar let out a collective howl.

'I don't suppose any of you know Jordan Kilby, do you?' she asked.

Heads turned and shook negative responses. The man with the tattooed arms mumbled, 'I know him but don't, if you see what I mean. I knew who he was but never really spoke to him. He used to hang with some of the Blithfield Wanderers mob.'

'You didn't see him in here on Sunday night?'

'Wasn't in at the weekend.' The man's mouth opened again as his attention was dragged back to the match.

Robyn left them to it.

Joe Harris was staring at her, arms folded. 'Finished annoying my customers?' he asked.

Robyn ignored the hostile comment. She approached the bar and studied the bar stool before deciding against sitting on it. 'I know you've already spoken to me about Jordan but I could do with your help. Now two young men have been murdered – both played for the Blithfield Wanderers and both used this pub as their local. Help me out here. I need to at least find justice for their families.'

Joe's eyes cast downwards. 'It's been a bloody horrible shock,' he said. 'I haven't got my head round it. It's upset me something rotten. Sorry. I didn't mean to be so off with you. I'm – oh, I don't know what I am – in shock, I suppose.'

Robyn offered him a smile and against her better judgement sat on the tatty stool, to appear less intimidating. 'It's been a shock to everyone. How long had you known Owen?'

'Years. This was his local. Been coming here since he was legally able to.'

'On Sunday night, Jordan and Owen didn't sit with the others. They were in conversation here beside the bar. I don't suppose you overheard any of what they said, did you?'

Joe scowled, his eyebrows dropping low until they met up and formed one long hairy line across his forehead. 'I didn't hear much of what they talked about. I had one eye on the match and wasn't paying attention. Might have mentioned going back to Owen's. Can't say for sure.'

'You didn't hear them discuss the Sudbury Dynamos or anybody called Darren Sturgeon?'

Joe picked up a tea towel and rubbed at a glass. 'No.'

Robyn gave him a smile of encouragement. Behind her, a cheer rang out as Villa scored.

'Were you at the match the week before? The match between the Blithfield Wanderers and the Sudbury Dynamos?'

'I was. What of it?'

'What happened between Owen Falcon and Darren Sturgeon?'

'Don't know what you're talking about,' he said, pushing out his bottom lip.

'There was some argy-bargy on the pitch.'

'Oh that! Nothing major. They lost their cool, that's all. It happens sometimes – testosterone, late nights the night before, words spoken in anger, tempers frayed. I've seen that sort of thing loads of times. They both got sent off.'

'I understand Jordan became involved too. He was behaving in a deliberately aggressive manner towards Darren.'

Joe shook his head. 'I don't recall that. He got sent off for arguing with the referee.'

'Did you know Darren was beaten up a week later, on Saturday 3 June?'

Joe stared hard at her. 'Was he? Gosh, I had no idea.'

Robyn changed tack. She'd get nowhere with this line of questioning.

'What did you think of Owen?'

Joe winced slightly before speaking. 'I'll miss that lad. He had his moments but he was a talented player. He'd not had the easiest time of it. Lost his mum when he was eight, got into a bit of bother as a teenager, then his dad passed on too, but I liked him. He had balls. Always stood his ground.' Joe stared into space, lost in thought. He cleared his throat and spoke again. 'He was sound. They both were. It's not going to be the same without them. Erm, do you mind if I serve now?' He nodded in the direction of a pleasant-faced man waiting patiently for a drink.

The match was coming to an end. She slipped down from the stool, gave the man a nod and thanked Joe for his time. She hadn't learnt a great deal to help her. She had, however, established that Joe had genuinely liked Owen, but had not taken such a shine to Jordan. He might well have known about Darren Sturgeon's beating, but if Owen had been involved in any way, Joe was certainly not going to drop him in it.

Robyn waited in her car in the lay-by down the road from the Fox and Weasel. The darkness seemed heavier here with no street lights, or ambient lighting from nearby residences. She used the time to think about what they'd learnt so far. She rang David and caught him still in the office.

'Darren Sturgeon is a trained carpet fitter and works for Grand Carpets, based in the unit next to Rugeley Electrical Centre, where Owen worked. Has a history of violence – involved in several altercations and fights. He was one of a gang known to police – the Young Threats. Most of that lot ended up doing time. Darren spent four years in a young offenders' institute for robbery with assault and was only released October last year. And, for the record, his uncle owns Grand Carpets.'

Robyn hung up and digested this latest information and wondered if they were closing in on their perp. Darren had a broken leg, which would make murdering either of the men very difficult, but he could have masterminded their deaths. He might have known individuals able to carry out the murders on his behalf.

She drew a deep breath and thought for a while longer before flicking on her mobile app to watch her cat grooming himself with extra care. Getting ready for her homecoming, she thought. She hoped she wouldn't be too much longer. It was already past seven. She considering calling Amélie for a quick chat but changed her mind as lights approached and a car pulled into the lay-by behind her own. She waited while the occupant got out, came to her passenger door and let himself in with a smile and a sigh.

'You were right, guv,' said Matt, the man who'd been behind her at the bar, patiently waiting to be served. 'They did talk among themselves after you left. They definitely think Owen and Jordan were responsible for the attack on Sturgeon. I overheard one saying those lads from Sudbury wouldn't let anything happen to one of their own, and only an idiot would take any of them on. Joe Harris wandered across after you left and checked they hadn't said anything to you. That guy with the tattoo sleeves reassured him. I kept my head down and pretended to be absorbed in the aftermatch discussion on the television. They didn't suspect a thing.'

Robyn nodded thoughtfully. 'Great stuff, Matt. Let's go and check out Sturgeon.'

CHAPTER NINETEEN

A group of teenagers on the wall outside the block of flats glared at Robyn and Matt as they walked in their direction. They reminded Robyn of a group of vultures, hunched as they were in black hoodies, dark eyes fixed on her movements. Empty bottles and cigarette ends littered the scrubby bit of grassed land in front of the wall.

One muttered something unintelligible as she passed by them and another sniggered. Matt stopped in his tracks to respond to the insult but Robyn shook her head at him. She didn't want to waste time on them.

They walked the three flights to Darren's flat and waited outside in a corridor that smelt of the remnants of a half-eaten Indian takeaway, foil dishes uncovered and exposing gluey contents.

'Put me right off my supper,' Matt muttered as they waited for the door to open. 'Shame, I like a nice Madras now and again.'

Robyn winked. 'I'll treat you to fish and chips on the way back to the station.' The opening of the door interrupted their conversation. A young woman with a toddler in her arms stared at the pair. She couldn't have been any older than late teens, her eyes heavily made up and her mousy hair scraped back from her face.

'Yes?'

The toddler, a bug-eyed child with a runny nose, gave Robyn a toothy smile that she felt compelled to return. She showed her credentials and introduced Matt.

'Is Darren Sturgeon at home?'

The young woman's shoulders slumped. 'You lot never leave him alone. Just because he's done time. You should give him a chance. Daz!' she shouted, moving away from the door and pushing it so Robyn couldn't enter.

Darren appeared a few minutes later, in a loose-fitting Metallica T-shirt and faded shorts, propped up on crutches, a large plaster cast on his leg. 'What's this about?'

'Could we possibly come in for a minute?'

He shook his head. 'No. My sister's trying to get the little one to sleep. He's not feeling well.'

'Then we'll have to conduct our enquiries out here,' said Robyn pleasantly.

Darren made no move to invite them in and leant further into his crutches. 'Keep it brief. Bloody leg's killing me.'

'Actually, we wanted to talk to you about your leg. You told officers you had no idea who attacked you.'

Darren's face scrunched up in a sneer. 'You here cos of my leg?'

'We've reason to believe you knew your attackers, Mr Sturgeon.'

His face now took on a look of surprise, eyebrows high on his forehead, mouth open. 'What? I don't think so. If I'd known who it was, I'd have said, wouldn't I?'

'Mr Sturgeon, we have good reason to believe Owen Falcon and Jordan Kilby set upon you on Saturday night.'

He shook his head vehemently from side to side. 'Absolutely not.'

'You had an argument with Owen on the pitch during the match last weekend.'

'That wasn't anything important.' Darren shifted to get comfortable. 'We had a few words that's all. Made it up once we got sent off the pitch.'

'Can you tell me what it was about?'

There was a moment of silence while Darren thought about his response, then footsteps as two of the youths who'd been sitting on the wall ambled into the corridor.

'Alright, Daz?' said one, eyes trained on Robyn and Matt.

'Yeah, fine, mate,' he replied.

They sloped past the trio and into the flat next door, banging the door behind them.

'Look, my leg really hurts.'

'Maybe you should sit down and we'll continue the conversation inside,' Matt suggested, quietly.

Darren looked up at the broad-shouldered officer, towering over him, and hobbled backwards.

Robyn and Matt walked into the tiny hallway, cluttered with a baby buggy, coats and shoes, and into a kitchen where Darren dropped down onto a plastic chair. He didn't invite the others to sit. Canned laughter rang out from somewhere in the flat. The room had a sour smell, as if it needed a good clean, or the rubbish bin emptying. Robyn wanted to get out and go home. She fired a series of questions at the young man.

'What did you say to Owen Falcon on the football pitch a week last Saturday, to make him lose his temper with you?'

'Nothing much.'

'It must have been sufficiently bad to cause him to foul you, and to involve Jordan.'

The sneer had reappeared on Darren's face.

'What was it, Darren?'

He played for time, gazed around the room, before speaking.

'I made some comment about him and Jordan – about them being bum chums.'

'And he lost his temper over that?'

Darren huffed. 'Must have been true cos he took it to heart. Kept going after me on the pitch. Said something to Jordan about it, and they both set about tackling me. I got pissed off with their antics. Told Jordan he was definitely Owen's bitch. That was all. We let our tempers get the better of us and were sent off. I apologised afterwards. We shook hands and that was that.'

'Darren, where were you on Sunday night?'

'Here. I got back from hospital in the morning and spent the day here. The doctor gave me painkillers and I took a couple and flaked out. Ask my sister. I went to sleep on the settee.'

'And how about on Monday?'

'I went into work for a while in the morning, but I wasn't much use. I can't do any fitting. Helped organise a delivery and then came home. I'm taking sick leave until I'm more mobile.'

Robyn looked at a list on her mobile. 'What about your team-mates, Darren? The lads who play with you in the Sudbury Dynamos: John Preston, Chris Davies, Mark Simpson, Craig O'Connell, Steven Hopper, Mickey Dickinson, Alan Russell, Rob Brindley, Max Quinn and Shane Chapman. Did you discuss what happened to you with any of them? Did they ask you about who attacked you?'

He ran a finger around the collar of his T-shirt. 'Course they did but I didn't know who it was. Look, I said the same thing to the coppers that asked me about it. I really didn't know who laid into me. I'd been out for the night. I'd had a fair amount to drink, stopped to have a piss on my way home, and got jumped. There were two or three of them. I can't be sure. One walloped me from behind before I'd done up my flies. I fell down and then one of them whacked me with something heavy – metal pole or wooden. I really don't know what was used.'

'Did they speak? Did they tell you why they were attacking you?'

He shook his head. 'Not a word. I blacked out pretty quickly. So, that's all I can tell you.

Fifteen minutes later and Robyn had made no further headway. Darren was sticking to his story. No matter how much he insisted he'd been randomly picked upon, Robyn couldn't shake the impres-

sion he was lying. She'd asked David to check out CCTV cameras
in the area but none had picked up the altercation or any of the
men walking to or from the scene of the attack. There'd been no
reason for the attack – no robbery or a hint of why he'd been the
victim of such a crime.

They left the block of flats with the uneasy feeling it was going
to be difficult to prove Darren Sturgeon had any involvement in
Owen's and Jordan's deaths.

She'd insisted on Matt clocking off and had been heading for home
when she got a call from Ross. His voice was shaky.

'Robyn, can you come to the office?'

'Sure. I'll be ten minutes. Everything okay?'

'I'll tell you when I see you,' he replied.

It wasn't like Ross to be downbeat. Something was up.

She flew up the stairs at R&J Associates and flung open the
door to find Ross in his usual chair, hunched over, with his arms
around Duke.

'What's going on?' she asked.

'It's Jeanette. She's got a lump in her breast. She's got to have
a biopsy to see if it's cancerous. She's known about it for ages and
not been to see anyone. She didn't tell me, Robyn.'

His face crumpled but he blinked back tears. Robyn scooted
over to him, knelt down and held onto his hands. Duke licked
her nose once, but sensing Ross's sombre mood, remained seated
on his master's lap.

'It'll be okay, Ross. This happens more frequently than you
realise to lots of women. It's normal procedure to get any lump
checked out and often they're just that – little fatty lumps. There's
no reason to suspect it isn't benign.'

His head bobbed slightly as if it required all his energy to move
it. 'Jeanette said much the same thing. Robyn, I feel dreadful. There's

Jeanette being brave and upbeat, and all I can think of is the worst scenario. I don't want to. I want to be there for her, like she was for me when I had all that heart trouble. I want to be the strong partner who comforts her and tells her not to worry, but I can't. I keep thinking of that word – cancer. I can't shake it out of my head.'

'Where's Jeanette now?'

'Home. She wanted to soak in a warm bath. I told her I'd take Duke for a walk. I came here. Thought about how I couldn't bear it if the operation reveals the lump is cancerous. The doctor explained everything – each step they'd take – but all I could hear was "cancer… cancer… cancer". I'm scared, Robyn. I can't imagine not having Jeanette by my side.'

Robyn's stomach sunk. Ross and Jeanette were inseparable. They were made for each other and had been together for years and years. It was unthinkable that anything could come between them. Ross had beaten a health scare a few years earlier when his heart had started playing up. He'd left the police force and moved into the field of private investigation to have less stress. His health had improved thanks largely to Jeanette who'd put him on a strict healthy diet and ensured he got plenty of exercise and rest. That particular crisis was over but now they were faced with another.

'Ross, listen to me. Go home. Jeanette is the same Jeanette she was this morning, and she won't want to be treated any differently. She knows you're concerned. She'll be anxious too, but it won't help either of you to worry. You don't need to do anything except maybe hold her, Ross, and treat her like you treated her yesterday. Behave normally. Nothing has changed. Until somebody tells you differently, there's no point in fretting.'

He lifted damp eyes. 'I'll try.'

'Want me to come back with you?'

'Thanks, but no thanks. I'd rather she didn't know I've told you.'

'Jeanette is a fighter, Ross. With you by her side, no matter what they find from the biopsy, she'll be fine. You know how strong she is. So, stop being Mr Miserable and put on your normal, cheery face.'

'You're being sarcastic now, aren't you?'

Robyn gave him a smile and released his hands. 'How did you guess? Listen, if you need me – if either of you need me – just ring. When is she having the biopsy?'

'Tomorrow but we won't get the results the same day. They'll come a few days later. We'll get another appointment to see the doctor for those. Thanks, Robyn. I feel better for having spoken to you.'

'The voice of reason. It's so easy to feel lost and alone in these matters. Sometimes a third party helps. You helped me, remember?' She planted a kiss on his stubbly cheek. 'Come on. Jeanette will be worried you've walked Duke's legs off him.'

Duke jumped from Ross's lap and shook himself, tail wagging all the while.

Robyn escorted Ross to his car and patted him on the shoulder as he ducked into it. 'Call me if you need anything – anything at all.'

'Cheers, Robyn. I shall.'

She waved him off, her heart heavy in her chest. She couldn't bear it if anything happened to either of them. Her inner voice told her to square her shoulders and get back to the case. Jeanette would be in the best possible hands and there was, as she'd told Ross, no point in worrying about what-ifs. If she did that she'd never get any results. Ross wouldn't be able to assist her in the case any more than he already had. However, she still had his file on Nathaniel; and now it was looking unlikely Darren Sturgeon was behind the murders, his notes might prove useful.

CHAPTER TWENTY

DAY FOUR – THURSDAY, 8 JUNE, MORNING

Robyn received the text before she set off for a run. It was from Ross.

> *Taken your advice and booked a few days with Jeanette in the Cotswolds. Going day after op. Doing normal stuff – walking the dog and drinking wine in quaint pubs – even promised her dinner at posh restaurant – blame you for this extravagance. Jeanette sends love. I fessed up and told her I'd seen you. X*

A smile tugged at her mouth. He sounded more like the Ross she knew and loved. She shrugged off thoughts of Jeanette's impending operation and jogged down the street, enjoying the mild morning as she crossed the road, and onto a right of way and upped her pace.

Her phone vibrated before she'd run too far; she answered it using hands-free.

'We've finished with Owen Falcon,' said Harry McKenzie. 'Ruptured ear drum, severe damage to the middle ear canal, considerable damage to cranial nerves and internal structures, including both the carotid artery and internal jugular vein. In essence, there was a massive bleed out in his brain, and he probably died moments after the screwdriver was driven into his skull. Whoever performed the act was quick. They hit him first with a blunt instrument and rendered him unconscious before hammering the screwdriver into place. There are indentations and light bruising, suggesting his attacker placed knees, and even entire bodyweight, onto his chest to hold him in place. It's my belief he awoke at the moment the screwdriver was placed in his ear canal and attempted to struggle, but it was too little too late.'

'Somebody bigger and heavier than Owen?'

'I would imagine so, although he'd have been too dazed and possibly concussed to have struggled too greatly.'

'Thanks, Harry.'

'I'd say it was my pleasure, but, of course, it isn't. I genuinely hope you catch this character, Robyn. Whoever it is has a nasty streak in them.'

She forfeited the rest of her run and instead returned home and changed for the day before heading for the office. Harry's news had highlighted the importance of the investigation and she didn't want to waste any more time than necessary. Once there, she'd run the names of all of the members of the Sudbury Dynamos through the police general database before her officers appeared.

Anna and Mitz were first through the door and before they'd removed jackets were by her desk ready to impart information. They relayed the conversation between them and Toby and Jane Marsh that had taken place an hour earlier:

Mitz speaks. 'Mr Marsh, we'd like to ask you about Mr Jones-Kilby.'

'There's not much we can tell you. I've spoken to him on a couple of occasions, that's all.'

'I understand you've recently had some dealings with him. Can you tell me what you discussed?' Mitz asks.

Toby Marsh turns his head away. 'None of your business.'

'I'm afraid it is because we're investigating the murder of his son.'

'Look, I found the body and I rang you. I'm not likely to have killed the poor lad and then rung the police, am I? I even kept the bloody crows away from him. Pecking him, they were.' Toby's voice rises in anger.

Mitz persists in the same quiet tone. 'That's not what I'm suggesting, sir. I'm asking about Mr Jones-Kilby. How well did you know him and why did you last meet him?'

'I don't see what this has to do with the murder.'

Anna gives Jane Marsh a smile of encouragement. 'It would really help us with our investigation if you could answer the questions,' she says.

Jane glances at Toby then speaks. 'About a month ago. He came to the house to tell us about the compensation we could expect.'

'I thought in these cases you were informed by the local authorities,' says Mitz.

'He was part of the delegation in favour of the HS2. He'd been influential in its outcome and came to advise us to take the money we'd been offered. I think he was concerned we would decline the offer.'

Anna's voice is tinged with gentle concern. 'How did you feel about the HS2 cutting across your land and having to give up your home? You've been here a long time, I imagine. It must have been hard for you to give it up.'

Toby shrugs his shoulders. 'I'm not getting any younger and we have no children to leave the farm to. I'd like to retire. They're offering us a handsome amount for this place – more than we ever dreamt of. What would you do in that situation?'

Jane picks up the conversation again. 'We want to move to Cornwall. We've seen a lovely cottage in Looe. It'll be so nice to have somewhere smaller and more modern to manage, and no more getting up at the crack of dawn. Toby's worked hard all his life. He deserves time off. We both do.'

Mitz furrows his brow. 'I thought most people around here are anti the new railway line.'

Jane nods. 'They are. We were too. Now we're not so against the idea. You can understand why. It's given us the chance to get out of this way of life and start afresh. We don't want any of our friends or the locals to find out we've sold out. At the outset, we were part of the campaign against the HS2. We protested along with all the others in Colton and we even lobbied parliament. The villagers will find out we're turncoats but hopefully not until we've got our money and left.' She looks shamefaced at Anna. 'You see why we don't want to talk about it? We don't want anyone to find out we've sold the farm and land. Not yet.'

'So, Mr Jones-Kilby came to persuade you to take up the offer?'

'He did, and Toby suggested they increase it by another £50,000,' says Jane. Toby throws her a look, and she says to him, 'It doesn't matter if they know. They're not going to tell anyone.' She turns back towards Anna and continues with the explanation.

'Mr Jones-Kilby was keen for us to agree to sell. He told us he'd see what he could do about increasing the offer. The next day he rang us and told us it had been agreed. He came by a few days later with the paperwork, and another person from the committee, and we signed. We're due to leave in three months' time.'

'You had no other meeting with Mr Jones-Kilby?'

Jane shakes her head. 'None. We suggested he didn't come here again, in case someone in the village spotted him and put two and two together. He understood. We've not spoken to him since.'

'And can you confirm your whereabouts on Sunday evening?'

Toby gives Mitz an incredulous look. 'We were here. We had a bite to eat and then watched television and went to bed at about nine. I have to get up early. I'm sixty-nine years old and I need my sleep.'

'Thank you. I'm sorry but we have to ask. It's procedure.'

'Bloody procedures,' Toby mumbles. 'Still, if it helps to catch the nasty piece of work who murdered that lad, I suppose we have to put up with it. We were both here. I can't tell you any more than that. I can swear we had nothing to do with his death if that helps.'

Robyn listened to Mitz's account and then spoke. 'It's not a cast-iron alibi and we can't entirely discount the possibility they're involved, but I find it hard to believe they are our murderers.'

Mitz produced a small snort of amusement. 'I had difficulty imagining either of them knocking Jordan down, dragging him across a field and hanging him up for the crows.'

'We'll leave them off our list for now and concentrate on other possibilities. I'm still keen to pursue the Jones-Kilby angle. Somebody might have killed his son because of his business dealings. Although Jane and Toby Marsh haven't any grievances against him, there might be others who do. Of course, this makes finding any link between Jordan's and Owen's deaths more difficult. I can't see any reason why somebody attacking Jordan because of his father would also kill Owen. The only person who might have a grievance against the two of them is Darren Sturgeon, a member of the Sudbury Dynamos football team, who was beaten up on Saturday. We have reason to believe Jordan and Owen were behind that attack. Now, he's saying he doesn't know who went for him that night but there's a chance he does – that it was Jordan and Owen – and he wanted to exact some form of revenge on them.'

Robyn faced the board and pursed her lips. As unlikely as it seemed that Jordan's father would be responsible for his death, she was having serious doubts about Nathaniel. Ross's report that detailed his investigation into Jordan's claims his father had murdered his mother only served to strengthen them. She told the team what she'd uncovered. David, who'd been working quietly behind his desk, let out a loud, 'Fuck me!'

'David?'

'Just came across something important. I was checking through Owen Falcon's list of friends, relatives and contacts on his mobile and found out his ex-girlfriend, Joy Fairweather, is personal assistant to Nathaniel Jones-Kilby.'

Robyn didn't move. Her heartbeat thudded steadily in her ears. They'd found another connection between the two dead men – one that was surely significant.

'Get hold of her. Meanwhile, Matt, can you look at these chaps? They make up the Sudbury Dynamo team. I'm having difficulty believing Darren Sturgeon was randomly attacked. It could have been to do with the stand-off on the pitch, and if some of these lads are as hard as their backgrounds suggest they are, they might, just might, have killed Owen and Jordan because they were the ones responsible for breaking Darren's leg.'

Matt took the paperwork from her and strode to his desk. There were photographs, names and contact details for each member of the Sudbury Dynamos. He read through each of them, noting that two of them – Mark Simpson and Alan Russell – had been arrested and fined for fighting on several occasions, while Shane Chapman had been cautioned for the same offence.

'John Preston was in the army for two years. Got discharged on medical grounds – an eye injury,' he said.

'I couldn't find out any more on him. I only managed basic information from the general police database. I'm sure there's a lot more we could learn. I'd rather find out if Owen and Jordan were responsible for breaking Darren's leg before we invest too much time checking these characters out.'

Robyn was about to speak again when DCI Flint stuck his head around the open door.

'My office, DI Carter.'

※

DCI Flint stood beside his window, hands behind his back. He made a series of small coughs before facing Robyn. His eyes were, for once, apologetic.

'I've had a complaint about you, Robyn. I have to ask you to lay off Nathaniel Jones-Kilby.'

Robyn drew herself up to her full height and pulled in her chin. 'Sir, with due respect, and whether he likes it or not, he has to be interviewed as part of this investigation. He was in Colton the night his son was murdered and his PA is Owen Falcon's ex-girlfriend. I'm not insinuating he's murdered these two men but he is in some way linked to them and therefore we have to make relevant enquiries.'

Flint gave a series of brief nods. 'I understand and I don't want your investigations to be compromised in any way, but Nathaniel Jones-Kilby has asked to be kept out of it. He doesn't want to speak to you or your officers.'

'And why doesn't he wish to aid us in this? His son has been murdered. Surely he'd want to cooperate fully?'

'It's not that he doesn't want to cooperate but he feels you are deliberately wasting time and charging about in the wrong direction. He informed me that you tracked him down at his house without an appointment and asked some leading questions.'

Heat rose up Robyn's neck. 'It wasn't quite like that, sir.'

'Did you go to his house without first ringing him?'

'I did, but you of all people know we have to chase leads as soon as we get them. His secretary was being evasive and I couldn't get him at work. I acted on my initiative.'

'And somewhat hastily. Look, don't get me wrong, Robyn, I have a huge amount of respect for you and the way you handle cases. Look at the results we've had thanks to you following your intuition. This time, you'll have to conduct the investigation more carefully. Mr Jones-Kilby has friends in high places. He lost his wife some years ago and now he's lost his son. He is the victim's father and, as such, deserves to be treated with courtesy and sensitivity.'

Robyn could barely suppress the snort of derision. 'Yes, sir. I don't deny that, but Nathaniel Jones-Kilby is not showing a great deal of grief or sensitivity himself. He's thrown his son's girlfriend and her child out of their home and not been terribly forthcoming about his business dealings that might, or might not, be behind this tragic event. We're trying to establish if somebody with a grudge against him killed his son. We can't do that if he refuses to cooperate with us.'

Flint unclasped his hands and rested them against his desk. It was impossibly tidy with files shuffled into a neat pile at one side of it and three pens lined up side by side at the other. He heaved a sigh. 'Sometimes we mustn't let our emotions cloud our judgement. I know Mr Jones-Kilby personally and he is a difficult man to like; however, he is a hugely respected businessman in our community and as such, we have to dance to his tune. He told me he gave you an alibi for his whereabouts on Sunday night. I think we have to leave it at that.'

'He said he was having supper with somebody but refused to tell me who that person was, or where they lived. From where I'm standing he has no alibi and that makes him a suspect until we can clear him.'

If Flint knew Nathaniel it could only have been through the Freemasons Society, of which he was a member. It was clear he didn't like the man any more than she did; yet she knew he was right. She'd have to back away from Nathaniel and conduct her investigation around him. She thought again of Amy, who'd been dragged away from her own investigations into his business dealings. The man definitely had something to hide.

'His alibi was weak, sir.'

Flint nodded and a brief smile flickered across his red face. 'I spoke to him about that. I'll vouch for his alibi. Let's leave it at that for the moment, shall we, Robyn?'

Flint knew more. Nathaniel had told him something that exonerated him from the enquiries – something he wasn't willing to share with Robyn. Or was Flint involved in Nathaniel's dealings and party to some corruption? She felt her fists tighten in frustration.

'I have to talk to his personal assistant, sir. She was Owen Falcon's girlfriend for a while.'

'Then tread carefully, Robyn. I don't want any more complaints about you.'

'Yes, sir. Thank you.'

His silence was a dismissal and she left quietly, fuming at Nathaniel Jones-Kilby, who could pull strings and manipulate those he knew. As far as she was concerned, Nathaniel was a cold, heartless individual and she'd get the answers she needed without his assistance. If she trod on his toes again, then bad luck.

CHAPTER TWENTY-ONE

DAY FOUR – THURSDAY, 8 JUNE, AFTERNOON

Joy Fairweather sipped her cup of green tea, her doe eyes looking forlornly out of the office window. She'd agreed to meet Robyn and Anna during her lunch break. The plastic tub of salad she'd brought to work stood forgotten on the table in front of her.

Robyn had established that Nathaniel wasn't at work before asking for some of Joy's time. She was pleased to see he had not arrived unexpectedly since her call. The door to his office was open and Robyn was surprised by its stylish modernity and soft seating in black, white and red, shaped like giant pebbles, that had been artistically arranged around a low white table. By comparison, Joy's office was very ordinary, with a wooden filing cabinet behind an oval desk on which stood a flat computer screen.

'I'm sorry for your loss,' said Robyn.

Joy put down her cup. 'We haven't stayed in touch since we split, but I loved him once upon a time. It's difficult to believe this has happened to him.'

'When was the last time you saw or spoke to him?'

'Spoke properly – months ago. Owen and I agreed it was best if we went our separate ways. Some couples can remain good friends but we both thought it would be better if we drew a line under our relationship. It hadn't worked out and we were different people by the time we split up. I saw him now and again. It's difficult to avoid seeing somebody when you live in the same area. The last time would be when he came here. He came to see Mr Jones-Kilby. Last week. Tuesday.'

'Any idea why?'

'There'd been a problem with a smoke detector at his house. It kept going off. I phoned Rugeley Electrical Centre on his behalf, and they sent Owen out here with a new one. He made arrangements with Mr Jones-Kilby to fit it.'

'Did you speak to him?'

'He told me he was going to Mr Jones-Kilby's house on Wednesday morning to fit the detector. I was quite busy at the time and didn't chat.'

'Did he often do work for Mr Jones-Kilby?'

'NJK Properties gets most of its electrical supplies from Rugeley Electrical Centre. They give us a generous discount. Owen often delivered parts to various developments or here to the office, for the electrical fitters to pick up. This was a one-off.'

The phone trilled and Joy answered it. While she was speaking, Robyn took a stroll around Nathaniel's office. His desk faced the window and over fields. She could imagine him on his mobile, discussing the erection of new housing on outskirts of villages, all the while looking out at pleasant green fields – the irony wasn't lost on her.

A set of red box files was propped up on black shelves to one side. She cocked her head to better read the names on the spines. One in particular stood out – Colton 2017–18. She moved back to Joy's office just as she finished her call.

'Can I ask you about Owen?' she said softly. 'Was he ever violent?'

Joy chewed at her bottom lip. 'He could be heavy-handed now and again. He never hurt me – beat me up or anything like that – but he was domineering. He had a bit of a temper.'

'He never struck you?'

'No. Not me. He was possessive though. He didn't like any other men talking to me. There was an occasion in a pub. The police were called.'

'We know about that. The charges against him were dropped.'

Joy nodded. 'Owen wasn't entirely to blame. The other bloke was drunk. He started it. First he came onto me, and when I rebuffed him, he called me a slag. Owen told him to apologise but he wouldn't. It got out of hand. The bloke went for Owen first. Owen was only standing up for me. He was like that. It was all or nothing with Owen. He didn't let me out of his sight sometimes. I think it's because he lost his mum so young. It was smothering at times. He'd want to know where I was going and who with. I got fed up of his clinginess followed by bad moods during which he wouldn't talk to me. We drifted apart.'

'Did you ever meet Jordan, Mr Jones-Kilby's son?'

'Only the once and that wasn't very long ago. He came storming in here, walked straight through to his father's office without saying a word to me, and shut the door behind him. There were raised voices and then he marched out again. The whole thing only took about five minutes, if that. Mr Jones-Kilby came out immediately afterwards, cancelled all appointments for the day and went out.'

'You have no idea what they were shouting about?'

Joy's eyelids fluttered. 'I like my job here,' she said. 'I've been working for Mr Jones-Kilby for six years and he's a good boss.'

'We're investigating a murder and we'd appreciate your cooperation,' said Robyn. 'Please tell us exactly what you heard.'

Joy thought for a moment before speaking again. Her voice was low. 'Jordan was shouting loudly, so it was difficult not to overhear it. He called his dad a liar – a dirty, rotten, cheating, murdering liar.' She flushed at the memory.

'Can you remember which day this was?'

'Last Friday, 2 June.'

'Did you know Owen and Jordan were friends?'

Joy shook her head. 'I've moved on since Owen. I'm not one of those ex-girlfriends who constantly checks up to see what their other half is up to – stalk them on Facebook or whatever. When Owen and I split up it was for good. I don't have any interest in his life, friends, new girlfriends or anything. I'm pretty certain he felt the same way.'

'Did Owen have many friends when you were together?'

'Work mates, football mates, biking mates, gaming mates – yes, he had lots of friends. He was often out and about with one or the other. Owen's a man's man. He enjoyed hanging out with men. He preferred going out with them to going out with me. That's one of the reasons I gave up on him – he wasn't that committed to our relationship. All water under the bridge now though. I've met somebody else and it's serious. I did love Owen though. And he loved me. Sadly, he didn't love me enough.'

She pushed her teacup away from her.

'Was that the only reason you split up?'

Joy nodded. 'I got so sick of his attitude I left him. I hoped leaving him would shock him and he'd change, but he didn't. He didn't chase after me, ask me to come back or even try to make it up.'

Robyn took in the sunken cheeks and sad eyes, and decided that although Joy had broken off the relationship with Owen, part of her would always love him.

CHAPTER TWENTY-TWO

THEN

The young boy fights to prevent his knees from knocking. He ought never to have lied. He knows the consequences of such an act of treachery.

His mother's face wears a grim expression of disapproval that makes the boy want to hurl himself to the floor and join his sister, kneeling silently on the hearth rug, hands together in prayer. Her eyes are closed and he sees her lips move as she mouths, 'Lord, forgive him. He knows not what he has done.'

On this occasion prayer is not going to be enough for him. He's committed one of the seven deadly sins that warrant the severe punishment his parents deem fit for his crime.

'You should have resisted temptation,' says his mother, her shrill tone vibrating through the boy's body. His mother is only five foot six but she has presence and seems far taller with her head held high. She has surprisingly strong hands and large, expressive eyes, and at present those eyes burn coal-black with anger.

'Mum, I couldn't say no.'

His mother raises two fingers and presses them to her lips and then holds them aloft. To some it would resemble a kiss, or a farewell gesture. The boy knows it to mean silence. He has said enough. He recalls the incident that has put him in this position and shudders at what is to come:

-☀-

'Come on,' said Larson, the freckles on his face standing out in the sunshine. 'Try it. They obviously don't want it or they'd have taken it inside.'

'No. It's stealing. It's dishonest. Don't do it.'

'You are such a goody-goody,' said Larson with a sneer. 'Or are you a scaredy-cat? That's it. You're scared.' He made stupid noises and laughed cruelly before reaching for the milk bottle on the doorstep, where he peeled off the foil top and chugged a mouthful.

He pulled a face. 'Yuck! That's disgusting! It's rancid. Been outside too long.'

He chucked the contents over the doorstep and left the bottle. 'Done the person a favour,' he said, nonchalantly. 'Come on, let's go to the park.' He scooted off, leaving the boy trailing in his wake, head down. The person who lived at number 32 was an elderly man and he would be unhappy his milk was gone.

-☀-

Larson doesn't seem to have a conscience. He does whatever the mood takes him and laughs and jokes and runs about without any cares. That's what the boy likes about Larson – he is free.

He usually waits for his sister to collect him from school and they come home together. However, she'd been held up at a school play rehearsal and so he'd chosen to accompany Larson.

They'd been spotted outside number 32 and been shopped. He wouldn't be beaten or receive a clip around the ear like Larson did. His punishment would be far worse.

He pleads with his mother. He promises he didn't touch the milk.

'Don't you lie to me,' says his mother, growing even taller in front of the boy's eyes. 'Mrs Hunter saw you. She wouldn't lie, would she? She's an honest woman – a fine, upstanding woman. Are you calling her a liar?'

'*No, ma'am.*'

'*Indeed. I should think not. Not only stealing but lying.*' *She shakes her head sadly. 'A week.'*

'*Please, no. That's too long.*'

His sister gasps at the harshness of the punishment.

'*Quiet!*' *Her mother's voice rises. 'You stay there and pray for his sins.*'

Tears spill over his eyelashes and down his cheeks. He's never done a full week before.

His mother places a cool hand on his naked shoulder, covered only with a grey blanket, and steers him in the direction of the back door.

It's turning dark outside and the temperature has dropped. The bright sunny day is turning into a long, cold night. He shivers, involuntarily, not on account of the breeze whipping around his bare legs, but through fear. In the distance stand the trees: huge, silent, black shapes where the crows live. A murder of crows. His teacher told the class that a group of crows is called a murder not a flock, or a group, and it has terrified the boy further. They'll arrive first thing in the morning. They'll smell his fear and land on the shed roof, cawing loudly and pecking their way with steely beaks through the soft felt to reach him.

'*Please, no. I—*' *He tries to wriggle free but she tightens her grip on him.*

It's futile to protest. His mother shushes him and unlocks the small shed, empty apart from a bucket for ablutions and a thin mattress. There's no window. There's no light. It will be his prison for an entire week. He'll receive food – small portions and some water – but no company. It will be him and the crows until his mother releases him.

'*Inside. Consider the evil you have done,*' *says his mother, flatly. She hands the boy the book – his sole companion for the next week – a copy of the bible.*

CHAPTER TWENTY-THREE

DAY FOUR – THURSDAY, 8 JUNE, LATE AFTERNOON

'It's no good,' said Robyn. 'We've asked every member of the Sudbury Dynamos the same questions and they've given identical answers. None of them know anything about what happened to Darren Sturgeon.'

'I find that difficult to believe,' said Mitz, twisting a ballpoint pen around in his hands. He was looking sunken-eyed and Robyn understood how frustrated he and the others felt.

'I agree but they all have airtight alibis for the nights of both murders and none were anywhere near Colton on Sunday or Monday. We've checked with their wives, girlfriends and parents. These guys have to be telling the truth. We're not getting anywhere with this line of enquiry and we should be looking at other possibilities.'

'Like what?' Matt said crossly. 'This was our strongest lead.'

'We've got others. Owen was at Nathaniel's house last Wednesday to fit a smoke detector. Now, I might be wrong on this but it strikes me as strange he'd fit it. Rugeley Electrical only supply goods, they don't fit them. Maybe there was another reason he went there, or maybe he found out something about Nathaniel while he was there that got him killed.'

Mitz shook his head. 'That means we'd have to go after Nathaniel and we can't do that. DCI Flint made himself clear on that, didn't he?'

Robyn nodded. She would certainly anger her superior if she conducted a full investigation into Nathaniel, yet now she knew about Nathaniel's wife and the fact Jordan had believed Nathaniel had killed her, she had further grounds to interview him. She was going to insist on talking to Nathaniel, and if Flint tried to prevent her again, then her suspicions he too was somehow connected to Nathaniel would be born out, and she'd have to investigate Flint as well. Just because he was her superior didn't make him exempt from corruption. 'I'm considering interviewing him and hang the consequences.'

Matt shrugged. 'Might not be a good idea, guv. You know what these poncey sorts are like. He could make trouble for you – for us all.'

'I'll only go for it if I think there's good reason. Let's hit the pub. It's been a crap day. The interviews took forever and you all deserve a drink.'

David pushed back his chair. 'Might give it a miss. Got to go home.'

'Everything okay?' Robyn asked. It wasn't like David to back out of a quick drink.

He pulled a face. 'Got a few personal issues to sort out. Heather's not feeling very loved at the moment. Says I spend too much time at work or out with friends. I said I'd go straight home tonight.'

'Sorry to hear that. Hope you get it resolved.'

'I'm in,' said Matt. 'No way am I going home to the dragon.' Matt always referred to his mother-in-law as a dragon but Robyn suspected he was quite fond of her and was playing for laughs. 'She's getting worse. Can't wait for her to drift back to Swansea.'

Robyn was last to turn out the lights and drifted out behind her officers. She'd only walked a few paces up the corridor when Tom Shearer called after her.

'Knocking off early, Robyn? It's only just after six.'

'Anyone tell you you're wasted here and should do stand-up, Tom?'

He swaggered towards her, his hands thrust deep in his pockets. He smelt of pine-fresh deodorant and his eyes twinkled as he spoke. 'I'm definitely wasted here,' he said with a grin that transformed his looks.

Robyn spoke before she could change her mind. 'We're going to the pub for early doors. You're welcome to join us.'

Shearer studied her face. 'Well, since you asked me so very nicely, I'd love to. See you there.'

She gave him a curt nod and strode after the others, who'd already disappeared, and wondered why she'd even thought about asking him along. She didn't dare acknowledge the truth – after two long years of mourning Davies, she was finally ready to think about male company and dating again.

CHAPTER TWENTY-FOUR

Dr Lucy Harding stretched and yawned. Her back was beginning to play up – one of the downsides to the job. She'd spent almost all day sat down, either stuck behind her desk or in her car, travelling between houses scattered all over Staffordshire, visiting those who were housebound and unable to make a surgery appointment. Like many medical centres, they were short-staffed and overburdened. She'd had to run the clinic single-handedly that afternoon because her colleague, Andy Trevago, had been called out to an emergency at the old folks' home in Hoar Cross.

Lucy stared at the computer screen and read back through the notes she'd typed about one of the patients she'd seen that day, and shook her head. Some days she felt powerless to help those who asked for her opinion – filled with fear and anxieties that she couldn't allay. She wasn't qualified to give them the information or treatment some required. She was a GP not a specialist in every possible field, and while she was well informed, some people appeared to expect miracles. Lucy, like her colleagues, was bound by red tape and the confines of an underfunded health system. She had to adhere to protocol – tests, examinations and procedures all had to be booked at local hospitals, as did specialists, and for many patients there would be huge waiting lists before they'd be seen. All Lucy could do was reassure each of them, treat the aches and pains for now, and hope they'd be seen soon.

She rubbed the base of her neck. She'd slept badly the night before and now had the beginnings of a headache. She picked up her mobile and using the FaceTime app called her young son.

'Mummy,' he yelled in delight. 'I'm watching Ninja Turtles. Nanny said I could before bed if I was good. Look, I'm ready.' He pulled at his pyjama top to show her he was dressed for bedtime.

'That's great. Not too much "cowabunga" jumping about the place though.'

He beamed a happy smile.

'Did you have a good day at school?'

The boy nodded.

'What did Nanny cook you for tea?'

'Potato spirals,' he said with satisfaction. 'And sausages.'

Lucy gave him a warm smile. 'Your favourite.'

He nodded again. They chatted for a while about school and what he'd done there before Lucy decided she ought to get going. It was after seven and she hadn't eaten since breakfast.

'Okay, give Nanny and Pappy a big kiss from me. I'll pick you up tomorrow from school. Night night. Sleep tight. Love you, Jamie.'

'Love you, Mummy,' he replied and blew her a kiss.

Lucy felt very fortunate to have her mum and dad to help out. They only lived ten miles from her, and they were always willing to collect Jamie whenever she took late surgery. They'd always been such a support – all the way through school and university and beyond. And now they'd stepped up to the mark again to help her with Jamie. Since the divorce she'd been dependent on them all over again. She owed them. It was her mum's birthday soon. She'd treat them to a weekend break away somewhere posh. They deserved that at the very least.

The surgery was empty apart from Lucy. The two duty nurses had left half an hour earlier. Lucy read back through a letter she'd written on behalf of a particularly poignant case. She didn't hold out much hope. The patient's condition was too far advanced and there simply wasn't sufficient funding in the NHS for the medication required to help them. *She emailed it and all the other letters across to her secretary to deal with in the morning before turning off her computer and pushing away from her desk.*

There was a chilled bottle of Pinot Grigio in her fridge back home and she needed a glass or two after the day she'd had. She collected her large leather handbag, snapped off the office lights and slipped out of the door into the car park behind.

The surgery at the end of a quiet lane backed onto a large cemetery. 'Best neighbours ever,' the practice manager had told her when she'd applied for the position. 'Never make any noise.' It was true. Hardly anyone used the lane that led to open fields at the edge of the village. There was rarely a sound, only from the birds and distant grazing cows, and Lucy often sat on the grassed bank behind her office to grab a few minutes' peace on sunny days. It was a far cry from the surgery she'd worked in before, situated in the heart of Derby. Here she could breathe.

She pointed the key fob at her Mini convertible – a present to herself after the divorce to help cheer herself up. It unlocked with a soft blip. She opened the driver's door and tossed her bag inside, then spun at the sound of a soft cough and her name being spoken.

'What is it?' Lucy squinted into the darkness and made out the figure standing by the large tree that hung over the grassy bank. 'Oh, hi again. Look, I'm really sorry about earlier.'

The figure approached with meaningful steps. 'Sometimes sorry just isn't good enough. You've let me down. And now you have to pay.'

Lucy glanced about. There was no one to shout out to. She was completely alone. The outside lights were on a timer, activated by her leaving the building, and would cut out soon. Then they'd both be plunged into darkness. 'Back off or I'll call the police. I won't be threatened by you or anyone.'

'I'm not threatening you, doctor.'

Lucy frowned. 'What do you want then?'

'Justice.'

Lucy had little time to register the object as it swung through the air and smacked her on the forehead. She crumpled to the ground, stunned, hand against her bleeding head. The figure stooped beside her and lifted the car key from where it had fallen on the ground. Lucy groaned. She was terrified. Paralysed by fear. And as she looked into the killer's eyes she knew she'd never make it out alive. Her assailant moved off and Lucy fumbled for her mobile phone. She had to alert somebody and get help. She paused as her car engine started, and she struggled to her knees as it reversed from its space. Agonising shafts of pain made her wince as she attempted to stand and she shut her eyes tightly as the car reversed, its headlight beams fully on her. They were stealing her car. Why? The Mini halted, then the engine revved angrily, and Lucy's car flew at her at speed, striking her full on. She was flattened beneath it, arms and legs pinned under the tyres. Thoughts scrambled in all directions but Lucy Harding was unable to move and, as she drew her final breaths, it repeated the manoeuvre. The driver left the vehicle and walked towards Lucy to study her ruined body before ambling up the silent lane.

CHAPTER TWENTY-FIVE

DAY FIVE – FRIDAY, 9 JUNE, MORNING

The following morning Robyn's first thoughts were about her cousin and his wife. It was likely he was at the hospital with Jeanette by now. She rang him and got his answerphone so she left a message sending them both her love and thoughts and wishing Jeanette well for the operation. As she ended the call, she mentally crossed her fingers. She couldn't bear to consider a negative outcome for them both. They meant far too much to her.

Frustration was building again. They weren't making sufficient headway. Robyn did what she usually did at times like this and headed out for a run before going to the office. Her chosen route was mostly along footpaths that followed Dyson Road, past office blocks, modern red brick buildings and huge glass buildings. It was approximately five miles long, relatively flat going, and didn't require much concentration. She fell into an easy stride and, ignoring the building traffic, followed the circular route.

Her thoughts jumped from Jordan to Owen. Could they have attacked Darren? And if they were behind the attack, was that the reason they were both dead? It didn't feel right. The deaths of the two young men had been planned. There had to be a greater motive behind it than revenge for beating a rival footballer. Surely, if any of the Sudbury Dynamos had gone after the Jordan and Owen, they'd have beaten the men, or knifed them in an aggressive attack. She wondered if drugs had played a part. Could somebody on drugs have murdered them?

Even though it was early in the day, the sun warmed her back. Forecasters were predicting even warmer temperatures and some of the highest felt in years in two weeks' time, which was when she'd be competing in the Ironman event. She'd not given the contest a great deal of thought or done any special training for it. The fact was, she was fit and would complete the gruelling course regardless of any extra effort she put it at this stage. She wasn't worried about how long it would take her to finish. What mattered was that she did it. It had become a focus and an annual challenge ever since the loss of Davies. Her training had helped her survive.

Before she realised it, she was almost back at her house and she was no closer to an answer as to who might have killed Jordan and Owen.

Her office was deadly quiet, even though the team was present.

'What's going on? It's like a morgue in here,' she said.

'Hangover,' said Matt.

'You left the pub at the same time as us. You didn't have that much to drink.'

'I hit the top shelf when I got home. Mother-in-law has left us in peace so we celebrated big style. When I say we, I mean me.'

Mitz looked across. 'Been going back through all these statements from the Sudbury Dynamos. Why would Jasper tell us about the attack on Darren Sturgeon if he didn't believe it was relevant? Do you think Darren was lying?'

'Could be. Try Darren's sister Fay, the girl with the toddler and baby, who lives in the same flat as him. She might know or be willing to tell us the truth about who attacked him. That is, if he wasn't randomly attacked. Something links Jordan and Owen, and that something got them both killed. I can't think what it could be, and chasing around after Nathaniel could be a waste of time, although, I still can't help but think he's something to do with their deaths.'

David, who looked like he hadn't slept all night, was tapping at his keyboard. Robyn sidled up to him and asked quietly, 'Everything okay?'

He shook his head and kept typing. She waited in case he wanted to elaborate but he ignored her, his attention on his task. Robyn eased away again. While she enjoyed good working relationships, there were some boundaries her team might not want her to cross. David would work it out with his wife and if he wanted to sound off, he'd no doubt talk to Matt or Mitz.

She still had to decide how best to approach Flint and demand she be allowed to speak to Nathaniel. She sat down with Ross's file once more and read up on his investigation into Sue Jones-Kilby's death. After fifteen minutes, she closed it again and pushed it to one side. He'd been right: it would have proved very difficult to establish exactly how she'd died. The car and her remains were unrecognisable, and only dental records had identified the unfortunate Sue. There was nothing in the file but circumstantial evidence. A witness overhearing a telephone conversation wouldn't be enough to convince Flint she had to speak to Nathaniel, yet it felt important. She had to question the man. He might just have been behind his wife's death. Jordan had thought so. Robyn had no idea if Nathaniel would be capable of such an act but he was certainly a man with powerful allies and friends who could protect him from investigations. She considered all her options but returned to the same conclusion. There was no way around it. She was going to have to go against her superior's wishes and speak to Nathaniel about this.

CHAPTER TWENTY-SIX

Connor Richards was on the phone. His voice was urgent and strained. 'Robyn, I'm on the outskirts of Abbots Bromley. DI Shearer's here, but you need to join us.'

'Whereabouts are you?'

'At the health clinic at the end of Bromley Rise – it's the new, purpose-built clinic just outside the village.'

She dropped the file she'd been reading back on her desk.

'Matt, you free? Murder at the health clinic at Abbots Bromley.'

It wasn't hard to find the clinic. The place was swarming with vehicles and police. Robyn and Matt headed swiftly towards the white tent erected on the car park where they found Shearer outside, dressed in his white suit. He lowered his mask and spoke.

'Victim's a doctor – Lucy Harding, aged thirty-six, divorced. She'd been working here for four months. Was run over last night. Not just once – her attacker ran over her several times with her own vehicle.'

He paused for a moment, his eyes twitching as he considered his own thoughts. 'Harry confirmed she died of internal injuries. She's still here. We waited for you.'

Robyn and Matt suited up before entering the tent. Shearer held the tent door open for them both. Robyn could hardly bring herself to look at the mutilated body in front of her. With arms and legs at impossible angles, it was clear that Lucy Harding's body had been crushed and destroyed.

'We wondered if Dr Harding's killer is the same one you've been hunting for.'

Robyn rested her gaze on the woman's mutilated form. 'It's possible. Unless we have two murderers on our patch.'

'Want me to report to DCI Flint and we'll let him decide how best to proceed?' Shearer asked.

Robyn nodded. 'What else do you have on her?'

'Lived in Colton with her five-year-old son, James. We've spoken to everyone she worked with here. Her body was found by a fellow doctor – Andy Trevago. Her parents are looking after the boy. He stayed with them regularly, whenever Lucy took the late surgery. They live Uttoxeter way. She moved from Derby to take up this position. Ex-husband's a barrister. He's in the Seychelles at the moment with his girlfriend.'

Robyn glanced at the body. Whatever made this killer tick? She was heartily sickened by the scene in front of her – more so knowing Lucy had a young child. She strode away quickly before her emotions could get the better of her. Outside, Connor's team were working on the Mini convertible car that had belonged to the victim. Connor followed her outside.

'Beastly, isn't it?' he said.

'That's one word to describe it. Christ, Connor, what gets into these sickos? What makes somebody maim and torture another human being like that? Some days, I feel so bloody sickened by it all.'

'Hey, you wouldn't be human if you didn't,' he said, softly. 'Take a deep breath. You'll pull it together.'

She wasn't so sure. Her stomach flipped at the thought of the spectacle hidden inside the tent – Lucy's shattered body – and she shuddered at the killer's total disregard for human life. Shearer emerged from the tent. His usual cocky air had been replaced by a more befitting sober attitude and his stance was of somebody weary of it all.

'We're moving her body now. Andy Trevago is inside – want to speak to him with me?'

'If that's okay with you,' said Robyn.

Shearer shrugged. 'Of course. I'll come with you.'

They both entered the surgery via the main entrance, passed the semi-circular reception desk and the hatch on the left marked 'pharmacy'. They continued past male and female toilets on the right, and through a pair of automatic doors that opened into a wide waiting room. Robyn was met by the scent of pine rather than the usual cloying smell she associated with such places. Small plug-ins puffed invisible clouds of the air freshener into the room, each puff accompanied by a soft hiss. A large television screen hung at the front of the room beside a door marked 'Doctors', and fifteen dark blue seats with plump, padded cushions had been arranged to face it. Robyn turned to Shearer.

'Nobody come in this way?'

'He shook his head. 'This side was alarmed and locked by the receptionist last night. Nobody broke in. Those doors automatically lock and alarm when it's set.' He nodded at the doors leading to another corridor set at right angles to the waiting room.

'What's down there?'

'To the left there are treatment rooms used by the nurses, and to the right are the doctors. Dr Trevago is in his office.'

Robyn noticed the white coveralls of forensic staff ahead. 'Is it clean or do we need to suit up?'

'It's clean. They checked as soon as we arrived. No break in this side either. It was locked and alarmed by Dr Harding when she left.'

-᠅-

Andy Trevago wore the look of a man who needed a long holiday. His eyes were hollow and his razor-sharp cheekbones stood out against his grey skin. Shearer made the introductions, then pulled out a chair and sat down opposite the man.

'Horrendous,' Andy Trevago said, shaking his head. 'Can't believe it's happened. Who in their right mind would do something like that?'

'That's what we'd like to find out. Thank you for waiting.'

'Least I could do.'

'How well did you know Lucy?'

'Only really in the professional sense. We passed the time of day together when we got the chance. We don't get a lot of time off – the schedules are tight and we have to meet our appointment times and quotas. We sometimes chatted after surgery if we didn't have to rush off. Patients really liked her. She didn't just give them the five minutes they're allocated. It didn't matter if she was running late; if a patient needed more time with her, she'd give it to them. Very dedicated.'

'Did she mention the names Owen Falcon or Jordan Kilby to you?' Robyn asked.

His brows knitted together in concentration. 'No. I can't say she did. I recognise Jordan's name though. Can't think how or where I know him from.'

Robyn waited while he thought a moment longer, then asked, 'He's not one of your patients?'

'Not that I'm aware of. Sorry. I can't put a face to the name. We have several hundred patients each and we haven't had time to get to know them all yet.'

Shearer waded in with questions of his own. 'Did Lucy appear to be unduly concerned about any of her patients, or anybody in particular? Maybe one of them had been disgruntled or even threatened her.'

'I doubt it. Our patients are fairly new to this practice and to us doctors. It was built to ease the strain on Yoxall Health Centre, so we've only been in existence a few months. Many of the patients were reluctant to be transferred to us and missed the old practice, and I've heard plenty of grumbles from my patients about being forced to change GPs, but I doubt any of them have had time to get that annoyed with us. There's only myself, Dr Winchester – who's getting close to retirement – and Lucy who work at the surgery. We're a small team and we cater for a very large catchment area.'

Robyn threw Andy a kindly smile. 'Tell me about yesterday. Lucy was the last person to leave here. Was that normal?'

'It's happened a couple of times before. It's because we're short-staffed. All three of us take morning surgery, which runs from eight thirty to twelve thirty, but the afternoon surgery, which starts at four and ends at six, is usually manned by only two of us. We rotate those shifts. Yesterday, I was working the afternoon clinic with Lucy, but I got called out to Hoar Cross nursing home – an emergency – half an hour into surgery, and I asked Lucy to take the remainder of my clinic, as well as her own. I felt really bad asking her because she'd already stepped in to take the morning emergency clinic for Dr Winchester. Anyway, she rose to the challenge. Said it wasn't a problem as her little boy was spending the night at her parents and she had no other plans. The receptionist juggled appointments about and contacted those she could by telephone, asking them to reschedule, but if they couldn't, or didn't want to, they were offered an appointment with Lucy.'

'In which case, I expect she finished her clinic later than usual.'

'Yes, we usually see our last patients around six and then there's always at least half an hour needed to write up notes and so on, so we get off at six thirty or thereabouts. I rang Lucy at ten past six to see how she was getting on. She had two more patients left to see at that time. I was at the nursing home until gone eight so I went straight home from there. If you need to check up on that, please do. I understand you'll want to cover all angles.' The corners of his mouth tugged outwards for a brief moment before he resumed his sombre monologue.

'Were there any other members of staff working along this corridor?'

'No. The nurses only work the morning surgery so all the treatment rooms were locked, as was my office and Dr Winchester's. Lucy was alone apart from the receptionist and pharmacist.'

'You were the first person on the scene this morning and found her.'

Andy gave a slight tilt of the head. 'I'll never get that sight out of my mind as long as I live. I've seen death in many shapes and guises, but I've never experienced anything as awful as the sight of Lucy in the car park.'

Robyn waited while he stared into space, his thoughts on his colleague. She gave him another smile. 'We'll need a list of patients that attended the clinic yesterday afternoon.'

He seemed to emerge from his reverie. 'I thought you might. I had to do something to keep my mind busy so I printed out the lists for you.' He slid sheets of A4 across his desk. 'These are my patients who saw Lucy yesterday, and these are her own patients.' He pointed at the two printed lists. Robyn read through the names. There were none she recognised.

'I don't know if they're of any use, but I also printed out the morning clinic attendees for all three of us.' He passed across more sheets, each headed with a GP's name. Robyn took them.

'Can you tell me anything about the last patient of the day? Mr Franks,' she said, glancing at the list in front of her.

'This gentleman's one of my more regular patients. He's in his late seventies and will have attended the clinic with his wife, who drives him about. He's somewhat immobile. One of his prescriptions was due for renewal. I asked Lucy to give him a quick check-up and write a new one for him.'

'What time did the reception staff leave?' Shearer asked.

'Jackie was working in the pharmacy and left at six. Our afternoon receptionist, Susanna, stayed until Mr Franks left the surgery at six thirty. She checked in with Lucy before she locked and alarmed the reception area, pharmacy and waiting room. It's for security. We can't have anybody wandering in if we're down here working. We'd never know they were there. We often isolate this section of the building and leave by the back door. That can't be accessed from the outside. I think one of your officers took the ladies' statements and one from Dr Winchester earlier, but if you need to talk to them—'

Shearer stopped him with a wave of his hand. 'That won't be necessary. You think Lucy alarmed the offices and left via the back entrance?'

'That was the normal procedure; the door was locked and no alarms were triggered within the surgery itself, so I assume so. There didn't appear to be any break-in.'

'But somebody might have got the alarm code from Lucy and broken into the pharmacy or the reception area from the office side of the building?'

'Not possible. You'd need door keys as well as the code. Susanna had one set and I had the other. Lucy didn't have a set.'

'I think that's everything for now. Thank you again for waiting behind. It's been traumatic for you.' Shearer glanced at Robyn to see if she'd like to add anything but she shook her head.

Andy slumped in his chair. 'I really can't believe this has happened. Have you any idea who could be behind this?'

Shearer stood. 'It's too soon for us to say but you've been most helpful, sir. You can rest assured we'll be doing everything in our power to find the person responsible.'

Andy pushed himself from the chair with effort. 'Good luck,' he said. 'I hope you track them down soon. Dreadful. Just dreadful.'

⚜

They came out the way they'd entered, through the doors and empty waiting room, through the second doors and past the pharmacy and toilets. Robyn took a look around. It was unlikely anybody could have hidden inside the building without being spotted. There were no places to hide along the corridor, and the door to the corridor was locked and alarmed. Whoever wanted to kill Lucy had waited outside for her to emerge.

Robyn caught up with Shearer outside the toilets. 'I want to walk around the place. See where the killer might have been hiding,' she said.

'I already checked that out,' said Shearer. 'The surgery's at the end of this lane so there's no access beyond it. This land was part of a huge farm but the landowner died and it was sold off. The house that used to stand here was demolished and this centre built in its place. Come on, follow me.'

They walked outside to the rear of the building, and Shearer pointed to the high brick wall that ran along the perimeter.

'That separates us from Abbots Bromley church, and the cemetery. There's no access, not unless you've got climbing gear and grappling hooks, and even then, you'd be spotted because there are CCTV cameras monitoring the graves – a deterrent for vandals. We've checked the footage and nothing showed up, apart from a hedgehog.'

'How can you access the church?'

'From the road that runs parallel to this one.'

'So the surgery can only be reached from this lane? And the road goes no further?' Robyn said, looking at the fields to the right of her.

'Exactly. Beyond it are crop fields and pasture land. A killer would have to walk miles and circumnavigate crops, farms and a field of bulls if they wanted to approach from the far side.'

'Which means the perp had to use Bromley Rise in order to get to the clinic.'

Shearer nodded. 'It's the only way.'

'Somebody must have seen him come along here.'

Shearer's left eyebrow rose in a quizzical arc. 'Did you spot any houses on the way here?'

'No. There aren't any along this lane, are there?' Robyn said.

Shearer shook his head. 'None. Nobody was about peering through curtains or on their driveways. The killer could easily have travelled this lane undetected.'

'Okay, what about in the village itself? There are houses near the T-junction. I spotted some.'

'Those buildings on the corner of Main Street and Bromley Rise belong to the old school and are currently being developed into housing. They're uninhabited. The ones opposite were recently developed and have no occupants.'

'Oh crap.'

'I know how you feel.' His head was lowered as he spoke. 'I'm going to talk to Flint. You want to come along?'

Robyn gave a brief nod and spoke quietly. 'You said Lucy lived in Colton?'

'Yes.'

'That's too great a coincidence. Both my victims were killed in Colton and one lived there. You know what we have here, don't you?'

'One seriously sick fucker.'

Robyn nodded. 'One seriously sick and dangerous serial killer fucker.'

CHAPTER TWENTY-SEVEN

DAY FIVE – FRIDAY, 9 JUNE, EVENING

DCI Flint dragged a hand across his forehead and let out a noise of depressed exasperation. 'Did either of these men know Dr Harding?'

'We haven't found that out yet, sir. We're looking into it,' said Robyn. 'We might be dealing with two killers, but I suspect these murders are related.'

DCI Flint scrubbed at his face before settling his gaze on Robyn. 'I want you to handle this, Robyn. I agree that these murders could well be connected. Do you want Tom to help out?'

Robyn looked across at Shearer. He shrugged lightly. They had very different ways of working that might hinder rather than advance the investigation.

'I'm okay handling it without his help, sir, if Tom's happy.'

The reply was hesitant. 'Sure. I don't have any problem with that.'

DCI Flint nodded curtly. 'I don't need to tell you I'm mightily concerned. We have an absolute lunatic who's plotting and executing grotesque murders. It's imperative not to divulge any of the pertinent details to the public. We don't want to incite panic and we definitely don't want any copycat murders. I'll notify the media team to prepare statements regarding the doctor's death.'

'Sir, I'd like permission to interview Nathaniel Jones-Kilby.'

Flint considered her request but shook his head. 'No. He's not involved.'

'How can you be certain?' Robyn was perplexed. Why wouldn't Flint let her talk to the man?

'You know where I stand on this matter. You're to leave him alone.'

Robyn wanted to push it but the look on Flint's face suggested it was wise not to say anything further on the topic. She wondered what hold Nathaniel had over her boss. She asked herself once more if Flint was also tied up in some suspicious dealings. Amy had hinted Nathaniel was unscrupulous. Could Flint also be involved with him?

Flint sent them away. Robyn walked away from the office, determined to get straight to work on the investigation. Shearer accompanied her in silence. As they reached her office door he spoke. 'You shouldn't have been so quick to dismiss the idea of me working with you. I know you think you can handle everything but you've got a right wacko here causing havoc. What if these victims are completely unrelated? What if this killer is randomly selecting folk for his own amusement? If that's the case, you'll have a heck of a task tracking him down. I personally think you need assistance.'

Robyn was about to shoot him down and say she was more than capable of handling the investigation until she caught the look in his eye. Tom Shearer was genuinely concerned. 'If I don't get leverage pretty quickly, I'll come to you and ask for help.'

He snorted quietly. 'No you won't, Robyn. That's your problem, you never do. You think you can manage everything single-handedly, or with the backing of your team. You don't know how to ask for help. Good luck. You're going to need it.'

⁂

The energy in the office was palpable, looks of concentration on the faces of all her officers. She marched to the whiteboard and stared at the photograph of Lucy Harding, her eyes open, her left cheekbone shattered. Three victims. Three vicious murders. Could one killer be responsible for all three? She folded her arms and considered the evidence: the nature of the deaths, all different but all equally brutal. There was no attempt to hide any of the bodies, and both Jordan and Lucy had been left in the open to be discovered. And then there was Owen. He'd been murdered at home in his garage. Had a different person committed that crime, or was Owen collateral damage, having unmasked Jordan's murderer?

She glanced around the office, wondering if she should bounce some ideas off the team. Her eyes lighted on David, who was twisting a biro around his finger and swinging from side to side in his chair. Robyn noted the uneasy movements. David was normally very laid back. She was about to ask if he was okay when Anna called across.

'Forensics have identified the fibres lifted from Owen's clothing. They don't match any of Owen's other clothing they found in the house. They're charcoal-grey, cotton bamboo fibres.'

'Bamboo?' The furrow between Robyn's eyes deepened.

'Cotton bamboo. It's super absorbent, feels very soft against the skin and bamboo is ethically sourced. It's becoming a popular alternative to man-made fibres,' said Anna, looking up. 'I bought some cotton bamboo workout kit for the gym. It's very comfortable.'

'Where did you buy it?'

'Amazon but you can pick it up from other outlets and even health food stores.'

'So our killer is eco-friendly,' David muttered.

Robyn registered the new information and then changed the subject. 'How much have you found out about Lucy Harding? Did she know Jordan or Owen?'

'Still working on it. Not found anything on that score yet, guv,' said Mitz. 'Jordan's girlfriend Rebecca isn't answering her phone, so I can't ask her.'

'Try her again in a while. She might be in the process of moving. She told me she'd found accommodation in Rangemore.' Robyn rummaged through the Post-it notes stuck on her desk. 'That's the address. Anna, you got anything for me?'

Anna scrolled through her notes. 'No red flags so far. Parents say Lucy was a workaholic and a hands-on mother. She split up amicably from her husband last year, moved soon afterwards and rented her house in Colton. No boyfriend. They said she didn't have much spare time for one, what with work and looking after her son. Also spoke to her neighbours, who confirmed she was a very quiet woman who spent most of her spare time with her child. She lived at the opposite end of the village to Owen Falcon. For the moment, I have nothing that indicates they were friends or even knew each other. I've got a phone number for one of her friends – Sarah Jones. I was about to ring her.'

'Would you mind me speaking to her? I'd like to get more of an idea of who she was.'

Robyn punched out the number, looking out at the car park below as it rang. Outside it was grey and wet again. June was turning into a month of warm showers. Sarah picked up on the fifth ring. Robyn could hear a baby crying in the background. She introduced herself and broke the news of Lucy's death.

'Oh, Lord, no,' said Sarah.

'I'm very sorry,' said Robyn.

'Do her parents know?'

'They've been informed and so has her ex-husband.'

'What about Jamie? Where is he?' Sarah's voice cracked.

Robyn explained the boy was with his grandparents. As she spoke she heard the baby's cries weakening.

'Sarah, are you okay to talk to me for a minute? I need to ask a couple of questions about Lucy. When did you last speak to her?'

'Yesterday, I called her during lunch to catch up but she didn't have much time to chat.'

'Was she seeing anybody – a new boyfriend?'

She heard Sarah swallowing hard. 'She didn't say anything about any new boyfriends. She was happy spending time with Jamie. There wasn't anyone else in her life. She went out on a date a month ago but it didn't work out. The guy wasn't her type at all.'

'Did she mention his name?'

'No. She jokingly called him Mr Dull. She came across him on a dating website. She met him in a café at a shopping centre – she wasn't taking any risks – decided to hold the first meeting in full view of everyone. She didn't like him though. Said he wasn't her sort at all. It put her off Internet dating.'

'Any idea which dating site she used?'

'No. She never said. Could be Tinder or any of them.'

'Did she share any worries? Was she troubled about anything?'

'Nothing. Apart from spending insufficient time with Jamie.' Sarah sniffed loudly, and unable to hold back any longer, began to cry. The soft cries became more intense until she gave only brief responses in between gulps of air. 'Poor Lucy... and poor little Jamie.'

Robyn tried hard to console the distraught woman. Her friend had been murdered and yet it became increasingly difficult to ask questions that would aid the investigation. Lucy hadn't mentioned Owen's or Jordan's names to her friend. She spoke for a few more minutes, ensuring Sarah was sufficiently composed to ring her own mother or friend for company, before hanging up.

'Can we check out Lucy's mobile?'

'It got crushed, guv,' said Mitz. 'It's with the tech boys. They might be able to extract information from it.'

'Who visited her house?'

'That was me,' said Matt. 'There's a forensic team going through it for any clues.'

'Did she own a computer?'

'An iPad. It's also in the lab.'

'Ask the lads to look for a dating app or website. She met somebody a month ago. Might be worth finding out who it was.'

Robyn thought back to the surgery at Abbots Bromley. On her return trip to the station, she'd followed Bromley Rise to the main road and stopped to check out the old school currently being developed into housing, in case anybody was still working there and had spotted any unusual activity the evening or afternoon before. She found it empty. Shearer had been correct. The place was a huge building site, cordoned off with high railings and no entry signs. It was impregnable and the back access was gated and locked so no vehicles could enter. However, she'd managed to drive her car into an off-road space in front of the school. It had set her thinking. She pulled up a map of Abbots Bromley on her computer screen and called Anna across.

'That's the old school, currently being developed into new housing. It's unlikely there'd have been any construction work going on after 6 p.m. on Thursday, or any activity in the vicinity once the men left for the day. I noticed a CCTV camera on the outside of the building that appears to cover a small drop-off area in front of the site. Can you get hold of the construction manager and take a look at any CCTV footage from it? They'd already left for the day when I was there. I'm looking for a vehicle that might have drawn up there around six, parked up and left an hour later.'

With her whole team busy, Robyn drummed her fingers against her desk. She was facing a huge task, trying to coordinate three investigations. If it began to spiral out of control, she'd be forced to ask Shearer for help, and she really didn't want to do that.

CHAPTER TWENTY-EIGHT

THEN

The thudding wakes him. It's the sound of heavy bodies landing above him. It must be dawn. That's when the crows come. They land one after another making excited noises. He hears them strutting on the roof, calling to others to join them. If too many come, the roof will collapse and they'll fall into the shed with him, where they'll flock him and peck his eyes and his heart from him.

He knows a great deal about the carrion. He's read up on them. They eat meat as well as fruit, nuts and seeds. He tried once to befriend them in the hope they'd remember he'd been kind to them, and spare him the torture each time he's incarcerated in the shed. He'd kept back bread from breakfast and walked to the bottom of the garden by the shed and spoken to the crows.

'This is for you. Take it and remember me,' he'd shouted.

The crows had remained in their trees, perched high, watching him beadily but not moving towards his offering.

He'd backed away and waited inside the house but still they'd not come. He'd tried fruit next but again the crows had stayed in their treetops, laughing at him.

His sister told him not to worry. The crows wouldn't attack him. They only liked small pieces of food. They liked nuts in shells and pieces of fat from bacon, or leftover meat. They wouldn't eat a small boy. The boy didn't believe her. She hadn't seen the way they watched him when he was outside, waiting – waiting for a time when they'd burst through the shed roof and devour him.

The squawking on the roof suddenly stops. A hundred wings flap in unison and the cawing lifts away and disappears into the distance. He hears a key in the lock and feels wet tears pouring down his face. He's survived. It's over. The door opens and light streams into the room, making the boy blink several times. He is almost too weak to stand but so, so grateful. His misery is at an end. He stands upright, head high as is expected. His mother says, 'Have you repented?'

'Yes,' says the boy. He knows what she wants to hear and he speaks the words he's learnt by heart. 'I was a sinner but I have repented and made peace with my Lord. Thank you for giving me the chance and for showing me the error of my ways.' He's said them before, many times, but they satisfy his mother, who nods and beckons him forward. He picks up his blanket and drapes it around his body, wobbles on unsteady legs and, pushing against the walls, attempts to walk forwards.

He stumbles and his mother puts an arm around him, tenderly whispering, 'Come home, my son.'

CHAPTER TWENTY-NINE

Matt scrubbed a hand across his chin, dark with stubble, and released a pained sigh. He drained a cup of coffee and stared at the bottom of the cup for a minute before speaking. Robyn was beside his desk, her lined face bearing similar signs of strain.

'Guv, I've been through the statements made by both the pharmacist and the receptionist at the surgery. The receptionist, Susanna, was the last to leave before Lucy, and didn't notice anything out of the ordinary. She said there were definitely no vehicles other than Lucy's in the car park when she left, and nobody inside the clinic. The killer stayed well out of the way until everyone had gone.'

Anna stood up, her notebook in hand. Robyn waved her over and carried on speaking. 'Any luck with the foreman for the construction site in Abbots Bromley?'

'Not yet.'

Robyn continued, voicing her thoughts to both of them. 'On a normal night, Lucy would have left the surgery earlier. Consequently, the killer could only have known she was at the surgery after seven that night if they'd been watching her movements. They must have known she had extra patients to treat and would be staying late to write up her notes. What time did the last patient leave again?'

'That'd be Mr Franks. He left at six thirty.'

Robyn shook her head. 'Someone knew Lucy was there after seven. Maybe her assailant was waiting for Susanna, if not outside the school, then maybe further along Bromley Rise perhaps, or parked on a verge. They must have known once Susanna left, Lucy would be alone.'

Matt considered her point. 'That would be logical. How do you want to play this, then? I've got contact details for the patients Lucy saw at the afternoon clinic.'

'We'll speak to each of them and see if anybody spotted unusual activity – people hanging about, either inside or out – anything that they might remember while it's still fresh in their minds. Ask if any of them noticed a car parked up along the lane, or even outside the old school. I'll help,' said Robyn, picking up Matt's sheet of contact details. 'We'll get through them faster that way.'

Ten minutes later, Robyn lifted the phone and dialled the last person on her section of the list – Lance Goldman, one of the patients who'd had an appointment with Lucy the day before.

The gentleman who answered sounded wheezy. Robyn introduced herself and explained why she was ringing.

'What a dreadful thing to happen,' said Lance. 'She was a lovely woman. I really liked her.'

'I was wondering what you could remember about yesterday afternoon. Who else was in the surgery when you were there, for example?'

The man drew a breath and began talking slowly, recounting every detail he could recall. 'My appointment was for four but Dr Harding was running late. Joyce Lincoln, who used to live three doors down from me in Abbots Bromley, was ahead of me – her appointment was for three fifty. She wasn't best pleased at having to wait. She was mouthing off to the bloke who works at the butcher's – Ed, I think he's called.'

Robyn had already spoken to Ed Caldwell and he'd seen nothing untoward.

'They both went in ahead of me and it was quiet in the waiting room for a while but then it filled up again pretty quickly. I didn't recognise any of the people who came in, although one was a man with a limp.'

'What time did you leave the clinic?'

'About quarter to five.'

'Did you notice anybody standing about outside or walking around, or even sitting in a car?'

The man on the other end of the phone wheezed heavily before replying. 'No. I don't remember anyone else being there.'

'You didn't notice any vehicles parked along Bromley Rise when you left, did you?'

'I can't say I did.'

'Did you go past the old school?'

'No, I turned left, towards the centre of town.'

The man had no more to add so Robyn ended the call and struck a line through his name on the sheet. None of the patients she'd spoken to had noticed anything unusual.

Matt looked across and shook his head. He was clearly having no luck either. 'I spoke to the last patient to have an appointment with her – Mr Franks. His wife accompanied him and waited outside in the car, listening to the radio while he went inside for his appointment. They both said the car park was empty apart from two cars – one belonged to Susanna Mitchell, the receptionist, and the other was Lucy Harding's Mini.'

'The killer isn't invisible. We've been assuming they drove up the lane to the surgery, but they could have walked or used another form of transport – bike, moped. It's about a mile up that lane from the village. We might have to ask residents if they spotted anyone. Any luck with the site foreman yet, Anna?'

'No, guv. He's not answering his mobile or his house phone.'

'Okay, keep trying. He might be out. Hope he's not incommunicado for the weekend.'

Hampered by fatigue and no fresh leads, Robyn had called it a day before they all became too disheartened.

Back home she couldn't settle. Even with Schrödinger beside her, and the television on, thoughts buzzed around her head. She got up and wandered through to the kitchen where she ended up standing against the kitchen top, mind fully on the investigation. It was coming up to seven thirty when she got a response from Rebecca's mobile.

'Hi, it's Robyn.'

'Hi. Have you been trying to get me today? I've got several missed calls on my phone.'

'Yes, that'll have been my officer, Sergeant Patel. We tried ringing you earlier.'

'We moved house today. It was an emotional and physical upheaval and I never want to go through such trauma again. Dylan's completely unsettled. He won't go to sleep. He wants to go back to Jordan's house.'

'It's understandable,' said Robyn. 'He's upset and this has all happened so quickly. He hasn't had a chance to understand what's going on. Dylan will eventually settle, especially when he finds out about the training grounds nearby. It'll take time. It'll be best to try and keep everything else in his life a constant.'

'Yeah. I hope so.' Rebecca sounded downbeat.

'I'm sorry to disturb you when you're going through so much, but I had a question to ask.'

'Sure. It's good to have somebody to talk to. I feel so alone,' said Rebecca.

'Would it help if I came over for half an hour?'

'Would you?'

'If it's not too late for you.'

'Not at all. It'll take Dylan's mind off the move too. What did you want to ask me?'

'It'll wait until I get there.'

Robyn ended the call and stroked Schrödinger's head. 'I'm going out for a while. You behave yourself. I've left you some tuna in your bowl.'

The cat studied her face as if listening and understanding her every word. Robyn smiled to herself as she pulled the door to and jumped into her car. She really was becoming a mad cat lady.

With her attention on what she was going to ask Rebecca, she reversed off her front drive and headed towards the main road.

The Audi driver released a soft groan as Robyn drove off. His plans were thwarted. He'd planned tonight carefully and now he'd blown the opportunity to confront her. He didn't know when he'd next get the chance to talk to her. His mind drifted back two years to the mission in Marrakesh, when he'd followed orders, knowing he had no choice in the matter...

The briefing room is hidden in the bunker and they descend into it via a lift. It's a highly secure unit, unknown to anyone other than those who work for the Intelligence Service. Peter Cross is alone. He sits at a large table. As they emerge from the lift into the room, he nods a greeting, signals for them to sit down and gets to business.

'It's as we expected. Our contact has confirmed Davies is the next target, and having already lost three of our most valuable assets the last few months, we can't afford for that to happen. Therefore, I'm implementing Operation Desert.'

Operation Desert is the code name given to getting Davies safely from Marrakesh back to the UK, where he's to be hidden at a secret destination. Hassan, trained in evasive tactics and a highly skilled driver, will drive Davies from Marrakesh to a landing strip north of Agadir across the Atlas Mountains to rendezvous with an extraction team, while a decoy jeep will be deployed to travel in another direction to Ouarzazate, where a team will lie in wait for the enemy and capture them.

Peter says, 'Once Davies has made good his getaway and is on his way to the safe house, we'll contact Robyn and get her on a flight back to the UK.' He nods in Davies' direction. 'As we discussed at our last meeting, she'll have to be kept in the dark for a while and she'll believe you're dead. Obviously, this isn't ideal, but we need her to respond naturally to the news. She's pivotal to the success of this operation. Her reaction will provide plausibility to the lie. The enemy will have eyes on her and we need the news of your death to be credible and circulated quickly so we can move on to the next phase and uncover who is behind the deaths of our operatives. Have you any questions?'

There's a heavy silence. They've been through the plan before. There's no more to add. Davies uncrosses his legs and leans forward, hands resting on his thighs. 'I don't like it, Peter. I said so last time. I'd rather you told her the truth. She doesn't need to be put through such trauma. I want you to tell her exactly what is happening. She's a police detective, for heaven's sake. Tell her or the whole thing is off. I'll put her off coming to Marrakesh with me.'

'Don't be hasty,' says Peter. 'It'll ruin the plan. Your life is in serious danger and we're doing what we can to keep you alive. I don't need to remind you who we're up against here. It's not just you we have to consider, but our other operatives as well. You might not care if you get killed, but there'll be others after you if we don't ascertain who's behind this. Their lives are in your hands.'

Davies doesn't break eye contact with his superior. 'For the record, I don't like it. We've never involved civilians in such matters before.'

'She isn't in any danger. We'll have an agent watching over her at all times. As soon as you've taken off, I'll tell her you've been in an accident and bring her home.'

'No. You tell her the facts or I'll tell her before I leave for Morocco tomorrow. You're overlooking the fact there's also my daughter to consider in all of this. I won't have her dragged into it. Robyn will look after her and make sure she suspects nothing, but for that to happen, you'll have to level with her.'

Peter lifts both hands up in a defensive gesture. 'Okay. You win. I'll be honest with her. I promise.'

'You better be,' says Davies, his face set in a determined expression. 'Or you'll have me to answer to.'

Peter gives a smile. 'No need for that, Davies. I'll handle Robyn personally and ensure she's not kept in the dark.'

The men are dismissed. Peter walks with them to the lift and holds out a hand to Davies, who takes it. They shake hands. Peter looks him in the eye. 'Good luck. Come back safely.'

Davies nods. The lift doors open and he enters it. Peter waits while the door closes and the lift whizzes back above ground.

The man in the Audi clenched a fist, his nails digging deep into his palms as he thought of all the lies he'd been told. Peter Cross hadn't kept his end of the bargain. The man had deceived them all.

The man drew in a breath and studied his face in the rear-view mirror. The beard he sported hid most of his disfigured face, as did the glasses and the recently dyed hair, but they'd track him down and it wouldn't take them long, especially if he remained in this town, filled with CCTV cameras that observed every movement. He needed to get on the move again and he was running out of time to contact Robyn to tell her the truth of what happened that day. He'd have to run the risk and return. He had to speak to her.

Robyn might never forgive any of them, but at least she'd finally understand.

Robyn found a space near the terraced houses in Rangemore, one of which Rebecca now rented, and squeezed her VW Golf into a tight space behind Rebecca's car. As soon as she shut her car door, a dog began barking – angry, high-pitched yapping Robyn associated with small lap dogs. She ignored it, marched towards number fifteen and rapped on the door. Rebecca opened immediately and beckoned her inside.

It was a small, clinical space that lacked homeliness. Rebecca had unpacked a few belongings but it was nowhere near as friendly and welcoming as Jordan's house had been.

'Hi. How are you?' said Robyn.

Rebecca had been crying. Her eyes were puffy again but she managed a brave smile. 'Oh, you know. Been a difficult day.'

'I can imagine.'

Rebecca gave her a warm smile. 'I've just opened a bottle of wine. Want to join me?'

'Just a small one. Can't afford to get pulled over for drink-driving.' She looked up as Dylan wandered in.

'Hey.'

The boy looked disorientated. 'Hi. Mum, I can't find Yoda.'

'He's in the box, sweetie. We packed him together.'

'I can't see him,' he whined. 'I want him.' His began to sniff.

Rebecca sighed. 'He's been like this all day.'

'I'll sort it,' said Robyn.

'Would you? I'll pour you a drink.'

'Come on, Dylan, I'll help you find him,' said Robyn.

Dylan looked up at her. His face was pale, and violet bags hung below his eyes. He nodded and she followed him into the sitting room, as sparse as the kitchen, furnished only with a settee, a chair and a television. A box of toys had been opened, and action figures and toys were strewn on the floor. Robyn's eyes lighted upon the Yoda figurine immediately, lying on the floor in front of the box.

'Look, there he is.' She passed it to Dylan, who blinked several times before taking it from her, his hand shaking as he did so.

'You feeling okay?' she asked.

He shook his head. 'Foggy,' he replied.

Rebecca came in carrying two half-filled glasses of wine. 'You found it,' she said, indicating the small toy.

'Dylan says he feels foggy,' said Robyn.

Rebecca's face became more serious. 'That's because you're tired, Dylan. It's been a long day. You need to go to bed. How about you get ready now Robyn is here? Then come down and say goodnight.'

'I'm not tired,' he said, dropping to the floor. 'I don't want to go to bed.'

Rebecca shrugged. 'I'm not going to make you go, but if you're too tired tomorrow, you won't be able to play football in the park like we planned.'

The boy stared at her for a minute then rose and left the room.

Rebecca watched him go. 'He's been acting up today.'

'It's the shock of it all. It's only to be expected. You've both had a terrible shock.' Robyn sipped her wine before speaking again. 'I know you've got a load on your mind but I wondered if Jordan knew somebody called Lucy Harding. She's a doctor at the Abbots Bromley surgery.'

Rebecca stared at her hard.

'Rebecca?'

'Sorry, I was a bit taken aback. I know her. Well, I've seen her at the surgery – slim, tall, with dark hair. We're all patients at the surgery but she's not our doctor. We're under Dr Trevago.'

'Did Jordan ever mention her?'

'No. He's not been to the new surgery. He's not been ill in all the time I've known him.'

'But you've been there?'

'A couple of times, with Dylan.'

'Dr Harding lived in Colton and might have known Owen Falcon. Did he ever mention her?'

Rebecca frowned and shook her head. 'Why are you asking about her?'

'I'm afraid she was killed in a hit and run last night.'

There was a sharp intake of breath. 'You don't think her death's connected to Jordan and Owen's, do you?'

Robyn knew better than to discuss investigations with any members of the public. 'I can't comment on that,' she said with a sigh.

'Oh, my goodness. And she lived in Colton. Another death in Colton.' Rebecca lifted her glass of wine and took a lengthy swig.

'No. She died outside the surgery in Abbots Bromley.'

Rebecca's eyes widened and she whispered, 'No. How awful.'

'Jordan never spoke about her?'

Rebecca shrugged a no. She sipped her wine then wiped a tear that had slid down her face.

'Sorry,' she said. 'It's been a rough few days. It's all too emotional. I'm finding the nights the hardest. I keep imagining what happened to Jordan that night in Colton – how frightened he'd have been, what he might have endured. Oh, Robyn, I can't get it out of my head.'

She looked at the wine glass. 'This is horrific. All this death. I didn't know Dr Harding at all, but that doesn't stop me from feeling awful for her and for her family. I know how much they must be hurting.'

'It'll get easier for you, Rebecca. Really it will.'

'Will it though?' Rebecca asked, her fingers caressing the glass. 'I can't imagine a time when it will feel okay again.'

Robyn thought about the pain she'd suffered too – the sleepless nights, the tears and the feeling of utter desolation she'd experienced following Davies' death. She reflected on how far she'd come on her own personal journey in the last two years and looked Rebecca in the eye. 'Trust me, you will. You've had a long, difficult day, but it's a start and you'll keep making little steps forward.'

Robyn drained her glass and made to leave. Spotting a folded pile of clothes on the floor, her thoughts flashed back momentarily to the bamboo clothing fibres found on Owen's body. Could they have come from clothing belonging to Rebecca? In Robyn's line of work nothing was taken for granted. She tried a subtle approach to steer the conversation in that direction. 'You could go the homeopathic route,' she said. 'You'd know more about that than me, having worked in the industry. I'm sure there's something you could use to ease the anxiety.'

Rebecca shook her head. 'We offered remedies and such-like at Longer Life Health. I'm actually not into alternative medicine or all those eco-friendly, gluten-free, organic products. They're very expensive and I'm not convinced of their benefits. Personally, I think it's all hype.'

'But you still sold them?'

'It was a job.' Rebecca shrugged.

Robyn offered up a smile. 'I don't want to keep you. You need to put Dylan to bed. He looks done in. You both do.'

Rebecca's face softened. 'It's no bother. Actually, it's nice to have company and talk to somebody who understands what I'm going through.'

'Haven't you spoken to Michelle Watson, the liaison officer, again?'

'I didn't want to. I have to stand on my own two feet and get on with my life. It's just me and the little champ again.' She swigged the pale-yellow liquid in one gulp. 'Top up?' she asked.

Robyn declined. 'I'd better get off. I hope Dylan settles soon.'

'Me too. I don't know what to do or say to him to make things better.'

'Just do what any mother does – love him and be there for him.'

Rebecca gave her a warm smile. 'I will – always.'

Robyn left Rebecca's house with a sense of unease. It was as if she had the puzzle pieces to a jigsaw but they were the wrong shape for the picture she was trying to recreate. She drove away, her mind flitting between the cases, all the while trying to work out what the link between the three victims could be.

CHAPTER THIRTY

DAY SIX – SATURDAY, 10 JUNE, MORNING

The day started badly. Robyn was getting ready for work when her mobile rang. Amy Walters could barely contain her excitement.

'A local resident rang me with news that a doctor was found dead in the surgery car park at Abbots Bromley. He said the police have cordoned off the whole area. Tell me. Is it the same killer?'

Robyn chose her words carefully. 'We agreed I'd speak to you when I could. We have to handle our investigations very carefully and can't afford to jeopardise them in any way.'

'That's your way of letting me know it is a serial killer, isn't it? DI Carter, I want this story. I need it for my book. It's perfect, especially as I saw what that person did to Owen Falcon. You have to help me. I let you have all my information on Jones-Kilby. Tell me something.'

'I appreciated your cooperation, Amy. We haven't been able to use the information you gave us, but I am still looking into it.'

'Jordan phoned me last week. He wanted to tell me something important and I think it was about his father. I believe that's why he was killed – to silence him. His friend, Owen Falcon, was probably murdered for the same reason, and now there's been another murder – the new doctor who also happens to live in Colton. Come on, DI Carter. This is a huge story. If you don't help me out, I'll have to do some digging of my own.'

'Amy, I can't comment.'

'I've already made connections between them.'

Robyn's brow furrowed deeply at the news. 'I don't want you interfering. I made that abundantly clear. If you mess up my investigations through meddling, I'll take—'

'Spare me your threats. I know what you'll do to me. I haven't meddled. I applied journalist logic. That new practice, the one that Lucy worked at, covers a wide area. Before it opened, Yoxall Health Centre was the only surgery for all the villages covering an area, roughly triangular in size, that stretched from Lichfield towards Uttoxeter and across to Rugeley. Due to the influx of new housing estates and an increasing population, it became overburdened, so the new clinic was built to deal with half of the patients, including those who live in Newborough and Colton. Take a look at the GP's patient lists. I bet you'll find Nathaniel Jones-Kilby is registered there. I'm convinced he's pivotal to this. If I'm right about this, promise you'll tell me, that's all I ask.'

'I'll think about it. I can't keep chasing after him because you have a theory he's up to no good. I need concrete evidence to haul him in.'

'Then find some, unless you want me to find it for you.'

Mitz, who'd seen Robyn pull into the car park, had walked outside to meet her.

'Had a breakthrough with the footballer with the broken leg – Darren Sturgeon – the one who denied being beaten up by Jordan and Owen. His sister, Fay, rolled up at the station first thing this morning, asking to speak to one of us. Matt's in the interview room with her.

'Great. Which one?'

'Two.'

Robyn tapped on the door to the room and entered. She recognised the young girl who'd opened the door with the baby in her arms. Today she looked even younger, barely old enough to take GCSEs. She looked up when Robyn entered.

'I told him everything,' Fay said. 'Darren got attacked by those two blokes you were asking after – Owen Falcon and Jordan Kilby. He told me to keep my mouth shut but I didn't see what harm it'd do to tell you. He should've reported them when it happened, and not kept it to himself. He deserves some sort of compensation and that Jordan bloke was filthy rich, wasn't he? His dad is, anyway. He should pay for Darren being off work.'

'What did your brother tell you exactly?' Robyn remained standing as the girl spoke.

'It was in the hospital. He was high on medication. I asked him what happened and he said he'd been jumped by the two "poofters" who'd had a go at him during the football match. Those were his exact words. I asked him who he meant and he said the rich kid and his mate – the hard-faced one – Owen Falcon.'

'You say he was on medication. He might have been mistaken.'

The girl shook her head. 'After you spoke to him, I told him he should've said something to you. He told me to shut up. He didn't want it getting out that he was done over by those two. He was well embarrassed.'

'Why?'

The girl flushed. 'He's got a thing about some men. He thought they were gay.'

'So he's homophobic?'

'I don't know what that means.'

'Your brother is prejudiced against homosexual people.'

'Oh yeah. He gets all weird about them.'

'To my knowledge neither of the men was homosexual.'

'Daz thought they were. Laughed about them. Said Jordan followed Owen about everywhere. That was before he got attacked.

Can I go now? I told the sergeant everything. Do you think Darren will get compensation?'

'I really can't comment,' said Robyn. 'You'd need to talk to a lawyer about it.'

Fay looked sulkily at Robyn. 'Oh, okay. Can you give me the name of a lawyer?'

Robyn folded her arms. 'I think we should talk to your brother first and see if that's how he wants to proceed.'

The girl shrugged. 'Whatever. I don't know where he is at the moment but he said he was going to the Fox and Weasel around lunchtime. Can I go now?'

'Sure, and thank you for helping us.'

The girl didn't reply. She edged her way towards the door, eyes flicking back to Robyn, and nodded briefly.

They found Darren in the corner of the Fox and Weasel, talking to some of the men they'd interviewed the day before. He rolled his eyes when Robyn and Matt approached.

'We'd like to talk to you again,' said Robyn.

'Well, I don't want to talk to you.' He picked up his almost empty glass of cider and downed the contents in one.

'We can do this in front of your friends or we can take it somewhere private. The choice is yours. Fact is we know who attacked you last Saturday.'

His friends looked towards Darren, who mumbled something incoherently and struggled to his feet. 'Okay, how about in there,' he said, nodding towards the door that led into a separate room. He hobbled across on his crutches, all the while under the watchful eye of Joe Harris, who'd been eavesdropping.

'Mr Harris, if you wouldn't mind leaving us alone,' said Matt.

Joe scowled at Matt. 'This is my pub.'

'I'm aware of that. I'd also appreciate a little privacy so we can have a quick word with your customer. We'll not be long.'

Joe slammed down a large bottle of gin he was getting ready to put into an optic and disappeared out the back. The other customers remained seated in the lounge bar and conversation resumed as the trio moved into the snug area.

'What do you want?' said Darren.

'The truth. You told us Owen and Jordan weren't behind the attack on you, yet it's come to light it was them.'

'How did you find out?'

'That's irrelevant. What is important is why you claimed otherwise.'

Darren sat back and sneered at Robyn. 'It's bloody obvious, isn't it? If you found out it was those two who attacked me, it put me in the frame for their murders. I had motive to hurt them, didn't I?'

'Hiding the facts is an offence. You are hindering our investigations. You ought to have come clean about it.'

Darren dropped his voice. 'I didn't want anybody to find out who did this to me. I didn't tell any of my mates. I have a reputation to uphold. I didn't want them to find out that pair had attacked me, so I didn't let on, then when you asked me about it, I didn't want to say anything in case you thought I'd killed them.'

'You only had to tell us the truth and we'd have cleared your name in this. Given your physical state it would have been difficult for you to have attacked either of the men, unless you had assistance. Did you?'

Darren sneered again. 'Course not. I had nothing to do with their deaths.'

'You didn't like them much though, did you? You riled them on the pitch, called them names, made wild accusations about their sexuality.'

'Wild accusations?'

'You claimed they were having a sexual relationship.'

'My bad. I was only taking the piss out of them. Anyway, maybe they were. They spent a lot of time hanging about together, just the two of them. I've seen them in the corner of the changing room, whispering stuff to each other. They could have been an item. I was only messing with them. That's what we all do. I've been called a lot worse than a poofter. I don't take it to heart.'

'What happened on the night of the attack?'

Darren pulled a face. 'They jumped me on my way home. Came out of nowhere. Owen was completely bloody mental. He was high, which made it worse.'

'High?'

'Drugs. He often took stuff. Didn't you know? Coke mainly. He sometimes took it before a match too. He could be a bad-tempered fucker at the best of times, worse after he'd snorted a line.'

'He appeared to have taken drugs that night?'

Darren nodded. 'Deffo. His eyes were all wide and rolling and he was well out of control. He and Jordan had tools – he had a hammer and Jordan had a large spanner. I laughed at first. Asked what they were going to do – fix a motor? Wish I'd kept my gob shut cos Owen pushed me against the wall and said he had a score to settle with me.'

'What part did Jordan play in this attack?'

'Watched mostly. To be fair, he tried to stop Owen but the lunatic was too far gone to be controlled by anyone. Owen said I'd crossed a line. I said I was sorry, that I didn't mean any harm and was only joshing, but Owen had that look in his eyes, like he wasn't listening, as if he wasn't in the real world. He kicked me and I went down, then it all went mental. He lifted the hammer and said he'd teach me a lesson and if I squealed he'd come back and smack my head with the hammer. Jordan rushed forward and pulled at his arm, but he pushed him away, and the next thing, he smacked me hard on the shin with the fucking hammer. I didn't feel anything at first. I heard the bone crack. Then my leg exploded with pain and I think I yelled just before I passed out. Next I knew, a paramedic was leaning over me asking if I was okay.'

'And Jordan didn't hit you at all?'

'Nah.'

'You say Owen took drugs.'

Darren nodded.

'Did Jordan too?'

'I don't think so. Difficult to know, isn't it? He might have cut a line or two with Owen. He certainly copied him a lot. Weird bloke. A right Billy No-Mates, apart from Owen and a few of the Blithfield Wanderers.'

'You should have reported this.'

'If I had, they'd have come after me again and done worse, wouldn't they?'

'But it might have saved their lives. If they'd been taken into custody for the attack on you, they might not have been murdered.'

'Yeah, but I might have been murdered by them.' Darren gave a shrug of contempt.

'Would you go through your movements that night again with Sergeant Higham, so we can eliminate you from our enquiries?'

'If I have to.'

Robyn left Matt to take a statement and wandered outside to get some fresh air. Darren's nonchalant attitude towards the victims had irked her. Although she doubted Owen and Jordan had been having sexual relations, she was puzzled as to why they'd be whispering together. Others had made similar comments about Owen and Jordan often being together in a huddle. The news Owen took drugs was interesting, especially as the blood screening that had been performed following his death hadn't revealed any substances in his system. Had his murder been in connection with drugs? Did he have a serious habit? Connor and the forensic team certainly hadn't uncovered any drugs at his house. This might be another angle to consider.

While she waited for Matt to wind up interviewing Darren, she rang Ross to find out about Jeanette.

'Hey, how's the patient?'

'She's okay. We're just about ready to leave for the Cotswolds. She's packed enough clothes for a month not three days. She's doing her hair at the moment. Want a quick word with her?'

'Nah. I don't want to delay you. Give her my love. When are the results of the biopsy due back?'

'Tuesday. We've got an appointment with the GP at midday. We'll drive back that morning and go there first.'

'Make sure you ring me as soon as you hear anything.'

'Goes without saying. Ah, she's here. Jeanette, it's Robyn.'

Robyn heard Jeanette shouting hello in the background.

'Best go. Duke's over-excited. He loves trips in the car.'

'Bye Ross. Love you both.'

She could hear the smile in his voice as he replied. 'Softie.'

She ended the call and again hoped the news was going to be okay. She didn't dare think otherwise.

Anna rang as soon as she'd put down the phone. 'I've been at the building site at the old school opposite the surgery all morning. We couldn't gain access to the site initially but we finally got a key. Anyway, I've been through the footage and a car did park up outside.'

'Good. Did you get a registration for it?'

'No. Sorry, it's not great news. The camera only caught a brief part of the front section of the car. I'm going to have to take the footage back to the laboratory and see if the tech chaps can identify the make and model for us.'

'What time was the car there?'

'The timings fit. It arrived at six fifteen and was there until seven forty. It might well belong to our killer.'

CHAPTER THIRTY-ONE

Robyn addressed the team in the office. David was at the back of the room on his phone when she began. He lifted two fingers to indicate he'd be with her shortly. She acknowledged him before speaking.

'Let's start with Jordan. Connor told me, in spite of an extensive search, they still haven't found the murder weapon; so, I think we can safely assume the murderer has removed it from the scene of the crime, along with Jordan's bicycle helmet. To date, we have no further suspects. His footballing teammates' alibis all stack up, as do the alibis from the team members of the opposing team, the Sudbury Dynamos, and Darren Sturgeon. This wasn't some vengeance attack for breaking Darren's leg.

'I'm keeping an open mind about the possibility this is somehow linked to his father, Nathaniel. We were prevented from questioning the man himself. However, I'll present our latest findings to DCI Flint and request the embargo be lifted. I don't see why we can't question him to clear him from this investigation.

'My latest information comes care of Amy Walters.' There was a soft groan from Mitz. She gave him a smile. 'I know, I know, but she's been providing us with help on this. She thought Nathaniel was registered to the Abbots Bromley surgery, the surgery where Lucy was killed. I've been through the patient lists for the practice, and she was correct. Nathaniel, Owen, Jordan, Jordan's girlfriend, Rebecca, and her son, Dylan, are all registered with the practice. However, Nathaniel and Owen were Lucy Harding's patients, and Rebecca, her son, and Jordan are her colleague Andy Trevago's patients.'

She rubbed at her forehead before she spoke again. She'd thought hard about the connection, and in the absence of anything else it was all she could offer. 'I don't know what to make of that information. It seems like it's relevant but I can't see what motive could possibly be behind the three murders. Moreover, I'm concerned about the planning and execution of these murders. They appear to be premeditated. The killer leaves no prints. He leaves no trace at all. He knew Jordan was in Colton the night he was murdered, that Owen was in his garage fixing his bike, and that Lucy Harding was alone late at night at the surgery. How? How could the murderer know that unless he was watching each of them?'

'I hate to say this, but although it appears the perp is well prepared, he might just be acting randomly – hunting and settling for any victim for no apparent reason – to act out some weird fantasy,' said Mitz.

'Sorry, but that scenario doesn't work for Owen Falcon, mate,' Matt said, raising his hands and shrugging.

'Exactly. Owen's murder was different to the other two. He was attacked inside not outside. The weapon used to kill him was one of his own tools. It's also come to light that Owen was aggressive, more so when he took drugs. I don't know what sort of habit he had, but it might be a significant factor in this case. I now wonder if we're dealing with two killers.' Robyn stared at the whiteboard, wishing it would aid her jumbled thoughts.

'We have one new piece of information regarding the death of Lucy Harding. We now know a vehicle was parked in small parking area outside the building site in Abbots Bromley between six fifteen and seven forty, which means the driver of that car would have been able to walk or jog to the surgery, kill Lucy and return to the car during that time. However, the CCTV footage is insufficient to identify the car and only shows a small section of it. From it we can only tell it's a dark blue car. The techies are working on it and will let us know in due course.

'I'd like us to interview all the staff at the medical centre again. That includes nurses and the other pharmacists and receptionists who work there. Susanna Mitchell was on reception in the afternoon but Alison Drew was the receptionist during the morning surgery. Speak to them all and see if any of them know anything or have an idea of who might have committed this crime.'

David joined the team, notepad in his hand. 'Guv, we've got another connection. That was Graham Valence, Jordan's manager at Speedy Logistics, on the phone. He said Jordan often took deliveries from Pharmacals Healthcare to the surgery at Abbots Bromley – at least twice a month. The last delivery was made the Friday before he was killed. Dr Lucy Harding signed for it.'

Robyn took a deep breath. At last, there was something more. This was different to what Rebecca had told her. Jordan had visited the surgery at Abbots Bromley regularly. He'd seen and spoken to Lucy Harding. That same day, he'd also visited his father and called him a cheating, murdering liar.

'What was in the delivery?'

'It consisted largely of wound dressing products.'

'Right. Jordan knew Lucy. Owen was one of her patients. Find out when Owen last visited the surgery. If it wasn't for an appointment, it might have been to deliver some electrical supplies. Also find out when Nathaniel last visited the practice.' She tapped her teeth with a pen, frown lines developing on her forehead. 'This might have something to do with the surgery, so while we're at it, find out when Rebecca last made an appointment to see her doctor. I might be going out on a limb here and be completely wrong, but our killer might even work at the surgery.'

A new thought struck Robyn. 'Mitz, can you find out more about Pharmacals Healthcare? Jordan took his delivery from there to Lucy at the surgery but I've just realised that Jordan's girlfriend, Rebecca, works there.'

'Sure.'

CHAPTER THIRTY-TWO

THEN

The bedroom door is slightly ajar. He can see his sister through the gap. She's face down on her bed, crying into her pillow, trying to muffle the sobs. She's been crying a lot recently and he doesn't understand why. She's older than him by several years and a whole lot more grown up. He usually goes to her when he's upset or frightened, but tonight, seeing her so unhappy, he decides to help her.

He pads softly into her room and to her bed, where he sits down. She feels his weight on the bed and pushes herself up, eyes wide with anxiety, until she realises it's him.

'You okay?' he says.

'It's nothing,' she replies, wiping her eyes with her nightdress sleeve. 'Bit down, that's all.'

'I heard you being sick again this morning. Is your tummy hurting?'

She gives him a kindly look. 'Yes. A bit. You won't say anything to Mum or Dad, will you? About me being sick?'

He shakes his head even though he thinks it's silly. Whenever he feels ill he goes straight to his parents and tells them. His sister must be a mind reader because she says, 'I don't want to worry them and I can't miss school. I have exams this week.'

'Maybe you have a bad tummy because you're worried about the exams. I always feel poorly when I have a test at school or have to read out loud in class,' he says.

'That'll be it,' she answers. 'It's nothing important. Off you go. I'll be okay.'

'Sure?'

She nods and kisses him on the forehead. He loves his sister. She's kind and good and is always nice to him. She's been making sure he doesn't get into trouble with Larson or his friends again. She doesn't want him to have to face the punishment again. When Larson started making chicken noises at him, she'd walked over and spoken quietly to him. The boy doesn't know what was said, but Larson shut up and sloped away and hasn't been a nuisance since.

He halts by the door. 'You sure you're okay?'

'I am. Don't fuss.'

He disappears into the corridor and into his own room. Downstairs his parents are holding a prayer meeting with their friends and it's best to stay out of the way. He wanders over to the picture of Jesus above his bed and traces the dark blood coming from his outstretched palms. His parents always ask Jesus for strength and for help.

The boy drops onto the rug beside his bed and asks the Lord to help his sister face her exams and for her not to feel so sick. When he's finished, he smiles. It'll be okay now. Jesus will help her.

CHAPTER THIRTY-THREE

'Darren Sturgeon's statement,' said Matt, dropping it on Robyn's desk.

Robyn read it out. Darren's statement matched the admission he'd made in the interview room. She looked up from the paper and said to Matt, 'Do you reckon Owen and Jordan used the tools from Owen's toolbox?'

'Probably. Why?'

'It struck me that these very tools were used against Owen himself. I'm leaning towards two different murderers here. I wonder if anyone witnessed the attack on Darren?'

Matt's face creased into a frown. 'There might have been a third party present at the scene – maybe somebody we haven't yet interviewed – who watched the attack and decided to avenge it.'

Robyn shrugged. 'They'd have to have a really good reason to kill Owen over it. Why not just shop the pair of them to the police? Unless it was somebody who already bore Owen a grudge and decided to kill him in the hope we'd conclude Owen had been murdered because of the attack. Does that even make sense?'

Matt gave a small smile. 'Not really, but that could be because we're reading too much into this.'

Robyn shook her head in dismay.

Anna came off the phone and crossed the room purposefully. 'The tech boys have only just finished with Jordan's laptop. There was a backlog of work and they couldn't get onto it immediately. They've not flagged up a thing. He really was obsessed with comic characters and sport. He visited hundreds of sites and forums and videos all to do with Marvel Comics characters, Comic Conventions, Marvel Universe and endless stuff on cycling and football.'

'Okay, cheers, Anna.' Robyn's phone buzzed and interrupted the discussion. It was Amy.

'Before you start, I'm not interfering. I'm helping you with your enquiries.'

Robyn grunted. 'And how are you helping exactly?'

'Don't be so ungracious. I was right about Nathaniel Jones-Kilby being a patient at the surgery, wasn't I? I've got something else for you: he was in Abbots Bromley on Thursday night, the same night Dr Lucy Harding was killed. You're in charge of this case. Do something. Drag him in for questioning.'

'How do you know he was in Abbots Bromley that night?'

'He was spotted there.'

'Were you following him, Amy?'

She took Amy's silence as confirmation.

'Are you for real? You're not only clutching at straws, you're misdirecting this investigation in the hope we'll uncover some facts about Jordan's father that you'll put into an article or your book. You're not a police officer so stop this interference immediately. I'm in charge of this investigation, not you, and I decide how to proceed. If you don't back off, I'll charge you. I mean it, Amy!'

Amy sounded slightly more contrite. 'I wasn't following him. I was chasing a lead and happened to see his car driving into the village around six.'

'That's not grounds for hauling him in here.'

'But this is important. You need to talk to him. I'm sure he's connected to all this. Don't forget: Jordan wanted to tell me something important. It was probably to do with his father.'

'Go away, Amy.' Robyn ended the call and threw the phone onto her desk. Amy's insistence the case was connected to Nathaniel was doing her head in, and clouding her judgement. But if Nathaniel had been in Abbots Bromley, it was essential she speak to him. She'd have to talk to DCI Flint about interviewing Nathaniel again. Flint couldn't possibly sign off on the man unless he was in cahoots with him and was crooked himself or, worse still, involved in the murders. She rang Flint's office but he didn't pick up. She slammed the phone down and turned her attention to other leads. She'd tackle the thorny issue of Nathaniel first thing in the morning. She'd get to the bottom of it, and if that meant flushing out Flint too, then so be it.

'Have you found out if Owen was at the surgery last week?'

Anna spoke up. 'He never visited the new surgery. The last appointment he made to see a GP was in 2014 in Yoxall, before his records were transferred to Abbots Bromley. The manager at Rugeley Electrical says they've had no recent jobs at the clinic although they supplied electricians when it was built. Owen wasn't employed on that job. I've spoken to the other pharmacists who work at the clinic and neither of them have anything new to add about Lucy Harding. She was a dedicated doctor, focused on her job.'

Robyn glanced at her watch. It was late again. They'd be too wrecked to work if they all continued like this. It was time to leave for the day and she told them so. She tidied up her desk before turning out the light and plodding down the corridor, her mind still far too alert to turn in for the night. As she did so, she remembered she was out of food again. She didn't feel like going to the supermarket. She'd stop off on her way home and get a takeaway and then join Schrödinger on the settee and watch a film on Netflix. There was bound to be something worthwhile.

-ᴥ-

Tom Shearer was standing at the entrance door, shrugging on his jacket. He held it open for Robyn.

'You fancy a drink?' he asked and gave her one of his rakish grins.

Robyn was about to refuse when she decided it would be standoffish. Besides, an hour with Tom would be a welcome break from the investigation. She accepted his invitation and accompanied him to the pub half a mile down the road from the station. Some of the vice team were in and in high spirits having collared a couple of dealers, and so Tom and Robyn joined them for some banter and a couple of drinks before heading further into town for some food.

The queue at the fish and chip shop was lengthy but worth the wait and they sat outside on the wall with cod and chips, discussing life at the station.

'It's quite tame here compared to some of the shenanigans we got up to in Derby,' said Tom, spearing a chip with his plastic fork and eating it with gusto. 'We used to have some right nights out on the piss. Especially after a good result. Mind you, that was what partly led to the break-up of my marriage – too many nights out with my team. I saw more of them than the wife. They were more fun!'

'Do you miss the old station? Your old team?'

Shearer pursed his lips and gave her a grin. 'Not any more. This lot are okay. They're a good bunch. Very dedicated. Even that dopey-arsed Gareth Murray's shaping up. Not sure he'd be able to keep up with one of my drinking sessions though. Derby's not far away but there've been quite a lot of changes there – a few of the old squad have left. It's not like when I worked there. Sometimes it's good to move on.'

'So you wouldn't go back?'

Shearer shrugged. 'Depends on the circumstances. If I went back as a DCI, that'd be fine. What about you? Fancy a change?

I thought when Louise Mulholland left for Yorkshire, you'd soon follow her.'

Robyn shook her head. 'I've got a great team here. I'm happy here. For the moment,' she said, catching the look on his face.

Shearer glanced at his phone that flashed with a message. He pulled a face. 'My son Brandon. I was supposed to take him to the football this weekend. He's just cried off. Probably got a hot date and doesn't want to hang out with his decrepit old father.'

Robyn saw the disappointment in his eyes. 'You're not a decrep, Tom. He's at university, isn't he?'

'Yeah. Keele. It's not far away but he may as well be in Kuala Lumpur for what I see of him.'

'Kids are, well, just kids. They do whatever they feel like. He's enjoying his freedom.'

Shearer gave her a smile that crinkled his eyes. 'You're right. He's just acting his age. I'd have been the same at his age. I was young once too.' He winked.

As Robyn drove away from the station she decided Tom Shearer wasn't the complete arsehole he sometimes pretended to be.

If she had bought the takeaway and gone home as she'd intended, she might have met the man who waited outside her house for three hours to talk to her. But as it was, he decided she wasn't coming home, gave up waiting and pulled away fifteen minutes before she returned.

CHAPTER THIRTY-FOUR

DAY SEVEN – SUNDAY, 11 JUNE, MORNING

Robyn wasn't feeling too alert when she entered the kitchen. She blamed the alcohol for the restless night that had caused her brain to whir with outrageous ideas. She thought about the three different crime scenes. There was something she couldn't put her finger on about them.

The cat's purring almost drowned out the sound of her mobile buzzing on the kitchen top. She carried him across and picked up the phone, juggling to talk and hold on to the cat.

'Have you seen the *Stafford Gazette* this morning?' Flint asked.

Robyn could tell by the icy tone it wasn't good news.

'No, sir.'

'Meet me in my office in half an hour.'

The article was far worse than Robyn expected:

> *The death of Dr Lucy Harding (36) outside the surgery at Abbots Bromley has rocked the inhabitants of the sleepy rural village. Local residents are shocked and outraged by what has taken place.*

Dr Harding's body was discovered in the surgery car park, early Friday morning, and her murder comes in the same week as the deaths of local electrical engineer, Owen Falcon (29), and Jordan Kilby (23), son of successful property developer Nathaniel Jones-Kilby (55).

Both men also died in suspicious circumstances in the village of Colton, only four miles from Abbots Bromley, and were both patients at the Abbots Bromley Surgery where Dr Harding was killed.

DI Robyn Carter of Staffordshire Police refused to comment on the cases. However, she hinted that the police are searching for one suspect in connection with the murders.

There have been many concerns and questions from locals, anxious about their own safety, and some fear DI Robyn Carter, who has suffered mental health issues in the past, is not up to such a task.

There's concern that DI Robyn Carter is out of her depth with this case. She has refused to act on information about a third party who might be connected to the three murders.

One resident declared, 'Staffordshire Police need to gain the public's confidence and tell us what they're doing about this. We have a right to know. They can't afford to ignore the possibility of a serial killer on the loose.'

Robyn's fists tightened. Amy had gone too far this time. 'This is Amy Walters getting her own back because I wouldn't share information with her, and because I wouldn't go chasing after Nathaniel. She believes he's involved in the murders. She rang me yesterday and I sent her packing. This is her way of retaliating and to get me to follow up on Nathaniel. You must allow me to talk to him, sir.'

DCI Flint remained seated behind his desk, eyes on the article. 'I can't say I'm any happier than you are about this, but she's set the cat among the pigeons.'

'I understand that, sir. The public is now concerned that there's a killer out there waiting to attack again and that I'm mentally unfit to handle the investigation.'

Flint didn't respond.

'You know she has made a grossly unfair accusation in that bit in the article about mental health issues. My fiancé and baby died. I took time off as any normal person would after such a loss, and when I returned to work, I proved myself to be a capable officer. I am not going to be sidelined in this investigation on account of this woman.'

'I'm on your side, Robyn. However, I'm stuck between a rock and a hard place here. I want to support you and I want you to head up the investigation, but she will have rattled the public with this article. I can't have the force lose face. I might have to consider setting up a unit to handle the investigation and let Tom Shearer head it. Let the dust settle. It doesn't mean I don't have faith in you, Robyn. I have to do what is seen to be right in the public's eye.'

'You would throw me off this investigation on account of this?' Robyn was incredulous. 'You know how focused I am. You of all people know how driven I am, and how I always get results. You pull me off this and I shall walk. I'll put in for an immediate transfer.'

'There's no need to be hasty about this.' Flint held up his hands.

Robyn threw him a cold glare, her heart thumping hard in her chest. 'I can assure you there is. My reputation is on the line here. This woman is casting aspersions on my ability to do my job, a job I love and one I'm bloody good at. Amy Walters is a jumped-up journalist who believes she can manipulate my investigation and sully my name while she's at it. She won't browbeat me. I ask for your support on this, sir. Back me up.'

'You see my dilemma, Robyn.'

'No, sir. I don't. This is my case and I want to see it through. Do I need to remind you who told me to leave Nathaniel alone? It's because I didn't bring him in for questioning that Amy has written this piece. Furthermore, I don't understand why you wouldn't allow me to interview him. You've never explained why he's been allowed to stay below the radar. Nor why he's been allowed to confide in you. I've never come across behaviour like this before. You've not even divulged the truth to me and I'm supposed to be in charge of this case. Nathaniel drove through Colton the night his son was murdered and he was seen driving through Abbots Bromley the evening Lucy Harding was killed. That's a big coincidence. You can't continue to keep my hands tied like this without good reason.' She kept her tone level in spite of the rage she was feeling. Flint was to blame for this situation.

Flint's head bobbed up and down slowly. 'Okay, okay. I'll talk to the press office and get them to handle this as sensitively as we can.'

'And you'll back my judgement?'

'You'll need to work fast. I won't be able to support my decision to leave you on this case for long if you don't return some results pronto. The superintendent will be breathing down my neck. Get back to your investigation, Robyn.'

'I insist on bringing Nathaniel in for questioning.'

'I told you he has an alibi for the night his son was murdered. He was having a late supper with a friend.'

'That's not good enough. Why won't you tell me who he was with?'

'It's a delicate situation. It's personal.'

'And this is a murder investigation.' Robyn was incredulous. 'Nothing is more important than trying to find out who killed his son and two other victims. The murderer is still out there.'

Flint looked her in the eye. 'Mr Jones-Kilby was with a married woman the night his son was killed. He does not want that to become common knowledge.'

Robyn rolled her eyes. 'Why didn't he just say so?'

'Because you'll want to interview her, and her husband will find out, and he's an extremely influential person.'

'Oh, for goodness sake. That's not reason enough. I want to speak to him and ask him about why his son accused him of murder two days before he died, and why he was seen driving through Abbots Bromley the night Dr Harding was killed.'

An indentation appeared between Flint's eyebrows. 'I'm not sure it's a good idea to question him. He has powerful friends.'

Robyn waited for him to speak further, and when he didn't she let out a sigh of exasperation. 'Are you saying he could go over your head here and maybe even get you and me fired? I don't care if he does. I have to be allowed to do my job. I owe it to the public.'

Flint appeared to take a lengthy breath before giving a curt nod. 'Then tread carefully.' He gestured for her to leave. She stomped along the corridor, fists still balled. She was torn between ringing Amy to scream at her and getting on with the investigation. By the time she reached the office, she'd decided. Amy could get screwed. Robyn had more than enough on her plate than get involved with Amy's games. She marched to the front of the office and coughed loudly to get everyone's attention.

'You probably know that Amy Walters is causing trouble. I want us to ignore it and push ahead with this investigation. We're under extra pressure now to get results. Anyone who can't manage to put in the extra time, please speak up. I'll understand if you have other commitments. If you don't speak up, I'll assume you're behind this 100%.' She glanced about the room. Everyone met her eyes.

'Good. Thank you. First off, I want Nathaniel brought in for questioning.'

Matt held up his hand. 'I'll do that.'

Robyn gave him a brief smile. 'Okay, team. Let's go.'

CHAPTER THIRTY-FIVE

THEN

His sister hadn't been waiting for him as usual when he finished school, even though her exams were over. She ought to have been sitting on the wall, but when he came outside, it was empty, and he had to run home to avoid getting swept up with a crowd of boys, led by Larson, who were headed in the same direction as him.

He enters the house and knows immediately something bad has happened. He creeps towards the sitting room where his sister, wet-eyed, is standing head held high, facing their mother. Father is standing in the corner of the room, head lowered. He never interferes in these matters.

'Pray for forgiveness, you cursed creature,' Mother shouts.

'No. I won't.'

'Jezebel!' roars Mother. 'Whore!'

'No!' his sister cries. 'I'm not. I love him. We're going to get married.'

Mother's face is a mask of fury. The boy edges closer to the doorframe, not daring to enter the room but too afraid to run away from the scene unfolding in front of him. His sister stands her ground and speaks defiantly.

'I'm not going to repent.'

Mother's eyes blaze with anger and she waves her arms wildly. 'You have sinned. Evil pours from you, you filthy creature. You are not my daughter. You are a wicked, immoral being that has infiltrated the body of my child. You have defiled her and must be punished.'

Her hands shoot out and grab hold of his sister's hair, tugging it hard so she screams in pain and drops to the floor. Mother doesn't let go. She pulls harder and drags her across the carpet, her howls increasing.

Mother catches sight of the boy. 'Get up,' she says to his sister, who drags herself to her feet, holding her head. The boy can see blood trickling down her face from where hair has been ripped from her scalp.

'You must face your punishment.'

'This is madness,' his sister says, between sobs. 'You can't do this to me.'

'Be quiet,' Mother shouts. 'Boy, go to your room.'

The boy stares at his sister, who nods briefly. He turns and scurries upstairs, where he looks out of his window. He watches as his mother marches his sister towards the shed and pushes her through the open door.

He sees the crows circling the treetops in the distance and he cries. He waits and he watches to make sure the crows don't land on the shed roof, until it is too dark to see any more.

CHAPTER THIRTY-SIX

DAY SEVEN – SUNDAY, 11 JUNE, AFTERNOON

Robyn's first task was to continue searching through the images she'd been looking at back home. There was something about the way the bodies were positioned that bugged her: Jordan hanging from a pole, his guts ripped open; Owen stabbed through the ear and the screwdriver left on show; and Lucy run over several times by her own car. It was as if the killer wanted to make a statement.

Matt tapped lightly on the office door. 'He's here and he's not happy.'

'I don't give a shit about that. I'm not happy either,' said Robyn, pushing back her chair and preparing to do battle with Nathaniel.

Nathaniel, in an apricot sweater and jeans, was leaning against the wall opposite the interview room door, his arms folded. His lips were pressed tightly together and he maintained his steady gaze as Robyn walked in with Matt. His lawyer, a middle-aged man in a smart two-piece suit, a crisp white shirt and dark blue tie, rose to shake their hands.

'Thank you for coming in,' she said. 'Mr Jones-Kilby, would you like to join your lawyer?'

Nathaniel glared at her. 'No. I would not.'

'We might be here a while, sir, and it would be more comfortable for you if you sat down.'

'I want you to know I object to being rounded up and brought here. I'll be putting in an official complaint to your superiors.'

'I quite understand. Unfortunately, I have to ask you questions that are relevant to our enquiries. New evidence has been brought to our attention. In light of it, I had no choice but to ask for your cooperation.'

Nathaniel let out a lengthy release of air.

'Please take a seat and I'll be as brief as possible.'

He released his arms and ambled across to the chair, hesitating before sitting down. 'I mean it, DI Carter. I'll be talking to your superiors about this.'

'Mr Jones-Kilby, you were spotted driving through Abbots Bromley on Thursday, 8 June, and I would like to know why you were in the village that night.'

He spluttered a response. 'None of your damn business.'

'I'm afraid it is our business. Please answer the question. A woman was murdered in the village that evening.'

'I didn't kill her.'

'Could you please explain why you were driving through the village at that time?'

'I was visiting somebody.'

'Who?'

'Again, it is none of your concern.'

'Would this be the same person you were visiting at around the time your son was murdered?' Robyn's voice rose as she spoke. Nathaniel flinched. 'Sir?'

'Yes,' came the reply.

'To eliminate you from our enquiries, I'll need to confirm this with that person. Who was it you were visiting?'

'I'm not prepared to divulge that information. I want to speak to DCI Flint.'

'That's not possible. I would like to remind you, you are obliged to tell us. If you withhold any evidence or impede our enquiries it is an offence.'

Nathaniel snorted. 'I want to speak to DCI Flint.'

'Mr Jones-Kilby, you are turning this into a difficult situation. We could resolve this very quickly if only you'd cooperate.'

She received silence as a response. She'd revisit the question in a while. He couldn't keep the information from her. 'Have it your own way, but you're making this problematic for yourself. I'd like to go back to Friday, 2 June. Jordan visited you at the NJK Property offices. According to your secretary, who overheard the conversation, he accused you of being a cheater, liar and murderer. Two days later he phoned a newspaper journalist asking to meet her to give her some vital information. What do you have to say about the incident on that Friday?'

'I don't know what he wanted to say to the journalist. However, it wouldn't have been about that unfortunate episode. It was no more than an angry outburst that was typical of him. He's said similar to me before. Jordan was prone to bad moods and often spoke without thinking. After the death of his mother, he became especially antagonistic towards me. He'd behaved that way before – many times.'

'Yet Jordan was sure you were involved in a murder – his mother's murder. He was so sure he hired a private investigator to look into it.'

He let out an exasperated sigh. 'He was wrong, okay?'

'I spoke to the private investigator Jordan hired, Ross Cunningham, and he told me there were grounds for suspecting you of murdering your wife: not least, you were overheard making a phone call during which you asked somebody to "make sure she's sorted once and for all". Less than an hour later, your wife was dead. Jordan believed you were complicit. Did he uncover further proof and challenge you about it last Friday?'

Nathaniel threw a look at his lawyer. 'No comment.'

'It really isn't in your interest to stay silent. We have to find out who murdered your son. If it is somehow linked to what happened to your wife, we need to know. DCI Flint won't be able to help you once we present all the evidence we've amassed. And, should any of this get into the hands of the press, it could prove disastrous for your business and any future dealings you have lined up.'

The lawyer said something to him in a whisper. Robyn couldn't hear what but Nathaniel shrugged and then spoke to her. 'I didn't murder my wife. I told Jordan years ago, when he first started hurling crazy accusations at me, that I had nothing to do with Sue's death. Of course, I couldn't tell him the complete truth. He was a very sensitive soul – too sensitive in many ways.'

'Could you elaborate, please?'

Nathaniel paused to collect his thoughts, and then with a serious expression, continued. 'Jordan was his mother's boy. He simply adored her. In his eyes Sue was perfect. Truth was, she wasn't perfect. In many ways, she was a lousy mother. She started drinking when he was a baby. I didn't spot the early warning signs – the depression, the lethargy. I was too tied up with the company to see what was happening to her. It was only when it began to get out of hand that I woke up to what was happening. When he was no more than a toddler, I'd come home from the office and find she'd forgotten to make his tea, or bathe him, or he'd still be up at ten and she'd be comatose in a chair. You don't need the full picture. Fact was she had a drink problem.

'I persuaded her to see a psychiatrist and give the drink up, and for a few years she eased up. Then Jordan started at primary school and she began drinking more heavily. He, of course, had no idea of what was going on. In his eyes, his mum was perfect. She'd let him eat whatever he wanted and stay up late watching films with a twelve or sixteen age rating, while she drank. She was the reason he got into all that comic superhero stuff. She'd get pissed and pretend they were both superheroes and then they'd charge about the sitting room like a pair of idiots, jumping off settees and pretending they were saving the universe. She was quite crazy after a few drinks. I'd come home and find furniture, windows and ornaments broken after they'd been playing one of their stupid games. She never told him off. Always took his side. She was the good cop and I was the bad cop in our house. In the end, once she started taking drugs too, I had to take matters into my own hands; I sent him to private school out of harm's way and told Sue to clean her shit up.

'She tried but I was rarely at home. The business had taken off and I had to devote more time to it. She got bored. She'd hang out with her friends all like her – bored, spoilt housewives with nothing to do but spend money on shopping, lunches out and recreational drugs. The drinking got out of hand again. This time, I told her we couldn't go on. She pleaded with me to help her, so I paid for her to spend a few weeks at a top clinic to dry out. When she came out she wanted things to return to how they'd been before, but I'd moved on. I'd found somebody else – my secretary at the time, Evelyn Morris – as it happened. We kept the marriage going, but we were both unhappy in it. It was a sham. Sue eventually found out about the affair and told Jordan. He was already struggling with his own personal problems at the time. He'd been expelled from school and was making a hash of his life. The news messed him up good and proper, and to cap it all, Sue turned him against me. She wanted to take him with her when she left me but I refused. Said I'd drag her through the courts to prove she wasn't capable of looking after him.' He stared into the distance, face lined with sadness at the memory.

'I broke up with Evelyn and she moved away. It didn't help matters. Jordan couldn't accept Sue had died in a lousy accident. He thought there was more to it. He was in denial for a long time and then he became angry. I tried so hard to make it up to him. I did everything I could, I even bought a house for him to live in, invited him to join the firm, begged him to consider it, but he turned his back on me. He didn't want to know me. However, he was my son and I loved him. I would have done anything to gain his trust and love.'

'Can I ask you about his expulsion from school? What happened?'

He sighed heavily and his forehead creased as he spoke. 'I paid the school to stay quiet. I suppose now he's gone, it doesn't matter if the truth comes out. Drugs. Jordan was caught handling drugs. It was an unfortunate incident. Jordan didn't find making friends easy. He'd always been such a mother's boy and lacked somewhat in confidence. He struggled with his contemporaries, but there was one kid he got along okay with – called Sean Corbett. Sean's parents were pretty well off. Dad worked in the United Arab Emirates in oil exploration. Sean was spoilt rotten. He got into drugs and had a thing going with a local dealer who'd drive into the village near the school. Sean would send Jordan down to the village to collect the drugs, thinking no one would ever suspect Jordan. On the day in question, Jordan got caught coming back onto the school grounds and was hauled in front of the headmaster. Jordan didn't tell him or me the truth. He kept silent for his friend's sake. It was only afterwards – about six months later, when Sean dropped him and no longer bothered with him – Jordan told Sue what had happened. By then it was too late to go back and point the finger of blame at Sean. He'd left school and gone to join his father abroad.'

'Did you arrange for Jordan to be interviewed about it? I read a piece in the paper about rich kids going bad and he was interviewed.'

Nathaniel nodded. 'I tried to talk some sense into him, and convince him to use the opportunity to come clean and say what really happened, but he refused. Said he was loyal to his friends. Stupid lad,' he said, heavy with sorrow. 'I had nothing to do with his death. I did not kill Jordan because he was angry with me that

Friday. He'd been angry with me many times before. And I did not kill him because he accused me of murdering his mother.' Nathaniel rested his hands in his lap. 'Satisfied now?'

'One more question about the last time you saw your wife. Who did you ring soon after she walked off that day at the restaurant? You were overheard and I'm afraid what was said might incriminate you.'

He heaved the sigh of a man tired of life. 'The phone call was to her doctor. I asked him to check her back into the clinic. She still needed help. She drank heavily at lunch and wouldn't listen to me when I asked her to stop. Much of the argument overheard that day was down to me trying to stop her drinking. I told the doctor to sort Sue out, once and for all. I can give you his name. He may still be able to confirm it, even after this length of time.'

'Thank you, sir. I'm sorry to have put you through this.'

He shrugged. 'And for the record, I had no idea Sue intended driving back north to her house. She told me she was staying at a hotel. I'd have confiscated her car keys if I'd had any idea. It would have saved a lot of misery.'

'I'd like to ask you about Owen Falcon, if I may? He went to your house last Wednesday to change a smoke detector. I wondered if you'd spoken to him while he was there.'

'No. I was at work. My cleaner let him in. You'll have to ask her about him – Sheila Marchington. She's worked for me for years.'

'Could you give Sergeant Higham her details in a minute, please? What did you and Owen discuss on the Tuesday he brought the smoke detector to the office?'

'We didn't discuss anything. I asked him to go to my house to fit the smoke detector for me and arranged for him to do it the following day.'

'And finally, I have to ask you again, Mr Jones-Kilby, why did you drive through Abbots Bromley on Thursday evening?'

Nathaniel's eyes flashed. 'I've already told you more than you deserve to know. You ought to be hunting for my son's killer, not making my life any more miserable than it already is. I've lost my son. We may have had our differences but he was my son. I want to know who did that to him and I want to know soon. I'm going to be laying him to rest next week. Think about that when you're racing about dragging in people, willy-nilly.'

Robyn stared at the man opposite with his chin jutting in defiance. 'I'm afraid you have to tell us or we won't be able to eliminate you from our enquiries.'

The lawyer shifted in his seat and spoke. 'My client has already told your superior officer where he was the night his son was murdered. He will tell DCI Flint his whereabouts on Thursday. I'm sure that will be sufficient to vindicate him.'

'I am heading this investigation, not DCI Flint, and I am asking Mr Jones-Kilby to explain his movements on Thursday evening.'

Nathaniel made a soft hissing sound before speaking. 'I was visiting a friend in Abbots Bromley – a married friend – the same friend I was having supper with the night my son was murdered. She will be able to vouch for me, and DCI Flint is aware of who she is. More than that I'm not prepared to say unless you wish to charge me. However, I don't believe you have grounds for that and you certainly wouldn't want to incur the wrath of Rupert McIntosh, with whom I am very good friends.'

Rupert McIntosh was the chief constable of Staffordshire Police. No doubt Nathaniel had threatened Flint with the same, and Flint, having only been at the station a few months, would not want to rock the boat. Robyn supressed a sigh. Both she and Flint had been muzzled because of an extramarital affair. Whatever Nathaniel's reasons for wanting it to remain a secret, she still had to run her investigation.

'I'll ask DCI Flint to speak to you.'

He returned a curt nod of his head and then looked ahead, ignoring her as she crossed the room and left. Outside she drew a long breath. Nathaniel had no motive for killing his son. Amy had been wrong. Robyn wrestled with the desire to ring Amy and tear her off a strip for her article before deciding against it. She had more pressing matters to deal with. She walked towards DCI Flint's office with determination, head held high. She would ask him to talk to Nathaniel and then she'd have to trust her superior's judgement and hope they were right to eliminate the man as a suspect. That would leave her with one big problem: finding the murderer before her superiors decided she had to be removed from the case.

CHAPTER THIRTY-SEVEN

DAY SEVEN – SUNDAY, 11 JUNE, EVENING

It seemed Harry and his assistant Laura were also working late. Harry rang Robyn just after eight to tell her of their findings.

'Lucy Harding was struck by a hard object on the side of her face before she was run over. The grazing on her flesh, along with some red-brick dust residue, have led us to conclude she was hit by a house brick.'

'Did that kill her, Harry?'

'No. That probably incapacitated her long enough for her murderer to take her car keys, climb into her car and run her over, repeatedly. She died of internal injuries – primarily punctured lungs from crushed ribs. I have a full report. Laura will drop it off for you in a while if you'd like it tonight.'

'If she doesn't mind.'

'She doesn't. She goes past the station on her way home.'

'Harry, do you think the same person who killed Jordan and Owen is behind this murder too? The killer used different methods to dispatch them?'

Harry didn't hesitate before speaking. 'I'd say there's a strong possibility the same person is responsible for all these deaths. The level of planning and the complexity of each crime – those must have been conjured up by a twisted mind. Laura studied profiling as part of her course. Ask her when she comes over. She'll be there in ten minutes.'

Harry was true to his word. Ten minutes later, Laura was shown into the office. She held a large manila file which she offered to Robyn with a tired smile.

'Shit way to spend a Sunday,' she said.

'I had nothing else planned,' Robyn replied with a weak grin. 'You want one of our infamously dreadful coffees?' She pointed at the coffee machine in the corner of the office.

Laura shook her head. 'I've drunk too much coffee today, thanks.'

'Harry said Lucy was hit by a brick. Forensics didn't find any bricks at the scene of the crime.'

'The extent of injury to her left cheekbone, combined with the markings on her flesh and the brick dust residue, substantiate that theory. Her body had been crushed but remarkably most of her face was untouched except for the damage caused by the brick. She'd have died soon after her ribs punctured her lungs. We concluded that was probably during the first attempt to run her over. However, her killer ran over her another couple of times. We examined the tyre marks on her body, and thanks to the direction of the thread patterns evident on her body and in the blood left behind at the scene, we concluded the driver had attempted to squash every part of her body – apart from the head. There was huge damage to her organs and a massive amount of internal haemorrhaging. She couldn't have survived such an attack.'

'Harry told me you studied criminal profiling?'

'Only for a term. It was offered as an extra on my course. It was fascinating; however, I prefer working with actual evidence rather than theoretical.'

'What sort of person do you think we're dealing with?'

'I'm not expert enough in this field and I'm sure I'd be telling you nothing you haven't already considered.'

'Nevertheless, I'd appreciate your thoughts,' said Robyn.

'I'd say you're looking for somebody who's very clever – clever enough to plan and execute these elaborate crimes without being spotted, and without leaving any traces.' Laura stared at the ceiling for a minute. 'I also think whoever did it is very angry. That person's harbouring a genuine hate for their victims. They've not acted in a red mist moment. They've been methodical. For example, the attack on Jordan wasn't a frenzied stabbing. Somebody had hold enough over him to make him walk those final steps to the middle of Top Field, and when they killed him, they aimed accurately and only struck once. They took time to hang his body on the scarecrow's post and position it. They were unhurried and confident they wouldn't be spotted.' She closed her eyes and thought some more. Robyn listened intently to her soft voice.

'That same person attacked Owen, knocked him out and then again took time to hammer the screwdriver into Owen's ear. They might even have ensured he stayed alive long enough to experience the pain. They did the same with Lucy. They could have crushed her skull with the brick but they didn't. They could have run over her once and still killed her, but they didn't. They ran over her three times and each time took a slightly different direction. It looked as if the car had trampled over her. Then, I believe they took the brick they used to stun her and either kept it as a trophy or disposed of it elsewhere.'

Robyn rested her elbows on her desk and bounced the fingertips together thoughtfully. 'You've voiced my suspicions perfectly. I think the murderer might be sending a message.'

'Any idea what?'

'Not yet but I don't want another death on my hands before I establish what it might be.'

'They're confident and dangerous – they're a risk-taker. They're a calculating murderer,' said Laura.

'And cold-hearted.'

Laura agreed. 'Without a doubt. However, your killer could be psychopathic and you'd never know if you came across him or her what they were truly capable of.'

'That's what frightens me most. That I've already interviewed our killer and not seen through them.'

Laura offered a kindly smile. 'I'm sure you'll unmask them. From what I've heard, you'll most certainly track them down.'

'I wish everyone had your faith in me,' said Robyn with a sigh. 'Me included.'

'*Nil desperandum*,' said Laura. 'You'll crack it.' She gave a quiet laugh. 'Listen to me. I sound like your number-one fangirl.' She blushed.

The corners of Robyn's mouth lifted. *Nil desperandum* was one of Harry's favourite expressions. His protégé was clearly taking all his teachings to heart. 'I'll take the ego massaging today. Thanks for the report.'

'Sure. I had to drive past. Seemed silly not to drop it off. Not good bedtime reading but it might help you get a better picture of who you're dealing with. I'd better leave you to it.'

With Laura gone and only the droning of the strip light to keep her company, Robyn read through the pathology report, then pulled out Jordan's and Owen's and read them again.

Robyn was still struck by the way each victim had been dispatched. There was reason behind it – what could it be? Thinking about Jordan and the way his body had been arranged, crucifix-style, she google-imaged Christ on a cross. As she scoured through the images she wondered if she shouldn't get a professional opinion on the matter. There might just be some link to religion. She thought of Benjamin Burroughs, a professor of philosophical theology and religious studies at Stafford University. She and Ross had done some private investigative work for him in 2016 when he'd asked for a nanny camera to be placed in his office, convinced one of the students was breaking in and stealing question papers. He might be able to assist her.

Using the Stafford University contact page, she was able to find Benjamin's number and was pleased when he picked up the phone call. She reminded him of who she was and how they'd met. He sounded delighted to have heard from her.

'What can I do for you, Robyn?'

'I need some assistance with a case I'm working on.' She explained her theory to Benjamin.

'Would it be accceptable for me to come to the station and view these photographs?' he asked.

'It would. When would you be free?'

'Are you there at the moment?'

'I am.'

'Then I can be with you within a few minutes. I'm on campus, not far away.'

Benjamin was exactly as she remembered him. He wore a small stud in the right ear of his suntanned face, and his grey hair was pulled back in a loose ponytail, giving him the impression of an ageing rock star. He sat opposite Robyn in her office, a cup of steaming tea in front of him, chatting as if they were old friends.

Robyn took a sip of her drink, winced and blew on the scorching liquid. 'I'd watch out for that if I were you,' she said. 'Bit too hot. I think the machine is playing up again.'

Benjamin gave a deep laugh. His Canadian accent hadn't been tempered over the years. His beefy hands cupped the mug as he took a slurp. 'Ah, can't beat a nice cup of tea no matter what time of day it is,' he said with a contented sigh.

'I really appreciate you coming in on a Sunday evening to help us out.'

'My pleasure. I don't have many students to deal with this time of year and my brain could do with a workout. What's this all about? You've certainly piqued my interest.'

Robyn showed him the photograph of Jordan hanging from the scarecrow's pole and explained what she'd already found online. Benjamin adjusted a pair of thin wire glasses and lifted the photograph to better see it, all the while nodding at Robyn's words.

'I think you're right on this,' he said finally.

Robyn then described what had happened to Lucy. 'Is there anything in the bible that tells us of a murder where somebody was trampled or squashed to death?'

Benjamin nodded gravely. 'The bible contains several grisly murders, none of which could be remotely connected to your case. However, the story of Jehu and Jezebel might hold some relevance.'

Robyn leant on the table, drinking in the details.

'There's a slight possibility your murderer knew of that story and felt the need to re-enact it – you can see he or she's not following it to the letter.'

Robyn persisted. She was onto something significant. She told him about Owen. It was almost ten but Benjamin wasn't in a hurry to leave. He'd brought his laptop with him and opened it on the desk.

'Now this does sound familiar,' he said.

As the strip light continued to hum in the background, Benjamin's fingers flew over the keyboard, dragging up the information Robyn needed: relevant passages from the bible and pictures.

'Right, what have we got here?' he asked, clicking through the images Robyn had been looking at.

'They're paintings of Christ on a cross. I saw one in the Louvre, years ago – this one,' she said, pointing at the relevant image. 'I can't find a picture where Christ is hanging in a similar position to the victim. In none of them is his stomach cut open and I can't see any blood on ground. Do you know of one?'

'I can't say I do.' He studied the photograph of Jordan again and noted the positioning of the body. 'You think the sheet was relevant?'

'I'm pretty sure it is. It wasn't laid haphazardly, you know, thrown down to catch the blood. It was almost like it had been loosely ruched.' She took his frown to mean he hadn't understood. 'Gathered in deliberate folds. At least that was my impression. I thought it looked like red waves at his feet.'

'Like waves, waves in a sea of blood,' muttered Benjamin. 'I see what you mean.'

Robyn waited while he stared more closely at the photograph. 'Your victim's head appears to be held back with a strap.'

'There was a belt holding his neck in position.'

'Okay. He was found in a field, right?'

'Strapped to a pole used for scarecrows.'

'And his stomach had been cut open?'

'That's right.'

Benjamin thought for a moment. 'This reminds me of a different picture: a fifteenth-century fresco of Judas – you know, the traitor.'

Using the search engine, he typed in the name Judas Iscariot, and clicked on the results. Robyn watched as he poured through the sites and images, finally sitting back with a small smile of satisfaction. 'I thought as much.'

Robyn looked at the screen and at the painting of a man hanging by his neck with entrails on display.

'This is the one.'

'There are similarities,' Robyn said. 'But he isn't in the same position as Jordan. He's hanging from a tree, and what about the sheet we found?'

'I have an explanation for that. You gave me the key words that got me thinking: field and blood and waves.'

He brought up a website that shared the theories of how Judas died. Robyn nodded slowly. They were onto something. Benjamin held up a finger and said, 'While we're on this, why not tell me how your other victims died?'

By the time they'd finished, Robyn was in no doubt the murders were related and certainly committed by the same killer. She thanked Benjamin and saw him out of the station, watching as his motorbike eased onto the road and listening as it growled into the distance. She returned to the office, printed out what she needed and prepared to go home to grab a few hours' sleep.

Laura had not only brought her a pathology report; she'd provided Robyn with enough information to make headway. Flint needn't think about reassigning her to another case. She was all over this and she would flush out the killer. No newspaper articles or threats would stop her now. She was close and getting closer.

CHAPTER THIRTY-EIGHT

DAY EIGHT – MONDAY, 12 JUNE, MORNING

Robyn was well prepared for the 7 a.m. meeting and was keen to share her thoughts. Benjamin Burroughs had also joined the team. She introduced him to everyone, passed out the pages she'd copied from the websites Benjamin had shown her and began immediately.

'Jordan was found hanging from a post in a field. At first, we thought he'd been left there deliberately to be mistaken for a scarecrow and to allow birds to destroy much of his body. For a brief while, we even suspected it was to hinder identification of his body. I was always curious about the sheet in front of the body, which we thought was to attract crows. As you see from the photo on page one, it's been set out at the foot of the post and was, as we know, covered in Jordan's blood. I now believe the killer positioned Jordan's body and the sheet for a difference purpose. The way Jordan's body had been positioned reminded me of a religious painting so I asked the professor for his opinion. Professor Burroughs?'

Benjamin gave a slight cough before beginning. 'The painting that Robyn is thinking of is *Christ on the Cross* by El Greco, but I was struck by the other identifiers: the way Jordan's head was held in position by the belt, for example. In most pictures of Christ on the cross, his head is hanging to one side. Also, the wound to your victim's abdomen, and finally, the sheet at the foot of the post conjured up an image of another death in the bible and a different religious painting. I believe the killer was arranging a tableau – one he'd either seen or fabricated in his mind – of the death of Judas Iscariot, who betrayed Christ, rather than of Christ himself.

'There are two versions concerning the circumstances of Judas's death: one is that he was hanged for his betrayal to Jesus, and his guts eaten; the second is that he fell and his guts spilled out over what is called the field of blood. I think your murderer set the scene to bring together both accounts, with the sheet representing the field of blood.'

On cue, Robyn picked up an enlarged photograph of a picture portraying a man hanging from a tree with his abdomen cut open and insides on display, and a hairy demon tugging a small Judas from it, and stuck it onto the whiteboard.

She took over from Benjamin. 'This might seem a little too deep or that I'm going off-piste, but bear with me. This is a famous painting by Giovanni Canavesio of a demon stealing Judas's soul. I've given this further thought since Professor Burroughs and I spoke about it last night. Many people associate crows with evil or death. It's possible our murderer did and might have chosen that spot deliberately, and attempted to encourage the birds to flock there to attack Jordan's body. When I look at this picture, I see similarities to it and Jordan's death: the field of blood, the positioning of the body and the demon pulling at Judas's intestines.'

Mitz spoke. 'And were the crows supposed to represent the demon in this picture?'

Robyn shrugged. 'I'm throwing it out there. It seems possible. What's more certain is that the killer created a striking visual scene of Jordan hanging from a stake with his guts spilled onto a field of blood. The more I consider this, the more I'm convinced our killer was trying to copy the scene in this painting.'

Matt scratched at his chin, deep in thought. 'Guv, do you think the killer felt Jordan had betrayed them, like Judas did Christ?'

'Professor, can you throw any light on that?' Robyn looked towards the man, his face screwed in thought.

'That's a valid point and one you should consider. I have an additional point to make about the field of blood. According to one story in the bible, it was so called, not purely because of the blood shed on it, but because it was purchased with money Judas received for betraying Jesus.'

Matt let out a low whistle. 'Top Field, where Jordan was found, was also purchased. It was purchased for the development of the HS2 line.'

There were nods of agreement and a general murmur from the team.

'This gets weirder and weirder,' said David.

'Which brings me onto Owen Falcon, who was found in his garage with a screwdriver protruding from his ear. I'd like you to look at the second sheet, a photocopy of a painting Professor Burroughs found for me.'

Each member of the team shuffled the papers and stared at Artemisia Gentileschi's painting entitled *Jael and Sisera*, of a woman holding a metal tent peg aloft, ready to drive it into a sleeping man's ear. Anna gasped in astonishment.

Benjamin spoke again, his voice strong and clear, as if addressing students at a lecture. 'This is a painting of a biblical character – Jael. The passage that refers to this murder comes from Judges 4 and 5.' He read the quote below the image:

'She put her hand to the tent peg and her right hand to the workmen's mallet; she struck Sisera a blow, she crushed his head, she shattered and pierced his temple. He sank, he fell, he lay still at her feet; at her feet he sank, he fell; where he sank, there he fell dead.'

'Shiii…it!' said Mitz, making the word stretch into two syllables.

Robyn nodded. 'Exactly. Our murderer is a bible reader, maybe very religious, maybe just obsessed with gory deaths in the bible.

He's replicating the murders or deaths from the bible, using modern-day tools.'

David asked, 'Could we be looking for a female and not a male killer, then?'

'We could be searching for either, or both. Take a look at the third sheet. It's some text taken from the bible.'

There was silence punctuated by another low whistle from Matt. 'Fuck me. This is one creepy killer.'

Benjamin looked at Robyn, who nodded for him to continue. 'According to the biblical story, Jezebel was once a powerful queen of Israel until an army captain called Jehu led a coup d'état on her royal house and killed her. The manner of her death is significant: she was thrown out of her palace window and then trampled to death by chariot horses driven over her still-living body. She was left to rot, and stray dogs consumed her corpse.'

Robyn spoke. 'The similarity to Lucy's death is alarming: she was struck by a brick and fell to the floor, and then her car was run over her body numerous times until she was dead as if she'd been trampled to death.'

'This is creeping me out,' said Anna. 'Why choose these methods?'

Robyn grimaced. 'I don't know. I can only assume the perp believed all his victims deserved to die this way. I can't draw any real correlations between those killed in the bible and our perp's victims. Benjamin?'

He shook his head. 'Jezebel died defending her lands. Judas died after he betrayed Jesus. Sisera was killed because he was trying to conquer lands, and Jael had the honour of killing him through trickery. I can't tell you any more than that.'

Matt made a suggestion. 'Maybe our perp has a large ego and believes he's clever too – that he can trick and outwit us.'

'Lots of killers believe they're beyond the reach of the law, but they make mistakes in the end,' said Mitz.

Robyn joined the conversation. 'I agree, but I don't want to wait until this one slips up. We haven't time. We have to work out why he killed Jordan, Owen and Lucy.'

'You mentioned land a few times. Those guys in the bible were defending land and Judas bought land. Could this possibly be related to the HS2 or even Nathaniel? He's bought up loads of land and built new housing on it?'

Robyn rested her palms on the nearest desk and looked at Anna, who'd asked the question. 'It might seem that way, but we also have to consider our other leads. Fact is we don't have much time to work this out. I have a nasty suspicion our perp will act again. He's confident, cool-headed and clever. Whatever the reason behind his actions, he'll strike again, and we have to stop him before he does.'

CHAPTER THIRTY-NINE

THEN

The boy is very excited. He's going to stay overnight with Oswald, a new friend. Mother and Father approve of Oswald and his parents, who are new to the area and have been coming to prayer meetings. It's Oswald's sixth birthday and they've invited the boy to come over for the night. He's never been away from home for a night before.

His sister is pleased for him and smiles. It's the first time she's smiled since her punishment. She's been so different since she was released from the shed. She was kept in there over three weeks. By the end of week two even his father had pleaded with his mother to release her and said she'd served her punishment, but his mother was adamant. She had to stay the duration. She was a sinner.

He'd watched as his mother had trundled down the path and taken food to his sister each morning. She'd unlock the door, push the tray in and close it again without speaking. Apart from the last morning — then, she'd opened the door and stopped in her tracks, dropping the tray to the floor. She'd gone inside the shed and for a moment the boy was terrified the crows had come during the night and murdered his sister. His mother had come running back inside the house, calling for Father, who'd rushed to the shed with her. They'd re-emerged a few minutes later, his sister between them, their arms supporting her as she walked the path. Her white dress was stained red with blood and she was crying.

She'd stayed in bed for several days. The boy had visited her but she'd not wanted to talk.

'Did the crows get into the shed?' he'd asked.

She'd shaken her head sadly. 'No.'

'But the blood?' he'd said.

'It wasn't the crows. The crows didn't attack me. They wouldn't have anyway. Now leave me to sleep.'

When she'd finally got up and left her bedroom, it was like she was empty. Mother had killed the evil inside her but not before it had eaten some of his sister's spirit.

'What time are you going?' she asks now, helping him to choose between his blue and green jumpers for the event.

'They're coming to collect me at four, after school. We're going to the cinema and then we're going bowling. There are six of us staying over at the house. We're going to sleep in the same room.'

She ruffles his hair with affection. 'That'll be such fun.'

'What will you do while I'm away?' he says, suddenly concerned that she'll be lonely without him in the house.

'I'm going out too.'

'Where to?'

'Nosey,' she says with a laugh. 'Nowhere interesting. Just out for the night. Now, are you taking these pyjamas with you?' she asks, holding up a pair with space rockets on them.

He nods. It's going to be exciting to stay at another house.

CHAPTER FORTY

DAY EIGHT – MONDAY, 12 JUNE, MORNING

David put down the phone and spoke. 'Nathaniel's cleaner, Sheila Marchington, says she let Owen into the house to change the smoke detector. She was upstairs vacuuming most of the time he was there, though she made him a cup of tea before he left. They talked about her nephew – he also plays for the Blithfield Wanderers. She didn't notice anything unusual about Owen's behaviour, although he did ask about a photograph of Nathaniel and MP Stewart Broughton, taken in Lichfield at a function last year, that was on the wall by the front door. He seemed quite interested in it.'

'I wonder why.'

'According to Sheila, it was the original of a picture that accompanied an article in the *Stafford Gazette*. Want me to get a copy of it?'

'Yes. Let's see if we can work out why he was drawn to it.'

Mitz stuck his head round the door. 'You ready to head off to Pharmacals Healthcare, guv?'

She took one look at the jumbled Post-it notes on her desk and nodded. A trip out might help clarify matters.

The security at Pharmacals Healthcare was as strict as Robyn remembered and it took quite a few minutes before they were allowed entry. They pulled up outside the main building in a wide space marked for visitors.

'Big Brother is alive and well here,' muttered Mitz, catching sight of a young man who was observing their movements.

A slim man in his thirties, dressed in a tight-fitting suit, white shirt and green tie, met them at the entrance. 'DI Carter,' he said, holding out a pale hand. 'I'm Neil Hardcastle, head of operations.' He guided them towards a seating area consisting of three tables and chairs that reminded Robyn of café furniture. They sat around the first table.

Mitz spoke up. 'We're investigating the death of a young man who managed deliveries from here – Jordan Kilby. He worked for Speedy Logistics. We understand he collected deliveries from you on a regular basis.'

'Ah yes. We use Speedy Logistics for all our local NHS and private clinic deliveries. They're very efficient. We have a good working relationship with the company. Jordan was one of two Speedy drivers we used.'

'Is there a reason you stuck to the same drivers?' Mitz said.

Neil's dark eyebrows knitted together. 'We prefer to use drivers who understand how we operate and who have passed stringent background checks. As you can see, we have an enormous site here – eight warehouses, each half a million square feet in size, and filled with stock – and everything has to run like clockwork. Our delivery drivers must arrive at their appointed slot time, load up and be out of the premises within a given time. You may have noticed lorries parked in the layby down the road from here. They'll be waiting for their allocated time. It's all worked out to the last minute, you see? On top of that, it's easy to get lost, and go to the wrong delivery area – we have thirty different areas, depending on what's being dropped off or collected. We don't need any confusion – schedules are tight. Also, it's more convenient for our security staff to deal with PH-approved drivers. We vet all our staff and our drivers carefully. Imagine doing checks on different drivers every day? It'd be a nightmare.'

'I expect you have some very valuable stock.'

Neil nodded. 'Our stock runs into millions of pounds. Hence, we're extremely careful who we employ. Some of the stock is exceedingly valuable.'

'Would Jordan have delivered such drugs to local clinics?'

'Not very often. The most expensive drugs – cancer-treating drugs, methadone for ex-heroin addicts and suchlike – only go to the private clinics, usually in London or other major cities. They're far too costly for the NHS to fund. The most expensive, the rarest and potentially dangerous drugs are kept securely in what we call "the vault" in warehouse G. The vault is monitored by CCTV cameras at all times, both inside and outside. Nothing leaves the warehouse without being signed for, and any prescriptions ordered by clinics have to be signed for on delivery. We run a tight operation here.'

'Are you saying it would be impossible to steal any drugs?'

Neil gave Mitz a solemn stare. 'I'm not saying stuff doesn't disappear. It's impossible to monitor everything and everybody, but we do what we can and we operate CCTV cameras in every warehouse. Each warehouse also has its own highly trained security guard who has also had to pass strict background checks. They perform random checks on the staff. It's impossible to get into the vault where we store our most valuable medication and drugs. Only the warehouse supervisors have the two keys and codes to it, and the codes are changed every month.'

'So, you think it would be difficult to steal those particular drugs?'

'Extremely difficult. Not only have the supervisors in warehouse G been through the most stringent of background checks, they've worked for us for many years. They too are subject to daily checks for stolen goods and the vault is monitored 24/7 by CCTV. Any suspicious activity would be spotted. They're not going to be able to walk out of there with so much as an aspirin without being found out.'

'We'd like to talk to anybody who had dealings with Mr Kilby if possible.'

'I'll check upstairs to see who he usually reported to. Bear with me.' He left them sitting at the table and took the stairs two at a time.

Robyn watched him peel off to an office at the top of the open staircase and at the same time caught sight of Rebecca going in the opposite direction. She called out, 'Rebecca.'

Rebecca stopped and turned her head to see who was calling, and peering through the stair risers, caught sight of Robyn. She descended to speak to her. Robyn was struck by how tired she looked. Her eyes were bloodshot. She was reminded of the first time she'd met the woman, dressed in bold colours with shimmering eye shadow and glossy hair. The woman in front of her wore a dark, shapeless cardigan and plain skirt, was make-up free and looked defeated. She'd changed greatly in the week since Jordan's death. Robyn wondered if that's what people had seen when they'd looked at her two years ago, after she lost Davies – a woman whose spirit had been shattered and who was lost in a world of pain. Mitz was staring at the entrance, where a lorry driver was leaning out of his cab talking to the security guard. Robyn spoke quietly to Rebecca.

'You okay? Sure you've not come back to work too soon?'

Rebecca gave a nod. 'I had to return. The rent needs paying. I have to carry on. It's been harder than I imagined.'

'I suppose there are memories of Jordan here too.'

Rebecca bit her bottom lip, turning it white before speaking. 'I sometimes caught sight of him when he pulled up at the entrance. Now and then, he'd spot me in the office and wave at me.'

Robyn could only offer a sad smile of compassion. 'What time are you finishing here?'

'I'm leaving at one. I got a call saying Dylan's not feeling too well and wants to come home. I'm going to collect him. I just cleared it here.'

'He's most likely disorientated, what with losing Jordan and moving out so soon afterwards. He might be better after a day or two in the new place,' Robyn said.

'I really hope so. I have to go now. I've got to take these invoices to accounts.'

'Sure. Take care.'

Robyn watched as Rebecca plodded up the stairs and disappeared from sight. Within seconds of her vanishing, Neil bounded back down the stairs. 'There you are. Names and contact details for the two warehouse supervisors who work in warehouse G and would have dealt with Jordan. We only have one supervisor per shift. Ben Taylor's on shift in the warehouse at the moment and I'd rather not have him disturbed, if you don't mind. We're behind target this month and need to get output increased. He'll clock off at six. You should be able to get hold of Clifford Harris. He's on nights this week so he'll be up and about after lunch.'

'That's very useful. Thank you,' said Robyn. 'I see Jordan's girlfriend is back at work.'

'Girlfriend?'

'Rebecca Tomlinson. She's an admin assistant here. She was living with Jordan.'

'Goodness me, I had no idea. I don't really know her.' He flushed slightly. 'We have thousands of employees here – some part-time, some full-time and many agency workers as well. I know quite a few of them but it's impossible to know them all. I deal mostly with clients and overseas customers. You know how it is.' He studied his fingernails briefly and regained his composure. 'So, if there's anything else I can do?'

'That will be all for the moment.'

Mitz passed Robyn the names of the two supervisors they were to contact as they got back into the car. She read them out loud, 'Ben Taylor and Clifford Harris, both from Burton-on-Trent. Put their names through the general database to see if anything's thrown up when we get back. Although, if what Neil Hardcastle told us is true, Pharmacals Healthcare will have thoroughly examined their backgrounds and deemed them trustworthy. Do it anyway. I'm not leaving any stone unturned.'

Robyn folded her arms and watched as hedgerows and fields flew past the windows. Her mind wasn't on Jordan and Pharmacals Healthcare. Instead she thought about Rebecca and wondered how long it would take her to recover from this. In her personal experience, it would be a very long time.

CHAPTER FORTY-ONE

Robyn's mobile buzzed. She looked at the caller ID and thought twice about answering it. It was Amy Walters. She stared at it briefly before touching the accept button.

'I have something,' said Amy.

'You've got a bloody cheek calling me.'

'Yeah, about that. I was pissed off you weren't taking me seriously. It was a knee-jerk piece.'

Heat rose up Robyn's neck. 'You wrote that piece of shit because you were pissed off at me? You thought it was okay to refer to my personal health and criticise me in public?'

'I didn't say anything that wasn't true.'

'Fuck you, Amy.'

'I've found out something that might help you. It's my way of saying sorry.'

'You can't say sorry. Didn't you consider the consequences of writing that article? Didn't you have the foresight to realise I'd be taken off the investigation? According to you, the public think I'm unfit to lead the investigation. My superiors wanted to allay the public's fears and remove me from the case.'

'Oh shit, they haven't, have they? I didn't want that to happen. I figured they all thought more highly of you than that. It was only a brief article in a local newspaper, it's not like I wrote to *The Times* about you.'

Robyn shook her head in dismay. The woman was so self-centred. 'As I said a minute ago: fuck off, Amy.'

'Fair enough but don't say I didn't try to help. I heard Nathaniel Jones-Kilby is involved with a married woman. It's all hush-hush and I can't find out who she is. Thought maybe whoever it was, her husband was after revenge. Possible, isn't it? I think you should talk to Nathaniel about it.'

'Oh, for crying out loud. I've interviewed the man. He's nothing to do with any of the murders. He's not a suspect. Now for the third and final time—'

Robyn pressed end call before she swore again and breathed deeply to relax the tension in her neck and shoulders. She shouldn't have allowed her emotions to kick in, but Amy had touched a nerve with her article. Robyn *had* been mentally unfit after Davies' death. Not many had known how ill she'd become. Many thought she'd taken time out to adjust and refocus. Hardly anyone knew the truth of the matter or the real cost to her health.

She scraped back her chair and headed to the changing room to get her thoughts back in order. There she initiated the nanny cam app and smiled, watching her cat as he first draped a paw over the edge of the settee then studied it through lazy orange eyes before licking it contentedly. Bloody Amy Walters. She oughtn't let the woman get under her skin. She watched Schrödinger for a couple of minutes. Was Amy onto something? It seemed a long shot to Robyn. If a husband wanted to enact revenge on his wife's lover, killing the man's son seemed an extreme length to go to. She let out an exasperated sigh and then turned off her phone.

What had they learnt so far that day? The answer was simple – nothing. They'd made no further progress and they were well into the afternoon. Flint would be prowling about soon, demanding answers and wanting to know how much closer they were to finding the killer. All they had was the link to biblical murders. She thought again about Amy's suggestion. It still didn't make any sense. An irate husband might, if he was unhinged, kill the son of his wife's lover, but why the son's friend and a doctor? Robyn dragged a hand through her long hair and tried to make sense of it all. A bat-crazy murderer who left his victims' bodies set up as some sort of a biblical tableau; somebody who hated Jordan, Owen and Lucy sufficiently to murder them in such horrific ways. What common ground did they share?

The answer wouldn't come to her in the time Robyn spent sitting on the bench in front of her locker. She only moved when she heard the clattering of boots and two officers entered the room. As she trundled back up the corridor she wondered how much longer she dared leave it before she requested assistance. If they didn't turn something up soon, she'd have to concede defeat and appeal to Shearer for help. Since their drink together they'd not really had a chance to speak again. She wasn't sure how to interpret that evening. Were they just friends and colleagues? The sight of Shearer rushing down the corridor ahead of her spurred her quickly into her office. She hadn't time to explore those thoughts and the case wasn't going to beat her. She wouldn't be asking Shearer for help anytime soon.

CHAPTER FORTY-TWO

'Bloody hopeless!' said Matt, shifting from side to side in his chair.

'We're all hacked off, Matt, but there's no point going off on one about it.' Anna appealed to his better nature, but he glared at her and paced the floor to the coffee machine.

'I know, but bloody hell, this is one of the worst cases we've handled. We're running around like headless chickens.'

Robyn shook her head. 'No, we're not. We're narrowing it all down. We've established the attacks weren't a result of a football incident on the pitch between members of the Sudbury Dynamos and the Blithfield Wanderers. We've determined the assailant is setting up his victims according to biblical murder scenes. We know Owen was aggressive at times and that he took drugs. We're still waiting for the lab results on Lucy's iPad. We know she had a date with a man that didn't work out but we're waiting for more information on that. Anna, give us a reminder and see where we are with that. I want to find out more about him. We're also aware that Jordan and Owen were best friends and we found out they both knew Lucy. We just need to fit all the pieces together.'

'I've received a copy of the photograph Owen was looking at in Nathaniel's house,' said David, pulling out a picture from an envelope. He studied it and shrugged. 'Can't see anything untoward in it. It's as the cleaner described. It's of Nathaniel with some others: Brian Turner and his wife, Maude; Chief Constable McIntosh and his wife, Deirdre; and MP Stewart Broughton and his wife, Vanessa, at some event.'

He showed it to Robyn, who studied the smiling faces and searched the background for any clues. She handed it back to David. 'Can't see anything. Take a magnifying glass to it. Check out what event it was taken at. Maybe Owen knew something about it or saw something significant in the photograph we've yet to spot.'

Anna let out a sigh and said, 'Lab boys say they can't identify the car parked outside the old school in Abbots Bromley. There's simply not enough to go on. All we have is a colour – dark blue. They apologise about Lucy's iPad. They're behind with work again and haven't been able to go through its contents. I reminded them we needed it as a priority and volunteered to check it myself if they were too hard pushed. I think they got the message.'

Robyn grimaced. 'Sod it. Another dead end. We could ask around the village and see if anybody spotted the vehicle while it was parked there.' She let out a groan. 'We really don't have time for all this.'

David looked up at the noise. 'By the way, while you were out of the office a gentleman called Lance Goldman rang. He said he spoke to you the other day. Wouldn't talk to me. Said he'd call back.'

'He's one of the patients from the surgery. Have you got that list of patient contact numbers? I'll ring him now.'

Mr Goldman sounded even chestier than the last time she'd spoken to him.

'I understand you've been trying to contact me,' Robyn said.

He wheezed his reply. 'I thought of something and wondered if I should have told you about it when we spoke. I was so focused on getting my facts right I neglected to mention a detail. When I was in the waiting room, I talked to Joyce Lincoln. Remember I told you she was annoyed about her appointment time being delayed?'

'I remember.'

'Well, she was complaining about how it would make her late for getting back to watch some programme on television she always watches and that she hated missing it.' Robyn resisted interrupting the man, who continued his lengthy monologue. 'I wasn't paying much attention, just biding my time, like I told you before, but she said something I'd forgotten about. She muttered something about her grandson being miffed too because he'd taken time off to drive her to the surgery and was waiting for her outside. I didn't see him when I came in but he must have been in his car in the car park. You asked me if anybody was in the car park. He was.'

Robyn pressed the phone more tightly to her ear to drown out the sound of her heartbeat, which had suddenly accelerated. 'Do you know her grandson?'

'Of course I do. Joyce used to live near me until her health went downhill and she moved in with her daughter, Hannah. I've known Hannah since she was a baby.'

'Mr Goldman, who is her grandson?'

'Oh, silly me, of course. It's an age thing. I sometimes forget what I'm talking about. Now let me see, Hannah married Rowan, what was his surname? Began with an F. Flint? No. Fletcher, that's it. The grandson's called Jasper – Jasper Fetcher.'

Robyn sprang into action as soon as the call ended. 'Bring in Jasper Fletcher. He was at the surgery the afternoon Lucy was killed. He's also a member of the Blithfield Wanderers, and friend to Owen and Jordan. The night Jordan died he claimed he dropped off two other friends who'd been at the pub with them – Dean Wells and Callum Bishop – and then went home to watch a film in his bedroom. I want details on Jasper, please. As I recall, he drives a dark blue Ford Fiesta. It was parked outside his house in Rugeley.'

Mitz stood completely still. 'The cross-stitch pictures,' he said. 'The ones on the dining room wall – they were all of biblical verses.'

'And his mother and grandmother had been to church the night he came home from the Fox and Weasel. Looking promising, isn't it?'

Robyn wrote Jasper's name on the whiteboard. 'I want you all to keep digging, folks. We're not there yet.'

She settled back at her desk, heart still thumping. She couldn't afford to play this wrong. Not only were there the victims to consider but her whole career. If she were to be removed from the case, she'd follow through on her threat to leave. She glanced at the faces of her team and prayed it wouldn't come to that.

CHAPTER FORTY-THREE

Jasper Fletcher sat with his hands folded on the table in front of him, leaning forward, mouth slightly agape in confusion. 'Am I under arrest?' he asked.

Robyn stared hard at him. 'You're helping us with our enquiries and you're free to leave at any time.'

'I don't get this. I was at home the night Jordan died. You spoke to my mum and nan.'

Robyn merely nodded. While they had both admitted seeing Jasper that evening, he could easily have left the house after both women had retired to bed, and returned to Colton to murder Jordan.

'And you say on Monday evening you were training at Riverside Gym but only one person saw you and that was when you were about to leave?'

'It's only a small gym. It's not always busy. It happened to be empty that night. I got there at six thirty and trained for an hour and a half. One of the regulars came in as I was leaving. He saw me there.'

'Aren't there any members of staff?'

'No. It's one of those gyms where you get an access code that opens the gym door. It's permanently locked and only members can get in.'

Even if Jasper had been seen at the gym it was only for a brief spell. He might only have been in the gym long enough to get a witness. Robyn wasn't convinced of his alibis.

'On Thursday you took your grandmother to her appointment at Abbots Bromley surgery. Did you usually take her?'

'No, Mum normally runs her about but she couldn't get the time off, so I did it instead. I wanted to finish early anyway, so I could get off to the heavy metal event – the Download Festival at Donnington Park. Why are you treating me like some criminal?'

'We're asking for your cooperation, Jasper. We have to ask these questions. You were at the surgery last Thursday afternoon. Doctor Harding was killed later that day. We're wondering if you saw anything peculiar while you were in the car park – possibly somebody hanging about?'

'I was watching YouTube videos on my phone. The surgery has Wi-Fi and you can pick up the signal in the car park. I didn't notice anything.'

'What time did you leave the surgery?' Robyn asked.

'Some time around half four. Nan was cross because we missed most of the antiques programme she liked, *Put Your Money Where Your Mouth Is*, and it was the last episode in the series.'

'And what did you do after you dropped off your grand-mother?'

'I got showered, had a bite to eat and then set off at about six fifteen.'

'For Donnington Park? Alone?'

'Yeah. I was meeting up with some mates there. We wanted to get good pitches.'

'You travelled by car?'

He nodded.

'You own a dark blue Ford Fiesta?'

'That's right.'

'What time did you arrive?'

'Traffic was really heavy, especially around Donnington. Took much longer than I expected. I got there about half eight. My mates were already there and set up. I pitched my tent, had a few beers and stayed there all weekend. Saw all the main stage acts. Saw Aerosmith, they were awesome – and came back in time for work.'

Robyn considered the possibility Jasper might have stopped at Abbots Bromley – only ten minutes away from his house – then after he'd murdered Lucy Harding, continued to Donnington Park, a journey of approximately forty minutes. It was viable. His alibi wasn't airtight. They'd need to track his vehicle using the traffic cameras along the route to see if it held up.

'Did you know Dr Harding?'

'No.'

'But you knew she treated your grandmother?'

'Nan never mentioned her doctor's name. Or, if she did, I didn't hear her say it.'

Robyn slid a photograph of Lucy across the table. 'Are you sure you don't know this woman?'

Jasper shook his head. 'I've never seen her before. Can I go now?'

It had been a long interview. They'd asked the same questions over and over but Jasper hadn't changed his story. He was adamant he didn't know Lucy.

Robyn sighed and decided to go out on a limb. 'Are you a religious man, Jasper?'

'What, me?' He sniggered. 'Can't say I am. Don't believe in God and angels and all that stuff, if that's what you mean.'

'Your mother and grandmother are, aren't they?'

'I suppose so.'

'They attend church regularly?'

'Nan likes to go to church. Mum goes with her sometimes to keep her company. Why?'

'Did you use to go to church when you were younger?'

'Never. Wasn't my bag. I used to go to football on a Sunday, not church.' He scoffed. 'If that's it, I have to go. My mum's expecting me home.'

'Thank you, Jasper. That's all for now.'

CHAPTER FORTY-FOUR

DAY EIGHT – MONDAY, 12 JUNE, EVENING

DCI Flint stood by his office window. Outside was dark, with only the occasional sweep of headlights illuminating the empty road.

'I can't determine a motive,' said Robyn. 'Jasper Fletcher has witnesses and alibis for the three murders, albeit weak ones – but the real problem I have is that I can't fathom out why he'd kill them.'

'Random?'

'Crossed my mind. We've trawled through safety camera footage and can place his car on the A50 headed towards Donnington Park at eight as he claimed, and traffic was congested. He could well be telling the truth and is nothing to do with any of this.'

'Where does that leave you, Robyn?'

'To be honest, sir, it leaves me with very little to go on but I'm not throwing in the towel yet. We're trying to establish if Jasper Fletcher's dark blue Ford Fiesta was the car parked outside the construction site in Abbots Bromley. We're also going back through evidence to see if we've missed anything. What I need to know, sir, is the name of the woman Nathaniel was going to see when he travelled through Abbots Bromley the night Lucy was killed. I have to speak to her and find out more. He's the only person we can place at two murder scenes and he was one of Lucy's patients. It always seems to come back to him. Even if he isn't responsible for the deaths, I have to know what I'm up against. Is he the reason these people have been killed?'

DCI Flint drummed his fingertips together, as he often did when considering a situation or request. 'This puts me – us – in a very awkward situation,' he said.

'I think you'll find I'm the one who's been put in a difficult situation. It's impossible to investigate a case when one of your suspects can't be questioned.'

'If I told you I'm satisfied he's not responsible in any way for the death of Lucy Harding, would that be enough for you?'

'Do I have any other options?'

He pressed his lips together. 'Not really.'

'Nathaniel told me he was friends with the chief constable and suggested if things didn't go his way, he'd make waves.'

Flint winced slightly, confirming her suspicions. Flint was frightened of losing his job. Nathaniel Jones-Kilby, and what he might say to Chief Constable McIntosh regarding the investigation, worried him. She wanted to challenge Flint about it and wondered how far she could trust him, but she had more pressing matters.

'Then I'll have to accept that,' she said. 'For now.'

'Suffice to say, Robyn, I allowed you to stick with this investigation because you were certain you'd get a result soon. It's been over a week since Jordan was murdered. I needn't point out the obvious, need I?'

'No, sir.'

'Good, because I'd hate to have to carry out my threat, and I might have to if the superintendent isn't happy with how things are progressing. He'll be expecting an update in the morning.'

'Yes, sir.' Robyn turned on her heel. She didn't need reminding at all. The clock was ticking – too quickly for her liking. Jasper might be their man but her gut feeling was he didn't have enough anger in him to commit the crimes. He'd been too laid back during the interview. She caught sight of Shearer in reception and reminded herself that most people wore a mask. Shearer certainly did. He'd be grouchy and offhand or bolshy and loud, but underneath he wasn't as confident as he tried to appear. She'd seen his vulnerable side in the past. Jasper might be one such person – an apparent innocent – and underneath be somebody completely different. It would be foolish to wholly discount him.

The whole team were working overtime and were leafing back through reports, statements and evidence. If they'd missed anything, it would be unearthed this evening. For the moment, she was stumped. The victims were bound by the clinic where Lucy worked, Jordan delivered packages and Owen was a patient. She couldn't see any other common thread, other than the village of Colton where two of them had lived and two had died.

A healthy aroma of freshly cooked pizza, olives and basil met her as she walked into the hectic office, cluttered with paperwork, bodies and cardboard boxes. Matt pointed at the one on her desk.

She gave him a thumbs up and lifted the lid, allowing the scent of spicy sausage to escape into the office. She pulled off a slice and popped it into her mouth. Robyn had written several questions on Post-its that she felt would lead to answers. 'I've got some ideas to throw out to you.'

'I'm in position,' said Matt, facing her and holding his hand out as if ready to catch a ball.

'Why did Jordan leave Owen's house that night? He'd told Rebecca, his girlfriend, he was staying the night. Why not wait until the morning? Owen said he'd planned on staying the night.'

'Maybe he changed his mind and decided to go home,' Matt said.

Mitz joined in. 'Fell out with Owen. Owen could have lied to us. They could have had an argument and Jordan stormed off.'

David looked up. 'He might have arranged to meet somebody.'

Robyn tapped the pen against her chin. 'That's what I wondered, David. If he'd drunk so much alcohol he had to stay at Owen's until he sobered up, it doesn't follow he'd be riding home in the dark at that time. His phone records didn't reveal any calls around that time so it wasn't a last-minute meeting.'

Mitz spoke. 'Owen could have arranged it for him.'

'They could have organised it with somebody when they were in the pub.'

Robyn let out a long hiss of exasperation. 'Too many possibilities, aren't there? Thanks anyway. I'll think about how to handle that angle.'

They hadn't found anything noteworthy on Jordan's computer, but she remembered Rebecca had asked for the device to be returned so she could download some photographs on it. Robyn picked it up to take to the lab where Anna was working on Lucy's iPad. The techies were still understaffed and overworked so Robyn had sent Anna to step in. Robyn was right to have faith in Anna because as soon as she walked into the lab, she was met with a shout of triumph.

'Eureka,' said Anna, brushing hair back from her flushed face. 'Lucy deleted all trace of it but I found it. She used a dating website called LonelySouls. Here are the profiles of the men Lucy was sent as potential matches.'

She turned the computer screen so Robyn could see too and scrolled down the list, stopping at one name. 'Really?' she said.

Robyn heaved a sigh. 'Looks that way.'

They both looked at the profile of the man who claimed to be a widow, seeking love, companionship and friendship, and who called himself Nath – Nathaniel Jones-Kilby.

'I'm going to have to interview him again,' said Robyn, rubbing the back of her neck that was beginning to ache dully.

'What's that you've got?' Anna asked, indicating Jordan's laptop.

'Rebecca wants to get some photographs off it. I thought you might take one last look at this before I head over there with it. Just in case the techies missed something first time around.

'Sure. Give it to me.' Anna caressed the machine. 'I love these things. There's always so much about people hidden on them – their lives, their thoughts, their secret desires.'

'You sure you're in the right department?' Robyn asked with a smile.

Anna grinned. 'If I did this all the time, I'd go mad. I need to be with people.'

'Good. When you're done, come and rejoin us humans. We've got plenty for you to be getting on with.'

When Robyn couldn't reach DCI Flint again, she decided she had no choice other than to ring Nathaniel. She tried his number but it went immediately to answerphone. It was after eleven. A trip to his house at this time of night would only rile him further, especially if he was in bed. Her options were limited. She'd have to leave it until morning – that was, if she was still on the case by then.

Mitz, in front of his computer screen, was chomping his way through a pizza topped with peppers and mushrooms. He swallowed his food and wiped his hand on a piece of kitchen roll by the keyboard. 'Guv, I went through the statements I took from Ben Taylor and Clifford Harris, the two supervisors at Pharmacals Healthcare. They didn't have anything to add about Jordan, but I've been doing some research on the pair of them, and Clifford is related to Joe Harris who runs the Fox and Weasel. He's his older brother…' He hesitated mid-sentence.

Robyn spun around to face him. 'I sense there's more coming.'

'There is. He owns a dark grey Ford Transit van. Did we find out anything more about that van in Colton the night Jordan died?'

David joined the conversation. 'Nothing. Couldn't find it on any safety cameras and nobody else spotted it.'

'Where was it?'

'By the village hall,' said Mitz as he pulled up a map of the village for her to look at. She squinted hard at the screen, her eyes sore now with tiredness. Mitz pointed to a grey shape. 'It's here in the middle of the village.'

'How far is that from Owen's house?'

Mitz did the calculations. 'Just over a mile.'

'We considered the possibility that Jordan was meeting some-body. If Jordan were travelling from Owen's house to a meet at the village hall, he wouldn't pass Top Field where we found him,' said Robyn, scratching her forehead.

'How about if he'd already made the meeting and was headed home to Newborough?' Mitz suggested. He traced a line along the road that represented the direction Jordan might have taken.

'Yep. That's an option. Where does Clifford Harris live?'

'Rugeley. On the huge estate on the left, as you head out of town towards Kings Bromley.'

'He married?'

'He was. Wife divorced him last year. He lives alone as far as I can tell. Nobody else is registered on the electoral register as living at that address.'

'David, check all the safety cameras from Rugeley to Colton after 9 p.m. on Sunday, 4 June. The van was seen in Colton at 10.30 p.m. or thereabouts. See if Clifford Harris's van shows up on any of them, and run a quick background check on his brother, Joe, will you? We could be trying to force pieces of this puzzle to fit together, but if Clifford was in Colton that night, we have grounds to be suspicious. Mitz, talk to Joe. Find out if his brother was at the pub Sunday night. Matt, fancy a drive out to Rugeley?'

CHAPTER FORTY-FIVE

DAY EIGHT – MONDAY, 12 JUNE, LATE EVENING

Clifford Harris looked exactly like a younger version of his brother, complete with a balding head and caterpillar eyebrows that rose high on his creased forehead when he read Robyn's ID.

'I apologise for disturbing you at such a late hour,' she said as he signalled for them to enter. Robyn stepped over a pair of dirty trainers in the front porch, and followed Matt into a sitting room immediately to the left. Clifford turned off the programme he'd been watching and regarded them with a baleful look. Robyn let Matt take the lead and glanced around the untidy room. It might once have been a family home but now it was a jumble of neglect, with books haphazardly stored on shelves next to pictures and ornaments. Sticky-looking coffee cup rings patterned the coffee table next to a settee, and a television stand and set were thick with dust. A pile of folded washing, yet to be ironed, filled one chair, and the dining table, crushed into the far corner of the room, was set up with an electric train set, complete with setting, platforms and scenery.

'Do you own a grey Ford Transit van, sir?' Matt asked.

Clifford rolled his eyes. 'You must know I do. I assume you've checked the DVLA website and seen one is registered to me. What's going on?'

'We are investigating a serious crime, sir, and would appreciate some cooperation. I'd like to ask a series of questions about Sunday, 4 June. Where were you between 10 p.m. and 1 a.m.?'

'Here – asleep. I was on the early shift so I went to bed at about eight.' He glared at Matt. Matt kept his cool gaze on the man and Robyn felt her pulse quicken. David had phoned them en route and they knew Clifford had just made his first mistake.

'I'm sorry, sir. I'm going to repeat that question. Please bear in mind that a Ford Transit van with the same registration as yours was seen leaving Rugeley at just after ten that night.'

Clifford licked his lips. 'Oh, Sunday – you mean the Sunday before last. I thought you meant the Sunday just gone. I went out for a drive.'

'It seems a strange time to suddenly go out for a drive. Where did you go?'

'I headed to my brother Joe's pub – the Fox and Weasel near Colton. Thought I'd have a chat and a pint.'

'Do you often go to the Fox and Weasel?'

'No but I hadn't seen him for a while so I thought I'd surprise him.'

'And what time did you arrive?'

'Don't know. I wasn't clock-watching.'

'How many people were in the bar when you arrived?'

'Not many. It was Sunday night so it was quiet. I didn't look around. I went up to the bar and had a word with Joe.'

'What did you have to drink?'

'A half-pint of Pedigree.'

Matt wrote something in his notebook and motioned with his pencil in a nonchalant manner. 'What time did you leave the pub?'

'Again, I can't tell you. I drifted back home after Joe had shut up for the night and went to bed. Maybe you picked up my van again on the cameras and could tell me.'

Matt ignored the comment and scribbled something down.

'What did you and your brother discuss?'

'Lots of things – life, my ex-wife, my kids, football and work.'

'Did he show you the new football shirts for the Blithfield Wanderers?'

'No. How is that question relevant?'

Robyn ignored the question. Joe Harris had been keen to show off the new shirts to the few members of the Blithfield Wanderers who were in the pub that night. Surely, he'd have wanted to show them to his brother and ask his opinion too?

'I thought he might have shown them to you since he'd just got the new logos on them.'

'Well, he didn't.'

'Mr Harris, did you stop beside Colton village hall at ten thirty before going to your brother's pub?'

Clifford's eyelids fluttered. 'I think I did. I received a text message from my daughter. I'd have stopped to read it. I don't remember where I stopped though. It might have been anywhere along that road.'

'Did you see Jordan Kilby that night?'

Clifford breathed long and loud. 'No. I did not. Is that what this is about? You think I had something to do with Jordan's death? I didn't. I swear I didn't.'

Robyn's mobile buzzed in her pocket. She excused herself and stood outside to take the call.

'Joe says his brother visited the pub that night – arrived about ten thirty just as he was thinking of shutting up,' said Mitz.

'Oh shit. What else did he say? Did you ask him what they were discussing or what he had to drink?'

'He had a half-pint of Pedigree and they discussed work and boring stuff.'

'Oh, double shit. That's not what I wanted to hear. Their stories tally. Is that everything?'

'I'm afraid so. Joe told me the place was quiet so they had a good catch-up and then he showed Clifford the new football shirts before he left. Thinks he went at about 11.45 p.m. or so.'

A small smile tugged at her cheeks. 'He said he showed Clifford the football shirts?'

'That's what he said.'

'Excellent. Bring him to the station, Mitz. We'll meet you there. And request a couple of warrants: one for his pub and the other for Clifford Harris's house.

CHAPTER FORTY-SIX

Matt marched Clifford Harris through the station doors, past reception and towards the interview rooms. He'd requested a lawyer and Robyn would have to wait for him to appear before she could begin her official questioning.

She took Clifford's mobile phone to the office and placed it on Anna's desk. 'Can you check his call history? I want to know if he received a text message at ten thirty or thereabouts on Sunday. If he did, who was it from and what did it say? Also, search for any suspicious activity, strange text messages, repeat calling – anything that you think you should flag up. I need this quickly. We'll be interviewing him as soon as his brief appears.'

Anna turned the device on and began thumbing through the keys with lightning speed.

'I really don't know how you do that,' said Robyn, with a grin. 'It takes me ages to compose a text message.'

'It's down to practise,' Anna replied with a straight face. 'And spending far too long playing *Candy Crush*.'

'Where's David?'

'He got a call from his wife. He's outside.'

Robyn followed the corridor to the back entrance and peered through the glass. David was leaning against a railing, a cigarette in his hand, staring into the dark. Robyn opened the door quietly and joined him. 'You want to get off, David? We've got this covered for now. We're waiting to interview the Harris brothers and it could be a while before we get the lawyers in.'

David drew on his cigarette and inhaled deeply.

'Didn't know you smoked,' said Robyn.

'Started six months ago. I used to when I was young but gave it up. Fancied it again,' he said, staring at the cigarette. 'I'm okay, guv. I'd rather be here where the action is.'

'You don't have to be.'

He looked at her. 'Yes. I do. I'm not expected home and I want to see how this plays out.'

'Cool. I'll see you back inside then. I'm waiting for Mitz to bring in Joe Harris. Fancy coming in on that interview?'

He took a final drag, flicked the cigarette onto the ground and crushed it with his heel. 'Definitely.'

Robyn headed back to the office and grabbed a cup of coffee. It was going to be a long night and she needed caffeine to see her through it. Anna looked over. 'Want one?' Robyn asked.

'I've had enough caffeine, thanks. Clifford didn't receive any text messages at ten thirty. No messages at all. I've linked his phone up to my computer and run a programme to see if he deleted them, but there's nothing. He made a few calls the following day. Several to one number in particular – Owen's.'

Robyn left her coffee on the top and scurried across. Anna was right. Clifford had contacted Owen numerous times on Monday. 'You find out anything else?'

'Nothing else at this stage. I'll need time to work through his contact list and establish who else he knows.'

'Did he ring Jordan at all?'

Anna shook her head. 'Can't see his number. I'll keep looking.'

'Great. Well, we have something to work with. Clifford has some explaining to do.'

Mitz marched in. 'I've left Joe with an officer. He's saying nothing more. Got a right face on him.'

'He won't be the first surly suspect we've handled, or the last,' said Robyn. 'What did you get out of him?'

'He isn't squealing. I tried all the tactics but he refuses to comment.'

'Bloody typical. We get them over a barrel and they clam up. We'll play it by ear.' Robyn sat in front of her Post-it notes and shuffled her thoughts into order. What was the connection between Jordan, Owen, Joe, Clifford and Lucy?

Mitz, now behind his own desk, reading information from the computer screen, voiced as much himself. 'What on earth links these people? Is this about Nathaniel or something else completely different? Joe, Jordan and Owen are connected through football. Owen and Lucy are linked by location. Clifford's linked to Jordan and Owen through his brother, Joe. Lucy to Jordan, only through Pharmacals Healthcare.'

'And they all know Nathaniel Jones-Kilby,' said Anna, earning a groan from Mitz.

The desk phone rang. David, who'd entered the room, picked it up. 'Clifford's lawyer is here.'

Robyn drew herself up to her full height. 'About time too. I'm not coming out of that interview room until I know what's going on.'

Clifford didn't exude the same confidence he'd displayed back at his house. Robyn studied his lawyer, a young, nervous individual, barely out of nappies, who'd been dragged out in the middle of the night to represent a man he clearly didn't know. Robyn asked the questions, speaking directly to Clifford, who only just managed to maintain eye contact with her. She decided to ease him into the questioning, and keeping her voice controlled and level, she said, 'Mr Harris, when we last spoke you told us you were in Colton on the night of 4 June. You went to visit your brother, who runs the Fox and Weasel, just outside the village. Is that correct?'

'Correct.'

'You were asked what you and your brother discussed to which you replied, "Lots of things – life, my ex-wife, my kids, football and work." Is that correct?'

'Yes.'

'You were also asked if your brother showed you the new football shirts he'd had made, to which you replied no he hadn't. Is that correct?'

Clifford gave a slight twitch. 'I can't remember.'

'You can't remember if he showed you the football shirts?'

'He might have done but I didn't register them. I was talking about my ex-wife. I tend to get blinkered when I talk about her. I wasn't paying much attention to Joe.'

'So, you now claim you can't recall looking at the football shirts.'

'That's correct.' Clifford lifted his face to hers. 'I can't.'

'How odd you now can't remember when before you were quite certain you hadn't seen them,' said Robyn.

'My client says he can't remember,' said the lawyer.

Robyn stared hard at him but he was unwavering. 'You were asked if you drew up outside the village hall in Colton at about 10.30 p.m. You replied, "Might have done."'

Clifford nodded. 'Yes, to read a text. I don't know where exactly I stopped.'

'The text being from your daughter?'

'Yes.'

Robyn's eyes glittered as she spoke. 'I'm afraid that's not true. You received no texts that night.'

'I did. I deleted it, that's all. It was there.'

'No, you did not delete it, Mr Harris. We've been able to ascertain you did not receive or send any text messages that evening.

However, you did make calls the following day to Owen Falcon, who was later found dead at his home.'

'Whoa. Wait a minute. I didn't have anything to do with that.'

'How did you know Owen?'

'I met him at the Fox and Weasel. He was one of Joe's football team. I met him there. Got along with him.'

'Is that so?'

'Yes, sure,' said Clifford.

'I'm afraid I don't believe you. You have nothing in common with Owen that we know of. You didn't work with him, or share any of the same interests. Therefore, it seems extremely odd you'd ring him several times soon after Jordan Kilby was found dead.'

'That's why I was calling him. To see if he knew anything about Jordan's death.'

'The first call you made to Owen was at six twenty in the morning. At that time, Jordan's body hadn't yet been discovered. I suggest, Mr Harris, you are lying, and might I remind you we are investigating three murders. Would you like to come clean or shall we charge you with murder or conspiring to assist a murder?'

'Fuck, no! I didn't kill them. Honestly.'

'I'm waiting, Mr Harris.'

'Can I talk to my lawyer? In private?'

'Make it quick or I'll charge you for wasting time too.' Robyn scraped back her chair and left the men to talk. Matt followed her, leaving an officer outside the interview room door.

'What do you think?' he asked.

'I think I need another cup of coffee. Want one?'

'Yeah, why not?'

A black lead stretched between Clifford's mobile and Anna's computer. She was examining numbers that streamed across her screen.

'He's been in regular contact with Owen since February 2016. Text messages and phone calls. Some only last a few seconds. There's definitely something dodgy going on there.'

An officer poked his head around the office door. 'Mr Harris wants to make a confession.'

'Does he? Does he indeed?' said Robyn, striding down the corridor and bursting into the interview room.

The young lawyer was sat bolt upright. Clifford kept his eyes downcast as the man spoke. 'DI Carter, my client wishes to make a confession. He'd like to confess to theft and distribution of drugs from Pharmacals Healthcare. He's admitting to falsifying documentation, stealing drugs and handing them to Jordan Kilby for delivery.'

CHAPTER FORTY-SEVEN

Robyn drew up to the station. The two hours she'd spent in a heavy, dreamless sleep had not been refreshing and she stumbled out of her car nursing a headache as bad as a hangover.

It was just after six and she still had some time before DCI Flint arrived and hauled her over the proverbial coals for having insufficient evidence to convict anybody for the three murders. Joe and Clifford Harris were still being held at the station and would be charged soon.

She snapped on the office light and winced at the smell of leftover pizzas. The crushed boxes tossed into the rubbish bin made her stomach flip. She lifted the bin and marched it down the corridor to the back entrance. Tom Shearer was outside the door and grinned when she came out and dumped the bin beside him.

'Given up detective work for refuse collecting – admirable choice,' he said and guffawed.

'Not now. I'm in a shit mood and my head feels like it's going to burst.'

'Thought you'd got two perps. You should be in high spirits. Desk sergeant said they're waiting to be charged.'

'They are, just not for murder. They've been stealing drugs from a company and passing them on for sale on the streets. What are you doing in so early?'

'Couldn't sleep. Thought I'd do some paperwork. So, not caught the person responsible for the three murders, then?'

'Not yet, Tom. But I'm not beaten so don't even think about wading in and taking over.'

He held his hands up. 'Hold on a sec. What makes you think I'd do that?'

'You would if you were asked to, wouldn't you? I know you're after promotion, Tom, so don't play games with me.'

'True about the promotion, but nobody's asked me to take over your case. So there's no need to get all hissy.'

'Well, if they do, refuse. I want this, Tom. I want it badly and I'm not going to pass it over.' She crossed her arms, waiting for a retort. None was forthcoming. 'Good. We understand each other,' she said and marched back inside, letting the door slam shut.

Downing two paracetamols and an entire bottle of water, she prepared for another interview with Clifford. Her heart was heavy. Surely, she couldn't have got so far into this investigation and still have unturned nothing. She shook back her hair. She'd get this over with and then consider her options.

David joined her outside the interview room. He'd been determined to return early and gave her a smile of encouragement before she opened the door.

Clifford, unshaven and still in the same clothes as the night before, looked drained. He'd aged twenty years since he'd confessed.

'I just want this over with,' he said as soon as she sat down.

His lawyer, wearing a pristine white shirt, sat in silence.

'Mr Harris, we're recording this interview and we'll be charging you at the end of the session. Are you clear about what is happening?'

He exhaled noisily. 'Yes, yes. Let's get it done.'

'On Sunday, 4 June, you drove to Colton and waited outside the village hall in your Ford Transit van. Can you explain in detail why you did so?'

'I'd arranged to meet Jordan outside the village hall between ten thirty and eleven.'

'What was the purpose of this meeting?'

'He wanted out and I was trying to prevent him from leaving.'

'Would you explain what you mean by that, Mr Harris?'

Clifford gave a heavy nod of his head and began the story…

Owen leans across the bar and hisses at Joe. 'Found somebody. Big Tony gave me a name of another delivery driver we could use.'

Joe looks around to check nobody is listening to the conversation. Luckily, it's a quiet night and the three punters at the far end of the bar are deep in their own conversation.

'His name's Jordan Kilby. He's Nathaniel Jones-Kilby's boy.'

'What, NJK Properties Jones-Kilby? Are you having a laugh? He'll be no good for us. If his father gets wind of what he's up to, we'll all be in the shit.'

Owen pulls a face. 'Nah. Hates his old man. Look, Jordan's a complete screwball. Big Tony says he's obsessed with three things in his life: gaming, cycling and football. Said the guy looks like he's dead scared of everybody. He goes into work, hardly speaks to anyone and scurries off home when he's done his deliveries. Big Tony arranged a meeting at a pub near where Jordan lives – in Newborough. Made it look like I'd come in by accident and left us talking. Big T was right. Jordan's football crazy. I said he should come along to our training on Wednesday and maybe try out for the team. He nearly bit my bloody hand off. He'll be so easy to manipulate. Once we befriend him properly, we'll be able to count on him.'

'Why would he want to get involved in this? Is he bent?'

'No, but he'd love to be one of the lads. I'm convinced of that. I told him I was game mad too and he invited me back to his house to play on his PlayStation. I tested out the waters and managed to steer the conversation towards drugs. I told him I took the odd E and skunk.

He didn't flinch. He even revealed he smoked pot at school, along with his best friend, but he got caught buying some and got expelled. He didn't dob his friend in, though. He took the blame alone. I reckon we could easily sway him. Get him involved in the team and then ask if he wants to be part of our elite group. He's got bills to pay. He isn't going to turn his nose up at some extra cash. All he has to do is sign the fake sheets Clifford gives him and then drop off the extra package with me. It's a great deal of reward for such a small amount of effort. You okay still to get the gear to the lads?'

Joe nodded. 'They know there's a problem with delivery and that it'll be resolved soon. They're not getting too edgy yet. I don't want to leave it too long or they'll find another supplier.'

Clifford, who's been listening to the conversation, puts down his pint glass and whispers, 'How long has this Jordan been driving for Speedy Logistics?'

'Since he was eighteen. He'll be ideal. Never put a foot wrong. All you need to do is mention him to the admin staff at Pharmacals Healthcare and they'll run the background check on him. Next you know, he'll be on the local drug run and we'll persuade him to follow in Big Tony's footsteps and get him on board.'

'Shame Big Tony moved away. It was going well,' says Clifford.

'You won't miss him once we get Jordan involved. Honestly, wait until you meet him. You'll be waiting to shake my hand.'

'You've done well to find a replacement if it works out.'

'It will. Make sure you keep fiddling those medical supply sheets and getting your hands on the gear. We're not going out of business just yet.'

Robyn listened in silence as Clifford revealed how they'd cajoled Jordan into helping them move drugs, taken from Pharmacals Healthcare to Joe, who'd then transferred them to dealers. Owen was the fixer who arranged the dates, the drop-offs and the money. Everything had run smoothly after Jordan replaced Big Tony: Clifford had continued to steal drugs in small amounts and fiddle the orders and delivery sheets, Jordan had ensured surgeries signed the altered delivery note and dropped off the stolen drugs with Owen, somewhere along his planned route for the day, thus eliminating the chance of suspicion falling on his shoulders.

'So, what happened on Sunday, 4 June? Why did you arrange to meet Jordan in Colton? Why not bump into him at the Fox and Weasel?'

'Jordan wanted out of the scam. He wanted to take his share of the money and stop making the drug deliveries. Joe and Owen couldn't convince him otherwise. I thought I might be able to.'

'You could have done so at the pub or at Owen's house. Why not there rather than late at night outside a village hall?'

'I didn't want anyone to see us together. I didn't want Joe and Owen to know I'd met him. Thing was, I was having second thoughts myself. I was the one with most at risk. I work at Pharmacals Healthcare. I have access to both keys and the combination codes to get into the vault in warehouse G where we hold the drugs. I arrange for drugs to go missing. The other two don't. They deal with them afterwards. They get it moved on. Jordan and I took the biggest risks – the other two profited from that. I've been doing this for over a year – since my wife left me. She took almost everything I had. Left me almost destitute. I needed the extra money and this was one way of getting it. But lately, I've been worried about who Joe and Owen have been dealing with. They wanted me to get my hands on some methadone so we could make some serious money. They've been talking to some serious players on the street, and I was starting to get concerned for my safety. It's one thing nicking a few pills and cannabis now and again and raising a thousand quid to share out among us, but the stuff they were talking about stealing is high-value stuff. It sells for thousands of pounds.

'When I heard Jordan wanted to drop out, I decided to talk to him and ask why. I thought maybe he knew something I didn't. I told him to keep the meeting quiet and chose a neutral point from where we both lived. I didn't want anyone to see us together or make any connections. Colton seemed ideal. He'd planned on going to Owen's house that night after the pub so they could discuss some stuff – there'd been some bother with a lad called Darren Sturgeon they wanted to talk about and Owen wanted to discuss drop-off points for the next batch of drugs. Jordan said he'd leave after Owen went to bed, meet me, then head home and no one would be any the wiser.'

'Did you meet him?'

'Yes. He turned up at just after eleven and he confirmed my suspicions. Said Joe and Owen were getting too greedy and he was especially concerned about Owen. Said the man was using drugs himself and had begun to act irrationally. He'd beaten up a footballer – Darren – and the incident had put the wind up Jordan. Claimed Owen was losing the plot and would get us all into serious trouble not just with police but with local drug dealers. I was concerned about what he told me. Joe's always blinkered when it comes to Owen. He has a soft spot for him so there was no point in telling him Owen had become a loose cannon. I told Jordan I'd speak to Joe and tell him they'd upped the security at Pharmacals Healthcare, changed the systems, and we wouldn't be able to work the scam any more. He seemed happy with that and left soon after.'

'And you?'

'I went to the Fox and Weasel to tell Joe it wasn't going to be possible to steal the drugs any more, but the lights were out at the pub and the door locked. I thought it could wait until the morning so I drove home.'

'You didn't pass or see Jordan, or anyone else?'

'There wasn't anybody on the road. I didn't see a soul. Jordan headed in the opposite direction, so I wouldn't have seen him anyway.'

Robyn waited to see if Clifford was going to offer up anything else but he sat, shoulders forward, a defeated individual. She ended the interview and returned to the office where Matt had given up interviewing Joe and was slumped in his chair. He looked across and held up his hands.

'Nothing. Bastard refuses to talk.'

'Give him time. We'll let him sweat a little longer then try him again. His brother has told us about the drug stealing. It's only a matter of time. We've got officers searching both their houses. We'll turn up something and he'll squeal.'

'However, none of this helps us with the murder investigation, does it?'

'Not unless Joe is behind the deaths.'

'You reckon he is?'

Robyn sat on the edge of her desk and considered the question. 'I really don't know. My gut says not, but we have to work on evidence, and Joe has a motive for killing Jordan. If Jordan was planning on shopping them all to the authorities, Joe might have decided to kill him, although why he'd turn on Owen and Lucy remains a mystery.'

A pink-cheeked Anna appeared. She placed Jordan's laptop on Robyn's desk with a smile and pointed at the LonelySouls website on the screen. 'I discovered a hidden cookie and found out somebody had accessed this website only a few days before Jordan's death – Friday to be exact. I hacked the account.'

'And?'

'It wasn't Jordan's account. It's Rebecca's. She's had it for two years and is currently active on the site. She clicked on hundreds of profiles.'

'So, she didn't want us to know she was dating online. She might have been embarrassed about it.' Robyn knew her words sounded hollow and she was trying to convince herself Rebecca was the woman she believed her to be.

Anna persisted. 'She's been on the site since Jordan's death. She updated her profile. I figured it was a bit soon to be dating again.

And… she doesn't mention having a son. Says she's a singleton who's not had the easiest time, but is searching for a caring person to share her life.'

Robyn drew a sharp breath as she wrestled with the news that Rebecca had lied to them.

'I also found this thread in a forum about comic conventions. Jordan posted a question about favourite venues and a couple of people replied, but the post didn't attract much attention and lay dormant until November when somebody added a comment, which led to a private conversation between them and Jordan. It was Rebecca.'

'What did she and Jordan discuss?'

'There was stuff about superheroes, Marvel Comics characters and films and then the conversation changed to a more personal nature. Take a look,' said Anna, pulling up a series of dialogue boxes. 'This was all I could retrieve, but it's sufficient to get an idea.'

Robyn read through each box. The conversation had taken place late November the year before:

Rebecca: That's mad. I can't believe we have so much in common – DS comics, music, films, football, gaming and we even think alike.
Jordan: We should meet up.
Rebecca: You reckon?
Jordan: Why not? I bet we hit it off.
Rebecca: Okay. Why don't we meet at the gallery at the Mailbox in Birmingham next Saturday at 11 a.m.? They've got an exhibition of limited superhero prints.
Jordan: Perfect. See you there.

Robyn skipped through some more conversations about what films they'd watched and which special edition superhero statues Jordan wanted to buy for his collection, until she reached one posted the second week of December, a week before Rebecca resigned from her job at Longer Life Health in Birmingham:

> *Jordan: You going to try that place I told you about?*
> *Rebecca: Pharmacals Healthcare?*
> *Jordan: Yes. Go for the job interview there. You're obviously really unhappy where you are, and your landlord sounds shit.*
> *Rebecca: He is horrible and I do hate my job but it's crazy to move. I'd have to find somewhere to live.*
> *Jordan: You can stay with me until you get sorted.*

'This is weird. Rebecca never mentioned meeting Jordan this way.'

Anna agreed. 'And she seems to love all the same things Jordan does. I wasn't under the impression she was as keen as all that on Marvel Comic characters.'

There was no question about it; Robyn had to talk to Rebecca again. 'You're absolutely right, Anna. I'm going to speak to her now. Keep me informed of any new leads.'

The corridor and reception were beginning to fill with officers and she nodded good morning to several as she slid back out to the car park and unlocked her car.

DCI Flint was parking in his marked space as she reversed and left without catching his eye. She didn't want to admit she'd made so little progress. Time really was running out for her and possibly her career at Stafford. She indicated and joined the traffic on the main road. She was up against it but she still had determination. She'd not failed yet and this case was going to be no different.

CHAPTER FORTY-EIGHT

Rebecca opened the door and smiled wanly at Robyn.

'Hey,' she said. 'Come in.'

Robyn followed her into the sitting room where Dylan was curled up on the settee in a brown fleece onesie, his eyes shut. They flickered open at their arrival and he mumbled something unintelligible.

'Is Dylan feeling all right?' Robyn asked.

'I think he's coming down with flu,' said Rebecca, sliding onto the settee next to him. She lifted him to her chest and rested an arm around his shoulders. 'Everything okay?'

Robyn nodded. 'In light of new evidence, I'm going to have to ask you some more questions.'

'Have you found the person who…' she didn't finish her sentence. Dylan stirred and Rebecca clammed.

Robyn shook her head. 'We examined Jordan's laptop and came across a thread in a forum about superhero characters.' Robyn watched as Rebecca looked away and smoothed a hand over her son's head.

'We uncovered dialogue between you and Jordan that began in late November last year.' Robyn waited for a reaction but all she noticed was a drooping of shoulders. 'You lied to us, Rebecca. You didn't meet Jordan at Longer Life Health.'

Rebecca lifted wet eyes to Robyn. 'I know. Seems so stupid now. I don't know why I lied to you. You looked so confident and important and I felt so – oh, I don't know – confused and I didn't want you to judge me. I'd told the same story to others when they asked me about how I'd met Jordan. I guess I was too embarrassed to confess we'd met thanks to a forum about comic book superheroes. At school, I was classified as a nerd and laughed at, and had real difficulty finding anyone to accept me as I am. I've never had luck with men. Dylan's father dumped me as soon as he found out I was expecting. He shattered what little confidence I had in myself. I hadn't been on a date since I'd had Dylan. I hit it off with Jordan immediately. He answered my comment and we got chatting and then we met up.'

'Rebecca, please don't lie to me again. I'm going to ask some questions and I need truthful answers.'

Rebecca's eyelids fluttered. 'Okay.'

'Did Jordan suggest you go for an interview at Pharmacals Healthcare?'

'Yes.'

'On the thread Jordan suggested you stay with him only until you found somewhere else. Was it a temporary arrangement?'

Rebecca's voice was heavy with sadness and her eyes damp. 'It was supposed to be a temporary arrangement, just until I found my feet. It had been a major upheaval coming into an area I didn't know very well. After the first week, he asked me to stay because he'd fallen in love with me.'

Robyn studied Rebecca's face, trying to judge if she was telling the truth. Rebecca picked up on her suspicions and spoke again. 'Really. That was how it happened. I'm not lying.'

'Did you have any dealings with Clifford Harris at Pharmacals Healthcare?'

'Who's Clifford Harris?'

'He's one of the supervisors in warehouse G where all the top-level drugs are kept.'

'Then no. I only work with the team in the offices. We have no dealings with any of the warehouse personnel. I'm on admin stuff. I deal mostly with spreadsheets and suchlike. I don't communicate with anybody other than my immediate boss, Nicky Boyce, and some of the team there. There are hundreds of employees at that place. It's difficult to know anyone.'

'Did Jordan ever mention Clifford Harris?'

Rebecca shook her head. 'Never.'

'Rebecca, we think Jordan was involved in smuggling drugs from Pharmacals Healthcare and selling them on to dealers. We've two suspects in custody and they've already admitted to their involvement and implicated both Jordan and Owen. I won't beat about the bush, here. If you know anything about this, now is the time to tell me.' She looked directly at Rebecca, whose head shook from side to side a number of times.

'I know nothing about this. Are you sure Jordan was involved? He can't have been. He wouldn't have kept such a thing from me.'

'Rebecca, if his death is down to his involvement in this, we have to know everything.'

'I didn't know,' said Rebecca. 'Believe me. I didn't know.'

Dylan started to moan quietly.

'He's got a temperature. I'm going to put him to bed,' said Rebecca. 'It might be best if you left. I really can't help you any more. I can't believe Jordan would be so dishonest. As for me – I'm sorry I lied. It was the spur of the moment. I can't bear people thinking I'm a failure because I'm a single mother.'

Robyn stood. 'Being a single parent doesn't make you a failure, Rebecca.'

Rebecca looked at her son. 'No, it doesn't, does it? I shouldn't care what people think about me.' Tears trickled down her cheeks.

'No. You shouldn't.'

'I don't know if I'll ever get over this, Robyn. I can hardly get through the days at the moment. It's all too much.'

'You have to be strong, Rebecca. You're strong enough. Just believe it.'

Robyn saw herself out. While she still felt sympathy for Rebecca and her sick son, she was now more distanced in the emotional sense from the woman. She'd made a fundamental error in handling this case. She'd allowed herself to become too involved. She'd drawn parallels between herself and Rebecca when, clearly, they were two very different people.

She arrived back at the station even more determined to get to the bottom of the investigation. She had to speak to Nathaniel regarding his possible relationship with Lucy Harding, and nobody was going to prevent her from doing so.

The liaison officer, Michelle Watson, was coming out of the station as she entered. She paused to speak to her.

'I've just been visiting Rebecca Tomlinson. She's still in a bit of a state. Her boy is ill. Have you got time to pop around and visit her?'

Michelle snorted. 'I don't think she'd want me to. She's chucked me out of her house twice. First time was immediately after she found out about Jordan's death. I accompanied her home but she told me to leave her alone. I put it down to being upset and the stress. I come across all sorts of reactions when loved ones are involved. However, the second time was the following day – the Tuesday – the day you came by and I played football with Dylan. About ten minutes after you'd gone, Rebecca asked me to leave. Said she didn't need my help and not to come back. I was told she'd moved to Rangemore, so I went to check on her on Friday, but she wasn't in. Are you sure she'd benefit from me visiting?'

Robyn scratched her head and puzzled over what Michelle had revealed. 'I must have misread the situation. I thought she needed support. Obviously, she doesn't. Leave it for now.'

As she walked back to the office she realised an important fact. If Michelle hadn't been with Rebecca on Monday, then Rebecca no longer had an alibi for the time of Owen's murder. Could Rebecca be involved at all?

Her ruminations were interrupted by a call from Ross. She steeled herself for the news she'd been dreading, that Jeanette's biopsy results had revealed something serious. She'd promised herself to be there to help them both through it. No matter what happened, they'd be able to count on her.

'Ross, tell me,' she said.

The relief in his voice was palpable. 'She's clear.'

'Oh, thank goodness,' said Robyn, releasing the breath she'd been holding.

'You have no idea how relieved I am – we are,' said Ross. 'I haven't been able to sleep for worrying about it. It's been the worst few days of my life and I've had some ghastly ones as you know.'

'I do. Hey, it's over. Jeanette's okay,' she said, hearing a sob rise at the other end of the phone.

Ross's voice was tearful. 'Oh, Robyn, it's been dreadful. I've gone through every awful scene imaginable. I worked myself up to the point where I was convinced she was really ill and I'd have done anything to help her if I'd had to. I'd have sold everything we owned to pay for private treatment to get her seen quicker – anything.'

'Come on, now, you don't need to think about it any more.' Her voice was gentle and she spoke as if to a child. She understood the relief he was experiencing.

'I'll be okay. Dash it! That's twice in a week I've bawled my eyes out talking to you.'

'Three times in forty years isn't a bad record, Ross.'

'When was the third time?' he asked. 'I don't ever cry.'

'At the school disco, when the love of your life at the time, Tina Linton, dumped you for Davy Townsend. You cried like a baby.'

Ross snorted. 'Only because she kept my prize-winning conker I'd given her as a love token. I really missed it. It was a fifty-times champion.'

Robyn ended the call and turned towards her office door. Mitz came bustling out, a disturbed look on his face. 'DCI Flint is in there. Wants to know if we've arrested anybody yet.'

'Crap. I've not got anything for him. Come on, let's go and talk to Nathaniel. I'll ring Matt on the way.'

As they raced up the corridor, Robyn tried to work out how best to tackle Rebecca. The more she thought about it, the more she decided they needed to question her whereabouts and look more closely at her. There'd been something in her conversations with Jordan on the forum about a landlord who she didn't get on with. She'd ask Anna to follow that up. Maybe Rebecca wasn't as nice as she appeared to be. That was the trouble with people; they often weren't what they seemed.

CHAPTER FORTY-NINE

THEN

'It could be the candyfloss,' says Oswald's mum to his dad. 'It was maybe too sweet for him, poor lamb.'

She feels the boy's forehead and winces. 'He's got a temperature. Maybe it's more than the candyfloss. We don't want the others to catch it. Better take him home.'

The boy feels too sick to care. He'd felt poorly the morning of the party but hadn't said anything in case his parents had prevented him from coming. He'd thought it was butterflies because he was excited but at school he'd felt hot and sick and by the time Oswald's parents collected him, he wasn't feeling quite as thrilled as he thought he would. Now he wishes he'd said something sooner. He only managed to watch ten minutes of the film before he had to run to the toilets and be sick. He gags and throws up again. Oswald's mother pulls another face.

'That's it. I'll ring his parents while you drive him home. I'll stay here with the other children. Oswald's having a lovely time and I don't want to spoil it.' She turns back to the boy and speaks gently. 'Oswald's daddy is going to take you back home. As soon as you feel better, you can come and stay again.'

The boy wants to cry but he knows there's no point. He's made a mess of his blue jumper and he wants to go home to his own bed. He nods dumbly.

Oswald's dad takes him to the big Volvo and he sits in silence as they drive. He likes Oswald's dad. He's got a big friendly face and he jokes a lot. The boy feels sad he can't stay at the party. Oswald's dad is kind and tells him it's more important he gets checked over in case he's picked up a nasty bug.

'Maybe you'd like to come over next weekend and we'll go out canoeing on the reservoir?' he offers. That cheers the boy and he says thank you.

His mother is concerned when she sees him and hustles him upstairs to bed, where he's given warm milk and a gentle hug. He asks for his sister but is told she's out for the night but not to worry, she'll be back in the morning. They fuss over him and his father sits on the side of the bed and tells him he'll soon feel better. He reads him a story – he hasn't read to him in a long while and the boy enjoys hearing his father's mellifluous voice. Eventually, he finishes the story and plants a kiss on his forehead.

'Night, night, son,' he says.

The boy mumbles good night to them both and they withdraw silently.

The boy snuggles down under the duvet covered in trains. His stomach is no longer churning, and he doesn't feel as sick as he did. He just feels sleepy – very, very sleepy. He shuts his eyes and drifts off to sleep. Tomorrow, he'll tell his sister about the candyfloss and how it made him sick, and about going canoeing with Oswald and his family.

The boy doesn't hear his parents turning in for the night – the running of taps as they clean their teeth, or the creak of the bed as they slip between sheets. He doesn't hear his mother's soft snores. He doesn't hear the distant calling of the crows, disturbed by the flames that crackle and begin to leap and dance in the kitchen, spreading rapidly throughout the house. The boy hears nothing.

CHAPTER FIFTY

DAY NINE – TUESDAY, 13 JUNE, AFTERNOON

With Mitz standing silently by her side, Robyn waited for Joy Fairweather to send them through to Nathaniel's office. The young woman kept her eyes fixed on her typing until her phone lit up, announcing Nathaniel was ready for them.

'You may go through, Detectives,' she said.

Nathaniel was less gracious. 'What now?' he barked as soon as Robyn walked into the room.

'I'm sorry—'

'Spare me the platitudes,' he interjected. 'Get to the point. I'm within a whisker of demanding you be removed from the investigation into my son's death. Make it quick.'

'Lucy Harding,' she said, waiting for a response. She got one. Nathaniel shut his eyes for a moment and exhaled silently through partially opened lips.

'Okay. I see why you think I might be involved, but I can assure you, I'm not.'

Robyn kept her fixed stare on the man.

'Lucy found me online. We chatted and got on well. So much so, I invited her out. She accepted. We had a pleasant enough time, but we struggled for conversation, especially towards the end of the meeting. We parted amicably but didn't stay in contact. Just as well, because soon afterwards, I had a letter telling me I was to be one of her patients at the new clinic in Abbots Bromley.'

'I need more details than that, sir.'

'What sort of details do you require? I'm not going into this chapter and verse. I haven't committed any crimes. I'm a single man who happens to enjoy female company. That's it. End of.'

'Where were you on Thursday evening, Mr Jones-Kilby?'

'Oh, for goodness sake. We've been through this. I didn't kill her. Now get out of my office.'

Robyn didn't move. 'I need to know your movements, sir. You've admitted to having known Lucy Harding and I can't ignore that fact.'

'I have a witness who knows my whereabouts. DCI Flint has been informed of that fact. I don't have to talk to you about this matter now, good day.'

It was futile to argue. Robyn stalked out of the office and back to the car. Mitz trailed in her wake, keeping his council. Robyn pulled out her mobile and rang Amy.

'Ah, DI Carter,' came the casual response. 'Have you phoned to kiss and make up with me?'

'Cut the crap. You phoned me because you had something on Jones-Kilby.'

'And you bummed me off.'

'You surprised after that article you wrote?'

'I apologised for that.'

'Did you find out who Jones-Kilby was seeing?'

'Last time we spoke, you told me to fuck off, well, now I'm telling you the same, only not so impolitely. I'm not pursuing that angle any more. I've found somebody who wants to talk to me.'

'Amy, you can't jeopardise an investigation.'

'And how's that actually going, DI Carter? You charged anybody yet with the murders? You carry on doing your detective work and I'll continue with mine.'

'It isn't connected to the murders, is it?'

'Sorry, DI Carter, this is a very bad line and I have to get to a meeting.'

The line went dead. Robyn growled at the mobile. Mitz gave her a brief look.

'If she messes things up, I'll make sure she pays.'

'She's arrogant and a complete pain in the arse to deal with, but I doubt she'd be that stupid,' said Mitz.

'I don't know. She's desperate to get ahead of the pack.' Robyn drummed on her leg angrily. 'That bloody Nathaniel is infuriating too. If only he'd come clean so we didn't have to keep working around him.'

'He's not the most charismatic, is he?'

'He's a hard-nosed businessman. I suppose he has to be that way in his profession. It's not helpful though. Amy said she had something else on him, but she's gone cold on me. I don't want to waste any more time chasing my tail with him. I need to check out Rebecca. Something isn't adding up there, either.' She dialled Anna's number.

'Got anything on Rebecca?'

'Still searching. I rang Longer Life Health where she used to work, and they told me her aunt Rose is back from her trip to Barbados. She also works there, and went in yesterday.'

'Have you an address for Rose?'

'I'll text it across.'

Within seconds, Robyn read out, 'Rose Griffith, 22 Ashdown Crescent, just off Vicarage Street, Water Orton.' She put the address into the satnav and they headed in the direction of Birmingham.

Ashdown Crescent consisted of a row of detached Victorian houses, most of which had been added to over the years and had been extended upwards and outwards so much, they were in danger of outgrowing the plots on which they stood. Number 22 appeared lonely and unaffected by comparison to the other houses. It retained its front garden with flower borders and original patterned brick exterior, slate roof and three-sided bay windows. A decorative bay tree in a pot stood in the brick-enclosed porch, a red ribbon tied around it and finished with a bow.

Rose Griffith was a pleasant-faced woman whose large hooped earrings matched her cerise lipstick and nail varnish. She could have passed for any age between thirty and fifty, although David had discovered she was in her mid-fifties. She reminded Robyn of Rebecca with her glossy black hair and clear, hazel eyes that regarded Robyn and Mitz cautiously.

'You telling me Rebecca's boyfriend was murdered?' she said in a honeyed voice as she poured water into three mugs for them, her hands trembling as she did so.

'I'm afraid so. Has Rebecca not been in contact?'

Rose sniffed quietly. 'That young lady made it quite clear how she felt about my "interference" when she moved out of this house last December.'

'She lived with you?'

'She'd been living with me since she was sixteen years old. Came here straight after her folks died. God bless their souls.'

Robyn thought back to Rebecca's online conversation with Jordan when she told him she had a horrible landlord. Another lie.

'She seems to be renting a place in the same area of Staffordshire for now.'

Rose handed the mugs to the officers and lifted her own mug to her lips before she spoke. 'No doubt she'll come back here in her own good time. DI Carter, why are you here?'

'We have to look into the backgrounds of everyone who was involved with Jordan.'

Rose nodded wisely, her eyes glittering. 'You suspect she might have had something to do with his death, don't you?'

'It's procedure,' said Robyn.

Rose placed her hands together, as if praying, and rested her chin on them. 'Rebecca's had a hard life. She's been let down and she's struggled to come to terms with huge losses. She can be a confused, hurt and even angry young woman, but she's not a murderer. She's had more than her fair share of bad luck. It's a struggle for her.'

'I understand. I've spoken to her a few times and met Dylan. She told me Dylan's father walked out on her when she found out she was expecting.'

'That's right. Gabriel Smith never wanted children. He was adamant from the outset but Rebecca believed otherwise. She wanted Gabriel's son and thought once he found out she was pregnant, he'd change his mind. He didn't. He was furious. Told her to get rid of the baby, and when she refused, he left her to it. It was a bitter blow. She thought such a lot of Gabriel. He was all she talked about for months. He was her first real love.'

'Does Gabriel live locally?'

'Not far away. I can give you his address. He's married now and his mother comes to Longer Life Health regularly.'

'That's where Rebecca worked too, isn't it?'

'She did. I got her the job there. She worked in the shop selling various herbal remedies and health products. I'm one of the therapists there. I perform various treatments: acupuncture, healing, reiki, among others.'

'But she left her job to be with Jordan, her boyfriend?'

'It was all very sudden. She came in one day and said she'd found another job, had been for an interview and was leaving. I wasn't very pleased with her. She might have at least talked to me about it before jacking it all in. I felt very awkward. I had to explain I was as much in the dark about her decision as they all were. She'd been acting strangely for a few weeks prior to it. She wouldn't say why. She could be quite secretive at times and I learnt a long time ago it did no good to pry.'

'So you were surprised she suddenly upped and left to live with Jordan?'

'Not exactly. She's done this sort of thing before. A year ago, she moved in with a man old enough to be her father – Hugo Morton. He owned a large engineering company and was widowed. She met him online and they started dating. He invited her to some big corporate events and even took her away to Paris and Amsterdam with him. Then he invited her to move in with him. Apparently, it was a massive mansion with six bedrooms and an indoor swimming pool. She was so excited. We said our goodbyes and I waved her and Dylan off to start their new lives. Less than a week later they were back home. It hadn't worked out. She flatly refused to talk about it. Luckily, her position hadn't been filled at Longer Life Health and she returned to work.'

'Would you say you were close?'

'It's very difficult to explain our relationship. Rebecca's my niece. I love her dearly. She is my sister's daughter and every time I look at her, I think of my sister Bethany. But Rebecca is not an easy person to get along with. She has her demons and she is, in many ways, still like a teenager. She won't open up to me. Lord knows I've tried often enough, but when you question her decisions, or try to guide her, she retreats into herself. She insists on doing everything her own way. It's like living with a sixteen-year-old all the time. I'm partly to blame. I've allowed her to become the way she has. I was always compensating for what happened in the past.'

'Could you elaborate?' Robyn asked.

'Where to begin? Rebecca's very bright. She could have done anything she wanted: gone into law, been a teacher, even run her own company I dare say. She had such potential – was always top of her class. We were all very proud of her. Then losing her family changed her in many ways. She wouldn't let anyone close to her – not me, not her friends, not anyone. She dropped out of school. Of course, I understood it was because she was hurting and I tried to make life better for her, but I had no parenting skills as well as my own sorrow to handle, and she drifted further away from me. I insisted she take the job at Longer Life Health. I couldn't carry on supporting the pair of us, so she did, and after a few weeks there, she met Gabriel Smith. Things improved. She started going out with him and began living again, but it all happened very quickly. One minute they were a young couple having fun and the next, she was pregnant.

'She went through with the pregnancy alone. She was determined to have Dylan but it left its mark. Rebecca's a woman who wants to be loved. She craves attention and love and is desperate to find a soulmate. Sadly, she never seems to find the right man. She's had a few boyfriends. Hugo Morton let her down and then she found Jordan. I had hoped this time she'd be lucky, but it appears bad luck follows her and she's destined to be alone.'

'Did she leave here on bad terms with you?'

'I'm afraid sharp words were spoken. I said what's been in my heart for some time. I've looked after Rebecca for the last seven years. I put up with her arguments, tantrums, selfishness and dogmatic attitude because I felt it was my duty to. I owed it to the memory of my sister. But Rebecca is a grown woman who's made decisions I haven't approved of, and who expected too much from me – her housekeeper, her guardian and even a babysitter – without giving much in return. I chose not to marry and have children. I wanted my freedom to be who I was. I had plans to travel, not to spend my life here bringing up children and being confined. When this house came up for sale, my sister who also lived in Water Orton suggested I buy it. At the time, it seemed a good idea. I could be near my family and my job, and they'd keep an eye on the place when I went away. Since the night they all died, I've felt trapped here. I stayed here for Rebecca's sake, not mine. But she doesn't need me any longer and I'm getting older. I'd like to return to Barbados and Rebecca ought to fend for herself.'

Rose's hand trembled again as she lifted the mug to her lips.

'You said, "They all died." I understood your sister and brother-in-law died that night.'

Rose shook her head with sorrow. 'And my nephew. Isaac was six when he died in that fire. He perished alongside his mother and his father. That was why Rebecca became so withdrawn. She and Isaac were very close. I mean extremely close. He was some years younger than her, and she looked after him like she was his mother. She did everything for him – took him to and fetched him from school, went to the park, played with him. I believe that's why having her own son was so important to her. In her mind, she was replacing Isaac with another child to love. She adores Dylan. I've seen many mothers with children in my life, but I've never seen one love a child with such passion as Rebecca does.

Robyn was astounded. Rebecca had never spoken about Isaac. 'The fire. What happened?'

'It was tragic. Bethany's husband, Joseph, asked if Rebecca could stay with me for a couple of nights. Said Rebecca was being difficult – teenage hormone problems – and it would help him and Bethany if Rebecca could spend a day or two with me. He was so apologetic the way he asked. Like he was frightened I'd say no or would shout at him. I never understood why Bethany fell for him. She was so vibrant and he was such a timid, little man – scared of his own shadow. Bethany was the strong, determined one who looked after them all. Anyway, I agreed and Rebecca came here. Sometime during the first night she was here, the house caught fire. The fire brigade put out the blaze but it was too late to save anyone inside. Bethany, Joseph, and Isaac all died of smoke inhalation.'

She blinked away tears. 'It still hurts to talk about it. Rebecca was heartbroken. Blamed herself for not being there to maybe save them or die with them.'

'It was an electrical fire?'

'Yes, the chief officer told us it was caused by a faulty toaster.'

'I'm so sorry.'

'It was a long time ago, but yes, it still hurts. To have only been a few streets away and not known anything about it until it was too late is difficult to live with.'

Robyn looked out of the kitchen window, down the garden and towards a brightly painted orange shed with a window box filled with yellow flowers, and thought about the young Isaac who'd perished in the fire. It was a sad story. Rebecca had certainly had her share of sorrow.

'Where was this?'

'Along Vicarage Street. The house was in such a bad state after the fire that it collapsed and had to be demolished. There's nothing left but the land, but you can see where it used to stand. It's fronted by a tall hedge and a large wooden gate. Rebecca owns it, not that she ever visits it. It holds too many painful memories for her. I told her she should sell it, but she won't. She said the land belonged to her parents and Isaac and she wasn't selling it to a developer for another family to live on. I couldn't persuade her even though I'm sure she'd have got a decent amount of money for it.'

Robyn thought she'd swing by and take a look for herself so she thanked Rose, who spoke.

'Rebecca won't manage on her own. She'll come back. I know she will. She'll turn up full of regret at what happened between us, and I'll forgive her. It's happened before. I know her. She'll return with Dylan and we'll try again, until she finds another man to chase after.' For a moment, her cheeks lifted.

Robyn returned the smile and thanked her again. They requested Gabriel's address and phone number and left Rose by the kitchen window, watching as they left, possibly hoping Rebecca would soon turn up.

⚜

Vicarage Street was at the edge of Water Orton and backed onto fields, edged by tall oaks. They drove past two houses well set back from the road and isolated before reaching a site that had undoubtedly belonged to the Tomlinsons. They drew up on the driveway in front of a tall wooden gate, padlocked and bearing a sign: 'Keep Out'. The thick foliage of a large hedge prevented anyone from seeing what was beyond. Mitz got out of the car and tried to peer through the hedge but drew back with a tut.

'Can't see a thing through this'

'I'll take a look,' said Robyn, managing to lodge a foot against the gate and lifting herself up far enough to see over it. There wasn't much to see. It was a neglected patch of land blackened in part, with no evidence a family had ever lived here. Nature was gradually reclaiming the land and huge forsythia bushes, rhododendrons and other large bushy plants had taken over what had presumably been the back garden.

She dropped back down and wiped her hands clean. 'Looks like a scene from *Day of the Triffids* out there.'

She climbed back into the car and rang Gabriel Smith, who didn't reply. She left a message for him to ring her and checked the time. It was after five and there was a chance that by the time they got to the station, DCI Flint would have left for the day. She instructed Mitz to return and mulled over the information she'd accrued. She was still no closer to finding her murderer and another day had almost passed. She fought back a sigh. She had to stick at it. There was no other option.

CHAPTER FIFTY-ONE

THEN

The girl tiptoes past the bedroom. She hears snores, indicating the occupant is fast asleep. It's 1 a.m. and she has been awake ever since she went to bed, waiting for this time. She's planned it perfectly.

The idea had come to her three days earlier. Her mother had been making them breakfast and suddenly let out a yelp of terror. The girl had turned towards the noise in time to see sparks leap from the toaster. Her father had been quicker still and jumped to his feet, unplugged it and wafted a tea towel at the tiny flames until they were extinguished, in what seemed to be one swift movement.

'I told you it was playing up,' said her mother, once she'd recovered from the shock.

'I could take it in for repair,' said her father.

'You'll do no such thing. It's lethal. It'll burn the place down. You saw what happened. Take it to the recycling tip.'

Her father pushed the plug back into the socket and watched carefully. Within seconds, sparks flew out. Again, he yanked out the plug and grunted. 'You're right. It needs throwing away. I'll put it in the recycling pile. We'll take it to the recycling tip next week when we take the other stuff.'

The girl saw it as a sign – a way to rid herself of her evil mother, who'd caused her baby to miscarry, and her weak-willed father who'd let it happen and hadn't stood up to her mother, the religious nut who ruled the house. That very same morning, her brother told her about the sleepover. If only she could wangle a way to be out of the house the same night as him, she could start a fire that would engulf their parents. She and her brother would never have to face the punishments in the shed again.

She'd decided to talk to her father and persuade him it'd be better if she spent a few nights away. She'd tell him she was desperately unhappy since the incident in the shed and ask if she could stay at Aunt Rose's house. It's only up the road. She only had to get her father to agree.

There was a way out of this hell. God had shown her the way. He wanted her evil parents to be punished and she would listen to his voice.

The girl slinks out of the back door and shivers in the cool night air. There are no sounds, only a rustling of the leaves in the trees at the bottom of the fields. The crows are sleeping. She hastens down the roads to her home, where her parents are sleeping, and enters via the back gate. Behind the house is a large cardboard box where her father stores plastic bottles, cardboard packaging and other recyclable materials, to be thrown out at the local tip. The toaster is in there. The girl lifts it out, puts her key into the lock and turns it. The only sound comes from the thudding in her chest. It will soon be over. She opens the door and creeps into the kitchen. Moonlight floods through the kitchen window overlooking the garden and the hateful shed. She shudders at the memory of being imprisoned inside it. However, she has more pressing matters. The moon is guiding her, its light shining brightly onto the kitchen worktops, where she feels for the three-pin socket she is going to use and prepares to insert the toaster plug. She inhales deeply. Her brother is out at his friend's house and she can hear no noises coming from her parents' room. They haven't heard her. It's time. She pushes the plug in hard with the flat of her palm and without turning back, races for the door, shutting it quietly, locking it behind her and then disappearing back into the night.

Tomorrow she'll be free. She and Isaac will never have to worry about the crows again. She'll look after her little brother and be a better mother than theirs ever was to them. She rushes down the dark roads, a shadow fleeing along the pavements back to the warmth of Aunt Rose's house, where she treads carefully up the stairs to her room and slides between cool sheets, happy for the first time in a very long while.

CHAPTER FIFTY-TWO

DAY NINE – TUESDAY, 13 JUNE, EVENING

Robyn clicked on Hugo Morton's profile on the Morton Engineering website and wondered what could have attracted Rebecca to the man other than money. He was in his early sixties, with a puffy face, broad nose and thinning hair – a complete contrast to Jordan's delicate features.

She dialled the contact number for the works and spoke to a receptionist who put her through to Hugo. After introducing herself, and explaining she was amassing information about people connected to Jordan, she asked about Rebecca.

His voice was quiet and unassuming, and he answered politely. 'I haven't seen Becky since June last year.'

'I was led to believe she moved in with you for a while.'

Hugo gave a small cough. 'Yes, that was most unfortunate. I rather rushed into the relationship. With hindsight, I ought not to have let my ego become so flattered, but she was a very attentive and attractive young woman, and she was so empathetic. I'd lost my wife, Kathy, to cancer the year before. Becky said all the right things – understood the misery of such a loss. I'm afraid I fell for her charm.'

'How did you meet?'

'At a garden centre, in Sutton Coldfield, of all places. I'm a keen apiarist and was invited to give a talk there about beekeeping.

Rebecca came along to it and stayed behind to ask some questions afterwards. She really was most interested in bees and their part in our environment. Soon afterwards, she sent me an email to say how much she'd enjoyed my talk and asked some more questions, and then we started a casual relationship.'

'This was all online?'

'Oh no. She came to visit me a few times. I showed her my own bee colony and we chatted about bee conservation. We went out together a couple of times and then, well, she stayed over after an event. It was the annual Morton Engineering Ball and she accompanied me there. She was a delight. Rather than ask her to find a hotel, I invited her to stay at my house and I'd say that was when things accelerated. I found myself swept along by it all – a lovely lady like her, interested in a fossil like me. And I knew it wasn't about my money. Not with her having been paid out all that insurance money. She had her own money. I felt we'd connected.'

'Insurance money?'

'Yes, from the fire that killed her parents. That's what she told me, and at the time, I believed her.' He sounded defeated.

'Can I ask why you broke up?'

'It was quite simple. She lied to me. I can't tolerate lies. I don't care if it was because she was afraid it would frighten me off. You shouldn't hide something as important as that.'

'I'm afraid you've lost me, sir.'

'Her son Dylan. I didn't know she had a son. She didn't mention him until the day she arrived with her bags, and him by her side. How crazy is that? I wasn't best pleased. Of course, I couldn't turn them away immediately so I let them stay in one of the spare rooms, but I told her it was over between us. She insisted I'd get to love him. I've nothing against children and, indeed, he was a nice lad, but it was the fact she didn't say anything to me about it in the first place. I wondered what else she'd keep from me and I couldn't maintain any relationship on that basis. Kathy and I had been completely open with each other. Kathy wanted me to find love again. She'd have turned in her grave if she'd known I'd been duped like that.

'At first Rebecca was tearful and said she thought I'd take to the boy in time, that surely I loved her enough to love him too. She hadn't wanted to frighten me off by telling me about him. It was utter lunacy. Then she begged me for help. She said she needed money and asked if I would loan her several thousand pounds, because hers was tied up in a trust fund. Of course, that struck me as nonsense. She'd lied about the insurance money and I wondered what other untruths she'd told me. I refused to give her any money and that was when she flipped completely. In fact, she became quite aggressive. Called me many names I'd rather not repeat and eventually marched out, taking the boy with her. I think I had a lucky escape there. Felt a complete bloody idiot though and haven't been on a date since.'

After the call, Robyn made some notes. Rebecca was a manipulator and a liar. Was she also capable of murder? Robyn rang her immediately to arrange a meeting but the phone went to answerphone and she left no message. She'd catch up with Rebecca very soon.

David Marker sat back in his chair and ran a hand over his tired face. He spoke to Robyn. 'I can't understand why Owen would be interested in this photograph. It's of a group of people, Chief Constable McIntosh, Councillor Turner, MP Broughton and their wives, with Nathaniel Jones-Kilby taken at a charity event at Stafford Town Hall. They're sitting at the table. It's no more than that.'

The photograph could be completely unimportant, but for now it was all they had to connect Owen to Nathaniel, and Robyn was still curious to know what he was hiding from them. Nathaniel was seeing a married woman. Robyn wondered if it could be one of the three women in the photograph.

'Check out the wives in the picture. See what you can find out,' she said.

David wasn't very long before he turned up some useful information.

'Guv, Vanessa Broughton lives near Tamworth with her husband but last month, she purchased a third-floor flat in Abbots Bromley in her name. It's in a converted schoolhouse, developed by NJK Properties, and it's bang opposite the construction site in Abbots Bromley where the dark blue car was parked the evening Lucy Harding was murdered.'

'Then I think we need to talk to her and see if she happened to be there on Thursday.'

'She could well have been because I also found out she's got an impending speeding fine from that evening. Her car passed through a speed camera on the A515 heading towards Abbots Bromley, touching sixty in a fifty limit.'

'What time did it clock her?'

'At 5.50 p.m. and Abbots Bromley is only ten minutes from there.'

'It's time we paid Vanessa Broughton a visit. We'll go via Abbots Bromley and take a look at where her flat is.'

David seemed cheered at the prospect of making progress. He regaled her with factoids about Abbots Bromley on the journey there. Every trip with David was a history lesson.

'Famous for the annual Horn Dance,' he said.

'What is that exactly?' Robyn asked.

'A folk dance that goes back to the Middle Ages. They perform it each September. They use reindeer horns. Worth seeing.'

'I'll bear it in mind come September.'

'It's a bit like watching you and DI Shearer when you have a stand-off,' he said.

She threw him a scowl that turned into an amiable grin when she saw the smile on his face. It was nice to see him looking more positive. In any case, he was probably right about her and Shearer.

They drew to a halt beside the construction site at the T-junction between the main road and Bromley Rise. The squad car's headlights skimmed a large 'No Entry' sign attached to the wall of a disused school building fronting the road as they turned into an area – a small, tight turning circle – that Robyn had spotted on Friday. Robyn jumped out and looked back across at the road, trying to ascertain how viable it was for a car to be spotted from a flat on the top floor, and decided an occupant there would have a partial view of this area, even though any vehicle stationed here was well hidden. An observant passer-by might also have noticed one, but would not have had a clear view of it. If Vanessa Broughton had been at the flat on Thursday evening, then she might have seen it; however, Robyn didn't hold out a lot of hope. The block of flats with its bare windows didn't yet appear to be occupied. She sighed at the futility of her quest and, joining David again, walked across the empty road to the flats where she rang the bell marked 'Penthouse' and waited for a reply.

'She's not here. She must be at her home address. We'll try there.'

The Broughton's house, in an affluent area north of Tamworth, was an individually designed, detached residence, hidden behind large laurel hedges and approached via a brick driveway. Robyn was pleased to see a hint of orange glow in a downstairs window, indicating somebody was at home.

After the third knock, a light came on in the entrance, and a few minutes later, a woman with tousled auburn hair, wrapped tightly in a dressing gown, appeared.

Robyn held up her warrant card. 'Mrs Broughton. I'm DI Carter and this is PC Marker. I'm very sorry to disturb you at this late hour but we're conducting investigations into a serious crime and think you might be able to assist us.'

The woman blinked at them. 'Can't this wait? It's late.'

'I'm afraid it can't. We wouldn't trouble you if it wasn't important.'

The woman folded her arms.

'Where were you last Thursday, the eighth?'

'What time?'

'The evening – after six.'

The woman looked down at her elegant mule slippers briefly before responding, 'Here.'

'I'm afraid your car was spotted elsewhere at that time.'

'Where was it seen?' she demanded, arms tightening further.

'Abbots Bromley. I understand you have recently purchased a property there.'

Vanessa cast a look behind her. 'Come inside. My husband is upstairs. Keep your voices down. I don't want to wake him.'

They followed her into a small sitting room, filled with two settees facing each other in front of an open fireplace. The room was painted pale blue, and turquoise scatter cushions filled the settee; the same heavily embroidered fabric hung at the windows.

Robyn tore her eyes away from the large green-and-blue Buddha sat in front of the fireplace and spoke. 'Mrs Broughton, we believe you were in Abbots Bromley on Thursday evening.'

'Yes. I was. I went to my apartment. I had a new table for it.'

'This is the penthouse apartment in the old schoolhouse?'

'Yes. Why?'

'Can you see the building site entrance across the road from you, from any of the windows in your flat?'

'The master bedroom overlooks the road and the site. Why?'

'Did you at any time that evening spot a dark blue car parked in the turning area in front of the construction site?'

Vanessa brushed away a stray hair, holding onto it for a second as she considered her answer. 'I don't recall seeing a car.'

'Did you notice anybody walking into that area, or leaving it?'

Vanessa nodded. 'I did catch a glimpse of somebody but I didn't see their car. I'd have had to be staring out of the window to see directly into that area, and I wasn't.'

'This person. Can you describe them?'

'No. I only saw them for a fleeting minute.'

'What time would that have been?'

Vanessa flushed again. 'About seven thirty.'

Robyn continued. 'If we showed you a photograph, would you take a look and see if it resembles the person you saw?'

Vanessa's shoulders rose in acceptance of the request. Robyn extracted a picture of Jasper Fletcher and showed it to Vanessa. One well-groomed eyebrow rose in surprise.

'No. It wasn't him. It wasn't a man. It was a woman.'

'A woman?'

'Yes. I think so. She had dark hair and was walking briskly. She turned off into that area. She might have come straight out again. I don't know. I wasn't really paying much attention.'

Robyn didn't know what to make of this information. It was something and nothing. The woman might have no bearing on the case at all. However, she might also have seen the dark blue car parked there. If only Robyn could identify her, it would aid her investigation. There was no other way: she was going to have to go door-to-door along the street and put in a request for witnesses for this woman, yet she didn't really have time. Flint wanted results and soon.

'Were you alone at the flat?'

'What are you suggesting?'

'Did your husband accompany you? If so, did he also see this person?'

'Oh, right.' Vanessa pulled at another hair, avoiding eye contact with Robyn. 'No. He was here. The apartment is an investment property. It's my pet project. There've been a lot of snagging issues to address and I've been there on and off to make sure the finishing touches are completed. I'll let it out in due course.'

Robyn was about to leave it at that when it struck her that she had an opportunity to ask about Owen. She pulled out another photograph.

'Do you recognise this man?'

Vanessa took one look at it and nodded. 'He's called Owen. He works at Rugeley Electrical.'

'How much do you know about him?'

'Not a lot. I wanted some ambient lighting fitted in the sitting room – those LED lights that throw out different colours. Owen served me. I needed an electrician and asked if he could fit them. He told me he was qualified but didn't usually do private jobs. The long and short of it is we came to an arrangement. He installed them out of hours and I paid him in cash. Hardly illegal, is it?'

'When was that?'

'Erm. It wasn't last week... the week before... Wednesday. Wednesday evening.' There was something about the way she'd become furtive that triggered a thought in Robyn's mind. This was the same day Owen went to Nathaniel's home to install a smoke detector and spotted the photograph of them all at a charity ball. Had he recognised Vanessa in it? Could this be the woman with whom Nathaniel was having an affair?

'Was your husband there that night too?'

Vanessa's neck flushed scarlet. 'No. As you may know, he's an MP. He was in London – some paper he had to vote on.'

Vanessa's obvious discomfort encouraged Robyn to pursue her line of questioning. 'I expect he has to visit London quite often.'

Vanessa's head bobbed up and down, her auburn hair bouncing as she did so. 'Yes, he does. Now, can I be of any further help?'

'Did you have any visitors at the flat that evening?'

'I don't see how that's relevant.'

'The man who fitted your lights was killed last week. It's important we talk to everyone who saw him those last final days.'

Vanessa spoke with reluctance. 'I did have a visitor. Nathaniel Jones-Kilby. He knows my husband well. He wanted to discuss something and had forgotten Stewart was in London. He stayed for a while. Nathaniel didn't see or speak to Owen. He was in the kitchen when I settled up with Owen and showed him out.' Her neck deepened in colour and Robyn knew the truth immediately.

'And Mr Jones-Kilby went to your flat in Abbots Bromley to discuss something with your husband? He didn't come to this house to see him?'

'I think you should leave now,' said Vanessa. 'There's nothing more to be said on this matter.'

'Are you going to pull in Nathaniel, guv?' David asked once they were back in the squad car.

'No. I think I've worked out why DCI Flint didn't want me to pursue Jones-Kilby's alibi. He's been having an affair with Vanessa Broughton. If word of that got out, or her husband got wind of it, it could be messy. Owen saw them together at her flat – maybe they weren't as discreet as they thought. When he saw the photograph of the three of them in Nathaniel's home, he put two and two together. I reckon he told Jordan about it and that's why Jordan went to see his father on the Friday afternoon. He was probably annoyed. We may never know. Either way, I don't think it helps our investigation. I'll confirm this with DCI Flint to make sure.' She heaved a sigh. 'We could do with finding the woman with dark hair, seen near the building site.'

They travelled back in silence until they reached the outskirts of Stafford and then David spoke up. 'We're seeing a marriage counsellor next week. I don't know what to say to them. I feel really awkward about it.'

Robyn cast a glance at him. 'That bad, eh?'

'Yeah. It's been on the cards for a while. Heather says I'm not dynamic enough. What sort of stupid bloody statement is that supposed to be? I've always been who I am.'

'Sounds like Heather's the one with the problem. She might be feeling unfulfilled. Some of us lash out at those we love when the problem is actually us.'

David kept his eyes on the road. 'Maybe.'

'The counsellor will help uncover the real issues behind her complaints. Be open. That's all you can do if you want to save your marriage.'

There was a long silence. 'Not sure I want to, guv,' came the reply. Robyn left it at that. David would work things out in his own way as he always did.

As they drove, a call came through. It was Gabriel Smith, Dylan's father. His voice was deep and lazy.

'You want to talk about Rebecca Tomlinson?' he said.

'I hoped you'd be able to tell me about her. Her aunt said you were very close at one stage.'

'She in trouble?'

'No, we're looking into the death of her boyfriend, Jordan Kilby.'

'Dead guy? I never heard of him. It's been a long while since I last saw Rebecca. A long while.'

'You don't have any contact with Dylan?'

'Why would I have any contact with the boy?'

'You're his father, aren't you?'

The laugh was long and resonant. 'She's been telling stories again. She's so good at that. I'm not the boy's father. Rebecca knows that. That's why we broke up.'

'She told us you left her when you found out she was expecting.'

'That's what she told a lot of people but it isn't the truth. Rebecca said she wanted a baby, but we were only seventeen and I didn't want a kid. She pressed me and pushed me and pleaded but I told her if she wanted a child, I wasn't the man for her. She seemed to accept that. I didn't realise then that Rebecca was like two people – she'd say one thing to my face and do another behind my back. She's seriously twisted. Within a few weeks, she said she'd fallen pregnant and didn't understand how it could have happened. I knew it wasn't my kid. I told her so and we had an almighty argument. I walked out, and a few days later I found out she'd been sleeping about behind my back the whole time we'd been together: one night stands with friends, strangers at raves – she'd been shagging anybody who wanted her. I don't think she even knows who the father of that boy is, but it sure isn't me. I took a paternity test soon after Dylan was born to find out the truth. She knows it came back negative.'

After Gabriel hung up, Robyn was about to ring Rebecca when she received a call from Mitz.

'Joe Harris wants to make a confession,' he said.

'We're on our way back. Wait for me. We'll be ten minutes.'

David floored the accelerator. Robyn was mindful of how quickly the time was running out before Flint insisted on bringing in Shearer. She would interview Rebecca again. If the woman was able to behave in such a deceitful way, she could well have been duping Robyn with an act, and Robyn Carter hated nothing more than being lied to.

CHAPTER FIFTY-THREE

DAY NINE – TUESDAY, 13 JUNE, LATE NIGHT

Joe Harris rested his hands on the desk, head hung forward. He'd refused a lawyer. He'd agreed to the interview being recorded and Mitz now sat alongside Robyn as Joe unburdened himself.

Robyn spoke. 'What did you want to tell us, Mr Harris?'

'I want to confess to my part in the drug-stealing operation. I received and handled stolen goods. There's no point in denying it any longer. Clifford is bound to have said something by now. I also want to help you with your enquiries. Maybe we could cut a deal.'

'What information do you have?'

'It's about Jordan and Owen.'

'I'm listening.'

Joe Harris kept his eyes fixed on the desk as he told them what had happened between the three of them…

It's the beginning of June. There's just the three of them in the Fox and Weasel. Jordan is chewing his thumb, nibbling at the skin around the nail, his face contorted. He stops for a minute and speaks again, his voice needy. 'Look it's not a lot to ask. We lift drugs and sell them on. All I want is something lifted for myself.'

Joe shakes his head. 'Nah, it's way too risky. We've got it all sorted the way we play it. Clifford knows what's coming in and falsifies the quantities; you pick them up and drop them off with Owen. It's the way we operate. If we all start putting in shopping lists of what we each want, it'll get messy and we'll get caught. We've just managed to work out how to get our hands on a lucrative amount of methadone. We'll be rolling in money once we get that out on the street. You can buy your own drugs once you've got the money for that.'

Owen crosses his arms and glowers at Jordan. 'See. Joe agrees with me. It's not going to happen.'

Jordan persists. 'Owen, for fuck's sake, this is really important. I can't buy this stuff even if I have got the money for it. It's only just come to the market. You know why I need to get my hands on it. I have to get it. Come on, mate. It can't be just about the bloody money, can it? Help me out here.'

'Drop it, Jordan,' says Joe, leaning across the bar. 'Owen says no, and no it is. You knew what you signed up for when you joined us. We call the shots here, not you.'

'Then I'm pulling out. You can find yourself another driver.'

Joe's voice oozes menace. 'We won't let you do that. You got into this with your eyes open. You do as we say and you keep doing as we say until we decide you can stop. Got it? The plan is to keep it up until Clifford retires and then stop, not beforehand, so don't you go rocking the boat or we'll have to make sure you stay quiet, permanently.'

Jordan's knuckles turn white as he clenches his fists.

Owen moves closer to him and puts a heavy hand on his shoulder. 'Leave it, Jordan. You're in for the duration. And we're not straying from the plan. You go to Pharmacals tomorrow and you collect the methadone from Clifford. You meet me in the layby as usual on the way to Abbots Bromley surgery and hand it over. Got it?'

'I thought you understood, Owen,' Jordan says. 'You're supposed to be a friend.'

'I do understand but we can't do what you want. It's far too risky. You want some real top-end gear that will be missed. Even Clifford won't be able to lose that in the system without suspicion falling on him. You see that, don't you? You're my mate. I don't like letting you down. If we could wangle it, we would, but it's too dangerous so drop it, okay?'

Jordan nods miserably.

'Go home, Jordan,' says Owen. 'I'll see you tomorrow.'

Jordan picks up his cycling helmet and leaves.

Joe waits until the door is closed before speaking. 'That's a fucking madcap idea. Stupid prick. He must be out of his tree if he thinks we'll try stealing that.'

'Fuck knows what made him come up with that one.'

Joe studies Owen's face and his heavy-lidded eyes that hide many secrets. Jordan revealed Owen knows why he wants the drugs, but Owen is remaining button-lipped. 'We got a problem with Jordan?' he asks, instead of pressing the issue.

'I'm not sure. He's been behaving really oddly recently. I blame that bitch Rebecca. She tugs his strings all the time and keeps making demands on him. He's always moaning about her to me. I told him to dump her but he says he can't. Fuck knows why not. I'd have chucked her out ages ago, along with that whiny kid of hers. Jordan doesn't even like the brat so no idea why he puts up with them both. If we have got a problem, I'll handle it. Best to keep an eye on him in case he decides to bail or dob us in to the cops.'

Robyn listened to Joe's account of the evening a few days before Jordan died.

'What drug did Jordan want Clifford to steal?'

'Never heard of it before,' said Joe. 'Brinera, or something like it.'

'Why was it so important?'

'I honestly don't know. I didn't ask. Owen knew. He was the only person Jordan confided in. He didn't share that information with me or Clifford, but I believe whatever the reason was, it was why they both got murdered.'

'I'm going to talk to a colleague and leave you here with Sergeant Patel. If you'd like a lawyer, please let him know. We'll interview you officially again once one has arrived and charge you. Are you clear about that?'

Joe grunted a response.

Empty paper cups were strewn on desks and there was a collective clattering of keyboard keys as the rest of her team continued working even though it was almost midnight. Robyn headed straight for her computer and typed 'Brinera' into a search engine and groaned. It returned no results.

'Anna, first thing tomorrow, find out if there's a drug called Brinera or one that sounds similar to that, and let me know what it would be used for. Okay, all of you go home. I'll need somebody to be fresh in the morning.'

'You staying, guv?'

'I'm going to interview Joe Harris again. He thinks Owen and Jordan were killed because of some drug Jordan wanted to get his hands on.'

'What sort of drug?' Matt asked.

'That's what I need to find out. Joe doesn't know its name and the one he gave me isn't yielding any results. All he could tell me was that it is a new drug.'

'Do you think Lucy Harding was anything to do with it?'

'I'm flummoxed for the moment. Neither Joe nor Clifford has mentioned her, but I'm going to ask them who they sold the drugs on to, and see if she could be linked to this in any way.'

'So, none of this is to do with Nathaniel?' said David.

'Doesn't look that way.'

'I wonder why Amy was so sure he was involved.'

'She doesn't like the man and was trying to dig up dirt on him. You know Amy, she'll do anything for a story.'

'Yeah. She'd sell her soul to the devil, that one.' David sniffed. 'Night, guv.'

'Cheers. Night. See you in a few hours.'

CHAPTER FIFTY-FOUR

DAY TEN – WEDNESDAY, 14 JUNE, MORNING

Robyn could barely keep her eyes open. She'd given up on sleep and come in early only to find Matt already at his desk.

'Don't ask. Poppy woke me up at four. She's teething again. Couldn't sleep after that,' he said. He shoved a bacon roll into his mouth and continued scrolling through a list.

'What you up to?'

'Searching back through the lists of all the patients who visited the surgery on Thursday, the day Lucy died. We only checked and spoke to the patients who attended the afternoon clinic.'

Robyn yawned and meandered across to the coffee machine. 'I'm actually sick of this bloody coffee,' she said.

'I'll do a coffee run and get you a hot chocolate from the café down the road, if you like. I could do with another bacon roll.' He stopped speaking. 'Whoa. Hold on.'

Robyn took a step back. 'What is it?'

'There are two surgeries a day, but there's also a half-hour slot for emergency appointments before the morning surgery. Look who attended.' He pointed at the first name on the list. 'Dylan Tomlinson. Isn't that Rebecca's son?'

'It is. Who was on reception duty?'

'Alison Drew.'

'Have we not already interviewed her about that day?'

'Only to ask her about Lucy Harding. She was one of those who said Lucy was dedicated to her job.'

'Get hold of her immediately. We have to talk to her.'

Alison Drew was extremely accommodating and since she only lived a couple of miles away, insisted on driving to the station immediately. Within five minutes, she'd arrived and was sat opposite Robyn and Matt. She removed her spectacles and polished them carefully with a patterned cloth from her handbag before replacing them and looking earnestly at Robyn.

Her voice was calm. 'I arrived at the surgery at seven fifty. There were already three patients waiting in the car park. I booked them in as soon as I was set up.'

'Don't patients need to book an appointment in advance?'

'It's different for the emergency clinic. We offer a handful of open slots and operate a first come, first served policy for the emergency clinic, although we have to ask the patients what their emergency is before we check them in, to ensure it really is an emergency.

'Doctor Harding arrived soon after me and buzzed the first patient through at eight. That was Miss Tomlinson. She was one of those who'd been waiting outside for the clinic to open. She said Dylan really needed to see a doctor. He'd had another fit and she was worried about his medication – thought maybe the dosage was incorrect. She's been in several times with Dylan over the last four weeks. She usually books appointments with Doctor Trevago but last Thursday she was very agitated and Dylan seemed disorientated, so I booked her a slot.

'I saw her leave. I looked up from my desk and noticed she wasn't her usual self. She marched towards the exit, tugging Dylan along behind her. He was crying and she wasn't paying any attention to his wails. That wasn't like her. Normally she's very gentle with him. I've spoken to her a few times and I've never seen her behave like that. I asked if everything was okay but she ignored me and stormed out. By then the phones were ringing and the doctors were getting ready to start their surgeries and it was very hectic, so I didn't get the chance to mention it to anybody at the time. After morning surgery, Doctor Harding dropped by reception to ensure some letters she'd dictated had been posted. I told her Miss Tomlinson had seemed perturbed. The doctors never discuss the cases with us but I remember her words because she seemed so sad when she spoke – like she really cared. She said, "People think we can work miracles but we can't. Some things are outside our control." I left soon after, at my usual time. I don't work afternoons. That was the very last time I saw Doctor Harding.' Alison looked down at her hands folded neatly in her lap.

'Alison, you've been very helpful. Thank you.'

Robyn strode down the corridor again, mobile pressed to her ear.

'Rebecca's not picking up,' she said to Matt. 'I want her brought in, and Dylan if you have to. We'll get him looked after while we interview his mother.'

She threw open the office door and marched to her desk. 'Quickly, folks, where are we with this?'

Anna was dragging up page after page on her computer at speed. 'There's no such drug as Brinera. There is, however, a brand-new enzyme-replacement therapy out of the US, called Brineura. It's only recently been approved.'

'What's it used for?'

Anna sucked in air through her teeth as she read the latest page she'd discovered. 'It's used to treat Batten disease, a rare and fatal inherited disorder that affects the nervous system.'

'You reckon Jordan or somebody he knew had this disease?' Robyn asked.

Anna scrolled down the document. 'Not Jordan. It occurs in children. It says on this medical site that early symptoms develop between the ages of five to ten when a previously normal child suddenly begins to experience vision problems or seizures, and their behaviour changes. The symptoms progress rapidly and the child will ultimately become blind, bedridden and demented. The disease is fatal with life expectancy no greater than late teens or early twenties.'

Robyn's mouth opened. She recalled Dylan trying to focus on his Star Wars figurine, unable to see it even though it was in front of him, and complaining of feeling foggy. The clarity of the situation caused a sharp pang. Dylan was dying. Jordan had been trying to steal a medicine that might prolong Dylan's life.

'Doctor Trevago is Dylan's doctor. Ask him if Dylan has Batten disease.'

Anna's face screwed up in puzzlement. 'Even if Rebecca got hold of the treatment for Dylan she'd need somebody qualified to administer it. It has to be injected into the cerebrospinal fluid via a catheter device surgically implanted into a child's head. This makes no sense, unless she didn't realise what the treatment actually involved.'

'Is there much information about it?'

Anna shook her head. 'No, this is the latest. I'm wondering if she didn't just stumble across a couple of pieces of information that hailed it as a revolutionary new treatment for rare diseases and not look into it any more than that.'

'Maybe she knows a specialist who can operate on her son and is willing to treat him with Brinuera.'

The comms unit burst into life and Matt interrupted the conversation.

'Rebecca's not here,' he said.

Robyn let out a groan. 'You sure?'

'I've knocked and knocked but there's no reply. Her car's gone too.'

'We'll see if we can pinpoint her location.' Robyn turned towards Anna. 'Can we get a location on Rebecca's mobile phone or car?'

'Sure. On it.' Anna rushed off to follow orders.

'Matt, we'll get back to you. Stay there for now.' Robyn rubbed the back of her neck to ease the tension that had suddenly mounted. Rebecca – was Rebecca responsible for the deaths? She'd lied to so many people and kept secrets, but was she capable of murder? Even though she had no alibis for the days in question, she had Dylan with her. She couldn't have taken him along. There'd been no sightings of her car in Colton the night Jordan had been killed, or in Abbots Bromley when Lucy Harding was murdered, although Vanessa Broughton had spotted a woman with black hair headed towards the dark blue car stationed at the parking area. Robyn shook her head to clear it. Rebecca's car was red not dark blue.

Robyn's thoughts tumbled over themselves: Rebecca was a woman who loved her son... a son who was very ill and who would die, but what would she achieve by killing Jordan, Owen and Lucy?

She concluded Rebecca had chased after Hugo hoping to extract money, presumably for treatment for Dylan. She'd manipulated Hugo from the start through flattery, all the while keeping her son a secret from him until he invited her to live with him. Robyn wondered how Rebecca could have known so much about Hugo. The answer was obvious: the Internet.

David can you do a general search on Hugo Morton and tell me what comes up?

While David tapped away at his keyboard, Robyn put Jordan's name into Google and read the results. A number of hits were from eBay where Jordan had sold several Marvel statues, including Spider Woman, Guardians of the Galaxy Vol. 2: Star-Lord, Black Panther and Captain America. His name cropped up in a few forums relating to Marvel Comics characters. There was also the article about rich kids written by Amy Walters. A simple search revealed Jordan's address and he cropped up on the Speedy Logistics website as one of their employees. There was a wealth of material here for anyone wanting to learn more about Jordan Kilby.

'Stack of stuff about Hugo Morton online. He and his wife did a lot of work for cancer-related charities and there's loads more about his campaign to aid bee conservation, his engineering business, and he's even got a Wikipedia page. He's on a list as one of the UK's top 1,000 richest men.'

'And is Nathaniel Jones-Kilby on that list too?'

'He's in the top 500 – number 409.'

Robyn screwed up her face in concentration. Rebecca could have used every piece of information she found online to her advantage. There was so much she could have gleaned to worm her way into their affections – from apiculture to comic book characters. Her aunt Rose had told them Rebecca was clever – top in her classes at school. It wasn't beyond her ability to find out about these men's interests, gen up on them and be able to talk to them on the same level – to come across as enthusiastic as they were. It was a cleverly calculated and executed plan, except it was flawed. Hugo wasn't prepared to accept Dylan into his life, and Jordan wasn't as rich as Rebecca had possibly hoped.

The picture forming was of a woman who sought and chased after wealthy men and lied to them about having a son until she'd wormed her way into their affections and lives. For what reason? Ross's words echoed in Robyn's mind. He'd spoken passionately about Jeanette and told her that had the biopsy revealed Jeanette had cancer, he'd have done anything to get her the best medical attention. There was only one possible reason for Rebecca to pursue these men: it was for the sake of her son. That made some sense but why kill Jordan, who'd been trying to help her get drugs, and why murder Owen and Lucy? Robyn's face creased in concentration as she tried to fathom it out.

Anna spoke out. 'Got a ping on her mobile. Thirty minutes ago in Newborough.'

Robyn scrambled to her feet. 'She must be at Jordan's house. Alert Matt and tell him I'll meet him there.' She tore down the corridor to the car park. She hadn't quite fitted all the pieces of this particular jigsaw together yet, but she knew she had to get hold of Rebecca. Her mobile buzzed as she threw the car into gear. There was a one-word text from Amy.

Help

She rang Amy's number but it went immediately to answer-phone. She tried again. Same thing. She was now only ten minutes away from Newborough. Amy wasn't the sort to mess about. She'd only text Robyn if she was in serious trouble. She rang the station and spoke to David. 'Amy Walters has messaged me. Sounds like she's in trouble. Try ringing her. If you get no response, get a trace on her phone and send officers to the location urgently.'

Robyn concentrated on navigating the lanes to the village, avoiding the odd wide tractor that lumbered towards her. Her nerves were jangled. What could Amy have got involved in that she needed to text Robyn? For once, Robyn was concerned about the woman and wished she could be in two places at once. For now, she had to focus on finding Rebecca, but as she entered the peaceful village and raced up the lane to Jordan's house, she was overcome with an ominous feeling that she might just be too late.

CHAPTER FIFTY-FIVE

WEDNESDAY, 14 JUNE, MORNING

Amy Walters checks her reflection in her compact mirror and tidies a strand of bleached blonde hair. If she's well turned-out, she will get noticed and listened to, and treated with respect. In her business, reputation is everything.

The mixture of youth and confidence matched with a certain chic style has opened doors for her, but she wants more. She's perched on the precipice of the big time. She's had enough of writing for smaller newspapers. She's been working on her novel about serial killers for well over a year now and it will soon be ready for publication. It will help propel her into the limelight and that is exactly where she wants to be. She yearns to write for bigger publications and maybe even move into television. Amy Walters, a news programme anchor woman. She smiles at the thought.

Her informant has been very cagey. The rendezvous point wasn't specified until the last minute. All very cloak and daggers, Amy thinks. Still, she'll do almost anything to pin something on Nathaniel and it looks like she might at last have something – evidence he killed his wife.

Her mobile rings. 'You there?'

'I'm here. Where are you?' Amy asks.

'Not far away. Wait for me. I won't be long.'

Amy studies her nails while she waits. The nail polish is lifting on one or two of them and she'll need to get them all repainted. She can't have untidy nails. Personal grooming is important. She eases back in her seat. She's never liked Nathaniel. Ever since he sent her packing and had her story about him quashed. She was only doing her job – investigating and writing about the truth. He's spoilt beautiful villages and areas of beauty, all for financial gain. Amy likes the rural calm of the area and objects to the vast, tasteless housing estates he's erected, especially the one that's destroyed her own village. Instead of being able to look across at green fields and trees she now stares at the back of houses.

The informant has not given a name but has been insistent about their information. It appears Jordan hired a private detective to uncover the truth about his father. That must have been what he'd wanted to share with her. She wonders if that was what had got him killed.

A car draws up behind her. Amy gives a smile. This could be the *story. It might be the very stepping stone to success she's been searching for. She opens her car door and swivels out. The occupant of the other car does likewise.*

Amy's brow furrows. 'I know you,' she says.

'You might well do. And I know you, Miss Walters. I've read many of your articles. I want you to write something on my behalf.'

'It doesn't work like that,' says Amy. 'I agreed to meet you because you told me you had something on Jones-Kilby.'

'That was to lure you here. It was bait. I wanted you to see me and talk to me face to face.'

Amy glowers. This isn't how she likes to work. She arranges meetings and interviews and decides what she writes. Nobody else. She puts her hands on her hips. 'I don't operate that way. And I don't appreciate being treated like this.'

'You haven't even heard what I have to say.'

'Is it about Nathaniel Jones-Kilby?'

'No. It's much more important than that man.'

This isn't what Amy expects at all. She tuts loudly. 'If you'd had something ultra-amazing to share, you'd have told me over the phone, rather than pretend it was about Jones-Kilby. I get it. You're one of those time-wasters, or attention-seekers. I didn't come here to do your bidding. I came for a scoop on Jones-Kilby and if you haven't got that for me, I'm not interested. Now, if you'll excuse me, I have to return to work.'

'Are you refusing me, Miss Walters? You don't understand. I haven't got much time and you must interview me before I get caught. I want to tell the world my side. Why I've killed. You owe me that much.'

Amy looks at the large knife that now glistens in the sunlight. She has two choices: agree and listen to what the lunatic has to say and she might have the story she's always wanted, or make a dash for her car. She weighs up the options – do the interview or flee. The woman in front of her might kill her after running the story. There's no guarantee she'll be allowed to live. Amy's smart enough to know that no story is worth losing her life over. Her car isn't far away and it's unlocked. She can reach it in time if she had the edge. She just has to be cunning. Amy is renowned for her cunning. She pleads with her eyes and raises her hands in a submissive gesture.

'Okay. Okay. We'll play it your way. I'll interview you and write up the piece. Put the knife down. You don't need it. I'm sure it's a good story. Sorry, but I was a bit annoyed. I expected a story about Jones-Kilby. You understand, don't you? Would you mind if I record the interview to write it up accurately?'

For a few seconds, her assailant looks away, time enough for Amy to spin around and race for her car.

She's within reach of the door handle when she's shoved and stumbles against the vehicle. There's a hiss of annoyance and a flash of metal. Amy closes her eyes but doesn't scream as the knife drives into her side.

CHAPTER FIFTY-SIX

DAY TEN – WEDNESDAY, 14 JUNE, AFTERNOON

Robyn swung her car next to Nathaniel's Mercedes, jumped from it and raced towards Jordan's front door. Matt drew up behind her as she thumped on the door. He was by her side almost immediately and only a second before the door opened.

Nathaniel was perplexed at finding them standing on the doorstep.

'What's this about?'

'We're looking for Rebecca Tomlinson. Is she here?'

'No, she isn't. She was here about half an hour ago. She came to drop off the house keys. She still had them, and the key to Jordan's car. There isn't a spare key for it, you see, and I have to sell it.'

'You spoke to her?'

'Yes. Of course, I did.'

'How did she seem?'

'A bit upset still about Jordan. Understandable, really.' He shrugged.

'How did you know her phone number? She told me last time you contacted her to ask her to leave the house, you rang the house phone.'

Nathaniel's mouth dropped open. 'To ask her to leave? I did no such thing. I'm not a heartless bastard. What made her say that?

She rang *me* the day after Jordan was found, to ask how I was. I thought she was a charming girl. She was so very understanding. Said it was a huge shame Jordan had never really made it up with me but that he'd mentioned me often to her and was sorry we hadn't patched up our differences.'

'You're telling me you never asked her to move out?'

'I most certainly did not. It was her decision to leave. She thought it would be better for her and her little boy to go. There were too many memories in the house. I understood what she meant. I told her to take her time. She could go when she was ready, but she found a place almost immediately. She gave me her number and said it would be nice to keep in touch and asked if I'd let her know when we were holding Jordan's funeral.

'I was here a couple of days ago, going through Jordan's things, and couldn't find a key to his car. I rang her about it. With all the upset of moving out, she'd absent-mindedly picked up Jordan's house keys and taken them with her to her new place. The car key was on the same key ring.'

Robyn thought back to the first time she'd visited the house. She'd asked Rebecca about some keys hanging in the kitchen and she'd said they were Jordan's. He'd left them behind. There'd been no car key attached to them, only three door keys.

Robyn flinched at another memory of a car outside on the drive when she'd visited the first time. She asked the question even though she knew the answer. 'What make of car did Jordan drive?'

'A dark blue Ford Fiesta. It's parked in the garage.'

She turned to Matt. 'Put a shout out for Rebecca.'

'What's she done?' Nathaniel asked, his face etched with concern.

'I really can't comment. I'm very sorry but I'll probably have to ask you to go back through this with us again later.' She looked at the man's face. His bravado that he'd first exuded several days earlier had been replaced by sorrow. His face was leaner and more drawn than she remembered it being. Fresh lines were etched along his face. Losing his only son had taken its toll on this man. He might not be able to express emotion very well but his pain was now visible in his features and his stance. He nodded in her direction.

'Thank you, sir.' Robyn strode away, towards Matt.

Matt spoke. 'A dark blue car, like the one parked in front of the building site in Abbots Bromley. Reckon she used Jordan's car to get there?'

'It adds up. And Vanessa saw a dark-haired woman in the vicinity at about the right time. We have to find her. Get Anna onto traffic cameras to look for her car and see if we can pinpoint her phone again.'

She got back into her own vehicle, her head slumped back against the headrest and eyes shut in concentration. Where would Rebecca go? It came to her in a flash. The one place she'd always returned to – her aunt Rose's house. She put her car into reverse, talking into the comms unit as she did so. 'Matt, I think she's gone to her aunt's – Rose Griffith in Water Orton.'

There was a silence and a spluttering of static before she heard his voice.

'Want me to go there?'

'Definitely. I'll call the station and get them to check the safety cameras between here and there.'

Robyn drove back towards the main road that would take her towards the A38 and Birmingham. Sunlight reflected off her screen, making her screw up her eyes as she navigated the lanes lined with thick hedges. Her phone buzzed with another text message. She glanced down and saw it was again from Amy Walters:

Meadow

She buzzed the station immediately on the hands-free and got Mitz. 'You got a trace on Amy's phone yet?'

'About a minute ago. She's somewhere near Yoxall.'

'Is there a road called Meadow something?'

'There's a Meadow Lane.'

'She's on Meadow Lane. Meet me there. She's in trouble.'

Robyn pressed the accelerator to the floor. Amy hadn't rung emergency services. Instead, she'd called Robyn. There was an important reason for that. Amy was smart. She wouldn't have contacted Robyn otherwise. It had to be something to do with the case. She raced towards Yoxall and prayed she'd arrive in time.

CHAPTER FIFTY-SEVEN

DAY TEN – WEDNESDAY, 14 JUNE, AFTERNOON

Meadow Lane skirted around the village of Yoxall and joined the main road leading to Barton-under-Needwood. Mostly used by dog-walkers or ramblers, it was wide enough for only one car. Both Amy's BMW and a red Nissan Micra, which Robyn recognised to be Rebecca's, were parked on the grass either side of the lane, facing in opposite directions. Robyn drew her car up in front of Rebecca's to block it and prevent her from making a quick getaway. It would be impossible for her to turn her car around and drive away. It was the best Robyn could do until Mitz arrived.

Using the comms unit she gave her position. 'Get backup here immediately and paramedics.'

She got out of her car unsure of which direction she should take. She peered through Amy's car windows. There was no sign of the journalist. She approached a stile leading to a path that would take her towards Wychnor Park, where there was housing and a country club. Robyn hesitated before crossing the lane to Rebecca's car. Again, she looked through the windows. There was nobody inside – not Amy or even Dylan. Was the boy with Rebecca and Amy? The Nissan was parked beside a field of sheep that'd gathered by the gate and watched Robyn intently, jaws chewing all the while. Her eye was drawn to the wooden step that led into the field. It had splashes of bright red on it. Robyn was sure it was blood.

She clambered into the field where the sound of water gushing from a small weir under the humpbacked bridge became louder. She felt she'd come full circle. She'd started the investigation in a field beside a different humpbacked bridge, and here she was again, beside another.

The sheep bleated in unison, their serious black faces fixed on her as Robyn walked towards the River Swarbourn, no bigger than a brook. She looked left and right but couldn't spot Amy or Rebecca.

Robyn sprinted a few metres along the bank looking for places where the women might be. The sheep had lost interest in her and were grazing again. She contemplated shouting for Amy but she didn't want to alert Rebecca to her presence. She slowed and walked a few more paces then spotted a small stone building – a shelter for animals.

She headed swiftly in its direction, aware of the need to exercise caution. She moved silently towards the open-fronted building, its stones weathered and grey, with soft green moss covering many of the larger stones. She approached from the near side and hugged the wall, her back against it, straining for sounds of life. She heard Amy's voice although her words were laboured as if she were struggling to speak. The second voice was instantly recognisable with its Brummie accent and low, even tone.

Rebecca spoke loudly. 'Make sure you print everything I say. I'm going to start my confession now. Are you recording it on your phone?'

Amy's response was barely audible. Robyn's mind deliberated her options as she half-listened to the interview that was taking place. Amy's voice was slurred as if she'd been drinking or was terribly tired.

Rebecca spoke again. 'I killed Jordan Kilby, Owen Falcon and Lucy Harding.'

'Why?'

'They had to be punished.'

'Jordan was your boyfriend. Why kill him?'

'He was never my real boyfriend. I didn't love him. He was my chosen one. He was to be our saviour. I discovered him online. He was the neglected and rebellious son of wealthy parents; he'd lost his mother. I was confident he'd fall for me. Lonely people are the easiest to dupe and he was lonely, mixed-up and searching for somebody to understand him. I was that person. My plan was to convince him to spend some of his fortune helping Dylan. It went perfectly. He fell for my bullshit and for me. I moved in with him, taking Dylan with me. Jordan hadn't expected that but he accepted it. He didn't turn me away as some before him had. I knew then he'd be *The One*. He'd let us both into his life.

'Then I discovered Jordan wasn't wealthy at all. In fact, he was a sponging waster who lived in a house his father had bought. He wasn't *The One*. I was furious. I'd wasted time and effort tracking him down, and for what? He wouldn't be able to fund a trip to the States where Dylan stood a chance of receiving treatment to save his life. I became disillusioned quickly. Adding to the disappointment, I discovered Jordan wasn't the man I'd believed him to be. He was a loser – an idle waste of space – who spent most of his time playing games online, watching superhero films, or playing football. Superhero! In his dreams. He was no superhero.

'I had to come up with an alternative plan and quickly. I considered getting to know Jordan's father Nathaniel and try the same tactics with him, but Jordan hated him so much, he wouldn't talk about him, let alone visit him with me. I was about to give up and hunt for another saviour when I uncovered his involvement in a drug-smuggling operation quite by accident. He was part of a small team, along with his friend, Owen Falcon, thieving expensive drugs from Pharmacals Healthcare and selling them to dealers who offloaded them on the street. Miss Walters, are you listening to me? It's important you get this all.'

'I'm in a bad way, Rebecca. I need medical attention. Please call me an ambulance.'

Robyn could hear the pain in Amy's voice. Her eyes lighted on a patch of red ahead of her on the grass near the entrance to the shelter. Amy was bleeding badly. Heaven knew how long she'd survive. Robyn needed backup and quickly, or she'd have to act alone.

Rebecca spoke sharply. 'No. Not yet. You need to know how I found out he was stealing drugs. I worked for Pharmacals in administration, and I came across some discrepancies in the stock at one of the warehouses containing the expensive drugs. The amount coming in didn't tally with the stock that went out. It could have been a computer blip and easily missed. I was going to report them but I noticed Jordan was the driver who signed for and transported the stock from the warehouse to the clinic. I took it as a sign. I'd been led to this man for a reason other than money. He was probably the only person who could help me. I brought the subject of the missing drugs up with him that night and it wasn't long before he confessed his involvement. He said they'd only been taking minor amounts of stock that Clifford Harris managed to "lose" in the system. He begged me not to report it and I said I wouldn't if he'd help me. I'd noticed a shipment of drugs from the US had recently arrived and I wanted him to steal some for me. Miss Walters! Ask me why. Ask me why I wanted the drugs.'

The only response she received was a lengthy groan. Robyn could wait no longer. She had to save Amy. She'd have to take a chance and rush Rebecca and hope to catch her off guard. Whether Dylan was also there or not, Robyn had to act. If Robyn was lucky, Rebecca might even have her back to the entrance. She took a deep breath and, palms against the wall, edged towards the front of the building. The stones were thick and wide and cool to her touch. She reached the end of the wall and waited. Rebecca was still talking, telling Amy why she had decided to kill Owen. She was engrossed in her story. Robyn eased around the wall and craned her neck to peer into the shelter and identify Amy's and Rebecca's positions. It was far gloomier inside the shelter than she anticipated. She adjusted her position and eased forward to better see. As she screwed her eyes to allow them to adjust to the darkness, there was a rush of blurred movement and Rebecca barrelled out of the shelter, catching Robyn completely unaware. Even with her quick reflexes she was no match for Rebecca, who shouldered her to the floor in one fell swoop and left Robyn on her back completely winded. She blinked back the stars that had exploded as she hit her head on the ground and struggled back onto her feet. The sheep had bolted, and at the far end of the field, Rebecca was climbing the stile and running towards Amy's car. Robyn pushed up on her knees to tear after Rebecca when she heard Amy's voice.

Torn between chasing after her suspect and saving Amy, she barked instructions into the comms unit.

'White BMW headed towards A515 in direction of Yoxall to Lichfield. Apprehend immediately. Suspect Rebecca Tomlinson.' She gave them the car registration and her location and rushed back inside the shelter. She was greeted by Rebecca's voice again, this time talking about Lucy Harding. The conversation was coming from a mobile phone on the ground, next to a familiar figure.

'Amy,' she said.

Amy was slumped against the far wall.

'Robyn… you came.' Her words were breathy.

'Don't speak. Save your energy. There's an ambulance on its way.' The sound of a distant siren accompanied her words.

'Crazy… bitch,' whispered Amy. 'Hard to… text. Interview. She wanted to listen to it. Wouldn't go… until she heard it.'

The mobile on the floor was showing the icon of a recording app. Amy had been recording Rebecca's confession. Rebecca's voice rose from it. Robyn turned it off.

The ground around Amy was dark red with blood. She'd lost far more blood than Robyn imagined. Amy's eyes shut and her breathing became shallow. She was slipping away.

'Amy, for fuck's sake, don't give up on me. Hang in there.' Robyn sank to the floor beside the journalist, noticing for the first time the blood-covered knife that lay next to her. 'I'm going to help you.'

She put her fingers gently against Amy's back and pulled them away, wet with blood. She yanked off her own jacket and pressed it hard against the wound in Amy's back to stem the flow, all the while talking to Amy, whose head had fallen to one side.

'It'll be okay. You're tough. You'll make it and then think of the story you'll have then. It'll be a real scoop – journalist helps capture killer.'

She was almost sure Amy smiled, then with sudden reality she knew she couldn't have. Amy was no longer breathing. 'Amy!' she yelled. 'Amy!' Her shouts reached the paramedics racing across the field towards the shelter, and accompanied by Mitz and Anna, they all tumbled through the entrance together to find Robyn performing mouth to mouth on Amy. She moved away quickly and passed over to the lead paramedic.

'She's only just gone. We can still save her.' Even as she spoke them she knew her words were false. Amy had lost far too much blood. It was an impossible situation. She walked away, unable to watch the paramedics.

Outside, the sun shone brightly and the sheep were watching the scene in front of them, their mouths moving as if speaking to her. A murder of crows flew up from a copse at the approach of urgent sirens. Anna exited the shelter, her face grave, and shook her head.

The weight of responsibility was tangible. She'd warned Amy to stay away from her investigation, but now she wondered if she shouldn't have been more assertive. Deep down she knew Amy was always going to follow a lead, however dangerous it was. She was like Robyn in that respect. She had ambition and determination. The irony of the situation wasn't lost on Robyn. Amy had been obsessed with serial killers and had interviewed two whom Robyn had arrested in the past. And now, here she was, a victim of another.

'She suffered a single stab wound to the back but it didn't kill her immediately. She bled out gradually. Quite some time.' The paramedic who spoke was no more than twenty-five.

Robyn nodded and swallowed hard. Amy shouldn't have died. Robyn couldn't bear to stay any longer and walked to the river's edge. The sheep had moved away and were at the far side of their field, their bleating drowned out by the rushing of the water. Robyn looked into the distance and blinked back tears.

'You okay?' Mitz was beside her.

'I'll be fine. I feel really bad about this, though. If only I'd gone in there immediately, I might have been able to save her.'

Mitz shook his head. 'It was too late. She'd never have made it. She'd lost too much blood by then.'

Robyn knew he was right but she couldn't shake off the feeling she should have done more.

'Any word on Rebecca?'

'We're still on the lookout for Amy's car.'

His words did nothing to lift her mood. Amy was dead and Rebecca had escaped. Robyn hadn't been able to prevent either from happening. She could do no more here. She had to use her skill to work out how to track down Rebecca, and the only place she could think to start was at Water Orton. She'd join Matt there. Rose Griffith might be able to provide her with some information.

'Will you and Anna deal with Forensics? The knife is in there, and make sure Amy's phone comes back to the station. She was recording an interview with Rebecca.'

She left Mitz and plodded back to her car, legs like leaden weights. As she started her engine, she threw one last look back at the field. She could just make out the roof of the stone animal shelter from here. As she pulled off the grass verge she spoke to the woman inside it. 'I'm truly sorry, Amy.'

CHAPTER FIFTY-EIGHT

Rose Griffith shook her head for the umpteenth time. 'I have no idea at all of her whereabouts. Honestly, if I knew, I'd tell you.'

Robyn had no reason to disbelieve the woman. Rose exhibited every sign of a concerned relative and was trying hard to assist. She'd rung Rebecca to no avail. She'd spoken to the few friends Rebecca had known in the past, trying to establish if they'd heard from her, and to all the staff at Longer Life Health. She rubbed her forehead anxiously before asking, 'Could she have gone abroad?'

'It's possible.' Robyn hoped it wasn't the case. 'Did you know Dylan was ill?'

'Ill? What do you mean by ill? He had the usual childhood illnesses and sometimes caught the odd bug, if that's what you mean.'

'We think he might have a rare illness called Batten disease.'

Rose shook her head. 'I've never come across that. What is it?'

'Symptoms include a loss of vision, clumsiness, acting strangely. They might not manifest until the child is four or so.'

'I remember he did have trouble with his eyes. He squinted a lot so Rebecca took him to the optician a couple of times. He said there was nothing wrong with the boy.' She nodded all the while. 'And Dylan did fall over a fair bit. I thought that was normal for growing children. They can be clumsy, can't they?'

'Rebecca never voiced her concerns about him to you?'

Rose lifted damp eyes to Robyn. 'I wish she had. I told you that girl kept secrets. She never confided in me about anything.'

'You told me last time it was all because of losing her family.'

'That's right. She was in the most dreadful shock for such a long time. She wouldn't even talk to me to start with. She stayed in her room for days. Wouldn't eat. I was so worried about her. She wouldn't visit their graves, either.

'We buried them here in Water Orton. They share a plot at the church. I go regularly to tend to the flowers on their graves. Rebecca hasn't ever visited it. It was as if by not going, she could pretend it hadn't happened. It was the same with the house. She never went back to it, not that there was anything to salvage.'

Robyn digested her words as she recalled the scrubby bit of land where Rebecca's family house had once stood, the blackened earth and the overgrown foliage that hid the charred remains from view. Her attention was drawn to her mobile that lit up with an incoming message to ring the station. She excused herself and made the call.

Mitz answered it. 'Forensics are at the scene and Amy's been taken away. Harry said she was bleeding for a long time. Probably a full thirty minutes. In all likelihood, she wouldn't have made it to hospital in time, even if you'd got her out as soon as you found her. We just listened to the recording on Amy's phone. Rebecca confessed to all three murders. She wanted Amy to write up her confession as an interview. I don't think she understood how badly injured Amy was.'

The weight in Robyn's chest increased tenfold. Amy had got her interview with the serial killer but it had cost her very life.

'I'll listen to it when I return. Thanks, Mitz.' She touched the red button and returned to the sitting room where she'd left Rose.

'If you can think of anywhere she might have gone, please let us know immediately, won't you, Miss Griffith? I'm leaving you with an officer on the off-chance Rebecca comes here.'

'She's in bad trouble, isn't she?'

'We need to question her.'

Rose studied Robyn's face before speaking. 'Try not to be too hard on her. She isn't a wicked person.'

Robyn gestured at Matt and they left. Once outside, Robyn gave him instructions. 'We're going to try the church and Vicarage Street, where her old house was. I have a feeling she hasn't strayed too far. She's become careless, sloppy, and knows she's going to be caught soon.'

She set off ahead of Matt, through the village towards Vicarage Street, where the Tomlinsons had once lived as a family. She parked on the weed-filled driveway in front of the heavy wooden gate that blocked the site from view. There was no other way onto the land. She rattled the gate but it was, as it had been the last time, locked. 'Give me a shove up,' she said to Matt, raising a foot for him to help power her on top of the gate. She clambered up and surveyed the land, making out once more the charred earth and shrubs that surrounded it. Beyond were more overgrown shrubs. 'I'm going to take a look,' she called before dropping to the other side and walking towards the remains of what had once been a small house. A glimpse of white caught her eye and she hastened towards it. Hidden behind a huge laurel bush was Amy's BMW. She rushed back to the gate.

'Matt. Get over here. Amy's car's here.'

There was some scrabbling and Matt's face appeared as he hauled himself onto the top of the gate and landed heavily beside her. There were no jocular comments from him. His face was pure concern.

'Be careful, guv. She could well have a weapon.'

'You too.'

They prowled side by side past the burnt area where the house had stood, and pushed through overgrown bushes into what would once have been a garden. It stretched a length and beyond it stood tall oak trees. The cawing of crows began almost immediately as they spied the pair and flew overhead to watch the intruders descend into the garden. Robyn saw the building first. It was covered in ivy and half-hidden by brambles but it was still identifiable as a shed, its roof sunken and misshapen.

She nudged Matt and pointed at it. They separated and in silence crept around the shed, one approaching from the front, and the other from the rear. Matt joined her at the front door. Weeds had been trampled down, evidence somebody had been here recently. He whispered in her ear. 'No windows.'

She indicated the door. Matt stretched out a hand and, simultaneously shouldering the door to open it and pressing down the latch, he launched his entire body weight at it. It flew open and, blinking in the dark, they entered the room.

Matt let out a deep groan, for sitting on a wooden chair with her head slumped to one side was Rebecca. Across her knees but still cradled in his mother's arms was a lifeless body.

Robyn bit her knuckles and spun towards the door for a second before regaining control and approaching Dylan. She felt for a pulse on the boy's wrist and shook her head. She knew immediately beforehand it would be hopeless. The boy was dead.

She tried Rebecca's wrist. 'I can't feel anything.'

'Try the neck.'

She placed two fingers where she hoped to locate the carotid pulse. She pressed gently and thought she could detect something very faint.

'I'm not sure. I might be imagining it. You try, Matt.'

He copied her actions and let out a breath. 'I think she's alive. I'll call the paramedics.'

He scooted off and thundered back in the direction of the gate. Robyn stood immobile, staring at the woman holding her precious child, and was struck by its similarity to the sculpture of *The Pietà* depicting the Virgin Mary cradling the dead body of Jesus. As she dwelt on this thought a piece of paper on the floor caught her attention. They'd missed it in the gloom.

She donned gloves, lifted it and read: 'Father, I deserve to be punished.'

CHAPTER FIFTY-NINE

DAY TEN – WEDNESDAY, 14 JUNE, EVENING

Amy's voice was weak. Robyn's nails dug into her palms as she listened to the rest of the interview between her and Rebecca. She'd heard the beginning before – while pressed up against the shelter in the field. Listening to it, she was reminded of that moment when she'd believed she could still save Amy, not realising it was already too late.

> Rebecca: Ask me why. Ask me why I wanted the drugs.
> Amy: Why did you want these drugs?
> Rebecca: They were for my little boy, Dylan. He's only six years old and was diagnosed a year ago with Batten disease. According to his doctors, there's no treatment for it. It's a fatal, cruel, neurological disorder that will kill him in the next year or two, or by his teens at the latest. I've spent every waking hour since he was diagnosed trying to uncover a treatment for my boy, and there's nothing that will cure it, but I stumbled across a revolutionary new treatment available in the US called Brineura that treats CLN2 disease, which is what Dylan suffers from. I was granted a miracle – a sign of forgiveness for all my past transgressions – a clinic in London had recently ordered a

large batch of Brineura through Pharamacals Healthcare. It was in the warehouse awaiting delivery and that was what I wanted Jordan to lift for me. I asked Jordan to talk to his contact and steal some, but he flatly refused, saying it was far too risky because it was too valuable, and he didn't want to get caught.

It's an injection for intraventricular use. There wasn't much information available online about it, other than it's recently received approval from the US Food and Drug Administration, and it's exceedingly expensive. I had to get it and try it.

Amy: You can't use it. You need... be... qualified.

Rebecca: Once I got my hands on it, I'd have made sure Dylan got it somehow, whatever it took. Jordan was given this opportunity to redeem himself but he tossed it away.

Amy: Redeem?

Rebecca: He sponged off a father riddled with guilt over a death he didn't cause. He used that guilt to get whatever he wanted – a house, a car and money. How else do you think he was able to visit Comic Cons in the States and Europe, or purchase valuable artwork, or own a mega-expensive bicycle? His father was bankrolling him, even though Jordan hated him and treated him with disdain. He was a despicable son.

Amy: Why not tell the authorities? Better than killing him. Can we stop? Please. I'm bleeding a lot now.

Rebecca: I'll call for help when this is over. You'll be fine. Jordan told me he loved me and would do anything for me but he lied and lies have to be punished properly. Ask me how. Ask me how!

Amy: How did you execute... your plan?

Rebecca: It was quite easy really. We'd rowed that day – big time. Our relationship had become strained since I'd found out about his involvement with the drug racket and he'd become increasingly wary of me. He thought I'd tell the police. He was frightened of me and wanted me to leave. On the Sunday he died, he told me he was going to stay at Owen's and when he came back the next day, he expected me to have packed my bags and left.

I knew where Owen lived so I did what I usually did when I follow Jordan. I gave Dylan sleeping pills to knock him out, and drove to Colton.

Amy: You followed Jordan?

Rebecca: Too right I did. I didn't trust him. He might have been seeing another woman on the side. I had to make sure he was being faithful. I also used to read his text messages and emails, which is how I knew he'd arranged a meeting with Clifford Harris that night. I waited in a lane off the main road for his bike to go past. I knew he'd be heading home. Once he passed me, I drew out onto the lane, followed him and nudged him off the road.

Amy: But he told you he was at Owen's.

Rebecca laughs quietly.

Rebecca: I'd texted him late that evening. I told him to come home or I'd set fire to his house, and if he didn't show up by one o'clock, I'd burn the place down. I knew he'd come home.

Amy lets out a small groan of pain.

Rebecca: Once he was off his bike, he was vulnerable. It didn't take much to persuade him to cross the field with me. I threatened him with a carving knife taken from his own kitchen. He cried and pleaded and promised me the drugs I wanted, but I knew he was a liar and I stuck my knife into his stomach and twisted.

Rebecca's voice becomes distant and dreamlike.

Rebecca: I trusted you with my world. But you let me down. And now it's time to pay…

There's a brief silence.

Rebecca: Those were the last words I spoke to him. He had to understand why he'd driven me to killing him. He was my Chosen One and he turned his back on me. I stole his phone and sent a text to his boss to say he wouldn't be going to work the next day then got him ready for his fate. I strung him up in a field of blood like the Judas he was. I'd brought along everything I needed for my tableau. I set him up in that field and I invited the crows to feast on his body like demons feasted on Judas.

Amy: Jordan was like Judas?

Rebecca: Oh yes. As I said, I read all his text messages and checked his call history. He was being very secretive that Sunday. He pretended he was ringing a friend but I knew from the look on his face, he was lying. He rang somebody else, didn't he, Amy? He rang to tell somebody about his crazy girlfriend who was trying to make him steal drugs so he could save face and protect his friends. He was going to turn me in. I checked the number he'd called. It was yours, Amy. The lousy son of a bitch was giving me up to the press to save his own bacon. And you, you deserve to suffer too for your part. Judas. He deserved to die.

Amy: He didn't.

Rebecca: Whatever. It doesn't matter now because you know the truth. He served his punishment. I've endured cruel and sadistic punishments for far less serious crimes.

Amy: What punishments?

Rebecca: No. They're irrelevant. What's important is that people should pay for their crimes. Jordan paid for his. And so did the others.

Amy: Owen?

Rebecca: Jordan believed my every word until Owen sowed seeds of doubt into his head. Owen never liked me and did his best to prevent me from getting too close to Jordan. He'd be around every week, making sure I hadn't sunk my claws deeper into him, inviting him out, keeping him away from me. He turned Jordan against me. He prevented Jordan from following his heart. He also ran the drug-stealing operation. He told Jordan they wouldn't steal the very drugs I needed for Dylan. Jordan was like a pathetic dog when Owen was around. He did whatever Owen asked. It was nauseating to watch. Owen could have agreed to pilfer those drugs but he wanted me to suffer. He had an opportunity to show compassion but he didn't. He didn't care that Dylan would die. He wanted us out of Jordan's life. He was cruel and heartless. He deserved no less than he received.

Amy: What about... Lucy Harding?

Rebecca: Dylan had begun to have seizures. They were part of his condition. My usual doctor, Trevago, had given Dylan a blood pressure drug that helped control them but it wasn't working. I asked for an emergency appointment that morning and saw Doctor Harding instead of Doctor Trevago. I wanted Dylan to be taken into hospital and looked after there, but she told me there was nothing the hospital or any surgeon could do. I asked her about Brineura and she told me it was way too expensive for the National Health Service to fund and that I had to be prepared for the worst.

Amy: But why... why did you kill her?

Rebecca: I don't know. I threw myself on her mercy. I begged her to help me save Dylan. I asked her if I could get my hands on the new wonder drug, would she be able to administer it to Dylan, and she looked at me as if I was completely crazy. Maybe it was that, or more likely it was because there was a photograph of her own happy, healthy son on her desk, beaming out at us with no cares in the world. Dylan was dying and Doctor Harding wouldn't do anything to help. She increased the dosage on his regular medication but all the while I could see in her eyes she knew it was pointless. Dylan was going to degenerate, go blind, lose the use of his limbs and die a horrible slow death, and her son wasn't. Her son was going to grow to be a healthy man and have a family of his own. Then there was the look she gave me. The pitiful look. I couldn't bear it. I wanted her to comprehend how much I hurt. How awful it is to know you'll never see your son grow up. What that feels like.

There's silence.

Rebecca: You will get this to the newspaper, won't you? I want everyone to know about this condition. I want people to wake up to what is happening to some children. I'm going now. I want to listen to the interview first to make sure it's recorded and then I'll go.

Amy: Where? What are you going to do?

Rebecca: I've sinned, Amy. We all are sinners in some way. Give me the phone. I want to listen.

There's the sound of rustling and a click as the recording is ended.

Robyn stood back against the wall, arms folded, as Anna switched off the last interview Amy Walters had recorded – Rebecca Tomlinson's confession.

Mitz spoke. 'Will it hold up in court?'

'If Rebecca refuses to confess again, it'll be enough,' said Robyn. 'Is she up to it yet?'

Anna responded. 'She's still in intensive care and groggy, but the doctors say she'll make a full recovery. They got her in time to pump all the pills she'd taken out of her stomach. Ten minutes later and it would have been too late.'

'Might have been better if she hadn't come round. She'll be banged up for life,' Matt said.

David shrugged. 'She murdered four people and her son. She has to face the consequences.'

'But she'll have to live knowing she took her own child's life. That's a horrendous punishment,' said Anna. 'She obviously wanted to die with him.'

Robyn heaved a sigh. 'That's the way it is. We aren't here to judge or decide fates. We do our job.'

DCI Flint tapped on the door. 'Visitor for you. My office.'

Robyn left the team still in a sombre mood and followed Flint to his office. Nathaniel was waiting for her. He held out a hand.

'Thank you, DI Carter,' he said. 'I owe you my gratitude for finding my son's killer.'

She shook his hand. 'Just doing my job, sir.'

'And very well you did it too. I'm sorry I didn't make it easy for you. You'll understand that it was difficult to provide an alibi. It was awkward, to say the least.'

She gave a curt nod.

'Anyway, I wanted to express my thanks and wish you well.'

'Thank you, sir. And can I say I am genuinely sorry for your loss.'

'I appreciate that.' He swallowed hard and the irritation Robyn had once felt for the man dissipated. His world had suffered a seismic shift since she'd first met him and, like her, he would have to learn to carry his loss with him for the remainder of his life. She'd been saddened to learn Nathaniel had continued to help Jordan out financially and yet received no gratitude or love in return.

Flint congratulated her again and she departed. She didn't feel worthy of congratulations or thanks. Flint had let her down with his behaviour towards her during the investigation. She felt downhearted. Amy's death had knocked her badly. Amy had, in her last hours, helped her solve the case but at too high a price. She walked outside and dialled the number she'd looked up earlier. The producer at the BBC was very interested in her story and asked if she could send further details. Robyn agreed. She'd work with the *Stafford Gazette* and provide all the information they could about the ace reporter who'd helped track down a serial killer. By the end of the conversation, the producer was promising a programme dedicated to Amy. Amy had always wanted to be a household name. The least Robyn could do was give her that.

CHAPTER SIXTY

TWO DAYS LATER – FRIDAY, 16 JUNE, MORNING

'Argh! Take it away. It's blinding me,' shouted David.

Anna gave him a friendly thump on the arm. 'Don't be daft,' she said.

'Yeah, don't be daft,' echoed Sergeant Mitz Patel. 'Hang on. That isn't daft. It's only natural it's blinding you. That rock cost me a year's salary.'

'Only one year's salary?' said Anna, grinning. 'I'd have thought I was worth at least ten years' wages.'

Matt looked across from his desk and shook his head. 'Oh dear. It's started already. You're on a hiding to nowhere, my man.'

Mitz's face broke into a wide grin. 'I'd better come to you then for relationship advice, eh?'

Matt puffed out his cheeks. 'I charge for my advice. It's like gold dust.'

Anna brushed her finger lightly over her diamond engagement ring.

Matt feigned shock. 'Whoa! Careful you don't rub it too hard. The artificial coating will wear off.'

'Pack it in, Matt,' said Robyn, trying hard not to laugh. 'Anna, it's a beautiful ring. Congratulations to you both. And we all know you'll make a fabulously wonderful married couple.' She raised her paper cup of coffee and toasted them. 'We'll take this good news to the pub tonight and celebrate it properly there. Matt, phone ahead and book a table. Right, that's the excitement over. Shall we get on to this morning's debriefing?'

The team settled down to work. Mitz was first to speak. 'There's not much else to add. As you know the search of Rebecca's house at Rangemore turned up Jordan's mobile and his bicycle helmet. The lab identified microscopic droplets of blood on the meat knife Rebecca claimed she used to stab Jordan, and there was a DNA and blood match – conclusive evidence it's the murder weapon.'

He passed over to Anna. 'The tech boys have been through her laptop we uncovered. Rebecca had not only searched extensively for wealthy single men in her area but had made a shortlist of possible choices, which she stored in a document entitled *The Chosen One* along with Internet articles about each man. It confirms our suspicions that she was learning everything she could about each man to woo him, so she'd appear the perfect companion for him. There were a vast number of searches about gardening, bees, conservation, and obviously Marvel Comics characters, Comic Con, Marvel Universe, Marvel artwork, superhero films and football. In summary, she educated herself on all of these subjects to appear more knowledgeable and enthusiastic about them.'

Robyn took over and summed up. 'As you know, Rebecca Tomlinson's been moved to a secure unit and been charged. I spoke to her yesterday and she admitted to murdering Jordan, Owen, Lucy, Amy and her own son, Dylan. Furthermore, she divulged intimate details of each of the murders.' Robyn recollected the interview from the day before: Rebecca, hollow-eyed, speaking without any intonation, dead inside…

'I formed my plan a week earlier. I'd pulled in beside Top Field after following Jordan to Owen's house and spotted the crows in the field.

They were flying around what had been a scarecrow. There was almost nothing left of it but I realised immediately they'd been sent to show me what I had to do. It was suddenly as clear as daylight. He wasn't my Chosen One any more. He was a Judas and had to be treated accordingly. The crows spoke to me. They told me what I should do with him. They promised they'd help. They'd gouge out his heart and eat it, like the demons did Judas's.

'I gave Jordan one last chance to prove he was worthy and asked him again to steal some Brineura for me. Once more, he refused and left for the pub. I spent time with my little boy, and when it was bedtime, I gave him a couple of sleeping tablets.'

'You set Jordan up on the pole in the field to emulate a tableau of Judas in the Field of Blood?'

'That's right,' Rebecca says

'Rebecca, would you say you were especially religious?'

Rebecca continues to stare unblinking at Robyn. 'No. I'm not. Not anymore. Maybe once upon a time.'

'Then why copy gruesome deaths from the bible: Judas, Jezebel, Sisera?'

'Each of these sinners had to pay for their evils. We all have to pay in the end.'

Robyn has been troubled by a thought for the last day or two. She feels it's time to ask. 'Rebecca, your family: your mother, your father and your brother all died in a house fire. Did they pay for their sins?'

Rebecca's shoulders droop slightly.

'Was it an accident, Rebecca? Was the fire an accident?'

Rebecca refuses to answer.

'You told Jordan you would burn down his house if he didn't return home that Sunday night. Rebecca, did you burn down your parents' house as punishment?'

'He shouldn't have been there.' Rebecca's voice is barely audible. 'He was supposed to be staying at a friend's house. I was freeing us both. I was meant to protect him and save him from any more misery.'

'Is this Isaac, your brother?'

Rebecca lets out a soft sigh. 'He was taken with them. He was never meant to die. For a long time, I believed I was to blame for his death, but then I was granted salvation. I was given Dylan. He was to replace Isaac. I was supposed to protect and love Dylan. Dylan was my gift to prove I'd done the right thing by letting my parents perish in that fire. But Dylan was also my punishment. I loved him so much and yet he was going to be stolen from me by a silent killer I couldn't beat. I was going to suffer the pain of loss all over again. I tried so hard to save him but I failed.

'I don't want to talk to you any more. Leave me alone. I have a lifetime of punishment ahead of me. You, DI Carter, have brought that about. I should be with my boys — Isaac and Dylan — now, not here, locked away forever to relive the pain of their loss over and over again. You're responsible for that, DI Carter, and I hope you're satisfied.'

Rebecca's eyes suddenly flash and she leaps to her feet. Two officers quickly restrain her as she thumps on the protective screen with balled fists. 'You're to blame. I hope you suffer as much,' she yells as she's dragged towards the door.

Robyn watches until Rebecca has gone and only moves when asked if she is ready to leave.

Robyn continued with the briefing. 'I understand from her aunt that Rebecca and her brother were brought up strictly. We don't know any ins and outs of it but apparently their mother, Bethany, was particularly pious. We may never know the true reasons behind Rebecca's methods of dispatching her quarries but we can surmise something happened in her past that seriously affected her. It's not been an easy case and, like you, I'm very glad it's over. Once I have your reports, we can wrap this one up. As always, thanks very much for your diligence.'

'Does that mean I can have time off this week?' asked Matt.

Robyn nodded. 'Sure.'

'The missus is away at her mum's. I'm going to spend the entire day in bed, fast asleep – no noise, no work, no wife, no baby – just peace, perfect peace.'

A familiar figure tapped on the door.

'Sorry to interrupt.' DCI Flint waved a sheet of paper like a fan. 'This requires immediate attention.'

'Sure. We're done here.'

'Can I have a word too?'

Robyn nodded. Flint stepped into the corridor. Robyn raised her eyebrows at her team and joined him.

'Sir?'

'It's about DI Shearer.'

'Tom?'

'He's put in a request for promotion. There's a vacancy come up in Nottingham.'

'Well, that's good to hear. He's a very good detective.'

'Yes, he is. But so are you. Robyn, I'd like to put you forward for it. How would you feel about that?'

There was a burst of laughter from the office. Robyn deliberated her answer. 'When do you need to know by?'

'How about Monday morning?'

Robyn agreed. Flint's lips stretched into a smile.

'Excellent. Well, give it some serious thought over the weekend, then.'

He meandered in the direction of the reception and Robyn thought fleetingly about what a promotion would mean. Career-driven Amy Walters would have yelled at her to seize such an opportunity with both hands. More laughter burst from the office and Robyn headed towards it.

Shearer appeared from nowhere and threw her a smile. 'Are congratulations in order?' he asked.

'For what?' Robyn was defensive in case he'd overheard any of her conversation with Flint.

'Resolving a murder case. What else?'

Robyn recovered quickly. 'I thought you'd heard about Mitz and Anna's engagement.'

Shearer rolled his eyes dramatically. 'They haven't, have they? I hope they make a better job of marriage than I did.'

'I think that's some way off yet. It's going to be a long engagement.'

Shearer grinned. 'You know what they say about marriage, don't you? It's not a word, it's a sentence.'

'You're such a killjoy, Tom.'

'Only kidding. I'm actually in a good mood. I might have some good news soon. Don't suppose you fancy a quick drink later, do you?'

'We're going out to celebrate the engagement. Come join us.'

'Really?'

'Why not? The more the merrier. Just behave yourself. No cracks like that earlier one.'

'I love it when you're bossy,' he said, with a wink. 'Laters.'

She shook her head in mock dismay as he departed and decided if he was promoted and went to Nottingham, she might actually miss him. Squaring her shoulders, she went back inside the office filled with an ambience she'd miss if she left. She wouldn't be working with this team forever. Each of her officers had individual goals and ambitions. Mitz and Anna wanted to make names for themselves, and at some stage in the near future, they would be offered opportunities to take on new positions, and then this team would be disbanded. She ought to give Flint's suggestion more consideration. She would when she got home. For now, she was here and she didn't want to be anywhere else.

EPILOGUE

Schrödinger sat in the window, face pressed to the glass, awaiting her arrival. He spotted her and marched up and down the windowsill in the expectation of caresses and food.

Robyn paid the driver and clambered out of the taxi, weaving slightly as she reached the door. It had been a good night that had gone on far longer than she'd imagined. It was a good thing she'd given the team the weekend off.

The taxi pulled away from the kerb and Robyn fumbled for her keys. Schrödinger was now on the other side of the door, and she murmured to him as she attempted to slot her key in the lock. She didn't see the man until he emerged from the shadows. She took a step back in surprise and stared at him hard.

'Hello, Robyn,' he said.

Her mouth fell open and the keys slid from her hand.

'Can we go inside? I don't want anyone to spot me here. I can't afford to be discovered.' He bent down and picked up the keys, holding them out to her. She nodded dumbly, suddenly clear-headed, shoved them into the lock and pushed the door open. Schrödinger greeted them both like long-lost friends. He stroked the cat as Robyn shut off the alarm.

'Hello, little chap. I've seen you a few times through the window, haven't I? You're very friendly. I keep missing you,' he said to Robyn. 'I've tried on a few occasions to talk to you.'

'*You* sent the photograph.'

'I did. I know it wasn't very clear but I wanted to get a message to you somehow that wouldn't incriminate me if it was picked up, and Davies always said you were great at working out puzzles.' The man with black hair and a disfigured face regarded her intently.

'Is he alive?' she asked. 'Hassan, tell me the truth.'

'I don't know. He was when I escaped, but I can't say for sure.'

'Sit down and tell me what happened. You want a coffee?'

'No. I don't have a lot of time. I'm being hunted and you know what that means. I have to keep moving. There's no other way. I have to be one step ahead of them. They'll soon work out I'm here and come after me. I've been hiding in the Peak District the last week. I want to get off this island and return to Morocco, but it's a risky strategy. I have friends who might be able to get me to France and from there I'll try to work my way back home where I'll be safe. I couldn't go until I'd seen you. I promised Davies. I couldn't let him down.'

'What happened? The last time I saw you, you were driving Davies to Ouarzazate for a meeting. I was told you were both killed in an ambush.'

Hassan looked down at his trainers. Robyn tried to avoid looking at his ruined face. The skin on the left side was puckered and red from a serious burn or acid attack.

'That was not what happened. Peter Cross lied to you.'

'Then explain what happened, Hassan, because I can tell you at the moment I'm at the end of my tether. I spent two years believing that shit and it fucking destroyed me, Hassan, and *you* were part of the deception. So, you'd better have a bloody good explanation for it all.'

Hassan held up his hands. 'Davies' life was in danger. He had to "disappear", lay low and let the world believe he'd been killed, and it was my duty to extract you from Morocco and tell you the truth.'

'He went into hiding? For how long? And what was supposed to happen afterwards? We were all to return to normal and hope nobody noticed Davies was back from the fucking dead?' She spat angry words at him. 'For fuck's sake. Are you guys even for real?'

She slammed a clenched fist into a cushion, angry tears filling her eyes. 'How dare he! How bloody dare he! He should have warned me. Or he should have broken up with me first and then pissed off to play dead.' Memories of the hurt she'd experienced, the baby she'd lost, combined with impotent frustration made her cry out.

'Get out! I don't want to hear this. Get out of my house and my home and never come back.'

Hassan's dark eyes were filled with anxiety. 'Robyn, please, listen for a minute. Davies loved you. He wanted you to know the truth…'

The call to prayers echoes through the red city of Marrakesh as they drive away from the main square through empty streets and along the wide boulevard that takes them towards the dark peaks of the Atlas Mountains. The sun is making slow progress, its brilliance lighting the sky, turning it shades of deep pink and orange.

Davies says nothing. He tilts his head back against the headrest in the jeep and shuts his eyes. Hassan keeps his on the road, checking his rear-view mirror constantly to ensure they're not being followed.

The jeep rattles and jolts along the roads as they become less even and the scenery becomes increasingly verdant until they reach a sand-coloured village hewn into the side of a hill, camouflaged against its brown background. They pass a man in a grey and white djellaba, tugging at a camel's reins. He watches the jeep as it speeds past, leaving dust clouds in its tracks as it hastens towards the foothills of the Atlas Mountains that grow in stature at an alarming rate.

They begin the ascent into the mountains and Davies, with eyes still shut, speaks. 'What's our ETA for Agadir?'

'Oh seven thirty hours. Half an hour before take-off.'

Davies grunts.

The vehicle climbs for another half an hour. There's no more conversation. The squeaking of the suspension increases as they navigate the rough path that meanders ever upwards. Steep drops appear either side of it. Below them are the occasional burnt-out husks of vehicles tumbled from the rock-strewn paths. Davies opens his eyes and stares at the scenery. The terrain is flattening out for a while as the landscape shifts subtly from forested areas to patches of brown earth where little grows.

'Pull over up there,' Davies says. 'I need a leak.'

Hassan does as requested and stops the jeep. He rests his hands on the wheel and waits for Davies to jump out. Davies undoes his seatbelt casually and shifts in his seat, turning to face Hassan. 'What's the real plan, Hassan?'

Hassan lets out a hiss and moves his right hand swiftly to the pocket of the light jacket he's wearing but he is too late. Davies is too quick for him and grabs the gun that's been hidden there. He presses it hard against Hassan's temple and orders him to turn off the ignition.

'So, what's the real plan?' he asks once more.

'I don't know what you mean,' says Hassan, a bead of sweat forming on his top lip.

'Don't try and bluff this out. You're part of Peter Cross's little plan to dispose of me permanently. What was it to be? Shoot me then push the jeep off the side of the mountain with me in it? There is no flight back from Agadir, is there? Cross knows I am onto him and he's enrolled you to do his dirty work.'

Hassan spits in anger. 'You're a filthy traitor. Agents' lives have been lost because of your deception.'

Davies' laugh is humourless. 'Oh, Hassan. You've got that so wrong. I'm no traitor. You've been played for a fool. There is a mole. Somebody has been selling information and is behind the deaths of three of our most valuable assets, but it isn't me – it's Peter Cross.'

Hassan hisses again. 'You're lying to me.'

'On my life, I'm not. Look. I'll prove it. I'm going to lower the gun and tell you the truth. Would I take my hand off this weapon if I was lying?'

Hassan glares at him.

'Peter Cross is corrupt, Hassan. I'm a whisker away from getting the information I need on him. I was supposed to be meeting somebody here in Morocco who has proof Cross has been leaking details of operations. Cross knows I am onto him. This is an elaborate plan to dispose of me. It's true somebody wanted me dead – it's him. I'm putting the gun aside now. I need your help, Hassan. Because of him some of our best agents have died and I need you to help me trap him. I wasn't sure I could trust you at first but I have to now. You believe me, don't you? You and I go way back, Hassan. You've been my brother through many a mission. Be my brother now.'

Hassan is unsure but Davies has rested the gun on his lap and lifted his hands from it. He has confidence Hassan will believe him. Could it be true?

Davies speaks again. 'I need time to expose him. I have to find my contact and get him put away. If I don't, many more agents will be lost – maybe even you. I'm not the traitor, Hassan. Cross is. What's it to be? You going to pick up that gun and shoot me or are you going to assist me?' He regards Hassan coolly.

Hassan thinks carefully before responding. 'I'll help.'

'Thank you, my brother. First, you must get Robyn out of this country. I know Cross said he would, but I want you to reach her first and tell her the truth. I don't want her told a pack of lies about me. Convince her to leave with you. Here. Give her this.'

He passes Hassan a signet ring. 'Robyn gave this to me. Tell her I'm entrusting it to her until I return and tell her "anemones". She'll understand. Get her back safely to the UK in case Cross decides to use her against me. I'm going to meet my informant and get the information I need from him. Clear?'

A movement catches Hassan's eyes. A car is approaching at speed, winding its way up the hill. 'We have guests,' he says.

Davies turns and sees the dark Mercedes on the road below them. The passenger window lowers and Davies spots the shining reflection

coming from a weapon being pointed at the jeep. 'Shit! Okay. Go. Tell
Robyn the truth. Promise?'

'Promise.'

Davies gives him a smile and then picks up Hassan's gun before
climbing over his seat into the back of the vehicle and escaping out of
the rear passenger door. He races to the opposite side of the road where
he launches himself off the mountainside, rolling and tumbling from
sight. Hassan doesn't wait to see what happens to him. He throws the
jeep into gear and floors the accelerator. The Mercedes is still racing up
the road, its occupants unaware that Davies has gone. A bullet pings
against the rear door. Hassan powers on to distance himself from the
vehicle but it has greater power than the jeep and he struggles. He makes
it to the top of the mountain – the highest point – and is descending at
high speed when he meets a bus headed in the opposite direction that
takes up most of the road. Hassan pulls hard to the left and the bus
clips the jeep, sending it spinning over the edge. Hassan is thrown in
all directions as the jeep bumps and clatters down the slope, tumbling
and turning all the while. The passenger door smashes against a rock
and is ripped off, leaving a gaping hole. Finally, the jeep comes to rest.
Hassan fights against unconsciousness but begins to black out, aware
of the smell of diesel from the ruptured fuel tank.

'The men in the Mercedes left me for dead in a blazing jeep.
However, I was most fortunate. A group of ancient Berbers in the
mountains rescued me and took me back to their village hidden
in the mountains. They tended to my wounds and looked after
me. It took time for me to recover, and when I did, I had to stay
under the radar. As far as Cross was concerned, Davies and I were
both dead.'

He regarded her with a sad smile and felt in his pocket. 'Here,'
he said. 'I was to give you a one word message, "anemones", and
hand you this to look after until he returned to you.'

Robyn fought back tears of confusion and anger. Anemones – the flowers Davies bought her for Valentine's Day – whose symbolism was tied in to Greek mythology but whose message was look to the future and never abandon the ones you love. He'd told her their significance the first time he'd offered them to her. They were her special flowers.

She looked at the ring in the palm of her hand, her eyes misting. 'That doesn't make any of this right. I'm sorry you suffered too, but you knew what you were signing up for when you joined intelligence. I didn't. I only happened to fall in love. I didn't ever want to be part of this.'

'I know. I know. I don't know what you were told about Davies, but it would have been lies.'

'The photograph?' she asked.

'Falsified. Davies didn't come back to the UK that day. I wanted to send a message to help you realise you'd been duped. I see now it was the wrong thing to have sent. It probably gave you false hope when all I intended was for you to question what Cross had told you.'

Robyn wiped at the tears, now tumbling. Schrödinger climbed onto her knee and sat there protectively. She rested a trembling hand on his soft fur.

Hassan spoke again. 'I've been here to your house before but each time I didn't dare wait for too long. I see now I should have. I should have imparted this knowledge sooner.'

She sniffed hard and looked him in the eye. 'So where is Davies?'

'Honestly, I don't know. He might be in captivity somewhere, been murdered or is still in hiding until he can find out what he needs to about Peter Cross. He wasn't safe while Cross was still in charge.'

Robyn suddenly blinked as her thoughts became clearer. 'Who's hunting you? Why are you on the run?'

Hassan's eyes blazed. 'I've killed Peter Cross.'

Robyn drew a sharp breath.

Hassan continued. 'I have my own methods of establishing the truth. Peter Cross sent an assassin after us. He wanted us both dead. Of course, I have no proof of his corruption. Without Davies' information, I can't prove anything, and so, I'm on the run from agents who believe I am nothing more than a murderer – an agent gone rogue.' He suddenly looked at his watch.

'I must leave now. I've stayed here too long and they'll be onto me. I'm truly sorry, Robyn. I know Davies would be too.'

The fight drained from Robyn. The champagne she'd happily drunk an hour earlier rose and soured in her gullet.

'Go. Don't come back,' she whispered.

'I won't. Take care of yourself, Robyn.' He took her hand and kissed the back of it. 'From Davies,' he said. He hastened to the door and into the darkness.

She didn't look up. Her fingers rested on Schrödinger's spine and she stroked his silky fur. Time stood still for a few minutes then a tremendous boom rattled her windows and the sky flashed white, followed by a collective wailing of car alarms as flames sprung from a black Audi parked down her road.

LETTER FROM CAROL

Dear Everyone,

I can't believe *The Chosen Ones* is the fifth in the Robyn Carter series and is my seventh book to be published by Bookouture. It seems only five minutes ago I embarked on this writing journey with Robyn and her team, and now I feel they're very much part of my life.

I'm indebted to you for purchasing and reading *The Chosen Ones*. I hope it not only entertained you but also provided you with some of the answers you've been seeking with regards to what happened to Davies. Of course, all is not always as it seems with my plots, so don't be surprised to discover further twists at a later date.

A hypothetical conversation set me thinking about the subject matter for this particular book. How far would somebody go to protect or care for someone they loved? Love is an extremely powerful emotion and relationships often complex. They can make us who we become and can be seriously damaging. While I don't condone the actions of the killer in this book, I hope I've presented a clearer picture of what can make a person commit a crime as heinous as murder.

If you enjoyed reading *The Chosen Ones*, please would you take a few minutes to write a review, no matter how short it is. I would really be most grateful. Your recommendations are so important.

If you'd like to keep up-to-date with all my latest releases, just sign up at the link below. Your email address will never be shared and you can unsubscribe at any time:

www.bookouture.com/carol-wyer

Thanks,
Carol

 AuthorCarolEWyer

 carolewyer

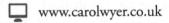 www.carolwyer.co.uk